DELTA HOTEL

Jon Swank

Cover Art by Jon Swank

ISBN: 13: 978-1543265866

ISBN: 10: 1543265863

ONE

"Ladies and gentleman, please buckle your seat belts, we will be landing at Ted Stevens Anchorage International Airport in approximately thirty minutes. The temperature is slightly different from what we left behind us in Honolulu, it's a brisk ten degrees Fahrenheit with a fresh coat of snow blanketing the city. I probably should mention sunrise is a little different too. We should expect to see the sun this morning at 9:57 a.m. On behalf of myself and the crew, I hope you choose Alaska Airlines for your next trip. It's been a pleasure to have you aboard."

Casey Link put his seat in the upright position and checked to make sure his belt was fastened. He was in the habit of always keeping the belt on after witnessing several passengers hit the top of the cabin during a turbulence flying over the Atlantic while returning to his first assignment at RAF Mildenhall in England. He moved his hand to feel the side of his face to make sure the two week beard was intact. It went well with the suntan he got after sleeping on the beaches of Australia for almost two weeks. He was supposed to get off his military hop in Hawaii to spend Thanksgiving with his parents and his sister, but decided at the very last moment to continue on with the USAF C 5 Galaxy's final destination to Australia. He had no trouble calling his mom from the bottom of the world with a story of how the hop changed its flight plan after departure. One more day and he'd have to give his face the razor treatment. He was to report to duty the next morning at seven in his Air Force Captain uniform. The Captain bars he wore were so new he had a hard time responding to someone calling him Captain.

Casey was a tall guy, just under six two, thin with dark brown hair and dark brown eyes to match. He moved in a way that made people think he was on the clumsy side. Like a thirteen year old boy who wasn't used to the tall body he grew into even though he was twenty-six years old. He also had a clumsy smile. Smiling didn't come naturally for him. His current boyfriend brought it to his attention. Before that, he thought his smile was as normal as anyone else's. When alone, he would practice in the mirror, and was quick to come to his boyfriend's same conclusion. His smile looked forced and quickly tired the muscles in his cheeks.

He loved the outdoors and choose the assignment at Joint Base Elmendorf Richardson, known as JBER for short. The Elmendorf side of the base was Air Force and the Richardson side of the base was Army. Casey kept in good shape by spending time on his mountain bike, sometimes even in the winter if the roads were clear. He liked it when the trails were covered in snow. It was his passion. Yet he realized he'd have to engage in other activities to keep in shape for much of the winter, biking was more geared towards the Alaskan summers.

At work, he was assigned as a registered nurse to the flight surgeon. He got his BRN degree at the University of Rochester School of Nursing on a Reserve Officer Training Corps (ROTC) scholarship. He grew up in Syracuse and while studying in Rochester, used the excuse of the Air Force to not have to visit much with the family. Summers were spent in Florida with the Air Force for training.

While Casey sat deep in thought thinking about his boyfriend Kevin after two weeks away, the Air Alaska Boeing 737 slammed its wheels on the runway and put on the brakes. Kevin promised to be there waiting for him. Kevin Lippman had no trouble getting away from his office job whenever he wanted since he was a sergeant police detective assigned to the department of cyber crimes. Besides the flight was arriving at 5:00 a.m. He was sure Kevin would be dressed and ready for work.

Casey went through customs in Hawaii. Departing the airport with his luggage would most likely be trouble free. He knew operations at the Anchorage International Airport were well organized. Getting out of his seat when the lights gave them all permission to do so was a task most tall people understood all too well. He slowly moved towards the exit of the aircraft following those in front to finally free himself of the cramped quarters he spent while returning from the bottom of the world on his journey to the top. It was snowing outside and was totally dark at 5:00 a..m. He moved like he was on auto pilot. So much so that he was caught off guard when Kevin pulled him from behind. Casey turned around to see the nice looking guy in his winter hooded goose down parka smiling at him and holding back from giving him a big hug and kiss.

"Woah! Just when I thought you couldn't be more sexy. Tell me you don't have to shave that off?" He had Casey's parka in his hand.

"Sorry. Air Force regulations. No facial hair other than a tiny Adolf mustache without a medical waiver."

"I'm glad you're back. I missed you."

"It's good to be back. You didn't have to pick me up. But I appreciate it. You're always so thoughtful." He half smiled while looking into his dark blue eyes. "Did you get a chance to have breakfast?"

"My place or yours? I'm hungry as hell, and I'm not talking scrambled eggs."

"Better idea. Let's hit the IHOP."

Their conversation was jolted by the sound of the luggage conveyer belt being thrown in gear.

"It's really early. I can come into work late?"

Casey put his hand on the lower sleeve of Kevin's parka. "If you don't mind too much, I'm really exhausted. Can we make plans for this evening after you get off work? I can meet you at your place."

"I guess I can wait. What's a couple of more hours after two weeks?"

"Thanks. I have a ton of things to do to get ready for duty tomorrow and I want to get a nap. I'm going to need a nap to be on top of my game tonight."

Keven recognized the brown canvas suitcase and moved to grab it. "Scrambled eggs it is."

Kevin Lippman was a few years older than Casey, but not much. He was thirty-one years old and anyone giving him a second look was half convinced he was getting ready for a cover shoot on a magazine like GQ or the Aussie's Men Style. He stood straight at five eleven and had light blond hair. Perfect skin on his face and a killer smile. He drew a lot of stares in any crowd, gay or straight.

Kevin drove a late model Honda CRV. Most anyone living in Anchorage drove some kind of four wheel or all wheel drive. Casey bought a new light green Subaru Forester upon arriving to this assignment. Those who didn't buy local shipped their cars from the lower 48. Some braved the drive north up the Yukon 1E highway before the snows set in. The two thousand three hundred mile trek north from Seattle that takes four or five days to complete.

The timing was just right. The IHOP opened at six and they pulled into the parking lot five minutes early. Kevin left the engine running while they waited the five minutes. He took off his gloves and moved the back of his right hand to feel the side of Casey's face. Casey jumped a little. "How was your Thanksgiving week with your parents in Hawaii?"

"It was nice. Better than a trip to Syracuse anyway."

"Looks like you got a lot of sunshine. I take it you skipped the bottle of SPF I slipped in your suitcase."

"I used it on my face. I forgot a couple of times on the rest of my body, but I didn't get a sunburn."

"I suppose I shouldn't tell you that a sun tan equates to sun damage to your skin, no matter where it is or to what degree you tanned?"

"I know. I'll be more careful for the next time. They're opening the doors, come on, I'm hungry and need some coffee." They got out of the Honda and walked to the door of the restaurant in the cold wind. Casey covered his ears with his hands.

After being seated, and getting their first cup of coffee, Kevin went through all the work events at his department while Casey listened. Kevin assumed he was too tired to talk about his vacation and decided to give him time. He could talk about his latest adventure after a good night's sleep and a healthy dose of long overdue sex.

Back in the Honda, Casey kept his eyes out the side window. Kevin smiled at him during every traffic light stop. He occasionally used his right hand to gently touch him someplace like on the side of his neck or on the top of his thigh.

"Home sweet home. I hope you get a good nap. What time will you stop by tonight?"

"Is six good for you?" Casey knew Kevin left the office at five if there were no emergencies to handle.

"Six is great. We'll make dinner at home. I'll surprise you."

"You always do." Casey leaned over to give Kevin a sweet kiss on the lips. "You're a great guy Kevin. See you at six" He got out of the car and opened the back door to get his suitcase and small travel bag. He walked up to the old wooden framed house where he rented the attic apartment. Not looking back, he found the side door and put in the key. Aware of the Honda still in the driveway, he gave in, turned around to throw Kevin a wave. Kevin smiled and put the car in gear to drive back towards downtown where he worked in the building for the municipality.

Casey pushed the door open. *You're a real asshole Captain Link. You just treated one of the nicest guys like crap and to top it off, you never gave lying to him a second thought.* He rented the attic in the old house with a nice fenced in backyard. The house was on McPhee Avenue in the small community of civilian houses bordering the South property line of the base. His attic apartment looked across the street into the forested area controlled by the military. It was once the Eagleglen Golf Course. The base closed the course and made it available for a military fitness training area. There were bike trails Casey frequently used, and in the winter, cross country skiing was a favorite for the military guys in the area.

Before Casey got up the stairs, Mrs. Gloria Atwell opened the door to let her dog Buddy out to greet him.

"Good morning Gram. You're up early."

"You know me honey. I'm always up early. Did you have a nice visit with your family?"

"Sure did. Thanks."

"I put your mail on the floor by your door. What did you do to your face?"

Casey felt his chin. "Do you like it?"

"Well, not really. You have such nice skin. Why cover it up?"

"It will be gone by tomorrow. Not allowed in the Air Force."

Gram was a real grandma type woman. She was usually wearing a cooking apron and the smell of cookies frequently made its way up to the attic apartment. Casey never complained. He always got some. Gram lived with her granddaughter who made a living cutting hair at the base barber shop. That's where Casey met her, made friends and was convinced to rent the attic apartment.

Buddy was Gram's dog. A mixed breed shepherd, male, four years old and weighing in at about fifty-five pounds. He kept nudging Casey with his nose.

"I guess you missed me." He stooped down to give Buddy a bear hug. Buddy retaliated with sloppy kisses on his face. Casey taught Buddy to run by his side while on the bike in the trails across the street. He was planning to teach him to pull him on his cross country skis while the snow was on the ground. Buddy loved his outings and spent a lot of his time in the attic apartment while Casey read on the couch.

"I missed you young man, but this guy has really suffered. He couldn't understand where you went. There wasn't a day that went by he didn't go up to sniff at your door."

"Well, I'm back now." He got up and pointed his finger at Buddy. "If you be a good boy, I'll take you for a run when the sun comes up."

Buddy barked and made two high jumps in the air without getting his feet on Casey. He was a jumper, but had the good manners to keep his paws off his friend.

"Oh dear, before I forget." Gram went back inside to grab a plate of sugar cookies in the shape of Christmas trees. "I made these thinking of you. I hope you like them."

"You know I will. By the way, did the lights work alright on the pine tree in the front yard?"

"They sure did. Candy said she owes you a free haircut for getting her free from her responsibility. I'll turn them on this morning so you can see how pretty they look in the fresh snow." Casey strung the outdoor Christmas lights before he left on leave, but it was too early to turn them on to see if there were any problems.

"Well, I better get up and unpack." He walked up the stairs with Buddy taking the lead to get there first. He unlocked the door and let Buddy in. Then he lugged his suitcase to the single bedroom and plopped down on the bed. Buddy followed and did the same.

"Buddy, you, I'm glad to see. I missed you." He rubbed the dog behind his ears. "I hope you realize your best guy friend is a total jerk. Just so you don't go and get surprised later on. This is me telling you now." Buddy cocked his head, probably wondering if they would take a trek for the snow covered trails across the street.

"I get it. Let me change my clothes and we'll go for a run. I don't think the dark will do us in. Nautical twilight starts in a few minutes" He got up, went for the closet to get on his running sweats and cold weather running gear. Buddy began twirling in circles at the sight of his shoes. “I bet you haven’t been for a run the whole time I was gone. Well, don’t worry now. As soon as I get my cross country skis, you’re going to learn to pull me up all the hills. Who said you have to be a Husky to pull a sled anyway?”

Buddy was getting stoked.

“Alright, let’s go and tell Gram where we’re off to.” He decided to run in the dark. The winter sun was well below the horizon.

After so many hours cramped into the tiny space on the Air Alaska flight crossing the near total length of the planet, he needed a good run to get his legs feeling the way they felt on the beach. But he needed the run more to clear his head. He knew the time had arrived to have a talk with Kevin, one of most caring, most gorgeous guys he ever knew. He prepared the talk in his head without any distractions. Dinner time was sure to be cause for a heavy dose of adrenaline pumping through his tall lean body, hopefully helping him find the courage to say what he wanted to say.

Buddy was well trained to stay at Casey’s side on the trails. Before they crossed the street to arrive back home, Casey put on his leash, told him he did a good workout and led him across McPhee Avenue to get home. He stopped to admire the lights on the pine tree, made a few adjustments with the line on the bottom, then proceeded to the back door. Buddy wanted to go back upstairs with Casey, but was pushed through the door to his own house. “You be a good boy and I’ll take you for a run when I get home from work tomorrow.”

After a long hot shower, the light of day filtered through the windows, minus the actual rays of the sun. Casey dried off, put on his robe and went to the kitchen to make coffee and try some of Gram’s Christmas tree cookies. He stopped to study the sunrise sunset chart for Anchorage. Anybody living in Alaska became acutely aware of a particular set of vocabulary to describe the light of day. He went over the times for December 7.

Twilight was the term to refer to when the Earth's upper atmosphere scattered and reflected sunlight which in turn illuminated the lower atmosphere. Both before and after the sunrise and sunset.

Astronomical twilight was to begin for the day at 7:05 a.m. and finish at 8:04 a.m. Just about the time he and Buddy left for their morning run. It occurred with the sun between eighteen and twelve degrees below the horizon. Before astronomical twilight in the morning there would be complete darkness. Same as after astronomical twilight in the evening.

Astronomical twilight was followed in the morning by nautical twilight. For December 7 it began at 8:04 a.m. and ended at 9:04 a.m. This occurred with the sun between twelve and six degrees from the horizon. During nautical twilight, most stars would be visible for navigation. The military referred to morning nautical twilight as BMNT, Begin Morning Nautical Twilight and as EENT for the evening. End of Evening Nautical Twilight. They used the terms for tactical Ops planning.

Next in the morning was civil twilight. It began for December 7 at 9:04 a.m. and ended with the sunrise at 9:57 a.m. There would be ample light during civil twilight for outdoor activities without the need for artificial light. It began in the evening at sunset, 3:45 p.m., and would be followed by the evening nautical twilight at 4:43 p.m. Evening astronomical twilight began at 5:42 p.m. and would end at 6:35 p.m. with total darkness.

The farther north one went in Alaska, the times would change. At the North Pole, twilight after the September equinox consisted of a few days with continuous civil twilight, followed by days of nautical twilight, until the days consisted of pure astronomical twilight. By the end of October, there would no longer be any twilight at all. It would be a consistent period of pure polar night until early March with the return of astronomical twilight.

Casey finished studying the times on the chart and sat at the table with his coffee. He could see the pine trees with the lights from his kitchen window and wondered if they would suffice for a Christmas tree inside the apartment. He thought to himself, *If I didn't put up a Christmas tree in England, why should I do it here?* Rubbing the side of his face, he remembered what Gram said in the morning. He decided to go to the base and get a free haircut from Candy. And a free shave too. He froze his fingers putting up those lights and was going to collect on the debt from his friend. Besides, he wanted her to see his two week beard.

The house where Casey lived on McPhee Avenue was very close to one of the JBER gates. All he had to do was drive east down McPhee Avenue to the end of the street and turn right on Pine Street, then left on Mountain View Drive to the Boniface Parkway Gate. G1 was only a mile and a half from his house. One of the reasons he took the apartment so he could ride his bike to work. That and the trails across the street.

It was a Monday, and the barber shop would not be so crowded at ten in the morning. He parked his Subaru at the Military Mall where all the shopping facilities were, along with the barber shop. It resembled a modern American mall in any city, along with a food court harboring many of the fast food chains found throughout the lower forty-eight. He walked over to the JBER Barber Shop and found Candy sitting in her chair, reading the paper. She saw him enter and put the paper down.

"What do we have here? Do I know this cute looking dude?"

Casey looked behind him jokingly.

"You know who I'm talking about. Get over here and give me a hug Captain Link."

"Do I have to?" Casey wasn't a hugger.

"You do if you want to collect on that free hair cut Gram told you about. She already called me to say you were back." Candy was anything but a plain Jane. She was medium height and kept her weight right where she wanted it despite living with Gram who spent so much of her days baking cookies, pies and cakes. She had light brown shoulder length hair, but dyed it bright red. Her left arm was tattooed from the shoulder down to her fingers with a red rose and green vine design. Gram never quite recovered from the shock of seeing it for the first time. Gram thought two ear ring piercings were over the limit. She made Candy promise not to get any piercings on her body and Candy agreed to make her happy. The promise took away some of the conflict around the arm sleeve tattoo. Candy was very outgoing and liked to do guy sort of things. She grew up labeled as a tomboy in high school. But she didn't mind because she realized the guys liked her that way. She had pretty green eyes and a very natural looking smile that made Casey envious. He asked her more than once to help him out with his.

Casey reluctantly approached her as she got out of her chair to give him a welcome back hug.

"That wasn't so painful, was it?"

"Only a little. Gram said you were going to give me a free shave too."

"What a shame. It looks so good on you."

"You know the regs. I report to duty tomorrow."

"Come on, sit down and let me get the electric razor first." He sat in the chair while she put the cloth cover over him to protect his clothes. "How did everything go with your family get together?"

"As well as to be expected. You know how those family reunions go. I did enjoy the beach though."

"Bah humbug. Doesn't sound like you had such a good time. But you did get a nice tan."

"I could have gotten darker, but you know who made me promise to use SPF."

"So how is that gorgeous cop doing anyway? Have you taken care of business yet?"

"Candy!" Casey looked around the room. It was practically empty. "What the hell?"

Candy shook her head and used her whisper voice. "You have been notified gays are allowed to freely serve in this country. Right?"

"They also have the right to stay in the closet if they want to. Regardless of whether or not the barber cutting their hair in the base barbershop is blabbing out loud about their personal business."

"Sooorrry! So did you?"

"You're helpless. By the way, any luck finding Mister Right yet?"

"Working on it. I got the best job to get it done. But I haven't scored yet. And that is precisely why you're taking me to Reilly's Irish Pub this weekend. This Friday night. That gorgeous guy can give you up for one night. Or better yet, bring him along. I have this really nice red dress I found at the Second Run thrift shop downtown. It had the original price tag on it, and it fits me like a glove. Talk about looking slutty in a classy way."

"Bad idea. I work with those guys. I know what I'm talking about."

"What guys?"

"You and I both know what I'm talking about. You got your mind set on a Zoomie. You'll be much better off with someone from the finance department."

"Come on. You know all those boys. They have to go through you to get to the flight surgeon." Casey worked in the hospital with all the guys who were on flight status. They had different medical requirements than the rest of the military. He worked under the flight surgeon managing their records and administering any medical procedures assigned to him by the doctor.

"And that is precisely why I said you'd be better off with someone from the finance office. Those guys are all type A personalities. Their daily goals include logging kill shots against their buddies and scoring with pretty girls to brag about the next day. Do you really want to be a notch on one of those guy's scorecards?"

"You got a bad attitude Captain." She began to use the electric clippers to cut his beard. Giving her time to talk while he was obligated to listen. "One of those boys could be my Prince Charming, and you're going to help me find him." She finished using the clippers on his beard and put a hot towel over his face while getting her razor ready.

Casey spoke through the wet fabric. "Are you sure you know how to use that thing?"

"Don't worry, I've seen it done before."

Casey sat up.

Candy pushed him back down. "I'm kidding. Yes I know how to do this." She removed the hot towel, foamed up his skin and began to scrape his face with the razor. He made like a statue. She laughed. "So, this Friday night. We can eat at home and take off about eight?"

"No."

"Please."

"No because we can eat at the pub. We can leave at six-thirty."

"You're a doll. Wait until you see me in that red dress. It really shows off my tattoo." They were quiet while she finished shaving his face.

"Don't blame me. I warned you."

"I can take care of myself." She began to give him the standard Air Force cut, not the Army version of the high and tight. Most of the young army guys cut their own hair with their own clippers. It was the Air Force guys that were the brunt of her business.

"Did you ever take Buddy for a run while I was gone?"

"Are you kidding? I work long hours you know."

"Poor guy. Did you take him for walks?"

"I took him for a thirty minute walk almost every night after I got home from work. Gram took him sometimes in the morning around the block. But that's going to stop now that you're back. Thank God. I told

Gram to get a poodle, but she wanted that big guy from the shelter instead."

"I'm glad she did. I really love him."

"I know. He loves you too."

Candy finished cutting his hair and held up the mirror. "Perfection. Agreed?"

"Agreed." He got up and pulled out his wallet. "Let me pay, I was only kidding about a free hair cut."

"No way. I hate stringing lights on those damn pine trees. You earned this one. But you better not change your mind about this Friday night."

"I won't. Thanks. I got to check into work and see what's going on. Then tomorrow I'm in uniform. I'm anxious to get back to work." He left her to her paper. The morning was so slow, there was only two other guys in the place getting a cut. Most of their business was at lunch time and after work hours.

Casey felt the skin on his face while he walked to his car in the parking lot. The cold air felt odd on the place that was for a short while protected by a slight beard. He imagined a full beard was great comfort to those guys in the North working outdoors. He got in his car and drove the short distance to the Joint Military Hospital only a half mile east of the Military Mall on Zeamer Avenue. It was before lunch time so he stopped off at his friends office first to check in.

"Hi Ian. How is everything going around here. Any disasters I need to know about?"

"Casey! When did you get back? Man am I glad to see you. Talk about being lonely around here. How was your family reunion?"

"Great. I didn't go."

"What?"

"I went, but I got a hop on the C 5 and made the decision to get off in Australia instead of Hawaii."

"No frigging way. You skipped your Thanksgiving family reunion?"

"I'll tell you about it later. Any gossip around here I need to know about?"

"Of course. I'll need a week to get you up to date."

"Anything I need to know about before I see the Doc?"

"No. He's been cool, as usual."

"Any TDYs planned for us since I've been away?"

"None that I know of." TDY was the term used to describe a deployment, a temporary duty assignment.

"Did you get a hop back from Australia?"

"No. I couldn't risk not making it back on time so I had to pay for a ticket. It's only money."

"Wow, that must have cost you a small fortune."

"Not too bad. Do you have everything in order for your leave?"

"Got my tickets paid for. Vancouver, ready or not here I come. Are you on tomorrow from seven to three?"

"I think so. I'm going to check right now. I'll catch you later."

"Glad to see you back Captain."

"Thanks Ian." Ian was a very plain looking type of guy. He told Casey he knew he was gay back in June when Casey first started his assignment. He said he saw him at a local gay bar in town. When Casey began to deny it, he cut him off and said it didn't matter to him. It took a few weeks for Casey to talk about it at the office. After he began to trust the guy. He actually began to like Ian and they soon became friends. Both enjoyed biking on the trails and frequently went on outings together during their off time. They kept similar hours at the hospital. When Casey asked if he was gay during one of their trail rides, Ian closed up and told him it was complicated. Complicated was a term Casey understood and left it alone.

Ian didn't have any boyfriends or girlfriends for Casey to meet. And Ian never made comments about anyone he might be interested in at work. He was average height, had black hair and kept in shape. He wasn't a muscular guy, he blamed it on his French Canadian ancestry. His dad was French Canadian and his mom was American. He grew up in Vancouver but had an American passport because his mom insisted. His dad didn't care.

Casey left Ian in his office. Ian was in charge of administration for several departments in the hospital and his duties kept him involved with the flight surgeon's office on a daily basis. This gave him time to develop a close relationship with Casey.

Down the hall, Casey found the flight surgeon's office with two guys in the waiting room. He knew one of them. An F 22 pilot from the fighter squadron and the other was in an army uniform. He was a chopper pilot he never saw before. Both guys were talking about the weather moving in.

The Sergeant at the main desk greeted Casey. "Captain, when did you get back?"

"This morning."

"You look like you got some sun. Hawaii right?"

"Right."

"You're on the schedule for tomorrow." Darius Tomlin was a Technical Sergeant. He was a friendly African American guy from Philadelphia. He was married and had a small son. His family lived on base housing. His wife was a teacher at the Mt. Spurr Elementary School on base. His mother in law lived with them to take care of their son while they both worked.

"Can I see the schedule?"

Sergeant Tomlin grabbed the schedule and passed it over to him. While he looked it over, he listened in on the two pilots talking while the one with the doctor came into the waiting room.

"How did it go Poker?" Asked the Captain waiting his turn.

"I'm grounded for a week. Or at least until I get rid of this crud." The Captain went to the desk to get the prescription for his chest cold. Pilots were not allowed to ever take over the counter medication without the permission of the flight surgeon's office other than aspirin. Taking any antihistamine or decongestant found in common cold medications would be grounds for temporarily taken off flying status.

Major Myers entered into the waiting room and saw Casey. "Welcome back Casey. I was wondering if you'd make it back in time. Looks like you got some sun. I hope you're ready to get back into the swing of things."

"Yes sir, I'm back and ready. I enjoyed the beach, but I'm happy to get back to work. I missed it."

"Good." Major Dave Myers was one of two flight surgeons on base. Casey believed he was easy to work with. A Southern guy from Montgomery Alabama. The second flight surgeon was Major Juan Martinez from Los Angeles. He was assigned to the general side of the hospital unless Major Myers needed his assistance. Casey barely knew him.

The Major looked at the other USAF Captain in the waiting room. "Captain Rogers, you can follow me." He led the pilot into the other room used for seeing patients.

"I got to go. See you tomorrow Sergeant Tomlin."

"Enjoy your last day of vacation Captain."

Casey left the office and found the exit to the hospital. He drove back to the Military Mall to get groceries at the commissary. He decided to cook lunch at home before his evening with Kevin. On the way he passed the barber shop to find the place mostly empty. Candy was between customers. He entered to ask her, "Did you cut one side shorter than the other? It doesn't feel right."

"No I did not, but you can be sure I will the next time."

"Just kidding. I got to go. See you later."

"Don't forget to take Buddy for a run Captain Link. I need a break."

"Got it." He left and entered into the commissary. While he was filling up his cart, he thought about his office friend Lieutenant Ian Tremblay. He decided not to pry on his personal life but was surprised after seven months of knowing him, the guy didn't open up. Especially since he began telling him about his personal life and his relationship with Kevin. He made his way to the cash register to pay. He bought extra steaks for Buddy. It was their little secret how Buddy liked steak. It was better than the dog food he had to eat in his house. Gram mentioned to him he was losing his appetite. Casey convinced her it was probably the winter blues. She agreed.

He got back into the car after loading the back seat with the bags of groceries and drove the ten minutes it took to get home. Buddy recognized the sound of the Subaru and was in the window, moving the curtains to get a good look at him leaving the car. He would run to the door at the sound of the key turning the lock.

Gram already let Buddy out to the stairway where he waited for Casey to get in. "Don't look at me like that. We already did our PT this morning." He opened the door and let Buddy outside. "Hurry up and go pee." Buddy ran to a bush and did what he was told. He quickly ran back to the door, not wanting to get left alone outside. Casey shut the door and Buddy scurried to the top floor door. It was a little after noon. He put the two grocery bags on the kitchen floor so Buddy could get his nose in to investigate. "That's right, we're having steak for lunch." Buddy wagged his tail. It had been two weeks since enjoying a good steak. Gram left the dog food dish full in her kitchen and Buddy was expected to eat when he was hungry. For sure she would notice the difference in his eating habits now that Casey was back.

After lunch, Casey grabbed a blanket and made way for the futon couch in the living room to get a nap with the soothing sound of the TV. He opened it up so Buddy could fit, and in a matter of ten minutes was fast asleep with Buddy snoring right next to him.

He awoke just as civil twilight was setting in. It was 4:30 p.m. His body was filled with nervous energy. He felt sick to his stomach. He wondered if he should take a shower or a hot bath. Buddy was giving him his best stare down. "You win. But we're not going to the trails.

We can take a run around the block a couple of times. I think we can both use it."

Buddy's ears perked up. He was sure the explanation had to do with going out.

On the way out the door, Casey stopped to let Gram know they were going for a run.

Gram put her hands on her hips while Buddy wagged his tail. "Two runs in one day. This must be his early Christmas present. Wear him out Captain."

"I will." They left the side door and took off towards the end of the street in the direction of the base gate. They both ran hard. As they approached the gate the MP came out to meet them. He had seen Casey run at the base with Buddy several times. While Casey stopped to regain his breath, the MP greeted Buddy and shook his hand.

"I haven't seen you for a while Lieutenant. Were you on leave?"

"Just got back today. And I made Captain last month."

"No disrespect meant. Congratulations Captain."

"Thanks. You guys ready for the snow coming tonight?"

"We're always ready Captain. Just a normal evening for us."

Casey regained his breathing and took off back in the direction of home, but with a much easier pace. He decided on a bath instead of the shower and laid out his outfit for the evening. Jeans, plain t shirt and a pullover cotton crew neck sweater with the Air Force logo.

Buddy was reluctantly returned to his house while Casey prepared himself a hot bath with bubbles. After his run, he felt better with the anxiety he was feeling ever since the Alaska Airlines jet slammed its wheels on the snow covered runway in Anchorage.

By 5:30, he was dressed and staring out the window at the two pine trees blinking red, green, yellow and blue lights. He looked around the kitchen for his car keys until he realized they were already in his left hand.

Leaving the apartment, he walked down the stairs, heard Buddy blowing air through his nose at the bottom of the door, and found his voice to tell him, "You be a good boy Buddy."

Buddy whined.

It was cold and snowing. The fifteen minute drive to Kevin's apartment was slow going with the fresh snow on the roads. Kevin lived just south of the University of Alaska Anchorage campus, in a nice place called Deer Park Apartments. He lived on the third floor with a balcony overlooking the mountains. There was always ample parking. He parked the Subaru and walked over to the steps leading up to Kevin's unit.

Kevin opened the door before he got a chance to knock. "I saw you parking your car. Were the roads bad?"

"Not really. Actually I zoned out with the music and didn't even notice." Kevin gave him a hug. "Are you hungry Captain Link?"

"Kevin, can we sit down, I need to talk with you?"

"I don't like the look on your face. Is this about the plans we made for your return? If it is, I can wait. Fucking isn't everything. Two months for some guys isn't enough."

"It's not about that. Come on, can we go and sit?"

Kevin led Casey to the kitchen table. "Do you want a glass of wine?"

"No thanks." They were finally both seated. Kevin went silent to hear him out.

"You're the nicest guy I've ever met. The best looking guy too. When I was on the beaches these past two weeks, I realized what I'm doing isn't right. Kevin, I'm being dishonest with you. I'm trying to make myself feel something I don't think I'm capable of feeling. I'm cold on the inside. I tried so hard, but I just don't feel it, and I want to stop this before you get hurt any more than what I'v already done."

Kevin folded his arms. "Did you miss me while you were away? I told you I missed you and you didn't say if you missed me or not."

"Kevin, I'm so sorry. I didn't. I felt relieved. Please don't hate me. I want you to be happy and any more time with me is wasting yours. I'm just not the relationship type of guy. God knows I wanted this badly, but it's not there." Casey got up while Kevin stayed seated. He grabbed his coat and moved for the kitchen door.

"Casey, if you work it out and I'm available, don't hesitate to look me up. Maybe if you went to counseling, I could help you out. I think you're worth it."

"Thanks Kevin, you're a wonderful guy." Casey left the door and shut it behind him. He slowly walked down the stairs and on to the parking lot to find his car. All the cars were covered in snow and he forgot where he put it. With the keys in his hand, he pushed the alarm button to help him out. Without putting on his gloves, he brushed away the snow from all the windows. He knew Kevin was watching from his apartment, but never looked up.

The Subaru took to the snow covered streets like a modern day snow mobile. Casey turned on the radio to listen to the news. He caught a glimpse of his face reflecting in the driver's side window. It was a face void of expression, not one of sadness or joy. *That's it. I will never try to have a boyfriend ever again. It's not fair to anyone my practicing feeling something while they are playing the game with a normal set of rules. It's so unfair.*

By 5:00 a.m. Tuesday morning, Casey was dressed in his winter running gear and hanging his Air Force blues on the back of the kitchen chair after using the iron to get all ready. He went for the door to do his morning run, not so much for him, but for Buddy. He stopped at the door Gram always left open for Casey to let Buddy out. His leash was hanging on the railing.

"Don't look so happy. We're not going for the trails this morning. We're going to run on the side streets and hope we don't get hit by a car. There must be a foot of fresh snow out there."

Buddy wagged his tail. He didn't care, just so they got out of the house. Casey heard Gram through the kitchen door. "Thank you Casey."

"No problem, Buddy is actually doing me a favor. He helps me run off all your cookies."

The roads on the base were all cleared off by the time Casey pulled past Boniface Gate on his way to the hospital. He parked his car and felt relieved to be getting back to his work schedule. Work was a great place to forget about the difficulties involved in his personal life. *OK, so work is my boyfriend. I feel good about that. And I can't go and hurt his feelings.*

At 6:45, astronomical twilight had yet to begin. It would be total darkness until after seven. Sunrise was to take place at 10:00 for the day. He made his way to the flight surgeon's office where his shift would begin at seven. The doctor, Major Myers was holding a cup of coffee as he entered.

"Welcome back Casey. Just in time, we have a bug going around."

"I'm ready. I missed work."

"Does that mean you're all fired up for your briefing at the fighter squadron after lunch?"

"Oh. Is that still on?"

"With three cases of Chlamydia this month, you better believe it. These guys need to understand the risk involved in fooling around. Thank God I'm married."

"Yes sir. I'm ready. Fired up? Not so sure. For some reason I don't think talking to a bunch of fighter pilots about sex is going to make my day."

The doctor laughed. "You can take it. We have a flight physical scheduled at ten. Look sharp, it's the Base Commander."

"Yes sir." The Major went into his office while Casey went into his to take of his winter uniform overcoat. He looked at his watch. He looked at his in basket filled with all types of folders and loose papers.

Two weeks worth of backed up papers. Then he left his office in search of his friend, Lieutenant Ian Tremblay. His office was just down the hall.

"Ian. You're early as usual."

"Good morning Casey. Are you ready for work?"

"I am."

"And what about your birds and the bees lecture you have scheduled at one today with those geniuses on the other side of the flight line?"

"So you heard about that? Damn it. I have to give them a lecture on STDs. The Major thinks they don't know about chlamydia."

"They probably don't. All anyone focusses on these days is the HIV virus. The list is so big, and some of that stuff can't be cured."

"They're going to eat me alive."

"Relax. Just do like I do. Picture them all naked."

"For real? You know my story Lieutenant."

"That's why I said that. Why not have a nice day at work."

"Bad idea. Really bad idea."

"So, are you going to tell me about your Thanksgiving reunion in Hawaii?"

"Yes. But I'll need a drink to get it all out."

"Tonight. My house. I'll fix dinner. Wine, and we can talk."

"OK."

"Casey, I also need to have a talk. You know, to get something off my chest. Would you mind if I took tonight to let it all out?"

"Of course I wouldn't mind. I remember you said things were complicated. I never pushed after that, but I'm here for you if you want to talk things out."

Ian inhaled making a whistle noise with the air passing his teeth. "God, I really hope you're an opened minded person."

"Ah, hello. I am gay."

"Is six OK with you?"

"I'll be there at six. And I'll bring the wine. Red?"

"Goes great with the lasagna I made. I've got a surprise for desert."

"I better get a move on. The Base Wing Commander has a flight physical scheduled in a couple of hours."

"Good luck with that. By the way, he doesn't fly anymore, why is he with the flight surgeon?"

"Because he's a full Colonel and gets to be where ever he wants to be."

"Of course."

Casey walked back to the flight surgeon's office to find two pilots sitting on the couch in their flight suits. They were both from the 525th Fighter Squadron. They flew the newest air combat jet, the F 22, otherwise known as the Raptor.

Casey looked at the schedule while he listened to the two guys talk shop.

"You're full of shit. That video was inconclusive on that shot."

"Sorry Wishboner, you put your ass right in my face. That was the easiest gun shot I ever took. And that means dinner and the drinks are on you this Friday at Reilly's."

"Fine Flexer, but I want a second opinion on that video. I say you didn't get the shot."

"Ask anyone of the guys. They'll all tell you the same thing."

"Good morning Captain Kelly. Captain Lethem. I see you're both here for drawing blood?"

"That's right." Captain Kelly was sprawled out on the couch. "We were here for our physical last week, and someone was away on vacation, so we couldn't get the whole thing done." Casey noted Captain Kelly spoke with a slight Southern accent.

"I guess they were short handed that week. But I can take your blood this morning and get you back to the squadron. Who's first?"

Captain Kelly offered up Captain Letham to go first. "While you got him in there, make him cough and be sure you got a fly swatter handy. He's been scratching all week."

"Very funny Flexer. I told you I had jock itch. It's all gone now, so you can relax and take care of me this Friday before I take you out to dinner."

"No problem, if the Captain here gives you a clean bill of health. Check him out good Captain Link. I don't want to be back in here next week."

"You both know I'm going to take blood samples this morning, that's all, right? I don't do the cough thing. That is the major's responsibility."

Captain Kelly sat upright. "Whatever." Casey couldn't help but notice the look Flexer threw him. He squinted his left eye almost shut while opening the right eye wider than normal. For some reason he wondered if anyone could do that or if it was a special talent that accompanied the fighter pilot's motor skills. The motor skills referred to as the stick and rudder ability. The ability to feel kinesthetically the movements of a super flying machine.

Casey pulled his eyes away from Nolan and took his first patient in to draw blood. After taking three vials of blood from Captain Lethem, he returned to the waiting room to get his next patient. Flexer.

"If you would follow me Captain Kelly. We should be done in a jiffy." Nolan Kelly followed Casey to the exam room to draw his blood. "Sit up here and pull down your flight suit. Do you want me to use your left or your right arm?"

"For a minute there I thought you were going to make me cough."

"Captain, the only way I can get to your arm is if you lower the top of your flight suit. Right or left?"

"You choose."

Casey breathed deeply and exhaled through his nose. "Are you right or left handed?"

"I'm ambidextrous."

"I'll take it from your right arm." He waited for Nolan to unzip his flight suit, remove his arms and lower the suit on the bench. Casey couldn't help but see the bare crack of his butt. He wasn't wearing any underwear. Casey fixed his right arm with the rubber hose. "I guess this is how you got your tactical callsign." Nolan had very shapely and hard biceps. They weren't huge or out of proportion for his body's size. Yet they were very noticeable. It was obvious he spent time on them with weights.

Before Casey could poke him with the needle, Nolan flexed his bicep to demonstrate the full magnitude of his arms. "Impressive, right?"

"Sure. Just don't go and do that for a couple of hours after we take this blood sample."

"So Captain Link, I saw on the schedule you're going to teach us on how to safely have sex after lunch today. Are you going to bring slides?"

"Well, I do have some nice blow ups of genital warts, but I'm not going to teach you how to have sex. I'm going to teach you guys what happens when you get reckless. The Doc's seen too many cases of chlamydia this month. And this is some real nasty stuff. It can hide for years in your body, while you pass it along."

"I say all one has to do is choose the right partner. Pick em clean."

"Don't miss the briefing after lunch. I have a feeling you need this."

Nolan turned his head as Casey poked him with the needle. "Are you going to be OK Captain Kelly? I can let you lie down if you wish."

"Did I say anything? Did I make a sissy noise?" He threw Casey that eye trick again.

"Just making the offer. I'm almost done here. Breath slowly and you'll be just fine."

Nolan did take slower and deeper breaths. Casey laughed to himself. "That's it." He placed the vials of blood on the counter and grabbed the clipboard. "How tall are you?"

"Five ten."

"And your weight?"

"I think I got weighed last week Captain Link."

"They must have forgotten to write it down. Don't worry, you don't look like a candidate for the weight program."

"178. I plan on breaking 180 before Christmas. I've got a bet to win with my brother."

"You can follow me to the waiting room. I'll see you at one."

"Bring pictures."

Casey smiled at the two fighter pilots as they left the office. He stood next to Sergeant Tomlin who was shuffling papers with his head down. Casey had free reign to watch both of the guy's rear ends as they left the room. *Neither one of those guys is wearing any underwear. What the hell is up with that? Are they afraid of panty lines or something?* "Sergeant Tomlin, we have Colonel Price coming in for his flight physical at eleven. Is everything in order?"

"Yes sir."

"Would you put those cookies out of sight until he leaves please?"

"Yes sir."

"Rumor has it he is a fanatic on diet and exercise. We don't want to get included in on his PT parties."

Sergeant Tomlin got up to put away the snacks that were on his desk top. Casey left his backlog of papers untouched and walked around making sure everything looked tidy for the Base Commander. By eleven sharp, Colonel Ed Price entered the room dressed in his flight suit, ready for his annual physical.

"Good morning Colonel Price. If you're ready we can get you started by getting your numbers and your blood work drawn."

"I'm ready. I owe anyone in my office with a better cholesterol count than me a free dinner at the Perma Frost Pub this Friday. Providing they can show me the official paper work." The Perma Frost Pub was the last vestige of any club on base serving alcohol. It was an all ranks club open only on Friday nights. Casey led the

Colonel into one of the examination rooms cleaned and ready for the Colonel. "Sir, if you would step up here so I can get your weight?"

"Let me take off my boots first. I got a bet going here too. I might have to ditch the flight suit. These things weigh over five pounds."

Casey panicked that the guy would strip nude in the room, he had him pegged for another free baller.

"Well, let me see the numbers first before I have to go there."

Casey read the numbers off. "198 sir. Seems like a winning number."

"It'll do, for now."

Casey took his height. "74? Does that agree with you?"

"All my life Captain. I haven't started shrinking yet."

"If you will have a seat here and lower your flight suit so I can take your blood pressure and draw blood."

The Colonel did as he was told, and sat on the bench. Casey wondered why the guy had such an old fashioned hair cut with his hair combed back and lightly greased. His hair smelled of coconut oil. "That's it for my part Colonel. I'll have Major Myers come in and finish with your physical."

Casey called Candy to see if she would meet him for lunch at the food court in the Military Mall where she worked. On his short drive over, he thought about the two fighter pilots in his office that morning. *What is it that makes those guys so obnoxious? They never have an off switch. And they think they walk on water.* He let his mind go to the two rear ends he observed leaving the waiting room. Especially that of the most obnoxious one, Flexer, or Nolan Kelly if he ever even used his proper name. Nolan was shorter than Casey. He had light brown hair, light brown eyes, and a dark four o'clock shadow early in the morning. One of the things that struck Casey odd was he sported an Army haircut, high and tight, while most of the other pilots had the type of cut Candy gave at the barber shop. Enough hair left for the necessity of purchasing a bottle of shampoo. His eyes were soft and had eyebrows lighter than the hair on his head. His nose was on the bigger side for the features of his face, yet straight and angular. And his lips were dark pink. Lips that had a smile every bit as tilted as his trademark look with his eyes. His ears were perfectly shaped and hard, lacking any traces of piercings. At least hard looking. In all, Nolan had the kind of face that gave the impression he was a guy caught between the stages of boyhood and that of a mature man. Casey let his mind wander to his arms. He had very shapely biceps that looked rock hard, even when not flexed. He wished normal procedure was for the rubber tube to be placed around the bicep, but the tube was tightened just above the elbow. Then there was the crack of his butt he quickly glanced at as he slid down his flight suit to get at his bare arms. If the biceps were hard, so was the two large slabs of muscles attached to his lower back. Casey shook his head free of the vision invading his thoughts. He pulled into the Military Mall's parking lot to find his friend for lunch.

"Hi Casey. Was it my imagination or did you and Buddy go for a run this morning in the snow?"

"We did. In the street on the tire tracks. No one had shoveled their walks yet. Buddy loves the snow."

Candy ordered a sandwich from Charley's Grilled Subs and Casey ordered a rice and chicken dish from Manchu Wok.

"I heard you come home last night. Only one pair of footsteps climbing the stairs, and I'm not thinking Buddy."

"Yeah. About that. I'm single again. This time forever."

"What the hell happened with you and Officer Perfect?"

"Me happened. My heart wasn't in it. I broke it off before I hurt him."

"You mean before you hurt him more."

"Yeah, that."

"Casey, Casey. What am I going to do with you? Here I am trying to get a date and you blow off the perfect opportunity for happily ever after."

Casey took a spoonful of his dish thinking of what Candy just said. "Some people weren't meant to have that special someone. I wasn't. I need to focus on that and live my life as it was meant to be lived."

"Bull shit. Pure bull shit."

"Are we still on for this Friday night?"

"I hope so."

"Maybe we should skip Reilly's Pub and go somewhere else?"

"No way. The fighter jocks hang out at that pub and like I said, I plan to snag one. One for my happily ever after."

"Fine. But I warned you."

"Yes you did. More than once I might add."

"What do you think about guys who go free balling?"

"I love it."

"Why?"

"Because a man who can go like that has to have confidence in himself. And he's not afraid of what he's got in his pants. Are you doing that today?"

"No I am not. And that doesn't mean I'm afraid of what I got in my pants."

"And the confident part? Forget I said that."

"I already did. Blink one of your eyes."

"You want me to wink at you? Is part of your plan trying to get a girl's attention?"

"Of course not. Now see if you can open one eye wide and barely open the other."

Candy tried, made it, but it took some effort. "Are you going to include me in on this?"

"Nothing to clue you in on. I was just wondering. Maybe the eye muscles are tied into the smile muscles."

"Oh, that again."

"No. I don't need it anymore."

"I better get back. Us civilians don't get to take off whenever we want."

"Boy do you have a lot to learn about the military. Thanks for meeting me today. I needed the positive energy. I have to go and work in the lion's cage at one. Wish me well."

Candy got up from the table. "You can do it. Whatever it is. See you later sexy."

Casey watched as she swung her thin body wrapped in a tight pair of jeans out of the food court and on to the barber shop a few yards away. *Damn, she is a looker,* he thought to himself.

Back in the car, he adjusted the rear view mirror, not to see the view from the back, but to see his face as he tried the eye thing. He couldn't do it. Then he tried the crooked smile. Knowing it didn't work for him, he readjusted the mirror and took off in the direction of the hospital to gather his notes and make his way over to the 525th Fighter Squadron, on the other side of the runways.

After driving around the end of the base to get on the other side, he found the building for the 525th, right next to the other fighter squadron on the base, the 90th. Parking was difficult, mainly because every spot had the name of some Zoomie hero painted on the curb. He had to park at the other end and on the side of the street. *My God, do they all need their names on a special spot around here? Talk about egos!*

Inside the building, he spoke with the Airmen at the desk.

"Yes sir, the Colonel is expecting you. Follow me please." The Airman took Casey to Lieutenant Colonel Walt Nelson's office. "Sir, I have Captain Link here for the briefing."

"Thank you Tom. Come on in Captain."

"Thank you sir." The Airmen left for the squadron's front desk.

"So we have a problem with STDs on Base?"

“Could be. But STDs are always a problem. The Major wants me to get the word out on Chlamydia. We’ve had a few to many cases this month.”

“Well, I think it’s a smart move to educate the guys. Follow me, I have you set up in the Alpha briefing room.” Casey followed him down the hall to the large room. It was better equipped than a fancy movie theater, with reclining rocking seats and a large screen for viewing videos. Not from Hollywood, but from the cams in their cockpits. The kind of videos that would prove their shots like the one Flexer was talking about with Luckybone in the office. Without the videos, kill shots would be nearly impossible to prove with so many guys thinking they are the best shot around.

The commander of the 525th entered the briefing room and all the guys jumped out of their seats to attention.

“Take your seats. We have a special briefing on safe sex this afternoon. I expect you all to give the Captain your best attention and courtesy. He might just save one of your rear ends. Captain Link, the floor is all yours.”

“Thank you sir.” Lieutenant Colonel Nelson left the room and once again the guys all jumped up to attention. “Take your seats,” he said while leaving the room.

“Good afternoon. I’m grateful to…”

A major got out of his seat to approach Casey. He was the second in command, the Deputy of Operations, called the DO. “Captain, let me interrupt you for a moment to personally thank you. You must be busy and the health of my pilots is important to us all. I’ll be in my office if you need me. I know these guys will give you their fullest attention. Some of them will need this brief more than others.” The Major left the room with a murmur of comments from the guys left in their seats. Most were captains, but there were a few first lieutenants too. None were women.

“As I was saying, I’m grateful to be able to get this information out to you guys. The flight surgeon has noticed an increase of what we call an STI, that stands for a sexually transmitted infection, not to be confused with the STD. Can I see a raise of hands for those of you who know about chlamydia?"

They all smiled and no one raised their hands.

"I get it. If you raise your hand, that makes you think the others will accuse you of having had it before. No problem. Chlamydia is called the silent infection. It affects both women and men. It is caused by the bacterium chlamydia trachomatis."

Someone from the back row called out, "Let me guess, it burns when you pee." Another guy called out, "And why didn't you raise your hand?"

"You're right Captain, it can cause a burning sensation when you urinate. In both men and women, but not always. Twenty-five to fifty percent of men who carry the infection will never experience any symptoms at all. But they can pass it on to their partners. Even more women will have the infection and will not have any symptoms. Sixty percent."

"Did you hear that Commando, I'm not going out with you again until you get a blood test."

"Your loss. Not mine."

"Actually guys, it's not detected in a blood test. You need to have a urine test without passing urine two hours before." Casey took a breath. "And there are two other test to take to find the infection. There is the throat swab and the rectal swab."

There was a rumble of comments not discernible from the front of the room.

One of the guys asked, "Is this thing curable, or is it like what Bellringer has, you know, herpes?"

"Up yours."

"It is very curable, but let me talk about the symptoms first. If you come in contact with the bacteria, it can take from one to three weeks to show itself. For women, there can be a vaginal discharge, yellowish and with a strong oder."

"Damn, there goes my lunch."

"Hey, with your looks, you have to take what comes your way."

Casey tightened his lips. He noticed Flexer in the front row with his legs stretched out throwing him that tilted eye look, followed by the tilted smile.

"And in women, there can be bleeding. If there is bleeding, intercourse is probably painful. In men with symptoms, there is commonly a clear fluid at the tip of their penis, definitely not pre-come or semen."

"Captain, don't you have any slides to share with us?"

"Yeah, cause he wants to see pictures of the clear fluid on the tip of a penis."

"Why not?"

"There can also be swelling of the testicles. Accompanied with a dull throb. If this is taking place, it indicates a late stage of infection. For both men and women, late stage infections can result in reproductive damages. In such a case there is probably a persistent low grade fever."

"What's with the anal swab test?"

"Well, if the individual was infected by engaging in anal sex, there can be anal swelling."

There was another roar from the guys. Flexer kept his smile on Casey like he enjoyed what he was having to do at the front of the room. It was a comical bit of bad luck.

"Lastly, for symptoms, I need to talk about chlamydia conjunctivitis."

"What, in the eyes?"

"Exactly. If infected vaginal fluid or semen gets in the eyes from an infected individual, the eyes will be infected."

"Oh, not the come shot in the eyes ordeal."

"Guns, guns, guns"

Casey noticed all the guys sat upright in their seats. The Commander looked in on the room as he passed by. "I guess now is a good time to tell you chlamydia is very treatable. Seven days of an antibiotic and you should be in the clear. We like to schedule a test three months after, since recurring infection is common. No sexual activity for seven days during the treatment."

"Give us some hope here Captain. What about prevention?"

"Good question. Use condoms for intercourse and oral sex. And cover your toys too."

"Captain, are you saying use a condom for oral sex with a female?"

Casey bit his lower lip. "Yes. They do have them for women."

"How?"

"Alright. You can use a latex barrier like a natural latex rubber sheet, a dental dam or a cut open condom to make a square. You put the barrier between your mouth and the vagina. You can also use plastic food wrap from the kitchen."

"What about rimming"

"Raise your hand if…" someone yelled.

All raised their hands.

"You can do the same with anilingus. But don't switch them around. You can't use the dam for one activity and use it for the other. You risk spreading infection."

There was another loud murmur of words Casey couldn't understand.

"Guys, if you don't have any further questions, I'll get back to the hospital."

"I have a question. Can crabs fly, because if they do, I'm brining a bottle to work. There is a whole lot of scratching going on around here."

"They can jump, but not fly."

"Captain, is it true you guys at the hospital keep any of this kind of information confidential. No leaks."

"We do. But we are required by law to report any cases of syphilis."

All the guys got out of their seats and began to leave the room, each one joking with another about the side effects of STDs and STIs.

Nolan passed Casey and patted him on the shoulder. "They're not so bad. They got the message anyway. See you around Stretch."

"Enjoy the rest of your day Captain Kelly." Casey gathered his notes and was more than ready for red wine at his friends house at six. He just gave the briefing from hell and planned to tell his friend all about it over lasagna and a surprise desert.

Ian lived only a half mile from Casey's apartment, a ten minute walk. So he walked to his apartment over a garage on 636 Mumford Street in hopes of enjoying enough wine to help wipe away the stress of the day. There was a large balcony patio leading to Ian's kitchen door. He knew it was usually open.

He stuck his head inside. "Ian, you home?"

"I'm in the back. Come on in and pour yourself a glass of wine." He knew Casey was bringing a bottle, but he had one opened and ready on the table to start things out. Casey did as he was told.

"It smells good in here. I'm starving."

"That makes two of us. Did you start drinking your wine yet?"

"Yes. Is there a hurry going on here?"

"Maybe. I want you to get relaxed."

"I am now. What are you doing back there?"

"Getting ready. I need you to get some of that wine in you first."

"What?"

"Take a deep breath."

"Fine. Now get out here. I have to tell you about my lovely briefing today with the fighter pilots."

"Alright. I'm coming."

Casey took another sip of his wine and grabbed the newspaper on the table. He looked up. "Oh fuck."

Ian stood before him and raised his eyebrows.

"I mean," he raised his voice to demonstrate support. "Oh Fuck in a good way."

Ian was wearing a short black wig, a navy blue dress, dark panty hose and a pretty pink sweater draped over his shoulders. He was several inches taller than what Casey was accustomed to. Wearing three and a half inch heels to match the dress in navy blue.

"Surprise." She turned around for Casey to get a full look. "Did I put on too much makeup for the occasion?"

"Ahhh, maybe just a little. But other than that, you look. You look pretty?"

"Thank you Captain. Do you mind if I practice my upper voice with you?"

"Not at all. You have another voice?"

"You don't expect me to talk all butch while I'm dressed up like this do you?"

"Of course not."

"Now you get it's complicated?"

"Yeah. But then what isn't complicated in this world. Trust me, I'm comfortable with complicated."

"I believe you."

"Ian, what did you do with your, with your, you know your bulge. That dress is a tight fit."

"It's not easy, but I have it all tucked back and away."

"Ouch?"

"Not really."

"When did you first know?"

"Know what?"

"About wanting to dress in women's clothing."

"This isn't about wanting to dress in women's clothing."

"I'm confused."

"This is about me wanting to be a women? And about when I first knew? I'd say when I was four, maybe three."

"Ian, are you transgendered?"

"That's me. I just started braving going out in public like this a year ago."

"If you get caught, do you get discharged from the Air Force?"

"Yes. But I don't care. There are rumors that the military is going to allow transgendered to serve open and freely, after complete transition, but not yet. I've decided to separate from the service when my four year commitment is up this coming March."

"What will you do?"

"Live. Start hormone therapy and begin the real life experience phase."

"Phase?"

"Yes. That is the phase you go to therapy and practice living as your new sex."

"What about a job?"

"I'll find something."

Casey took a gulp of his wine. "This is big. But I'm happy for you. You're on the path to finding the truth in your life."

"Thank you for that. You're the only person I've told about this. It feels great to talk about it."

"Sure. I get it."

"And now it's your turn."

"My turn?"

"Yes. Your turn. Come on, get it off your chest. I know something has been eating at you since you got back from your family, and I repeat, family vacation."

"Oh, that. It's complicated."

"Complicated is why we're sitting here drinking wine, right?"

"True." Casey paused for a moment before speaking. "How about if I work on it and make you a promise you'll be the first one I talk to?"

"OK. But I hope for your sake, you don't ignore it for too much longer. How's the cop?"

"Gone. I ended that when I got back."

"No! The most gorgeous guy in Alaska and you ended it?"

"I did. And I vowed he would be the last. I'm not cut out for having a relationship."

"Wait a minute." Ian got up from the table and went to the living room. He came back and placed a business card in front of Casey. "I really like this guy. He's gay, out and is good at what he does."

“A therapist?”

“Why not? He really helped me see some things in my life I never saw. Maybe he can do the same for you. Casey, for you to sit there and tell me you plan on never finding that soul mate in life is proof you really need this.”

Casey picked up the card. “These guys always have a waiting lists for months before they can see you.”

“Nope. This guy is new in town, and he could get you in the same week.”

“Maybe I’ll give it a try.”

Ian got up from the table and took off his heels. “God these things are torture, but damn, they make the calves look so good.” He took the dish out of the oven. The conversation changed to office politics and the briefing from hell Casey gave to the 525th Fighter Squadron.

“What about the 90th?”

“This week too. I can’t wait. At least I have a heads up on what kind of questions to answer.”

Ian set the table. Casey rubbed his hands together with enthusiasm. “This smells great. When do you tell me about the surprise desert?”

Ian went to the fridge and pulled out a pan to place on the table. “There’s a new bakery in town. They make the flowerless chocolate cake. Have you ever had this before?”

“I don’t think so.”

“It’s to die for.”

They dug into the lasagna and kept the conversation lively. It felt good to be able to talk and be in the open.

“I have a favor to ask.”

Casey finished chewing. “Sure.”

“It’s concerning your friend, that cute girl from the barber shop.”

“Do you want to ask her out?”

“Good God no.”

“Does that mean you like guys, and not girls?”

“Did I forget to mention that? Guys.”

“Forgive me for changing the subject, but will you be gay or straight in your transition?”

“Since my mind is female, that makes me straight. But get your mind off the labels. Now back to your friend, Candy right?”

“Right, Candy.”

“I was wondering if you could talk to her and see if she could help me out with the makeup ordeal, and the dressing too. I don’t have anyone to help me here. Unless you are an expert?”

“No. But I’m expert enough to realize you do need a little help. That lipstick is the wrong shade for you. Dark purple, really?”

“So you’ll ask her?”

“Of course I will.”

“Will she keep discreet?”

“I know she will. Candy is a special sort of person. Sometimes she makes me wish I was straight.”

“Bite your tongue.”

“Hey, Ian, if you ever want me to go out with you in, in drag, can I say that?”

“No. I’m not a drag queen or a transvestite.”

“OK, well, if you ever want me to accompany you on the town while dressed in a dress, I got no problem with it.”

“You’re a good friend Casey. I’d love that. Does that offer include coming to Vancouver with me?”

“I don’t think so. Not that I wouldn’t love to visit. I’ve heard the city rocks.”

“Shoot. I’ve decided to take all this home with me. I’m going to give my mom and dad the fashion show.”

“Do they know?”

“Not yet, but they will before Christmas.”

Casey walked home by 9:00 p.m. He already took Buddy for his evening run before his dinner date with Ian. All he had left to do was get into his sleep wear and watch a little TV before waking and getting ready for a new day at the hospital.

The rest of the week proved to be what Casey wanted most. To get back into the routine. He almost wished he could have the evening to himself with a nice book, some TV and a good run with Buddy from his house to the main gate and back. But he promised Candy, and she was a good friend.

"Hi Casey. TGIF, right?" Ian now looked somewhat different to Casey, but not any worse or better. Just different.

"Hi Ian. You got that right. My first week back after two weeks of loafing around and I'm beat. By the way, I talked with Candy."

"And? And? Come on."

Casey got a laugh. "She said she would be happy to help out. She asked if this Sunday would be good for you."

"That's in two days. This is going to be so great. Can you be there? I feel a little awkward not knowing her too well."

"My house, this Sunday at one. OK?"

"One it is. What am I supposed to bring?"

"Well, do you want to come dressed or do you want to bring your clothes?"

"In the daytime? Damn. Maybe I better bring my stuff with me in a bag. I don't think I like the way I look in the daylight."

"That has got to change. Candy is exactly what we need."

"I am so pumped for this. I can't thank you enough. Or her. By the way, what are your plans tonight, now that you're back on the single's list."

"I promised to take Candy to Reilly's Pub tonight. Dinner, and hunting for eligible boys."

"Good luck with that. Are you both hunting, or just you?"

"I told you, I'm single for life. She's the one with the big idea of finding a Zoomie at the pub. God help the poor thing."

“I agree with you on that. I have to get back to my desk. Thanks again. See you at your place this Sunday. Be careful tonight.”

“Later Ian.”

Ian turned to leave his office.

“Ian?”

He turned around to see what Casey wanted.

“I got a good feeling about what you’re doing. I really believe this is going to work out good for you.”

Ian gave him a smile and left.

Casey decided to skip lunch and make a visit to the barber shop at the Military Mall. *Maybe she will be so tired from the week’s work she won’t want to go out tonight.* He parked his car and walked over to find her.

“Hey sexy. We’re on for our date tonight right?”

“If you’re not too tired.”

“I’m not. And you haven’t seen my little red dress yet.”

The young Senior Airmen getting his hair cut braved a comment to Casey. “Captain, you are a lucky guy. Candy is the prettiest girl on the base.”

“Thanks Airmen. She is.”

“Are you trying to get a free haircut young man?”

“No. Just being honest. You are the prettiest girl on the base.”

“Fine. You just got a free haircut.”

The Airmen laughed.

“I’ll see you at five Candy. I’m going to take Buddy for a run when I get home.”

“OK sexy. Don’t go and twist your ankle in the snow. I’d hate to have you wobble your way around the dance floor tonight.”

Casey turned around before leaving the shop. “You didn’t say anything about dancing?”

The Airmen laughed again. Casey shook his head and left for the main BX.

He entered the store and went for the men’s department. Looking over the selection of jeans, he felt someone slap him on the shoulder. It startled him and he jumped back.

"What's up Stretch? A little jumpy today, aren't you?"

"Hello Captain Kelly?"

"You do know my name is Nolan. Or Flexer will do too."

"I know."

Nolan was dressed in a faded pair of jeans and a brown worn out leather jacket. "Shopping for a new pair of jeans?"

"Maybe. What about you." He noticed Nolan had a two pack of underwear in his hand.

"Just some jockey shorts."

"I thought fighter jocks didn't wear underwear." *Shut the fuck up Casey. Did I just say that?*

Before Casey could recover from his embarrassing comment, Nolan smiled and had the front of his jeans unzipped. "Proof. Jockey shorts. I don't need my boys all over the place in a tight pair of jeans." He gave Casey his tilted smile and zipped his pants up as fast as he had them down before anyone could even notice.

"I can't believe I said that. I just noticed with the guys that come into the doctor's office in their flight suits, most don't wear any underwear."

"And you also noticed I didn't have any underwear on the other day too, right?"

"I can't remember."

"Fire."

"Fire?"

"The flight suits are fire retardant. Underwear aren't. Some of the guys wear silk because it won't melt into the skin in the worse case scenario. I just prefer to not take the risk. Cotton burns too."

"I guess I just learned something new today."

Nolan gave Casey the smile again. He slapped him on the shoulder. "Got a go Stretch. My brother gets in tonight. See ya around."

"See you around Captain Kelly."

Nolan was gone in a flash. Casey watched him as he left the men's department until he was out of sight. *Alright, so the guy does wear underwear. Green underwear. And tight jeans. I wonder if he makes his 180 pounds and wins the bet with his brother?* Casey shook his head, decided on a plain pair of Levi jeans and left to find his car to get home, get in a good run with Buddy and maybe a small nap before his date with Candy.

Buddy used all four of his legs to nearly push Casey off the open futon where the two were having a nap. Casey laughed since Buddy was pushing him while he was asleep. By 4:30, he was ready to roll off the couch and take his shower. Buddy reluctantly jumped down to follow him to the bathroom. By 5:00 p.m., he was sitting on the kitchen table dressed and ready for his night on the town with Candy.

There was a tap on the door. "Casey, you ready?"

"Come on in, the door is open."

"You? Have you forgotten where you live?"

Buddy wagged his tail and approached Candy for a scratch behind the ears.

Candy made a full turn. "What do you think?"

"I think you really are like that Airmen said today. And you were right about the dress. Hot. Really hot." The red dress was tight fitting, sleeveless and not too low at the neck line. Only a small amount of cleavage was showing. Candy had breasts on the small side. "Actually the dress isn't all that special. It's how you fit in it."

"I hope it does the trick. If it doesn't, I might have to look up that nineteen year old Airmen who got a free haircut today."

"Well, he was cute. And polite."

"Right. If I was looking to rob the cradle."

"I'm ready. And hungry. But I did twist my ankle after work while running with Buddy."

"Of course you did. And I believe you."

They all three left the apartment. Candy had to cover her dress with a lightweight goose down jacket from Eddie Bauer. It was tight fitting and well designed to keep the body warm enough for bar hopping in the Anchorage winter. Buddy was disappointed he couldn't come along.

"You go inside and keep Gram warm," Candy told him as she pushed him through the kitchen door.

They both got into the Subaru at the same time.

"How nice. You cleaned your car for me."

"No. My car is always clean." Casey put the key in the ignition and took off towards downtown where the Irish pub was located.

"I watched that old movie Top Gun last night in bed."

"Thank God. That means you're gonna to take my advice and look for a boy from the finance department?"

"No it doesn't. I really liked TC in that movie. But there was something I don't understand."

"Why they were all like little boys instead of like grown men?"

"No. Why don't they have an officer's club on base where they can let off steam and have fun like they did in the movie?"

"Oh that. I never experienced that part of military life. By the time I joined the Air Force, the officer's club as an institution had already disappeared."

"What happened."

"Well, some of the guys that have been around for a long time told me the stigma for an officer hanging around in a bar and drinking began to affect their career. The young officers picked up on it right away. And getting stopped by the MPs while getting a DUI on base was a real threat. It was an immediate career ender, so the guys found their own places off base to drink and let loose, with less of a chance of getting caught with a DUI."

"They can still get caught off base."

"Yes they can. That's why I'm on soda tonight. You get to let your hair down. By the way, your hair looks great tied up like that."

"Thanks. So what you're saying is the base commanders closed the officer clubs?"

"Not really. They started losing money. So they first combined the NCO clubs with the officer clubs, but they continued to lose money so they made them all ranks clubs like the Perma Frost Club on base. The only place one can get alcohol now."

"What a pathetic excuse for a club. It's only open one day a week? Really?"

"Yeah, and not that I got something against the young enlisted troops, but how is a senior officer going to relax with a few drinks while the junior enlisted guy is watching his every move."

"And hitting on his wife."

"Oh damn."

"So is this world wide?"

"That's what they tell me. The officer's club is dead with all the branches of the armed services. Just a Hollywood story now."

"Shame. So here we are off to an Irish pub downtown to find us a cute fighter jock."

"Not we, you. You."

"Look, we're early. There's plenty of parking in the lot."

"Good. I don't want to wait to eat. I'm famished. What are you doing?"

"I'm leaving my puffy jacket in the car. Do you think I want to cover this work of art?"

"You'll freeze your butt off. Let's go."

They left the Subaru and walked into the pub to find it mostly empty at five to six. They were quickly seated to get their dinner. It was steak night, with a baked potato and sour cream. The desert was apple pie that came with the special.

While they waited for their dinner to arrive, Candy drank red wine, and Casey drank a diet cola. "Candy, I don't want to inflate your ego, but, damn, you look stunning."

“Thank you my dear. Now keep your eyes out for a nice looking Zoomie.”

Dinner arrived and they both enjoyed the lively conversation while eating.

“You’ll never guess what I learned today.”

“I’m listening.”

“Do you know why so many pilots are free balling under those flight suits?”

“I told you. Because they are a confident bunch of guys.”

“Wrongo. It has to do with the flight suits being fire retardant. And underwear are not.”

“I don’t know if I buy that. Their butts look so good without the underwear getting in the way and they know it. I’ll have to think about this one for a while.”

The time went so fast, so much so that the apple pie was right in front of them before they knew it.

“This pie is great.”

Casey shook his head in agreement. “It needs some ice cream, but it is great.”

They paid the bill and walked over to the bar side of the pub to enjoy the crowd.

Casey was surprised in the same manner for the second time in one day with a hearty slap on the shoulder. “Hey Stretch.”

After jumping a little he turned to face Nolan.

“Hello Nolan.”

“Still a little jumpy? Don’t fret. We all got our quirks. And who is your lovely girlfriend?”

“Friends.” Candy quickly jumped into the conversation. “We’re not dating, we’re just good friends.”

Casey threw them both his trademark eye trick. “This is my twin brother Chester.”

“Hi. Nice to meet you.” Chester couldn’t take his eyes off Candy and she picked up on it right away.

“He’s a pilot too, but not a fighter jock like me. He flies the C5 Galaxy on the run to Australia.”

Casey extended his hand. "Nice to meet you Chester."

"Actually, I think we already met a couple of weeks ago. You're the Captain who got the hop on my flight to Australia. I remember, because you decided at the last moment not to get off in Hawaii."

Casey glanced sideways at Candy.

"Australia? I thought you were in Hawaii?"

"Long story, I'll fill you in later."

She gave him a suspicious look. Then returned to pour on the charm with Nolan's brother.

He asked her, "Do you work on base?"

"Yes. I cut hair in the Military Mall Barber Shop. I can't help but notice you have a nice haircut. Really different from your brother."

"I know. He's had that Army grunt haircut ever since he was twelve. Go ahead and ask him where he gets it cut."

Nolan ran his hand over the top of his head. "I cut my own hair. I'm resourceful."

Chester pulled his brother's left ear. Nolan gave him a backhanded fist to the gut. "Can I get you guys a round?"

Candy answered, "Thank you Chester. I'm drinking red wine."

"What about you Casey?"

"I'm fine. Thanks."

Chester went to the bar to get Candy a glass of wine. Both he and Nolan still had a full bottle of beer.

"So Nolan, Casey told me about why you guys don't wear underwear at work."

"Did he tell you what color I had on in my civvies?"

She looked at Casey. "You left that part out."

"That's because I forgot."

Nolan did the eye trick again. "So?"

"So what?"

"What color were they?"

"Pink satin lace."

"Please, not another smart ass in the group. My brother is enough."

"Sorry. I didn't mean to say that." Nolan crossed his arms and tightened his lips. "Green. But I wasn't looking."

Nolan threw Casey the side smile and pulled back his head.

Chester came back with Candy's glass of red wine.

"Thank you Captain."

"You're welcome Candy."

Casey remembered the bet he had with the other pilot in the waiting room. "What happened to winning your bet with Wishbone?"

"You need to call him Wishboner like I do. He was put on call. I'll collect later, don't worry."

Candy was intrigued by the two guys. "So, you guys are twins?"

"Yes we are," answered Nolan. "But I'm the better looking one. Stronger too."

She thought about it. "If you two are twins, why does Chester have a strong Southern accent and you don't?"

"Go ahead Nolan, would you explain that please. We both grew up on the same farm, the same parents, and shared the same tiny bedroom all our childhood, so please, would you explain to the pretty lady why you sound like a Northerner?"

Nolan growled at Chester and refrained from giving an answer.

Casey took a gamble and asked, "Who's going to win the bet this Christmas?"

"What bet?" Candy hoped it wasn't about conquest.

Chester took off his jacket and handed it to Candy. "Will you hold this for me please?"

"Sure."

"Nolan here thinks he has bigger biceps than me. Go ahead Casey, you be the judge."

Nolan looked at his brother with the tilted one eye open, one eye half closed. "Fine." He took off his jacket and pushed it towards Casey who had no choice but to grab it. Both guys were left in nice tight fitting t shirts. They looked at Casey while flexing their right arms.

Nolan was the one to ask, “So?”

Casey stuttered a little. “I guess if I have to pick,” his eyes went from one to the other. Both guys had really hard and shapely biceps. He wished the contest was for which one was the hardest. “I guess I’d have to say by a small fraction,” his eyes took extra time. He was silently enjoying the view. “I guess maybe Chester, by only a little.”

“Yes.”

“No way Stretch. You need your eyes examined.”

“I thought your bet was for whoever reaches 180 first.”

“It is. And I’m going to beat him. We weigh in next week.”

“You’re dreaming Nolan. I got you beat already.”

Both guys grabbed their coat. Candy asked. “Is it true that if your right handed, your right arm will be bigger?”

Casey answered, “Usually, but Nolan is ambidextrous.”

“No he’s not.”

“Boys, you hash this one out. I have to visit the ladies room.”

“Yes I am.”

“Bull shit. Casey, go ahead and ask him what hand he uses to jack off with.”

Casey frowned. “Chester, really. He’s shy. You’re embarrassing him. As usual, no manners.”

Chester pinched Nolan on his nipple. Nolan threw him a dirty look, but their inevitable brawl was interrupted by the return of Candy.

Conversation went on for the next half hour the same way. It was obvious to Casey and Candy that the two brothers were steadfast competitors.

Chester ordered a tonic water. "I'm flying out tomorrow at noon. Tonic water here on out for me. So what do you two have planned for the night?"

"We're going dancing."

"No we're not. I told you I twisted my ankle on my afternoon run."

"Well, so much for my dance partner."

"I like to dance." Chester beamed his bright smile. He was built very similar to Nolan, but had lighter brown hair and his face was more narrow with a smaller nose. It was obvious they were brothers, but definitely not identical twins.

"Really?

"Especially with a pretty young lady."

"Are you OK dancing with gay people on the dance floor?"

"As long as you protect me."

"Casey, what do you say? We make a run on over to Mad Myrna's?"

"Count me out. Are you sure you don't want to come home with me?"

"This is my first night out in this new red dress. I am sure."

"Dude. The keys." Nolan drove a four wheel drive Dodge Ram truck. A new model.

"And how in the hell do you expect me to get home?"

"Casey. You don't mind, do you Casey?"

Casey opened his mouth to answer, but before he could, Nolan told his brother, "You better return that truck with a full tank of gas or it will be the last time I let you take it."

"Deal." He still had his hand held out.

Nolan took the keys out of his jacket and slammed them in his brother's hand. "You wreck my truck and you buy me a new one."

"No problem." He held out his arm for Candy to take.

"Candy, grab your coat out of the car before you go. It's not safe to be in car without a jacket."

"OK. See you at home."

They were gone. Casey had a worried look on his face.

"Don't worry about your friend Stretch. My brother is as honorable as I am. My mom and dad raised us right."

Casey gave him a look of no confidence.

"What?"

"Nothing. It's just that you have a sort of reputation on the base."

"Are you talking about my nickname Delta Hotel?"

"Yeah. A little."

"Look, I'm not a dick head. Those guys just accuse me of it because I never take any shit from any of them. Sometimes it gets ugly."

Casey exhaled deeply. "Alright. But if anything happens to my friend, I'm holding you accountable for it."

"Deal." He threw Casey his smile and a soft punch to the gut. "Come on. We're both pretty cool guys."

"OK. Where do you live?"

"About a half hour north of town. In the suburbs."

"Isn't that the pricy area for renting?"

"I'm not renting. My mom and dad own a cabin in Anchorage. I just stay there to save on rent. Why not, right?"

"So you live with your mom and dad?"

"No. It's a vacation home."

"Let's go."

"Please tell me you have a truck or an SUV?"

"A Subaru."

"That will do. Let's get out of here."

Casey led the way to his car. Nolan immediately changed the radio from the public radio station to one with rock. "Just head north on Highway 1. Do you know how to get there?"

"Yes."

Nolan leaned back and listened to the music. Then he startled Casey without the need of a surprise shoulder slap.

"Fuck."

"What?"

"Chester has my house keys. And I don't have a spare."

"So what are you going to do?"

"Turn around. I guess I'm on your couch tonight."

"How do you know I have a couch?"

"I sure as hell hope you do for your sake because if you don't, we're sharing a bed, and I ate beans tonight."

Casey mumbled something under his breath.

"Don't get pissed at me. If you want, give my brother some hell the next time you see him. This is his fault."

"He leaves tomorrow. Will I see him again?"

"Probably, we both have some leave coming before Christmas. My mom and dad are flying in to be with us. Then we both have to be back on duty for Christmas Eve."

"Don't you guys go down to min manning?"

"That's me."

"Me too."

The remainder of the ride back to Casey's house was quiet. Until he pulled up in the driveway.

"Is this where you live? Damn, right by the base. You could run to work."

"I do. I bike too."

"Hey, I love to mountain bike. Maybe we should hit the trails together sometime. I just bought the Rockhopper."

Casey kept quiet and parked the car. The TV light was lit in Grams's room, but she slept all night with the TV on.

"Are you afraid of dogs?"

"What, you got a poodle up there?"

"Yes. So are you?"

"No."

Casey saw Buddy watching from the window. "I live on the second floor. Candy lives on the first floor with her grandma. We call her Gram."

"Where are Candy's parents?"

"She doesn't know."

"Oh. Sorry."

"She's OK. Gram is a ton of love and support. For me too." Casey opened the door and let Buddy out. Buddy rushed out and gave the new guy a stare down. He looked at Casey's face and realized the other guy was no threat, so he wagged his tail and went over to smell his crotch.

"Whoa, that's no poodle. Is he friendly?"

"I don't know. I guess we're about to find out."

"I guess he is. What's his name?"

"Buddy."

"Hey Buddy, we gonna be friends?"

Buddy wagged his tail some more and ran to the top to get in first.

"Just a minute big guy. You got to pee first."

Buddy came back down to the open back door, ran out to water the bushes and ran back in to make it to the top floor before the other two could.

Nolan followed Casey up the stairs. "Is he your dog?"

"No, he's Gram's dog. But we're best buddies."

"So how many best buddies do you have anyway?"

"Follow me."

"I know you got a spare tooth brush and razor. Correct?"

"Correct."

"Good, I don't want any of that crud you briefed us about this week."

Casey turned around to give him a dirty look.

"Chill out. You're both jumpy and touchy. It was just a joke."

"STDs are nothing to joke about."

"STIs, not STDs."

Casey threw him another dirty look.

"What? I bet you thought I didn't pay attention." He followed Casey inside. "Nice place." He opened the fridge. "Good. We won't starve tomorrow." He grabbed the carton of milk, opened the top and smelled. "Good. I like milk in my coffee."

It was a little after 9:00 p.m. "Make yourself at home."

"You got cable?"

"Yes. Go ahead, the remote is under the TV. I'll get your pillow and blankets. It gets cold in here at night."

"So maybe we might have to employ the survival routine?"

"I'm not going to ask what that is."

Nolan laughed and mouthed the words under his breath, "Damn, so touchy." As Casey was in the other room looking for something Nolan could sleep in, Nolan walked around and shouted into the bedroom area, "Something is missing in here."

Casey shouted Back, "What, I said the remote was by the TV."

"Not that Scrooge. Something else."

"What?"

"You realize it's December eleventh, right?"

"I do. So what?"

"What is it most people have inside their house by December eleventh?"

"Are you talking about a Christmas tree?"

"Bingo. So where is it?"

"I don't have time for that."

Nolan threw Casey the eye trick.

Casey placed the pillow and blankets on the chair by the futon. He handed Nolan a pair of sweats to sleep in.

"Thanks Stretch. I usually sleep in the nude, but since you said it gets cold at night, I better put these on." He got up and stripped off his jeans in front of Casey who had no choice but to watch. He gave proof that his legs were as muscular as was his torso. Definitely not on the hairy side.

"What? So they're blue, not green. I do change my undies every once and awhile."

"Want some wine?"

"Got any beer?"

"Sorry, just wine."

"Sure why not." Nolan played around with the remote until he found the channel he wanted. Casey listened to him from the kitchen as he poured the wine. "I'll be right back, I have to take Buddy downstairs." He called the reluctant Buddy to follow him back to the first floor. Buddy was preoccupied watching Nolan wondering if they were to become friends.

"What a big pussy. He makes it all the way to the warped wall and can't get his hands on the top. If I had the time, I'd blow all those clowns away."

"What are you talking about?" Casey put his glass of red wine on the table in front of the Futon.

"The American Ninja Warrior. The warped wall at the end."

"You watch that?"

"Of course I do. If I was on that show, they'd change the name of Mt Midoriyama to the Nolan Kelly Mountain."

Casey sat down on the chair opposite the Futon and tried watching Nolan without getting caught. "What's it like?"

"It's this crazy course that you have to be in really good shape to make it through. Like me."

"Not that Ninja stuff, flying the fighter jets."

Nolan turned off the TV, grabbed his glass and thought of how to answer him. He stared at the blank TV. "Have you ever ridden a motorcycle?"

"Good God no."

"Hum." He kept his eyes on the blank screen. "When you drive a car, you're like a guest on the inside. You sit comfortably, change the radio station, move the gas and brake pedal when you need to. Sometimes you even relax your feet while the car goes with the cruise control. There's the vehicle, and there's you. But when you fly a jet like the F 22 Raptor, you're part of the machine. A motorcycle is the same way. If the bike leans to the left, you have to lean to the left also. In the jet, the human body is like an extension of the aircraft, or the aircraft is like an extension of the human body. We even have a visor in our helmet that let's our eye movements communicate with the computer system of the aircraft. We're one, not two."

"I guess it takes a special kind of person."

"It does. Don't tell my brother I said this, but he doesn't have what it takes. He's a good C5 pilot, but not a fighter jock. He won't give in to the machine with trust like you have to."

"I won't tell him."

"Dude, you need a Christmas tree. This just isn't right."

"I have to hit the sack. It's been a big week for me. See you in the morning."

"I hope so. You're making me breakfast."

"Good night Captain Kelly."

"Good night Captain Link." Nolan mumbled, "damn, always so formal like."

Casey left for his bedroom, took off his sweats and crawled under his large double goose down quilt. He thought about the guy known as Delta Hotel on his futon. Then he fell into a deep sleep.

By about 2:00 a.m., the covers moved and he felt someone crawl into the other side of his queen sized bed. He sat up half a sleep and half terrified.

"Go back to sleep. It's frigging freezing in that room."

Casey slid out of his side of the bed and grabbed his sweats on the floor. He left the bedroom for the futon.

"Suit yourself. You'll freeze your ass off out there."

Casey crawled under the blankets on the futon and swore to himself. *How in the hell did I manage to get myself into this mess? Candy. I am really going to give her hell if I ever make it out of this.* He curled up into a ball, put the covers over his head and fell back asleep.

By five, the heat kicked on. Casey and Gram worked out a schedule for the heat that worked well for him. He liked sleeping under the goose down in a cold room. By 5:30, Casey was awakened by a smell and an erection pushing up both covers. He was confused by the smell until he realized there was a strange guy in his bedroom who left his trademark scent on the pillow he had under his head. It was a smell he couldn't define, but not an unpleasant one.

Trying to push back his morning wood, he quietly made way into the bathroom for a shower. He locked the door behind him. Happy to find urinating did the trick to rid himself of the unwanted bodily reaction, he showered, shaved, and brushed his teeth before his morning coffee and breakfast. Leaving the bathroom, he heard the TV as he entered the living room.

"Do you always lock the bathroom door when you shower? I had to piss in the kitchen sink."

"Oh my God. You didn't?"

"Sorry, I had a hard time finding your guest bathroom."

Casey went to the kitchen to turn on the faucet. Nolan got up to follow him.

"You got coffee, I hope."

"You realize there is an S curve under this sink that keeps the waste water right where we can smell it."

"Just keep running the water, I'll tell you when you can stop. I'm an old pro at this. You don't grow up with one sister and four brothers and not learn how to piss in the kitchen sink without your mom finding out. "

Casey gave the guy a look of disapproval.

Nolan gave him his sideways smile in return. "Now. You can stop now. The pee pee water is all gone bye bye."

Casey took a deep breath and moved to put on the coffee. Nolan sat at the table. "So Stretch, what's for breakfast?"

"Eggs and toast. That is if it's alright with you?"

"Eggs and toast it is. Do you have any peanut butter?"

"Yes."

"Honey?"

"Yes." Casey was on auto pilot as he pulled the honey, milk and eggs from the fridge. He got two cups and put one in front of Nolan.

Nolan spread out and slid back to relax. He grabbed his phone left on the table and called his brother. "Good morning Numb Nuts. Is my truck OK?"

Casey poured his coffee and listened in on the conversation. He noticed Nolan was speaking with the same strong Southern accent his brother had at the pub.

"No I'm not at home, you took my frigging keys. I had to spend the night in a cold apartment on a lumpy futon mattress."

Casey made sure Nolan saw him lowering his brows.

"Yes, I'm at Casey's apartment. And yes I do have a spare key, but some dumb ass took the key and never put it back where it was supposed to be. Now I wonder who that would be? Where the fuck are you anyway? What is all that talking in the background?"

"At the North Star?" The North Star was the Air Force Inn on base used to house guys TDY to the area. "I thought you were supposed to be at home to help clean the place for mom and dad." Nolan held the phone away from his ear while there was some loud swearing coming through from the other side. Nolan smiled at Casey. "He's a little touchy this morning." They both heard Chester say, "The truck is parked on base," and the sound of silence. He hung up. "Jeeze, what the fuck's eating him today?"

Casey was mixing the eggs in a bowl. "So you had a rough night last night?"

"No. But it won't hurt him thinking I did."

"Have you always disliked your brother?"

"Who said I dislike my brother?"

"You fight all the time."

"That's not fighting. We love each other. It's not like we throw punches. Well, not all the time. When we lived at home we rolled around in the dirt sometimes. My mom tried to stop us, but my dad told her we were equally matched and should let us be. So she finally gave in. But not all the time. He's cool. I love him."

Casey shook his head. He grabbed the plates, put the toast in the toaster and finished setting the table.

"What about you, do you have a brother to squabble with?"

"No."

"Any sisters?"

"One."

"This smells good. I'm going to have to do a payback."

"Not necessary."

Casey watched as Nolan put a heavy amount of peanut butter on his toast and followed with an equal amount of honey.

"What time do you get lunch at the hospital?"

"Why?"

"Oh, I don't know. Would you rather talk about your sex life instead?"

"Usually at noon if we don't have an unexpected rush of sick Zoomies coming in."

"Zoomies? That is so lame."

"Is the coffee strong enough?"

"Sure. You gonna give me a ride to the base so I can find my truck?"

"Yes."

"You said you had a spare tooth brush and razor."

"I did."

"Maybe I'll skip the razor. It's a Saturday and I have Sunday off." He rubbed his beard. "What do you think?"

"I think you need a shave."

"Cool huh. I bet I could look like a mountain man in about a week if I didn't shave."

"Don't the girls complain about that?"

Nolan chuckled. "No. Never."

Casey survived Breakfast. Nolan belched, excused himself and got up from the table to stretch. He slipped off his t shirt and faced Casey bare chested. Casey tried hard to keep his eyes on Nolan's.

"I need to shower. Don't go anywhere Stretch."

He left the kitchen with his t shirt in hand, and wearing the sweats Casey gave him the night before. Casey knew what his arms looked like. But this was the first time seeing what was in between. His chest was heavily muscled, just a patch of light brown hair in the middle. His nipples were dark and shapely. His back was void of any hair and covered with a thick layer of muscle as was the front.

Casey shook his head as he watched Nolan walk to the bathroom. He heard him shout, "If you have to take a leak, don't worry, I don't lock the door."

Casey went to the futon and folded the blankets, put the pillow back in the closet and went for his cup to watch TV. He thought he heard something in the bathroom, so he put the TV on mute and walked to the door to listen in. Nolan was singing in the shower the theme song from Toy Story, You've Got a Friend in Me. Yet he was singing with the same strong Southern accent he heard him use with his brother on the phone.

He's not only the Delta Hotel, but he's crazy too. Casey listened in for a while until the shower was turned off. He went back to the futon fearing to get caught. He got up to put more coffee in Nolan's cup with milk, no sugar, and put it on the coffee table by the TV.

He jumped when he heard the bathroom door open. Nolan came out in his jeans and t shirt. He smelled his pits before sitting down. "I hope I don't stink too much. You'd be sure to let me know if I do, right?"

"No. That would be rude."

"Whatever, even if you'd be doing me a favor."

They both smelled at the same time. Nolan asked, "What the Dickens is that?"

"Gram. She must be baking cookies."

"Will she give us some?"

"That's why she's baking."
"What are we waiting for?"
"Wait a minute." He went for his cell to call Candy. "Candy, Casey. Are you home?"
"Yes I'm home, is this you snooping?"
"No I'm not snooping. We smell Gram's cookies."
"We? You devil you."
"Funny. His brother had the house keys, so he crashed here on my couch."
Nolan gave him the eye trick and spoke out loud to himself, "Now who's bullin?"
"I had to call because I didn't want to explain to Gram how I got home and you didn't. So it's all clear to head down?"
"All clear. You're going to get fat." She hung up.
"All's clear. Follow me." They left for the first floor.
"Hi Gram. We smelled the cookies. Chocolate Chip?"
"Good morning Casey. Yes they are. Sit at the table and let me get you boys a glass of milk. And who is this handsome young man?"
"Gram, this is Nolan Kelly. He's a pilot from the base. His brother took his keys by mistake so he had to sleep on the futon."
"Nice to meet you ma'am. And I slept in his bed. The futon was too lumpy."
Candy was standing at the door and gave Casey a look.
Gram poured the milk. "Well, how nice of you Casey. I think it's nice when two guys are not so uptight about sleeping in the same bed. For goodness sakes, what's the big deal anyway?"
Candy was smiling. "Yes I agree. I think two guys can share a bed with no problem."
Nolan swallowed. "So we all agree. These are great cookies."
"Thank you young man." Gram left the room to turn off the TV.

Nolan took the opportunity to ask Candy. "Do I need to pound my brother's ass, or was he well behaved last night?"

"No need to pound him. Chester was the perfect gentleman. We had a real nice time."

"Good. My mom and dad raised us right."

Buddy was nudging Casey with his nose.

"Sorry Buddy, I'll take you for a run this afternoon when I get my shopping done." Buddy sat and pawed at his lap.

"You run with the dog?"

Candy answered for him. "He sure does. Gets me off the hook. They bike together in the summer too."

"I'm going to teach him to pull me up the hills on my skis."

"Hey, I like to ski. Maybe we can get together for an outing."

Candy was holding back her look by the door.

"Well, I think we better get going to the base."

Gram came back into the kitchen. "Where are you boys off too? You just got here."

Nolan thanked her. "These are the best. Can I take a couple with me?"

"Of course you can dear. And I hope to see you back here soon."

"Great. I'll take you up on that offer." Casey rolled his eyes at Candy who kept the same look on her face.

"Candy, don't forget our date tomorrow at one."

"I'm ready."

They left the kitchen for the second floor to get their coats and car keys.

The sun was finally up at 10:02 a.m.

Some snow fell during the night, but not enough to make the roads difficult. "Start the car. Where's your brush? I'll clean the windshield."

Casey tossed him the ice scraper and brush. Nolan hummed a tune to himself while he cleaned off the top half of the car. It was cold outside. Twelve degrees with no wind.

Nolan jumped in the car. “Damn, it’s cold. Get this heater going.”

“Thanks. I should have tossed you my gloves.”

“Next time. Let’s go and find my truck.”

Casey put the Subaru in reverse to get out of the driveway. He headed towards Boniface Gate 1, keeping silent the whole way.

Nolan was the one to talk. “Drive over to billeting. I think he probably left it by the North Star Inn.”

“Is your brother stationed at Travis?” Travis AFB was about forty miles southwest of Sacramento California.

“Yes. But he spends a lot of time up here with that run to Hawaii.”

“Does he spend enough time at JBER to have a girlfriend from up here?”

“You’re getting ahead of yourself Stretch. They went dancing.”

“I know, but Candy had a different look on her face this morning. I think she likes your brother”

“Of course she does. What girl wouldn’t?”

“Is that your truck?” Casey saw a large dark brown truck with a full back seating area.

“That’s my baby. 6.4 Liter V8 engine Laramie Longhorn.”

“Longhorn?”

“You know, the model of the Ram. It’s a Laramie Longhorn.”

“Don’t trucks get stuck in the snow?”

“You do understand the concept of a powerful engine with a four wheel drive, right?”

“Not really.”

“Jeeze. Pull over there and wait for me. Numb Nuts might have forgotten to leave the keys inside.”

Casey pulled up to the truck. His Subaru looked like a kid’s toy next to the giant vehicle. He watched as Nolan opened the door, looked on the floor, and raised his hands to show Casey the keys. He found a note on the dash with three dollars on top. Casey could hear him.

"Son of a bitch. Three dollars for gas. I'm going to kick his ass good."

"Is everything OK? Can I leave now?"

Nolan got out of the truck, changed his face to a nice smile and leaned his arm on top of the car. "Don't forget Stretch, I owe you lunch."

"No you don't"

"Yes I do. Hand me your phone."

"Why?"

"So I can put my number in it? Jeeze."

Casey reluctantly gave him the phone.

Nolan gave him his.

"What am I supposed to do with this?"

Nolan laughed. "Ah, I don't know, maybe stop being such a pain in the ass and put your number in it?"

Casey shook his head but did as he was told. They returned the phones. Nolan got into his truck and roared up the engine. It started on the first try. Sometimes vehicles had a hard time starting cold. Casey had the block heater adaption to plug his car into heaters at the parking lots. It helped on days below zero. Nolan smiled and waved at Casey as he pulled away. *Finally, my night from hell is over. Candy really owes me one after this.*

Sunday proved to be a good day of rest. Casey took a good morning run with Buddy on the trails across the street and had time to read on the futon before his visit with Ian at one.

He was dozing off when the phone rang. "Hello?"

"Hi Casey, I'm by your car."

"Hi Ian, the back door should be open, come on up." They hung up and Casey heard Ian climbing the stairs.

Ian tapped on the door before opening it. He entered with a large bag of his clothes and makeup.

"Come on in, I'm in the living room."

Ian passed through the kitchen to find Casey sprawled out on the couch. "I think God made couches for Sundays."

"I agree. Sunday is my chill out day. On the couch."

Ian looked around. "Where's your tree?"

"Not you too."

"Are you sure Candy is alright with all this?"

"I'm sure. Besides, she owes me big time."

"May I ask?"

"Remember we had a date to hit the town this Friday?"

"Yes."

"Well, we had a nice dinner at Reilly's Pub, and she tried to trick me into going dancing. But I faked a twisted ankle. Then you'll never guess who we ran into after dinner."

"The base commander?"

"No! Delta Hotel."

"Oh God. Captain Kelly?"

Yes. And Captain Kelly."

"What?"

"He was there with his brother. And would you believe it was his brother who flew the C 5 Galaxy I took to Australia. And he spilled the beans to Candy about me skipping Hawaii, now I have to explain to her why I fibbed."

"You mean lied?"

"Thanks for the support."

"So what about Captain Kelly?"

"Not much. We spent the night together. He slept in my bed."

"Ohhhh. Are you telling me? Are you saying he's gay?"

"No of course not."

"Then you're saying he's curious?"

"No. When he crawled under my covers, I jumped out of the bed and made way for the futon."

"Alright. I'm totally confused."

"Nolan's brother is his twin, but they don't look exactly alike. But they are built the same way, almost. His brother, that would be Chester. I think Nolan has slightly bigger biceps. But they both have the same rear end, as far as I could tell."

Ian wrinkled his brows at Casey. He still didn't understand. "That Delta Hotel does have a great butt. He moves it like he knows it too. Not too big, but hard enough to get his flight suit caught in the crack sometimes."

"I knew you watched those rear ends."

"And you don't?"

"Back to the story. So Chester offered to take Candy dancing after I told her I couldn't, due to my recent injury. Before I knew what hit me, Chester had his brother's keys to the truck in his hand, Candy on his arm and they were out the pub's door, leaving me behind with Delta Hotel. And guess who had to give him a ride home? Me."

"OK, so how did he end up in your bed, if I may ask?"

"Half way to his house, he realized the keys to his house were with the truck keys and he didn't have a spare, so he told me to turn around and announced he'd be spending the night with me."

"Damn, I have to ask, that guy has a really thick beard, does he have a big bush between his legs?"

"Ian? What the hell?"

"Sorry."

"No I didn't get to see his bush. But if you must know, he took off his t shirt in front of me, and he has a really incredible chest. Not hairy. And really beautiful nipples. Damn, did I just say that?"

"Don't feel guilty. Who doesn't like a nice pair of nipples on a hot guy?"

"That's it. End of story, I hope."

"Like hell it is. How did he end up in your bed?"

"Oh. He said it was too cold on the futon, so about 2:00 a.m., he just crawled in."

"Was he naked?"

"No! He was wearing my sweat pants."

"So you just left him there?"

"Yes. Was I supposed to stay and keep him warm?"

"Or him keep you warm?"

“I went to the futon and spent the night there. Ian, yesterday was the day from hell. It’s taken me most of this morning to get past it.”

“Damn, what I wouldn’t give to see that guy in the buff. Do you think he has a hairy ass crack?”

“Ian!”

“Sorry.”

“Let me call Candy, she’s expecting us.”

“Oh right. Now you have me all flustered.”

“Well, get over it.”

In a few minutes, Candy entered into the kitchen with her makeup kit. “Hi boys. You must be Ian? I’ve cut your hair before.”

“Hi Candy, nice to formally meet you.”

“So, you’re interested in making a few changes in your appearance?”

“A few.”

“I’m just the right person to come to.” She moved her hands towards Ian. “May I?”

“Of course. I’m all yours.”

Candy took her hands and messed up his combed hair. She moved it around from the side part he had. “You need a cut. And I have an idea. I’ve seen some very awesome female models with short guy haircuts. I could change your cut so you could wear it one way at home and then you could comb it for your uniform.”

“Really? But it’s so short?”

“Doesn’t matter. We get rid of the part, wear it messed up and we have the look we’re pushing for. Casey can I cut his hair in the bathroom?”

“Of course.”

She took out her comb and scissor and they all three went to the bathroom. Casey watched as she totally changed the look of his cut in a few minutes. “You have a good texture to pull this off.” She used a little water to move his hair where she wanted it. The end result was an even cut with crooked bangs and an uneven back. It looked different.

"Candy, I don't think I can be in uniform with this look."

"Yes you can, watch this." She used more water, combed the hair with a part on the side, and the look immediately changed.

Casey commented. "That is really cool. A real Jeckyll and Hyde here."

"More like Lucy and Ethel. I love it." Ian beamed.

Candy used the back of her hand to feel the side of Ian's face. "Did you shave this morning?"

"Yes, why?"

"Because you are lucky you don't have a thick beard. I just met a guy this weekend with a really dense beard. If that guy wanted to dress like a women, he would have a really rough time with it."

"I think I know him. Are you talking about Delta Hotel?"

"Who's that?"

Casey laughed. "It's what we call Nolan at work. Delta Hotel is the phonetic spelling for the initial D and H. D for dick and H for head."

"Are you guys saying you think Nolan is a dick head?"

Both guys shook their heads up and down in agreement.

"That's not very nice."

They both shook their heads again, but this time back and forth to demonstrate the opposite of the affirmative.

"Well, his brother is a real angel. A good dancer too." She went back to feeling his face. "Do you know how to put on foundation?"

"No. One of my problems is I didn't grow up with any siblings and my mom never wore makeup."

"Well, let me show you all about the foundation." She fumbled in her makeup kit looking for what was needed. "You know I read some blogs on the internet about guys who made the transition. One of them had some really good advice. She said the biggest mistake she made was to go for the breast before completing her electrolysis on the facial hair. She said laser was a waste of time. As she was already dressed like a women with breast implants, she had to let the beard grow out a little for the electrolysis to work."

"I can't do that in the Air Force. We have to be clean shaven in uniform."

"Could you take leave to get it done?"

"Maybe. But I plan to leave the Air Force in a few months. So maybe I can wait for that part."

"You can. You shaved this morning, and even though you have black hair, there is barely a trace of beard. This is going to work."

Casey watched with a cup of coffee as Candy worked her magic. When she finished she handed Ian the mirror. "You're a magician."

"So are you Ian. It just takes a little practice. And do not, I repeat, do not over do it. You don't want to end up looking like a call girl. The best part of makeup is to have it on and have people think it's not."

"OK."

Casey asked, "Candy, what do you think about purple lipstick?"

"No way."

Next Candy worked on Ian's choice of clothes. "Let me see that dress."

Ian handed her a black dress, tight fitting on the top and like a skirt on the bottom.

"This is nice. And you got a great body for this. Casey, can you imagine trying to get those two brothers to look nice in a dress. My God those boys got some serious muscles. Did you happen to notice?"

"Yes Candy, I did notice." He rolled his eyes at her and she laughed.

Candy saw the strap was coming undone. "Ian, go and get dressed, I can sew that strap when we finish. You don't want the strap to break and have a wardrobe malfunction when you're out on the town. By the way, you have been out on the town?"

"A couple of times. Only to Mad Myrna's in the cover of night."

They spent the next hour working on Ian and giving him all kinds of advice, from his eyelashes to his choice of shoes. He left Casey's apartment with his bag full of women's clothes and a big smile on his face. Candy gave him some great pointers and promised to be his coach for anything else he might need. She even promised to take him to the big thrift store downtown.

The work week began as routine. Hump day finally arrived to find Casey sitting at his desk early in the morning staring at the business card Ian gave him the week before. He arrived early to work and no one else was in the office. He made up his mind to call at seven, expecting to get a recording machine and a good excuse to hang up and forget all about it.

"Good morning, this is Sawyer, can I help you?"

"Is this a recording?"

"No. I'm a real person. But be prepared, I do have an answering machine I use when I'm with a client."

"My name is Casey. I got your name from a friend of mine, Ian Tremblay."

"Yes, he gave me a heads up. Would you like to come in and get some things off your chest?"

"I think so. Actually, I thought I'd be getting your answering machine, and I would be able to change my mind and hang up."

Sawyer laughed. "You still can. I won't be offended if you do."

"No. I don't want to hang up."

"So, I have an opening tomorrow at 6:00 p.m. What do you say?"

"Tomorrow?"

"Is tomorrow too soon?"

"No. But I'm getting butterflies in my stomach."

"Casey, sometimes talking things out brings a whole suitcase of feeling in your stomach. But if you face them without fear, you'll be better off in the end."

"OK. So then I'll see you tomorrow at six."

"Nice. I'll be looking forward to meeting you."

"By." Casey hung up the phone and stood up. He put his hands on his chest and took deep breaths. *Oh my God. Am I really going to do this?*

Casey spent the morning on auto pilot. He managed to put the six o'clock appointment in the back of his mind. By 11:45, the office was empty and he was looking for things to do.

"Hey Stretch."

Casey jumped. "Good morning Captain Kelly. Do you need to see the doctor today?"

"No I do not."

"Do you need to get some records?"

"No I do not." Nolan almost broke out in a laugh. "Come on, it's lunch time, I owe you lunch."

"No you don't"

"Yes I do. And I'm cooking. Get your hat."

"Captain, I can't leave base. I don't have that long of a lunch hour."

"Who said we're leaving base? Come on, get your hat."

"Do you have a room at the North Star?"

"Stretch, your coat and hat?"

Casey reluctantly got his coat and hat. He told Sergeant Tomlin at the front desk he was stepping out for an hour.

Nolan led the way. "How's your week going?"

"Nice. And how about you?"

"Same. I flew training missions Monday and Tuesday. Nothing today or tomorrow."

They walked to the parking lot. "I don't see your truck."

"Over there. The white Ford Super Duty, the one with the camper on the back."

"You have a camper?"

"No. It's my mom and dad's. But I use it whenever I want. It's great for camping up here." He led Casey to the camper. Opened the door. "After you." Casey climbed into the back of the camper via a side door. Nolan followed him.

"Have a seat on the Sofa and hold on. I know you can be a little jumpy." Casey sat on the sofa at the very back of the interior and Nolan pushed some buttons. The sofa moved back and the dining table moved out to the side, making the interior space like that of a small one bedroom apartment. "What do you think?"

"Amazing. And I didn't jump."

"Is it warm enough in here for you?"

"Yes."

"Go ahead, take off your coat. I'll set the table and get started with lunch."

"So you cook?"

"Get ready. I'm making my speciality. Grilled cheese sandwiches. And we have a healthy salad too."

Casey saw the container from the Commissary with the salad inside. He took off his coat and watched Nolan prepare lunch. "Does this thing have a bathroom?"

"Right behind that door. If you want, you can shower."

"I don't need it. I just wondered."

The large bed was over the top of the truck. "Do you sleep up there?"

"I sure do. Trust me, it's plenty comfortable for two."

"Did your mom and dad buy it up here?"

"No. This summer, I picked up my truck and we all drove the Alaskan Highway. It took us ten days."

"I thought it was only a week's drive."

"My dad."

"Does he drive slow?"

"No. But every time he sees water, he has to stop and throw in a line. He's a fishing maniac."

"I bet it was fun."

"It was. I love my mom and dad."

"Nice."

Nolan stopped cooking his bread and cheese. "Casey, do you know about me?"

"I've heard things. But I already told you that?"

"Are you still on the Delta Hotel kick?"

"A little."

"I'm referring to my family. Have you heard anything about that?"

"No. Why?"

"Do you ever listen to country music?"

"No. Not really."

"Have you ever heard of Bobby Kelly?"

Casey got a blank look on his face. "Yes. Everybody knows who Bobby Kelly is. Wild Rose on the Fence Line?"

"Bobby Kelly is my dad."

Casey stared at the dining area situated to the side of the camper. He watched as Nolan placed the sandwiches on the table.

"Want milk for lunch?"

"So you're a celebrity?"

"Who? Me? Good God no. My dad is."

"How can you be a part of such a family and not be a global celebrity?"

"Ask my dad. He made sure we had as much of a normal life as possible. When Chester and I were seven, he retired from the music industry, stayed on our farm way out in the sticks of Western Georgia, wrote songs for other singers, raised his kids and fished. Can't forget that part. My mom told him not to, but he said being a country star was just an unplanned turn in life. What he wanted most was to be a great dad. And he really is. So he just quit."

"But I think I saw him winning a music award a few years ago."

"You did. He went back after his kids were all grown up, about six years ago. He won the CMA Entertainer of the Year his first year back."

"Are you rich?"

"Do you want to see my truck payment sheet from the credit union?"

Casey got off the couch and sat at the table. Nolan poured two glasses of milk.

"Did you grow up in a mansion?"

Nolan laughed. "An old farmhouse. Dad had an add on built for a bedroom. Get this, one room with a bathroom, three shower stalls and three toilets. Shared by five boys. Lots of privacy. My Grandma Milly and Pa Roy lived right down the lane on our farm. I spent the night with them several times just to get some privacy in one of their bedrooms."

"How did you keep the press away?"

Nolan shook his head up and down. "The farm was fortified. We were insulated with over 500 acres." He waited for Casey to take the first bite. "Let's go camping this weekend. We can make it a cross country ski event."

"I can't. I have a previous obligation."

"Break it."

Casey looked up at Nolan with those eyes doing the fancy one eye open, one eye nearly closed trick.

"The sandwich is good."

"Thanks. So Stretch, you know about my family, what about yours?"

Casey stared at his glass of milk.

"Mom? Dad? You said you had a sister?"

"I grew up in Syracuse New York. This snow around here is nothing new for me. It's colder though."

"So snow is your family?"

Casey swallowed the last bite of his sandwich. "Nolan, I can't. I don't know how."

"What?"

"I don't know how to tell anyone about my life. Can we just leave it?"

"Sure. I didn't mean to pry."

"It's alright." Casey made an obvious attempt to look at his watch. "My lunch hour is almost over. Can I help you clean up?"

"I got it."

"I better get back."

Nolan gave Casey his side smile. "So you'll think about camping?"

"Sure." Casey gave any answer. He just wanted to get out. He stood up. "Thanks for lunch." Walking to the door, he turned around. "I want to apologize."

"For what?"

"For referring to you as Delta Hotel. It wasn't very nice of me."

Nolan slid down in his place and smiled again. Casey left the camper. He walked back to the office from the parking lot to reach the security of his work space.

Inside the hospital he ran into Ian in the hall. "Captain Link. Just the person I'm looking for." He grabbed Casey by the arm and pulled him to the side by the wall so they could talk in private. "Candy just called me. Guess what?"

"Oh no. I'm afraid to ask."

"She said we were all three going out to the Irish pub this Friday night. And me all dolled up."

"She did, did she?"

"She's trying to call you right now. Can you get used to calling me by my new name?"

"What new name?"

"Ines. It means chaste in French?"

"Chaste?" Casey grabbed his phone and made a word search. He handed the phone to Ian. "Read this." The word chaste had the definition, abstaining from extramarital, or from all sexual intercourse.

Ian handed back the phone. "Minor details. I got to go. This is going to be great." He smiled at Casey and turned around to leave.

"Ian, I did it."

He walked back. "You called the cop?"

"Good God no. That card you gave me. I called for an appointment. I go tomorrow at six. I just wanted you to know. Remember, I said you'd be the first person I tell? I might have to break that promise now."

“You don’t worry about that silly promise. You tell me whenever you want. Hey, it looks like we’re both off in the right direction.”

“Maybe you’re right.” They turned and walked in separate directions.

Casey called Candy from his office. “Hello Candy, is there something you wanted to ask me?”

“No. But there is something I wanted to tell you. We’re going back to Reilly’s this Friday night. I want to start training Ian in social situations.”

“So go with him. What’s this got to do with me?”

“For real?”

“No. I’m sorry, I’m just a little jumpy this morning. I’ll go. And I think it’s nice of you to put forth the time and effort. This is huge for Ian.”

“Thank you Cutie. Maybe lay off the coffee with the getting jumpy, huh?”

“Yeah, that’s probably it.”

“And I’m still waiting.”

“For what?”

“For you to tell me about your family reunion without me having to ask.”

“Oh, that. It’s complicated.”

“Of course it is. I guess I wouldn’t understand complicated family situations.”

“Alright. I get it. I got to go. See you later.”

“Bye Sweetie.”

“Bye.” He hung up.

Sergeant Tomlin came to his office. “Captain, we have an Army warrant officer in the waiting room to see the doc.”

“I’ll be right there.” Casey left his office to take care of the Army helicopter pilot. “Mr. Brooks, would you follow me please?”

All Army warrant officers were addressed as Mister in the Army. They were a special rank apart from being an officer or an enlisted. Brooks was a flight warrant officer.

"Have a seat and let me get your information into the computer. We're having a slow day. The doctor, Major Myers will be able to see you right away." Casey got into the data base with the records of Brooks. "So, Mr. Brooks, what is the problem today?"

"My left ear. It hurts like a son of a bitch. I think I got an ear infection from taking my kid to the pool on base."

"Ouch. Let me get your vitals and I'll get you taken care of."

Casey spent the whole next day pacing the floors. He wanted to be totally immersed in his work so as not to be bothered with the appointment he had for six. Three different times he dialed the number to cancel but hung up before the number got connected. He was a nervous wreck. The only one who knew about it was Ian. He even skipped lunch. It was like this the whole day. It passed until he found himself leaving the therapist's office with homework he didn't want to do.

Thursday night, after his run with Buddy, his day of work and his appointment with Sawyer, he sat on the couch and drank his second glass of wine. Sawyer gave him a large plain looking book filled with lined paper. It was a journal. His homework was to write. More specifically, he was to report the following week after writing his first memory of the troubles, as he referred to them with Sawyer. He sat in the quiet living room and began to write. By two minutes into the new day, he closed the journal, put aside the pen and placed the journal on the table. He wanted to talk to Ian, and realized his labor would free him of having to do so. He found the sticky notepad from the kitchen, wrote 'Read Me' and stuck it on the cover for Ian to read.

Casey went to Catholic grade school for his first three years. His mind was conveniently filled with the images of angels and saints from the holy cards the nuns would give him as a reward. He also had the image of the devil right next to the other images in whatever part of the brain those things got stored.

Under the security of his double goose down quilts, he fell into a deep sleep. He awoke to find the devil staring at him from the bedroom door. Lucky for him, there was a big knife on the dresser, but he forgot to place it on the nightstand. The devil had glowing red eyes and slowly walked towards his bed. Casey was too afraid to get out and run. He glanced at the knife, but decided to hide under the covers and play dead. He awoke for real in a cold sweat. His heart was beating fast. He got out of bed to walk in circles around the apartment. That helped get the images of the dream out of his head. When he was in the fourth grade, he saw a black and white drawing of the devil flying over a French city by Eugene Delacroix in 1828. It was the same image that used to visit him frequently in his dreams at night. After leaving home, the dreams subsided to a two or three time annual event. This was one of those nights.

Damn it, I haven't had that dream for almost a year now. Gram's cookies. A glass of milk. He walked to the kitchen table to pour a glass of milk and have two of Gramm's Christmas cookies covered in multi colored little beads adorning the shape of bells. The next morning he awoke ready to reach the security of his job.

"Morning Ian. Or should I say Ines?"

"No, not here. You'll have to wait until tonight."

"The black dress?"

"No. Damn it anyway, Candy won't let me. She said I have to get comfortable as a women in jeans also. So I'm wearing hiking boots, tight fitting jeans and a nice frilly button down top. Candy said she was going to show me how a few rings and bracelets can really help push the envelope."

"Isn't she amazing?"

"My savior. You too. So how did it go last night?"

"It went, I hated it. I thought my heart was going to explode while I was waiting for him to open his office door. I might not go back."

"Can you give it a few days before you make that decision?"

"I don't know. I had a rough night. Things were going just fine before."

"I suppose you're right. After all you had great ability to dump the perfect guy with the excuse of feeling something."

Casey gave him a twisted jaw look. "I got to go. By the way, I'll be the designated driver tonight. I really don't want to get foggy on booze. I need to think clearly."

"Great. Let's just hope this work day gets over. I'm so excited about tonight."

Casey turned around to head for his department, but Ian called him back. "Casey?"

Casey turned around. "What?"

"I doubt if anybody from the base will be able to recognize me tonight. But what about you?"

"I don't mind. Really, I don't care if the base commander sees me. I know how to keep myself in the closet. This isn't the eieghties. Transgendered persons are finally getting some recognition."

"Thanks to Caitlyn and Chaz."

"Don't forget my hero former Navy SEAL, Kristin."

"So true. See you later."

Back in his office, he met Major Myers in the patient waiting room. "I don't know about you Captain, but I for one am damn glad it's Friday."

"Same here. It's been a rough week for me."

"Got any plans for Christmas?"

"Dinner with a friend and her grandma. A lot of loafing around and reading on the couch. Playing with the dog."

"Sounds like a plan. If you don't have anyplace to go, you're welcome at our house. We have our dinner on Christmas Eve, then we go to church at midnight."

"Thanks."

"Was that your friend's rig in the parking lot?"

"Yeah."

"What a beauty. Lance makes a great camper. How many does that sleep?"

"Four." Casey didn't like talking about Nolan as a friend. It was the first time anybody made the claim. He needed time to think about it.

After his run in the trails with Buddy, a hot shower and watching the local news on the TV, his phone rang.

"Casey, I'm here. Is the door open?"

"It's open. Come on up."

The door opened and he heard Ian climbing the stairs. He knocked.

"It's open."

Ian smiled as he came through the door dressed in the jeans he and Candy picked out at the Military Mall Exchange on his lunch hour. They managed to try on the jeans without anybody noticing, and Candy paid the lady at the cash register.

"Nice! Turn around."

Ian turned around and held out his hand to show off a pink and blue fake diamond bracelet. He painted his fingernails pink.

"How in the hell are you going to get your nails back to normal?"

"No problem. Meet Sula, it's a water based nail polish that you can peel off without any chemicals. It's only ten bucks a bottle on Amazon."

"You're getting to be a real expert at this."

"I have a long way to go, but yes, I have learned some things."

They both heard Candy at the door. "Are you boys descent?"

"Get in here. Descent!" shouted Casey.

Candy came in and immediately began to inspect Ian. "Turn around." He did as he was ordered to do. "I was right. Casey, look how those jeans fit his butt."

"And the front too. I can see his balls."

Ian looked down, turned and ran to the bathroom. He returned in less than a minute.

Candy smiled at him. "By the way, what are your future plans with those?"

"You mean," he paused, "I know what you mean."

Casey widened his eyes. "So?"

"This is just between us, right?"

Both shook their head yes.

"I'm working on that with my therapist. It's an area I don't understand with myself. Most guys in my position hate their genitals. And I don't. It's a mystery I have to solve."

Candy shrugged her shoulders like it was nothing. "So keep them. It's not like you want to be a stripper or anything like that. And besides, what if you find Mr. Right and he likes what you got. People come in all shapes and sizes."

"I didn't think you could understand."

"I do too." They all sat in silence for a few moments absorbing the mystery of Ian's lack of hate for his penis. "Guys, I found out something today that blew me away. I wasn't told to keep it a secret, so I'm telling you but please let's keep it between us?"

Candy raised both her thumbs on the air, "I'm in."

Ian confessed, "The more secrets, the closer we become. I'm in."

"I had lunch with Captain Kelly today in the parking lot."

Candy lowered her eyebrows. "A bag lunch in the freezing cold?"

"No, in his camper. You should see this thing. When you get inside, he pushes this button and the walls start moving. The couch to the back moves farther back and the dining area moves out to the side. In a split second the place is like a small apartment."

"Why did he make you lunch?" Candy was spinning the wheels in her head.

"Long story, I made him breakfast, so he insisted he owed me a lunch, even though I insisted he didn't."

"Right, that was the morning he woke up in your bed."

Candy twitched her lips. "We haven't had the chance to talk about that yet."

"Later. Now get this. He asked me about his family. He asked me if I knew anything about them. Do you guys know?"

Ian shook his head no and Candy said, "No."

"What is his last name?"

"Kelly," they both said at the same time.

"Wild Rose on the Fence Line?"

Ian opened his mouth, Candy gasped, "No way!"

"Way."

"He's related to Bobby Kelly?" Candy was the only one of the two able to respond. Ian still had his mouth open.

"Bobby Kelly is his dad."

"STFU! He's pulling your leg. After all, you guys call him the Delta Holly." Candy didn't believe it.

"Delta Hotel. And about that, I apologized for calling him a dick head. Maybe you guys can join me and stop the name calling with him. He's super obnoxious, but he's not a dick head."

Candy sat back in her chair and folder her arms. "Somebody here has the hots for a fighter pilot."

"What? No way. I told you he's very obnoxious. But he's a little bit considerate."

Ian finally found his voice. "If it's true, the guy is filthy rich."

"Wrong. He wanted to show me his bank statement from the credit union. The one with the huge truck payment."

Candy sat back up. "Alright, we keep this a secret. If it's true."

Casey got up. "Come on guys, I don't want to wait for a table. Steak night at Reilly's Pub is popular on Friday nights. I'm the designated driver."

"Give me a second. I want to visit the little girl's room." Candy left for the bathroom.

Casey left the kitchen to get a book and show it to Ian, who was still sitting at the table. "Look. I did my homework. I want you to be the first to read it. OK?"

"Read Me. Cute. I can let you read mine also. Sawyer said it helps to share those thoughts with someone you trust. I'm so glad we trust each other."

"Same here." He went back to put the journal on the side table by the futon.

Casey parked his light green Subaru Forester in the lot. They made it to the pub before six. Getting a table would be fast. Most arrived after seven.

Candy was in the back seat. She put her hand on Ian's shoulder. "Just relax. You look great."

Ian adjusted his short black wig. "Thanks. I'm ready." They all got out of the car and walked over to the side door. The pub was all lit up with green and white Christmas lights. There was a tall skinny real tree at the entrance that smelled like the pine forest. They were immediately seated and ordering drinks.

The waitress approached the table. "Merry Christmas guys. Can I get you something to drink?"

Candy nudged Ian on the arm. "Go ahead Ines, you go first."

Ines used her high voice he'd been practicing for years. "I'd like a glass of red wine please."

Candy followed. "I'll have what she's having also."

Casey did his best to hold back a smile. "I'll have a diet cola, no ice."

The waitress left the table to get their drinks. They soon found themselves having the same special they had the previous Friday night. But this time the desert was pumpkin pie with whip cream. Candy brought up the subject of famous transgendered persons. "Ever since you guys asked me to be Ian's personal coach, I've been reading blogs and looking for videos. Have you guys seen on Netflix that movie about the former Navy SEAL that became a women? It was called Lady Valor."

Ian answered first. "Wasn't that amazing?"

Casey added, "Kristen showed the world that it doesn't matter what sex you feel like on the inside. She was one of the world's superhumans for over twenty years with the SEAL Team Six. And now she's helping others make the transition with pride. Kristen is one of my biggest superheroes."

"Same here," added Ian.

"I can see why." Candy understood.

"You will never believe what I read online yesterday? It might be just a rumor, but I was thrilled to hear it anyway."

"What?" Casey didn't like being kept in suspense.

"I heard that the Defense Secretary Ash Carter was interviewed saying he planned to announce in June of next year that being transgendered will no longer be reason for not allowing anybody to serve."

"No way."

"Honest Candy, supposedly he said that anybody trans would have to be stable in gender identification for at least eighteen months before entering the service."

Casey shook his head, not buying it. "Don't go and get your hopes up, that would be a huge step. One the military might not be ready for yet."

"I know. But I can still have hope, can't I?"

Candy put her hand on Ines'. "Yes you can. And so can we." She changed the subject, "Damn, if that didn't hit the spot." She took a sip of the coffee she ordered to go with the pumpkin pie.

Ines shook her head in agreement.

"I like Gram's pumpkin pie better. And she makes whip cream from scratch."

"And it's twice as fattening."

"Who cares, I got Buddy to take care of the extra calories. What should I get him for Christmas?"

Candy wrinkled her brows. "Are you for real? You're getting a dog something for Christmas?"

"And why not? He's one of my best buddies."

Ian smiled.

They paid the bill and moved to the bar section of the pub to enjoy the crowd and have a few more drinks.

"And who is the pretty tranny?"

They looked back to see three big guys standing right behind them.

Casey pulled Ian by the arm. "Come on guys, let's move." They moved to the other end of the bar and the three guys followed them with their beers.

"Don't go away. We were just getting to know each other." The one in front put his fingers between Ian's legs at the back. He jumped and turned sideways.

Casey didn't see it, but he figured as much. "Keep your hands to yourself and leave us alone. We don't want any trouble."

The other guy spoke for the first time. "Come on, no harm meant. Just a little fun. That's what trannies want anyway. And we're here to offer our services."

Candy got red in the face. "You are disgusting. Get lost or I'm going to put my boot right between your legs."

The third one spoke. "You two can have the tranny. I want that one."

The bartender overheard the conversation. "Guys, do I need to call security?"

Casey looked at the first guy to speak, he was the biggest, but also a little on the overweight side. He didn't look like he was in super shape. "I'm not sure. Do we need to?"

The big guy smirked "We'll see you around. The green Subaru right?"

Casey gave him a dirty look as the three guys moved to the other end of the bar.

The bartender told them. "You guys better be careful around those three. I've never seen them in here before."

"Thanks." Casey kept his eyes on the guys as they found a spot to stand. They were giving high fives and laughing.

"Casey, how do they know what kind of car you drive?"

“I don’t know Candy, but I don’t like this.”

“Would you believe this is just a normal day for transgendered people. I think we get the brunt of violence in the LGBT community.”

“I think you’re right.”

“Great. Now what the hell are we going to do. Call the police?” Candy wasn’t sure if she still didn’t want to boot the guy between the legs.

Casey thought of Kevin. He knew Kevin would drop whatever it was he was doing and fly over to the pub to help him out. “Hold on, I got an idea.” He pulled the cell phone out from his pocket.

“Hello Stretch. What are you up to?”

“Hi Nolan. Sorry to bother you. Are you at home?”

“Yes. And I put my number in your phone to call me whenever you want. Cut with the bother me crap. So what’s going on?”

“I’m in a little trouble.”

“What?”

“I’m at Reilly’s Pub with Candy and a friend. We were having dinner.”

“And you can’t pay the bill?”

“I wish it were so simple. There’s these guys who want to mess with us. I don’t think we can safely go to my car without ending up in a brawl. And these guys are on the big side. Mean too.”

“Stay inside by the bartender. I’ll be there in fifteen minutes.” He hung up before Casey could say thanks.

Candy was the only one of the three who kept her eyes on the group. “Nolan? I thought you were calling the cops.”

“I have a feeling the way Nolan is built, it will be a deterrence to those kind of jerks. He looks tough.”

“Is his brother coming with him? I think his leave started this morning.”

“I didn’t ask. Nolan said to stay by the bar and not go outside.” Casey looked at his watch. “He said it would take him fifteen minutes.”

“Guys, I am so sorry I got you into this. We should have gone to Mad Myrna’s instead.”

“Nonsense. We have the right to go wherever we want just like anybody else in this town. Don’t you go and start thinking we don’t.”

Casey had his eyes facing the bottles lining the back of the bar. “Are they still looking at us?”

“Yes. That big one is doing some disgusting gesture with his tongue. If Nolan doesn’t show up soon, I’m going over there to kick him in the nuts.”

“He’ll be here.”

Candy looked at the other patrons in the pub. “Why aren’t there any other pilots in here tonight. This place is usually crawling with them on a Friday night.”

“They had an exercise recall this afternoon. We won’t be seeing anybody unless they’re on leave like Nolan is.”

They spent less than twenty long nervous minutes saying little until they felt the air pressure change in the bar. The main door swung open and in walked two guys, jeans, t shirts and no jacket. They approached Casey and his friends while most of the patrons followed their path with their eyes.

“Are you guys OK?” Nolan was standing straight and spoke with a sense of urgency. Chester stood at his side saying nothing.

“Now we are. Thanks for coming.”

“Where are they?”

“See those three guys at the other end of the bar? The big one has on a hat with the Confederate flag.”

Nolan and Chester both turned their heads. The three guys knew their interest group summoned some backup. “Who are the other two?”

“The tall one with a green jacket and the other one is just to his left. With the black beanie on.”

“You guys stay here. Come on Chester, time to teach those dudes a lesson.”

As they walked over to the three, Casey got worried. "I didn't want a fight. I was hoping they would see us and just leave."

Candy kept her eyes on the event. "Hush up and watch. This is really hot."

Ines kept quiet.

The three saw them coming and moved their attention to the back of the bar so as to appear like they were clueless. Nolan came up behind the big guy, grabbed his right arm with lightning speed and pulled it up high behind his back. The guy moaned and lowered his torso to relieve the pain. Nolan took the opportunity with the guy's lowered head to use his left hand and smash his face against the surface of the bar. He broke the guy's nose.

With his right hand forcing the guy's right arm high up his back and his left hand holding on to his head of hair, he explained, "If you ever threaten or disrespect my friends again, I'll break your fucking neck." Nolan's deep Southern drawl poured out of his mouth.

The other two were in shock at how fast their leader was taken out. Then they gave it a thought to go after Chester. Chester held up his finger and pointed it at them. His muscular arms and torso were right on display. "Don't move. Unless you want the same treatment as your friend."

The second guy took a step forward, the third took a step back. "I'm warning you, I'll break both your fucking arms if you take one step closer."

The guy stopped. The other guy moved further back. "Chill out dude. We were just having a little fun. We didn't do anything."

Casey pulled the bleeding and moaning big guy from off the counter of the bar and aimed him towards the door. "Get the fuck out of here and don't ever come back. This is our hangout, and I hope to hell you follow my advice because the next time, it won't be pretty." He pushed the big guy towards the door who used his hand to stop the bleeding and followed the other two out.

As soon as the three were out of sight, the patrons began to applaud. A few patted them on the back as they went to find their group. The bartender smiled, took a wad of paper towels and proceeded to wipe the blood and spit off the bar top.

Chester spoke first while looking Candy in the eyes. "You alright?"

"I am now. You two are amazing."

Nolan looked back at the door. "We better get out of here. Someone might have called the cops. If the commander finds out I was in a bar fight he'll kick my ass and put me on some kind of stupid duty assignment. He might even cancel my leave."

Chester asked, "What if those guys follow us?"

Nolan handed Chester the keys to the truck. "You take Candy and follow us to Casey's house. Candy, keep an eye out the back to make sure we aren't being followed. I'll go with Casey. We'll take the lead. If I think we're being followed, we'll drive over to Boniface Gate 1, it's right by Casey's place."

"Sounds like a plan. Come on Candy."

Everyone watched them as they left the pub. There were a few nice comments of support. They stood in the parking lot looking for any signs of the three, not knowing what kind of vehicle they drove. Then they got in the Subaru and the truck to head towards Casey's.

"I didn't mean for you to get into a fight. I thought they would see you and leave us alone."

"They would have, but I wanted to teach them a lesson. I think they might stay away from Reilly's now."

Ines finally spoke. "I need to thank you Captain. This was all my fault."

"You're welcome."

They drove the rest of the way in silence, the headlights of the big Ram truck were right behind them. Casey spoke to Ines when they were about a mile from their house. "Ines, you're welcome to stay with me tonight if you want?"

"I'm OK. I got a loaded gun in my place if they want to come and find me."

"Good move," said Nolan. "Casey, do you have a gun?"

"No."

Casey gave Nolan the directions to the street where Ines lived on top of the garage. "Thanks again, to you both."

"We'll wait until you're inside. If for any reason you feel something isn't right, give me a call and I can be over here in ten minutes. Lock your door, I have your key. See you later."

Ines left the back seat of the Subaru and walked up the stairs to her place while Casey and Nolan watched. The headlights from the Ram truck were right behind them. Ines was on a training mission with Candy and Casey to learn how to act in the straight world. He got the training he would need. Violence against transgendered persons was always a real and serious threat.

Ines turned, waved at the two vehicles and went inside. Casey wanted to make a comment but held back in respect of his friend's privacy.

"Come on. Let's get you home."

Casey shook his head and pulled around to find his street. He parked the car. "Can you guys come in for a bite to eat or a drink? I bought some eggnog and rum for such an occasion."

"Sounds like a plan." They got out of the car. Candy and Chester were right behind them.

Casey invited them both up. They met Buddy by the back door waiting to join the excitement.

"Damn. Does he bite?"

"Not if you're nice to me he doesn't," said Candy.

Casey led the way, behind Buddy. "Have you two eaten yet?"

Chester said yes, Nolan said no. Chester changed his answer after getting a dirty look from his brother.

“Come on in. Throw your coats on the chair by the TV and we’ll put something together.”

“Do you have eggs for an egg sandwich?” Nolan opened the fridge door.

“Sure. Anybody want an eggnog with some rum?”

“They all did.”

Sitting at the table while Casey was preparing the egg sandwiches for Chester and Nolan. Nolan announced his plan for security. “I think we better stay here tonight, just in case.”

Casey stopped cooking and put his mind in gear. “Do you guys mind sharing the futon? It opens up into a full?”

“We don’t mind, but I want someone downstairs. Candy do you have a couch?”

“I do.”

“Will Gram mind if Chester sleeps on your couch?”

Chester held back a smile from his brother’s ingenious plan.

“Of course not. She’ll cook a great breakfast for us all.”

“Good. Then Chester will cover the first floor and I’ll cover the second.”

Casey remembered the difficulties with the last sleep over. “Candy, will you set the temperature for 68 and leave it there? It gets too cold for the Captain in the living room at night. I don’t want him to be uncomfortable.”

“I wasn’t uncomfortable the last time I slept here.”

“I remember.”

Candy changed the subject. “So, Chester, has your Christmas leave started yet?”

“This morning. I’m off until Christmas eve.”

“Same for me.”

Candy was braver with the questions than was Casey. “Do you have company showing up for Christmas?”

Chester gave Nolan a look. “My mom and dad fly in this Monday at noon. Then they fly out to get home by

Christmas day with my other brothers and sister. My Grandma Milly and Pa Roy too."

Nolan got sentimental. "We had some great Christmases on the farm when we were growing up, didn't we Bro?"

"Sure did. Remember the year Dad got us the dirt bikes and Mom didn't know about it?"

"Never forget. We tore up those woods the next day. I bet the trails are still there."

The conversation went on for about an hour after eating, while each having two Christmas eggnog drinks. Candy was the one to break it up. "I'm wiped out. My first time as the damsel in distress has had its effect on me. I need to call it a night. Chester, you can watch TV in the living room as long as you want, Gram always sleeps with the TV on in her room. It won't bother her."

"Should you say something in case she wakes in the night and finds a stranger on her couch?"

"I will. Don't worry." They got up and left for the kitchen door. "Keep her safe Bro."

"Same goes for you." They left with Buddy right behind them.

"So. Captain Kelly, want to watch TV?"

"Sure Captain Link. Don't you think friends should call each other by their first names instead of by their military rank?"

"OK. Just habit. I don't have too many friends."

"You got one more now than you had before. Come on Stretch, let's go and watch some TV." They made way for the living room.

Casey went for the routine sweat pants, two blankets and a pillow. "If you want, I have another blanket. I really don't want you to get cold in the middle of the night."

Nolan threw Casey his eye trick. "Don't you go and bother yourself about me. I know how to take care of myself."

Casey knew he was referring to the incident at the bar. "I could tell. Too bad we can't all be like Batman."

"It's not too bad because we're not all supposed to be."

Casey slid down in the chair and watched the screen of the TV.

"Hey, did I just piss you off?"

Casey kept his eyes on the screen. He waited a second before answering. "No."

"Because if I did, I didn't mean to."

"I'm just embarrassed. Tonight makes me feel like a helpless wimp. But I won't take it out on you. I really owe you big time."

"Don't be so hard on yourself. You grew up with a sister. I grew up with Chester. How in the hell would you learn to be tough like we are if you didn't have any brothers?"

"I'm going to learn. I'm going to quit something I recently started and sign up for self defense classes."

"It's your money. But I could do it for free." They both watched the TV as Nolan switched channels without any regard to stopping. "So, you said you owe be big time?"

"Yes I do."

"Go camping with me tomorrow."

Casey waited before answering. "That thing really has a shower?"

"Yes it does."

"Would we go where there is cell phone service?"

"Why?"

"For emergencies."

Nolan laughed. "For our first camping trip, we can go to the base campgrounds. They have electrical hookup, and yes, cell phone service."

"What time do we have to leave?"

"After we have breakfast with Gram's cooking downstairs."

"I want to pick up my skis from SkiAK's. They called me to say they were ready."

"No problem."

"What time do we come back?"

"Sunday afternoon. I need to get a tree and get it decorated or my ass is in big trouble. My mom gave me strict orders. I flipped a coin toss and lost with Chester. He won't be helping me this year."

"What will we eat?"

"Grilled cheese?"

"Deal. But we go shopping at the commissary first. Better we lay off the grilled cheese. Get some variety."

"So what you're saying is you're gonna be in charge of the food?"

"Do you mind?"

"Hell no. I got a good book I'm reading."

"Are you sure you don't want that third blanket before I turn in?"

"I'm sure. Why not give your friend a call first. He, she might have a bad case of the nerves."

Casey went to the kitchen table where he left his phone. "Hello, Ines?"

"Hi Casey."

"Are you OK?"

"I'm fine. And thanks for asking. Have a good night."

"You too." Casey put the phone back on the table. He walked through the living room and stopped at the hallway to his bedroom. "Nolan, thank you for tonight."

Nolan smiled at him and threw a salute. Casey turned and went to his bed.

The next morning Nolan awoke first, on the futon, not in Casey's bed. He decided to make coffee and returned to the living room. With the TV off and the side table light on, he spied a large journal with clear directions of 'Read Me' written on the cover. Nolan followed the clear instructions, opened up the book and began to read.

December 17
Dear Diary

This is crazy. Don't go and expect me to fill many of your pages with ink. You'll be lucky to get five lines. So here goes.

Did I mention I really hate this?

Summer, 1994, humid and hotter than hell on my Grandma and Grandpa's farm in Northern Indiana. In the cornfields about seven miles out from the nearest town. Bremen. About forty-five minutes southeast from the big Catholic University Notre Dame in St. Joseph County.

It was the summer before I started kindergarten, so I was five and a half.

My dad taught school in the Syracuse Public schools and had summers off. He was the physical education teacher in a junior high. My grandpa promised to take my grandma to Mexico for years and finally bought the tickets. But he needed someone to look over the farm while he was on his two week excursion south of the border. My dad loved the farm and was more than happy to farm sit while he was away.

It was early in the morning, breakfast wasn't ready yet and I was outside playing in the barn inside an old model truck. Abandoned after years of reliable service to the labor of the land. I was with my sister, who was proudly the star of the class in her second grade where the nuns awarded her the academic medal of the year.

"Mom said you can't go to kindergarten this year. You can't go until you learn to behave. Maybe you'll never get to go to school."

"Yes I will. I already saw my teacher."

"That doesn't mean anything. When the teacher finds out you wet the bed, she won't let you in her room. Too smelly."

I picked up a corn cob and threw it at her face. Realizing I was going to be in big trouble, the skin above her right eye began to turn red. She cried and went running to the farmhouse to tell.

I followed her. My mind began to enter into the world I frequently visited, even though I had control of my arms and legs. For some stupid reason I followed her into the house instead of finding a place to hide behind the hay in the barn.

My sister was crying more as she entered. "Look what he did to me."

I stood there after passing the flimsy storm door that shut behind me. Separating the screened in porch from the kitchen.

"She said I couldn't go to school."

I saw the blur of a man passing the corner to the kitchen. I knew the routine well. Safely in my other world, my body took flight as I passed through the glass door and landed on my back in the screened in porch. I stayed there. My body took another journey to the ceiling, a place I visited often, followed by a final journey to the old fashioned swing at the other end of the porch. My father gave up on his rage, somewhat fearful of the blood. It was one of my good fortunes in life that the sight of human blood made him faint, so he left the porch and walked to the barn. I left the zone when my mother grabbed me by the arm with the kitchen towel. I was bleeding only a little.

"Now look what you did. If I've told you once, I've told you a million times. You're the bad seed of the family. Every family has one. Donna was the bad seed in my family and you're the bad seed in this one."

She scrubbed the blood off my arm and decided a bandage wasn't necessary on the farm.

"Get outside and don't come until it's dark." She left to attend to my sister's scratch above the eye.

I calculated the best place to go, so I found the silo with the corn. There was a place behind it secluded and easy to hide. I played with a grasshopper for an hour before I was interrupted by my sister who also knew the hiding places. She had a very dramatic bandage on her forehead.

"You asked for it. You always do."

"Now the Boogeyman is going to visit me tonight. And it's your fault."

"I told you there is no such thing as the Boogeyman. How do you expect to go to school when you believe such stupid things?"

The rest of the day passed in peace because they left me alone. I peed in the hay and drank water from the faucet to the side of the house. I was called in at dinner time. No one talked at the table.

After dinner, I was sent to bed, in time to prepare for the Boogeyman who would surely visit late in the night. I had a plan. To play dead. It usually worked. If I were to scream, no one would come anyway.

Not knowing how to tell time, I awoke in the far bedroom all by myself. My sister had the other room by the stairs. It was him again. I played dead. I could sense he was standing at the doorway for several moments, wondering if he would come any closer. This night as many he did. He sat on the edge of the bed, but I outsmarted him. I played dead. Surely a Boogeyman wouldn't want anything to do with a dead child who hadn't even been to kindergarten.

Like a stone, I felt the bed slowly begin to move in a pattern all too well recognized. I kept my eyes closed. The Boogeyman moaned and there was a strange smell. But I still played dead. The Boogeyman left and I was free once again to face another day in paradise.

Alright Diary, so you got one of my first memories. Don't go and get all excited. This might be the last. In fact, I'm almost sure it will be.

Nolan closed the book and stared at the wall beyond the TV. He sat there with only a few seconds to absorb what he read. Casey stood by the entrance of the living room, looking at the guy with the journal in his lap.

"Oh my God. Did you read that?"

"Yeah. Casey I'm really sorry."

Casey looked at the big note 'Read Me' on the cover. He put his hands on top of his head and went to the bathroom, shut and locked the door. Placing his head against the mirror on the inside, he closed his eyes and kept still for a brief moment. He moved to the other mirror above the sink. Remembering the words of Sawyer during their session. "It helps to share your journal with someone you trust."

Casey unlocked the door, entered the living room and moved to the kitchen. "Did you already make the coffee?"

"I did."

"Thanks."

"Do you have a sleeping bag?"

"I actually have two of them. Should I bring one camping?"

"Do you have one that opens up like a quilt?"

"Yes. And I have one of the body shaped goose down ones too."

"Bring the other one. It won't get cold in the camper, especially with electric heat."

The two sat in the living room with the TV off. Sipping their coffee and saying little. Both were trying to adjust to the uncomfortable situation of the morning. Nolan was desperately searching for the right thing to say. "Why were you so shocked I read the journal?"

"I wasn't. I was embarrassed. It's an ugly past most normal people could never understand. Especially people who love their parents. "

"I get it. I won't understand, but I can listen. Whenever you want."

"OK. But not today. I have to take Buddy for a morning run. Candy won't do it and Gram is too old."

"Guess what I have in the back of my truck?"

"Artillery?"

"No. My winter running gear. I can go running with you this morning."

"It's cold." Casey got up to look at the thermometer outside the kitchen window. "Seven degrees."

"What are we waiting for? Let me run down and get my bag."

They put the leash on Buddy who was sitting by the backdoor waiting. He wagged his tail at the sight of Nolan. A pack of three was more exciting than a pack of two. They ran in the dark towards the Boniface Gate, and back taking the long way around, adding about a mile to the trip.

Walking the last quarter mile, Nolan made a comment about Casey's body. "What else do you do to stay in shape?"

"I bike, ski, run, walk, sometimes I do sprints."

"All aerobics. What about strength building?"

"You mean like weights?"

"Or pushups, pull ups and stuff like that."

"No. What do you do to get big muscles?"

"Weights in the gym and chin ups. I have a bar at home and do ten sets of fifteen every other day. I got weights in the garage too."

"Is there a difference between chin ups and pull ups?"

"Chin ups are more of a total body work out. I'll show you when we get to my place if you want."

"You have a bar at your house?"

"You can buy them to fit above any door. You should get one. Mix up your routine."

They arrived to the front of the house. The light was on in the kitchen. Gram was probably cooking breakfast. She stuck her head out the door as they climbed the stairs. "Breakfast will be ready in about an hour. Chester is taking a shower."

"OK. We're going to do the same and should be down in thirty minutes."

Buddy was already at the top waiting to get in.

"Do you want to shower first?"

"That might be a good idea. I get the feeling you aren't to happy with me peeing in the kitchen sink."

"You remember the color of your tooth brush?"

"Orange." Nolan felt his beard. "I'm not shaving until I go back to work." He got up to go to the bathroom and left the door unlocked.

Casey turned on the TV to get the weather report. He had some kind of fear they'd be buried in an avalanche while camping at the military campground. He was hoping for some kind of natural disaster to get his mind off of the main event of the morning.

They drove the Subaru north of town to find Nolan's cabin. He left Chester with the truck keys and plans to go shopping at the thrift store downtown. Chester also agreed to taking Candy to the Fifth Avenue Mall.

"I can't believe Numb Nuts is going to the mall. He hates shopping."

"Nolan, really?"

"What?"

"There's a girl."

"Are you saying he's already pussy whipped?"

"Could be."

"I'll be damned. And here I thought I had him trained."

It started to snow, the roads were covered. The Subaru hugged the road. It took thirty minutes to get to the cabin. Casey pulled up into the drive.

"You live here?"

"For now I do. Cheap rent."

"Where's the camper?"

"In the garage."

"The camper fits in the garage?"

"Yes. Over there."

Casey looked to the far end of the large wooden cabin, with the full deck around the whole second floor. The front of the cabin was all glass up to the pointed roof.

"Follow me." They got out of the car and walked to the front steps.

"Why isn't there any snow on the steps or the deck?"

"Electric heating. But I have to use the snow blower on the driveway."

Casey expected as much. After all his parents were millionaires, several times over, even if they arranged for their kids to live a more normal life. He decided not to make any wow kind of remarks.

Nolan opened the front door. "This is it. My mom and dad's cabin, don't go and think this place is mine. You know what kind of paycheck we both get."

"It's very nice. Do you use the fireplace much?"

"I sure do. Splitting logs is my therapy. Keeps my feet on the ground."

Casey tried not to gawk at the interior of the cabin. There were two large dark brown leather couches facing the fireplace, with three other matching leather chairs. The interior of the cabin was made of shiny yellow logs.

The open kitchen to the side looked like something out of a fancy big city restaurant. The upper face of the fireplace was guarded by a huge brown bear skin, head in tact. He looked up to the second floor railing. The mountains were in view from the front glass windows.

"Follow me, I want to show you something." He followed Nolan to a room housing the washer and dryer. The chin up bar was secured on top of the door frame. "This is the bar I was talking about."

"You don't need any screws to get it up?"

"None. Now watch me." Nolan put both his hands on the bar with the palms facing outward. He completely lowered himself with both arms fully extended. "Count for me."

Casey watched as his powerful torso lifted himself up and lowered himself down, one right after the other. The shoulder muscles looked rock hard. He began to slow at thirteen, finished with the count of fifteen. "How many sets of those do you do every day?"

"Ten, but every other day. It's important to give the body a day to recover. Come on, give it a try."

Casey put his hands the same way with the palms facing outward. He managed to do three. "I guess I need some practice."

"Practice makes perfect. What time does SkiAK's open?"

"Nine."

"What do you say we go shopping for the food around here and skip the commissary? We could go to the Red Apple Market instead."

"Alright. I've heard that place is really nice. Do you drink hot chocolate?"

"I sure do. We need to get a gallon of milk. I got the hot chocolate in the camper. My mom sent it to me."

By 10:38 a.m., they were in the camper showing their IDs to the MP at Boniface Gate. Base personnel were trying to clear the snow from the roads. Over six inches fell during the night.

"This truck does great in the snow."

"It's a Ford Super Duty. And the weight on the truck really helps." They drove down Otter Lake Road north of the base and turned left on Circle Road. "This is a nice wooded area, they plow the roads and it's a great place to ski. We're on base, but you get the feeling we're in the wilderness. Good training for our next camping trip."

Casey didn't respond, but wasn't sure he liked the idea of becoming camping buddies with Captain Kelly. They turned in to find a spot with electrical hookup. "Nolan, why are we the only ones here?"

"I don't know, maybe because it's winter and almost below zero?"

"Could be. You sure the heating in this thing works?"

"With electric hookup, camping is a breeze. Without electric, it gets tricky."

Nolan parked the rig by the main entrance. There was no sign of any people anywhere. Just what Nolan wanted.

"You ready Stretch?"

"I am." It was before noon. "What should we do first?"

"Try out your new skis?"

"OK. Do you ski much?"

"All the time around the cabin. On my days off. Usually alone. I got to say, time off here is somewhat lonely."

"You might want to try and find a girl like your brother is."

"I might."

Casey followed Nolan to the side and hooked up the electric. They went inside to push buttons, move walls and get the heat going. Casey loaded the fridge and emptied the grocery bags. "I think we might have overdone it on the food."

"Cool."

They left the warmth of the camper and went outside to put on their skis. “Do you know where we’re going?”

“Of course I do. Follow me.” Off they went further north on clean untouched trails. Casey kept his ski tracks inside of those made by Nolan. It was dead winter quiet. The two pairs of skis made a unique crunching noise in the snow that became hypnotic for Casey. It helped him forget about Nolan reading the journal. It’s what he wanted. There were no missions planned so the jet noise didn’t interfere with the wilderness experience.

After an hour of moving north, Nolan stopped and sat on a fallen tree. Casey maneuvered his skis to sit next to him.

“Stretch, don’t go and think I’m getting all in your business, but I know you’re gay. It doesn’t matter to me.”

“Maybe I’m not?”

“OK. Whatever you are, I’m OK with it.”

They sat in silence. “What if I was asexual?”

“Don’t matter.”

“What if I was transgendered?”

“You’re not.”

“Alright I am.”

“Trans?”

“No. Gay. But I try to keep in the closet.”

“Fine.” Nolan kept quiet waiting for whatever Casey would say next. After nothing. “Do you have a boyfriend?”

“No.”

“Why not. I bet you’re some guy’s dream.”

“Because I’m damaged goods.”

“The journal?”

“Maybe.”

“Maybe not.”

Casey stood up and stretched his long arms. “Where to now?”

“Follow me. There’s a nice creek just ahead.”

Although Casey gave the impression he was on the clumsy side with his walking, he managed the skiing with a natural sense of grace. They skied for two hours before they returned to the camper. Still the only rig in the area.

"You're in charge of the food, but I'm in charge of the hot chocolate."

"I like it. Do we get to loaf around and read for a while before lunch?"

"That's my plan. The best part of camping."

They leaned the skis against the side of the camper and went inside. "I think we can throw our winter gear on the couch and use the dining area to relax, or take a nap on the bed up on top."

They got in their socks, Casey sat at the table while Nolan made the hot chocolate. He sat sideways and grabbed a book from the cubbyhole under the table. It was the graphic novel, Capan Iceman, the ninth edition.

"Do you read Capan Iceman Novels?"

Nolan looked over at Casey, put his hot chocolate on the table and sat on the other bench. "I do. What about you?"

"I've read them all. When I was a kid, Capan Iceman was the guy to rescue me from the Boogeyman."

Nolan shook his head slowly up and down. "He was my hero too. More than you could ever imagine."

"Did you need a superhero? I mean, you had a superdad."

"True, but there were things Capan Iceman could do for me that my dad couldn't. He understood me. Provided me with a role model. It was him who made me feel proud of myself no matter who I was."

"I get it. Sometimes a fantasy hero is what we need. Growing up with a dad who is a celebrity must have had its challenges."

"Something like that." Nolan grabbed his book. "I'm going to go up and read. You OK?"

"Yes. Thanks. What are you reading?"

"I got this book on my Kindle, 'The Lieutenant Don't Know.' It's about this Marine in Afghanistan with the logistics convoy. He published it last year. The book is awesome."

"Isn't it like reading about hell on earth?"

"Casey, I got a brother over there right now. Sandy. He's a second lieutenant in the Army."

"You have another brother who is an officer?"

"He's the only other one. We tried to get him to apply for the Air Fore Academy, but he wanted the Army instead, like our Uncle Wade. So he went to West Point. Chester and I make fun of him, but he knows we're really proud of him. He wrote us last week to tell us he got accepted into training for the Army Special Forces."

"The Green Berets?"

"Yep. Damn, he wants to be like Uncle Wade."

"What about this uncle?"

"He's a Green Beret General. Retired about four years ago. Three stars. Now he runs a security training facility down in Texas."

"Who else do you have coming out of the Georgia Farm?"

"Not Chester and me."

"You're not from the farm?"

"Yes and no. We were born in Berlin right after the fall of the wall. My dad was stationed there. That's where he met my mom and married her. She was a high school teacher at the Berlin American High School. Get this, my dad says we were made the night the wall came down. He might be making it up though."

"So you're German?"

Nolan laughed. "No, we were born on base. Left before we were walking. My dad separated and pursued his music career. You know the rest of his story."

"So, are there any others?"

"My only sister, Ann. She's twenty-four and teaches German in high school. Then there's the twins."

"More twins?"

"Yep. By the grace of God, not fertility pills. And these two are identical twins."

"How old are they?"

"Colt and Preston are twenty now. And you'll never guess what their career aspirations are."

"Let me guess, military officers?"

"Nope. They want to break into the country music scene. They can sing really good. Dad says they can do it. But he said he would only help if they finish school first, so they're studying music in Atlanta. They bitch about it, but Mom said they really like it."

"You're a lucky guy Nolan. I guess that's why you're like you are."

"How am I?"

"Cocky, obnoxious…,"

"Hey!"

"Alright, let me finish, confident, honorable and…"

"And?"

"Didn't you want to get to that book you're reading?"

"I'm on top if you need me. There's room for two up there in case you want a nap."

"I'm OK."

Nolan grabbed his Kindle and crawled up on top to read. Casey remained at the same spot on the bench for the dining table. He had a book in his backpack, but preferred to sit and think. It was quiet, and he felt safe in the camper to ponder the issues in his life. He debated whether he should or should not continue with his counseling sessions. He moved over to the couch, curled up and fell asleep using Nolan's winter coat as a pillow and his own as a cover. His long body made it impossible to stretch out on the camper sized couch, but Casey was accustomed to sleeping in a tight ball like a turtle. A habit learned as a small child. His makeshift pillow had the same fragrance he recognized from his pillow a little over a week ago. He liked it. For some reason it made him feel safe.

His hour nap was interrupted with the sound of the camper toilet flushing in the little closet like room. Nolan tried to shut the door without making any noise, but Casey's eyes were already open. "Hey Stretch, did you get a nice nap?"

"Yes." Casey slid sideways to sit up. "Did you?"

"I guess I did. It wasn't my plan, but what the hell, we're camping, right?"

"Should I start lunch?"

"Do I get to help?"

"Depends. Do you take well to being ordered around?"

"Depends. Why not give it a go."

"Here goes nothing." Casey got up and looked at the bathroom door. "Do I need to get certified on the bathroom?"

"Come on, I'll show you." He opened the door and showed Casey where the flush button was. He laughed at the image of Casey inside with the door shut. "Damn, you got long legs."

"Shut the door behind you please."

"You can lock it if you really want." He left Casey to pee and wash his hands.

Closing the door behind him, he looked for the bag of items in the cupboard they bought in the morning. "I hope that microwave works?"

"It does."

Casey handed him two containers. "Can you read the instructions and cook the rice?" He had organic brown rice in two small bowls.

Nolan had to brush against the backside of Casey to get to the microwave. It was impossible to pass each other in the kitchen space without getting some kind of body contact. They were both in their t shirts. Casey froze with the feel of Nolan's muscular torso sliding past his back.

"Where do you keep the pans?"

"Below you."

Casey stooped over to get what looked like a sauce pan with a cover. "Can you cut that onion and green pepper?"

"Yes sir."

Casey took the package of cut chicken from the little fridge to cook in the pan. He washed the mushrooms in the small sink. Nolan once again had to move to the other side to get the knife out of the drawer. This time he avoided sliding past Casey with his torso, but had to slide past with his hips. Casey shivered.

"You cold?"

"No. I'm fine."

It took about twenty minutes to finish the chicken sauce to go on top of the brown rice. "Can you set the table?"

"Yes sir. See, I can be told what to do. Sometimes I like it."

"You drinking milk?"

"I'll have what you're having."

"Milk is good for me."

Nolan had to move behind Casey once again. "Can you imagine working in a sub?"

"I don't think I'd like that."

Nolan smiled at Casey and looked him in the eyes. "It might be fun."

The table was set. They sat down to have lunch. "Since you cooked, are you going to make me wash the dishes by myself?"

"You helped. So I'll help."

"Teamwork." They both dug into their plates. "Twilight starts at 3:40. Should we go for another ski outing after lunch?"

"We bought cake for desert. I think we better." Casey kept his eyes on Nolan as he ate. He liked the way the guy leaned over his plate and chewed. "Like it?"

"Sure do. Do you like to cook?"

"Yes."

"Are we making those filets for dinner?"

"If you want."

Nolan watched as Casey finished his plate. Nolan finished first.

Casey looked up to realize he was being watched. "What?"

"I didn't say anything."

"Am I chewing with my mouth open?"

"No." Nolan made the eyes move the way Casey first noticed.

"What then? And what's with that look you always have?"

Nolan moved his eyes to the normal position. "What look? You mean this one?" He did it again.

"Yes. That one."

"Don't know what you're talking about."

"You really have a thick beard. Did you start shaving in the sixth grade?"

"No. Believe it or not, Chester started shaving before me. It nearly killed me, so I had dad show me how to shave even though I didn't have any whiskers to speak about. I guess I was a late bloomer, aside from ample cover up front in the private department. Then after I graduated from high school, my beard really began to grow. Do you like it?"

"How do we wash dishes in that little sink?"

"We leave them until after we get back from skiing."

Outside the camper, they grabbed their skis and poles. "Where to now?"

"Follow me."

Casey was once again in the tracks of Nolan. Following his tracks made the work of sliding in the snow about twice as easy. The sun was below the horizon, sunset was at 3:41 p.m. for December nineteen. It would be dark by 6:37.

Nolan led Casey to another area where there were large rocks to lean against for a break. "Remember when you asked me what it was like to fly the F 22?"

"Yes."

"How do you feel on the skis?"

"Good. Almost like they're not there, but they go gliding through the snow."

"Like they're a natural part of our body, right?"

"That's true."

"Well, that's what I was trying to tell you about flying the F 22. It feels like it's a natural part of my body."

Casey stood by the side of Nolan and kept his eyes off to the mountains. They were losing their color and definition at the end of civil twilight.

Nolan was the talkative one. "I wish you and I were neighbors when we were kids."

Casey got a puzzled expression on his face and looked at Nolan who was already looking at him. "Why? You grew up with brothers and sisters. And a brother the same age as you. I can't imagine it was a lonely childhood."

"Because if we were neighbors, I think I could have protected you from the Boogeyman."

Casey grew up alone in the world. He buffered his adult life the same way. The concept of having someone other than Capan Iceman to protect him was never on his mind. But Nolan protected him the night before and was in front of him wishing he could have done it in the past. When he needed it most.

"That's, that's," he searched for the word he wanted, "that's really honorable of you. But reality is another story in this world. I had many descent people around me who took the easy road. They all pretended like nothing was wrong. Aunts, uncles, even grandparents. And some descent friends of my parents too. Not to mention my sister. She turned out to be the best pretender of them all. She wants to secure having grandparents for her kids when they grow up."

"I'm not like that. I don't play those kind of games. I would have done something. Not sure what, but definitely something. And Chester would have been my wing man."

"It's getting dark. We better get back. I bet I can whip your rear end in a game of cards?"

"Gin Rummy?"

"You're on." Casey went to move.

"One second here. You're dealing with the Flexer. What's the wager?"

Casey had no clue what to bet on. "Does there have to be one?"

"Of course there does." The question sounded absurd to Nolan. He let slip out his strong Southern accent.

Casey looked off into the distance. "I got it. If I win, you have to accompany Candy and myself on our next night out with Ines. And keep discreet about it."

"Fine. If I win, you help me decorate the tree tomorrow."

"Sounds fair."

They moved with their skis. What Nolan referred to as the extension of the body. Leaning their equipment up against the truck, they entered the warm camper to get ready for the duel. "I think we can have some hot chocolate, start the card game, take a break for dinner, and then we can finish. I plan on whooping your butt good. And I expect to get a high rating from my mom."

"I might want a double." They threw their coats on the little sofa, Casey sat at the table and Nolan prepared the two cups of hot chocolate by the stovetop.

The plan was to make dinner half way through the card game, but the stakes were too high to quit.

Casey laid down his cards. "Alright, so you win this time. But it was close."

"Sorry Stretch, but close doesn't count. And thanks to my excellent card game skills, I don't get my ass chewed out by my mom. I sure as hell hope your Christmas tree decorating skills are better than those you got with cards."

"Funny Mister Zoomie. Very funny."

Nolan pulled the rig up to the huge garage door made especially for a camper. He hit the button and the door opened. “Looks like Chester is home. A little warning, he will not be helping out with the tree.”

They left the camper inside the garage with the door closed and entered the cabin by the inside garage door.

“It smells nice in here.” Casey smelled the fire Chester had going in the fireplace. It was early in the day. A little after noon.

“Hello Numb Nuts. Did you get the tree?”

“It’s in the bed of your truck. Have fun decorating it, I picked the biggest one I could find. You might want to get the ladder out of the garage.” He gave Nolan a second look. “What the hell Mountain Man, did you lose your razor?”

“Hi Chester.”

“Casey. Did you survive my brother’s gas attacks in the camper?”

“I don’t think there were any.”

“Thank you Casey, my brother gets confused sometimes. He forgets about the saying, the skunk smells his own hole first.”

“So Casey, you going to help with the tree?”

“I am. What about you?”

“No fucking way. Not my thing. And my little brother here should learn to stop making bets with me. He always loses.”

“Sure I do. And about little, tomorrow we weigh in. Don’t go and call me your little brother yet. I’m sure I got you beat. Besides you need to respect your elders.”

“Elders?”

“Go ahead Chester, tell our guest who’s older here. You or me.”

“By less than three minutes.”

“That’s right, I was in this world by two minutes and forty-one seconds longer that you.”

Casey sat by the fireplace. “Chester, are you sure you don’t want to help? It will get you into the Christmas spirit?”

“Sorry Doc. I can get into the spirit just fine by watching you two.”

Casey put his mind to work. “Nolan, if I can convince your brother to help us decorate the tree, including getting it out of the truck and on the stand, do I get my bet we made in the card game?”

“Wait a minute. If you can make my brother help us decorate the tree, I go with you and your friends out on the town?”

“That’s right.”

“Deal.”

“Chester, If I can get you to help, you buy us pizza, two extra large, toppings of my choice for the decorating party. If you don’t, I buy the pizza while you sit back and watch.”

“This is fucking great. Some guys just never learn. Deal. Go for it. But if I win, I get to choose the toppings.”

“Deal.”

Nolan shook his head at Casey. “Dude, I think you just made a big mistake here. You under estimate just how stubborn that redneck can be when he puts his mind to it.”

“Maybe.” Casey got up and pulled out his cell phone. “Candy. It’s me, how are you doing?”

“Fine. How was your camping trip?”

“Great. What I’m calling about is a little problem we have. I’m with Nolan and Chester at their house, and we have to get a tree decorated. None of us have a clue how to do it right. Can you come over and help us out?”

“Sure. You said Chester is there too?”

“Yes he is. And he would really appreciate it if you could come. I’m sure he’ll let you be boss and tell us just what to do.”

“Why not. I’m just sitting around and watching TV. What’s the address?”

“Wait a second.” He asked Nolan. “Is it safe to follow Garmin GPS out here?”

“Yes. It’s reliable.”

“Candy, Nolan said you can follow the Garmin. It won’t dump you off the side of the mountain.”

"OK Sweetie, see you in a few."

"Great, I hope you're hungry, Chester has agreed to spring for the pizza. That guy is so amazing." Casey hung up the phone.

"What the fuck was that? I didn't agree to help."

"Suit yourself. But that won't leave a very good impression on Candy. Who wants to be around a Bah Humbug for Christmas?"

"Yes!" Nolan got up and gave Casey a high five. "Nice move. Come on Numb Nuts, let's go and get the tree out of the truck."

"Son of a bitch!" Chester threw the pillow from the sofa onto the nearby chair and followed Nolan and Casey out the front door to get the tree.

It began to snow again. Heavy large slow falling snowflakes. One landed on Casey's nose and stayed there until he used his hand to wipe it away, dissolving into a drop of water. Both brothers grabbed the eight foot pine tree and made way for the front entrance. Casey ran ahead to open the door.

Chester asked, "Where in the hell are we supposed to put this thing?"

"Mom said she wants it in front of the window. In the middle." They moved to the center of the floor to ceiling glass wall and set it upright. Nolan asked, "Which one of us is going to get the stand out of the garage?"

"Heads," Chester said first.

Nolan nodded his head at Casey. "Flip a coin. And I want to see it on the floor."

"I don't have one."

"In my front right pocket."

Casey froze. He moved towards Nolan and looked at his pants. "It won't jump out and bite you Stretch."

Chester laughed. "You better hope not, that dude has one hairy snake in his pants."

"Go ahead and tell him who got the hairy ass."

"Better than having the Amazon jungle up front. The chicks hate that."

Casey first placed a blank expression on his face before putting his left hand down the front pocket of Nolan's jeans. His thigh was rock hard and the jeans were too tight. He pulled back his hand. "Let me hold the tree, your pants are too tight. You flip the coin."

"Whatever." Nolan waited for Casey to grab a branch, stood back and put his hand in his pocket. "Damn, where did I leave my change?"

Chester answered. "By your truck keys and wallet."

Nolan walked over to the kitchen counter to grab a quarter. He tossed the coin up in the air in front of Chester. George Washington stared up at them both. "Fuck. I'll be right back."

"Get the ladder while you're out there, Bushman."

"Anything you say, Grizzly Ass."

Casey was left holding the tree with Chester who took the opportunity to ask him about Candy. "You been friends long with Candy?"

"Since I got here this summer."

"Do you think I have a chance with her?"

"Depends. If you treat her right you might."

"I can do that. Will I have to win over her grandma?"

"Yes, but eat her baked goods and you'll be half way there."

Nolan returned with the ladder on one arm and the tree stand on the other. He fixed the stand where they wanted to put the tree and placed the tree firmly in the middle. He tightened the bolts. "That's it. Now we sit, watch the tube and wait until the boss shows up. After about a half an hour, the doorbell rang.

They all looked at the glass door. Chester moved fast to let Candy in.

"Nice place. You guys must get extra hazardous duty pay to afford this place."

"It's my mom and dad's."

"I know, just kidding. Now that is a tree. Who gets the extra points for picking it out?"

"I did." Chester answered before his brother could take any credit.

Casey handed Chester his phone. "I want one of them with mushrooms, onions and green peppers. You can choose for the other extra large."

Chester gave Casey a secret dirty look and called the Pizza Shack to get their party food delivered.

"Well boys, what are we waiting for?" Candy began to order the three around. "Where are the decorations?"

Nolan went to the garage and returned with a large box recently mailed from somewhere in Georgia. "Mom sent the lights and decorations."

Chester begged, "Please God, let there not be a theme to this thing?"

Nolan opened the box to find lights, extension chords, and all ornaments in silver. "Looks like the theme this year is silver bells."

Candy looked in the box. "What color are the lights?"

"They might be all white."

She shook her head in approval. "I think someone has a mom with good taste. Now who's on the ladder?"

Chester moved fast to get to the ladder first. Nolan laughed a laugh that only the twins could understand.

While Chester was on top of the ladder, the pizza guy arrived. From the top, Chester asked Casey to get the door.

"And where is your wallet Captain Kelly?"

"I'm a little occupied up here Captain Link."

"Your wallet?"

"Next to the microwave." He swore under his breath.

Casey smiled. "Good thing for the pizza guy Captain Kelly is a good tipper."

Chester threw him an extra dirty look from the top of the tree. Nolan folded his arms and smiled from ear to ear. The idea of making it two against one was very appealing.

It took a couple hours to get the tree decorated the way Candy wanted it. She made Chester go outside to the end of the driveway to check on the lights being evenly spaced. Although Candy was busy getting the tree right, she had enough spare mental energy to watch Nolan and Casey. Half the pizza disappeared as they worked.

Candy walked around the first floor of the house. She went to check the bathroom. "When are you guys going to clean the house? You said your mom and dad arrive tomorrow?"

Both Chester and Nolan looked at each other. Nolan asked, "Why, we already did?"

"For real? Did you forget to clean the bathroom?"

"Chester, you loss the coin toss on that one."

"And that is why I cleaned the bathroom."

Candy shook her head. "What flight are they coming in on tomorrow. Delta?"

Chester answered. "They chartered a jet from Atlanta. The jet refuels in Seattle. They said they would call us from Seattle to let us know the estimated arrival time. We're guessing around noon."

Neither Casey or Candy commented. They both wanted not to appear in awe by the lifestyles of a famous country singer. "Well, I think you both better spend a little more time cleaning up. Your mom won't want to spend the holiday cleaning house."

Casey helped Nolan put the ladder and the unused decorations in the garage. As Nolan placed the ladder against the wall, he told Casey, "Thanks for helping out."

"You won fair and square."

"Would you have helped if there was no bet?"

"Probably."

"Bet or no bet, I would have said yes to going out with you and your friends. Come on, we better get back. My brother might be planning some gag for losing with the pizza."

Casey followed Nolan back to the living room from the garage door. He watched the backside of the guy move with extra attitude. He remembered how it felt to get his hand inside the front pocket.

Chester had a good fire going. They all sat by the fire and drank a beer. After a few minutes of listening to the wood in the fire crackle, Chester got up to get his clothes out of the dryer. Nolan put down his beer and followed him out.

"So Cutie, I want to get home before dark."

"You can follow me. Want a cola? I don't want to finish this beer."

"I'm fine."

Casey got up to go to the kitchen, next to the laundry room. He was going to ask Nolan where he got the pull up bar when he heard the two brothers whispering loudly. It appeared Nolan won another bet.

Casey laughed to himself. He never saw two people make more bets than did the Kelly brothers.

"I don't care, you can pay up with cash or a check. One hundred dollars."

Chester argued. "I'm not convinced. Are you sure he's gay?"

"Yes I'm sure. I outed him and he admitted it, so you owe me one hundred dollars before the end of leave."

"Fine. Before the end of leave."

Casey lost his breath, he moved back to the kitchen and opened the fridge to look for a cola. The blood in his ears began to rush so fast that the noise almost drowned out Nolan's words. "Want another beer?"

"I'm good. Actually Candy and I were just saying we wanted to get back before dark. She's going to follow me home."

"So soon? You can spend the night in the guest room."

"I'm on duty tomorrow at seven." He left the open kitchen and approached Candy. "You ready to go?"

"I am."

Chester's heart skipped a beat. "I owe you dinner before Christmas for helping. Can I call you?"

"I guess that won't hurt."

Casey grabbed his backpack and his bedroll. He kept his eyes away from Nolan. He led Candy out the front door. Nolan tried to make a nice thank you and goodbye, but Casey moved too fast. He got in his car and waited for Candy to pull up behind him. He never gave Nolan or Chester a glance back.

On the way to his house, his safe house with Gram, Candy and Buddy, he felt like crying. Something he'd not done since he was a little boy. *Snap out of it Captain Link. You knew the guy was a dick head before you went camping with him. One hundred dollars. And he gets hazardous duty pay. This wasn't about the one hundred dollars. He just wanted to beat his brother at another bet.*

The roads were clear. They made it home during astronomical twilight. Before complete darkness. Casey was feeling sick to his stomach. He parked and Candy pulled right up beside him. They both saw a guy walking down the side of the street. It was Ian.

"Did you two just get home?"

"Yes," answered Casey.

"I needed to walk off some ice cream. Got time for a visitor?"

"Actually, I'd appreciate it if you both could come upstairs. There's something I want to show you."

They all climbed the stairs. Gram let Buddy out to join the pack. "Guys, have a seat." Candy and Ian sat at the kitchen table. "Candy, remember I'm supposed to tell you about my family Thanksgiving reunion in Hawaii?"

"I remember."

"Ian, you already know, but not the details." Casey went to the living room to grab the journal. He came back into the kitchen. "Ian, I want you to read this first then pass it to Candy. I'm going to take a shower."

"Alright. Are you sure you're ready?"

"I'm ready. But only for the two of you, no one else." Casey left the kitchen to take a shower. He first went to the bedroom to find his sweats. He noticed the pair of sweats he gave to Nolan. Thinking about placing them up to his face, he decided against it. The hot shower was what he needed most.

I wish you and I were neighbors when we were kids. Son of a bitch. Delta Hotel! I need to get back on track. I know what I want in life. I know how to get it. Work. Nothing more, nothing less. I just want to do my job.

He went through the motions of getting ready for work usually reserved for the first event of the day. He even shaved, wanting to make sure his two friends had time to read the journal, and with time left over to discuss it. He wasn't planning on including himself in on the conversation.

With his sweats on, he joined Ian and Candy at the table. They were having egg nog, with a touch of rum added.

"Any egg nog left?"

"Of course we left you some. You'll have to add the rum if you want it."

"Thank you Candy." He sat at the table, put a splash of rum in his egg nog and took a taste. "Christmas and egg nog. What a great invention, right?"

Ian nodded his head. "Casey, good move on your trip to Australia. I knew you were doing the right thing even if I didn't know why."

"Thanks."

"You and I got shit families in common."

"Maybe, but you and Gram make the nicest family of them all. And the best part is she's always got leftover for me."

Candy put her hand of top of Casey's.

"OK guys, here's the thing. I wanted you to read that, but I'm not ready to talk about it. I hate lying, especially to my friends, but the truth is, I don't know any other way. I mean, how in the hell do you respond when someone asks you how is your family? I thought of saying they were dead from the very beginning. I still might invent some event like a plane crash or a tornado. But there I am again, faced with the lie. So I'm sorry for lying to you." He took another sip from his egg nog. "Is it true we're supposed to have a snow storm for Christmas Eve?"

Ian answered. "That's what the news is saying."

Candy tried to move on. "Can you imagine being caught in that camper during a snow storm?"

"Dear God, don't give me anything to have nightmares about. If I was stuck in that camper with the Delta Hotel, I'd probably slit my wrist."

Ian frowned, Candy spoke up, "I thought we…"

"Forget I said that." Buddy nudged Casey with his nose.

"I'm sorry Buddy. Tomorrow morning, before work I promise."

"Hey, don't go and play that game. I took you for a good long walk this morning. I swear that dog is like a kid."

Casey laughed and rubbed him behind the ears. "Do you think Gram would mind if he spent the night with me?"

"She won't. Well, I better get on my way. You guys take care. Ian, let me know when you want to go the mall. In the daylight."

"I'm working on the nerve. I'll stop in and see you at the barber shop this week."

She got up and left the kitchen.

"I'd better be off as well. Are you going to be OK?"

"Sure."

"If you want to talk about the Delta Hotel, let me know."

"I don't. See you at work."

Ian got up to leave. "Casey, I hope you continue on with Sawyer." He left Casey and Buddy alone.

"Come on, you have to go pee, then we're hitting the futon with some cookies and Netflix." Buddy wagged his tail and made it to the door before Casey could get out of the kitchen chair.

After the exciting go pee event, Buddy sat on the futon with Casey who had a plate of Gram's cookies. There were six. They divided them in half. Casey grabbed the remote and pointed it at the TV without pushing any buttons. He gave the plain looking diary a second look. Put down the remote, grabbed the pen by the TV stand and began to write.

Dear Diary
December 20

You screwed up big time. How could you let that guy open the book?

So Delta Hotel rushed to the pub to save our asses. Or did he? Maybe Chester heard Candy was with me and led him on. Maybe the guy likes to fight. I might never know now that I intend to keep that guy as far away from me as possible. He confuses me. He's obnoxious. He is the most conceited guy I've ever met. He's over competitive. He's straight. He's considerate. He's handsome and strong. Fuck.

This stops here.

Casey closed the journal and threw it across the living room. Buddy's ears perked up, wondering if the book was like a square ball.

Casey kept his promise and had Buddy running along side of him early in the morning, with the temperature hovering around twelve degrees. They both had frost freeze around their mouth after breathing heavily. Back at the house, Casey gave Buddy a hug and pushed the dog with four stiff legs trying not to move through his door. "You be a good boy and we might go skiing on the trails when I get home."

It was so cold that not an inch of Casey's body was damp with sweat. His skin was dry. After a fast breakfast of scrambled eggs and toast, he left for the hospital in his freshly ironed blue uniform ready to immerse himself in work and hopefully forget the Delta Hotel that was invading his thoughts.

He parked his Subaru in the parking lot and walked in the dark to the hospital. It was only 6:30 a.m., and his shift started at seven. A quick trip to the hospital cafeteria for a large coffee was in store. Ian was already there, enjoying a coffee and toast.

"Hi Casey. Is it still snowing outside?"

"A little."

"Cheer up. Today's the twenty-first."

"So?"

"It's the first day of winter. Starting tomorrow, the days get longer."

"I'm worried about that snow storm. I haven't got Buddy his Christmas gift yet."

"A ball? Get one from the Exchange."

"I might but I wanted a large beef knuckle bone. I'd have to drive in town to find one."

"Stick with a ball."

"Is the exercise recall over?"

"Yes. Everything should be low key until after Christmas now.

Casey sat with Ian after getting his coffee. By 6:45 he felt his phone vibrate with a text message. He read the message. *"Good morning Stretch. I had a great time with you this weekend. Let's do it again soon!"* He put away his phone and twisted the corner of his mouth.

"Dare I ask?"

"It's nothing more than a mild case of fleas."

"So he pissed you off this weekend? Are we surprised? I mean, I am so grateful for his saving our butts this Friday but he's still, he's still Captain Kelly." Ian refrained from using the more established nickname.

"I know. He has his good qualities. And he has the others too. That guy needs to find a girlfriend and let off steam. Way too much testosterone to take care of with Manuela."

"Are you on duty this Christmas?"

"Yes. The Major said to take off at noon on Christmas Eve. I'm on call for Christmas day. He's on duty Christmas day and Major Martinez is on duty Christmas Eve."

"Good move on us renting so close to base."

"It was. Well, I have to get on my way. Drop in later if you're not too busy."

"I will. See ya."

Casey walked to his office. He decided to ignore the message from Nolan. Sitting at his desk, he turned on the feed for BBC Radio while he filed papers.

"We have it from a reliable source that two American F 16 fighter jets based out of Incirlik AB Turkey came within twenty miles from Russian fighter jets over Syria. They reported saying the U.S. will divert any jets away from the mission in the presence of Russian Fighter jets. U.S. officials don't want the Russian pilots to make an error."

Damn. Nolan said his little brother was over there. In Afghanistan, but over there could mean anywhere over there. And the guy is infantry.

By seven, Sergeant Tomlin was on duty. "Good morning Captain. Do you think Santa will make it this Christmas? Sounds like we have a big storm coming our way."

"I hope so. You better get over to the Exchange if you're not finished."

"I'm finished."

"Me too. Other than a nice rubber ball."

"That big dog you run with?"

"Yes."

By 1:00 p.m., Casey was getting bored. He felt the buzz of his phone. *"Hey Stretch, my mom loved the tree. Tell Candy I said thanks."*

Casey put the phone back in his pocket and drove over to the food court. Candy had her break at 1:30.

"Hi Sweetie. Everyone is talking about the Snowicane that's supposed to hit on Christmas Eve."

"I know. Good news is there will be high winds to blow it off the trees so we don't end up with downed power lines."

"I got a text message from Chester. He said his mom loved the tree."

"That's nice to know."

"It was fun, wasn't it?"

"Sure was."

"Alright, what happened yesterday? You were as happy as a lark until the very end, then you acted like someone died."

"No."

"Yes."

"Alright. Nolan showed his true self. But I don't want to talk about it right now. I'll tell you over a drink."

"Casey, I get it. But you don't have to keep secrets about everything. You have to open up a little more with the people you trust. Your friends."

"I know. I'll tell you, but I don't want to do it here, I promise."

"Good. But don't keep me in suspense for too long. I end up losing sleep over these kind of things you know."

"About Christmas. Do I get to help in the kitchen?"

"I hope so. That will give me an excuse to watch TV. Three don't fit well in the kitchen. Especially with that dog at your feet."

Casey felt his phone vibrate again. He read the text message. *"Have a nice Christmas Casey. I miss you."* It was from Kevin. Casey tightened his lips.

"I won't ask Mister Secrets."

"Kevin. He needs to move on. I already hurt him enough."

"Are you sure? Maybe you could go out for a coffee or something."

"Candy, I don't have any feelings for him. It would be dishonest and unfair. I've already done enough damage."

"OK. I have to get back. All the boys want to look nice for Christmas."

"See you later." Casey watched as Candy walked back to the barber shop. He rushed over to the Exchange to get a ball for Buddy, then back to the hospital.

On the way to the flight surgeon's office, he felt the phone vibrate. Another text message from Nolan. *"Yo Stretch. The days get longer tomorrow. More time for skiing. Give me a call, we can plan our next camping trip."*

The next day, Casey made it to work right at seven. Major Meyers was talking with Sergeant Tomlin, both with a cup of coffee. He turned his attention to Casey as he walked into the waiting room. "Everything ready for Christmas?"

"Yes sir. Mission accomplished as of yesterday."

Sergeant Tomlin asked, "Does everyone have the kitchen stocked in case we all get snowed in for a couple of days."

"My wife took care of that."

"I better check. Can you imagine running out of coffee in a snow emergency?" He made a mental note to call Candy and make sure Gram had the kitchen fully stocked. With both essentials and snacks.

The Major stretched his back. "I guess we're going to have a slow week with everyone on minimal manning for Christmas. No complaints here." He grabbed his cup and returned to his office.

Casey walked to his desk just in time to feel the phone vibrate in his coat pocket. Another text message from Nolan. *"My brother is driving me insane. Meet me for lunch."*

Casey made a call. "Candy, what time do you have your lunch break today?"

"I don't know, one maybe."

"I think we should go to the commissary and stock up on food, and snacks too. Ask Gram to make an inventory and give you a list of anything she might need for Christmas dinner, and the next few days after that. We might get snowed in for a while."

"Good idea, I'll call you from work to let you know when I can get away. We're busy for Christmas."

"Later." He hung up.

By Thursday morning, Christmas Eve day, Casey was alone in the office, awaiting noon to go home. He and Candy made sure to fill up the house with all sorts of essentials and non essentials to have a fun calorie filled couple of days off. He was on call.

He leaned back in the chair in the reception room and watched live news coverage of the snow storm. The winds already were gusting up to twenty-three miles per hour and it was snowing. Candy called him on his phone.

"Casey, are you going to make it out of there?"

"I have the Super Subaru. And If I have to, I'll walk. There's no way I'm missing Gram's dinner tomorrow."

"I'm worried about you. Call me before you take off."

"Don't worry. I've got my cold weather gear in the trunk and I could walk home just fine."

He hung up and before he could get his mind back on the news, the phone buzzed with another text message from Nolan.

"Stretch. Come on. Can't you give a gay guy a break? What the F? You haven't returned any of my messages since Monday. Dude, you're smashing my feelings."

Give a gay guy a break? Damn it anyway. He picked up the phone and wrote a text message to send back to the Delta Hotel. *"Is this some kind of sick joke? You won your one hundred dollars with your brother about me being gay, now move on. Find the next victim in your sick little games."* He pushed send. Got up and walked in circles around the waiting room. The phone rang. Casey ignored it.

This time Nolan left a voice message. "I knew something wasn't right. You got it all wrong. Come on, pick up the phone. Fine, I'm coming right over. I'll be there in ten minutes."

Fuck, he must be on duty. And there's no one here to stop him from making a scene. Damn it if I don't step in it all the time.

He thought about turning off the lights and locking the waiting room's door. *Grow up Casey. Compose yourself, and get rid of this guy once and for all.*

True as to what Nolan said, he was walking through the door ten minutes after sending his voice message. He was dressed in his flight suit, minus a winter coat. "Casey, that bet. You got it all wrong. I don't know what you heard, but it wasn't like that."

"I heard you talking with Chester in the laundry room. Do I get ten percent of your money? I earned it."

"Damn it Casey, I'm telling you, you got it all wrong."

"You're joking never ends. What's with the give a gay guy a break?"

Nolan looked around the room. "Are we alone here?"

"Yes."

He looked around again before speaking. "You're not the only one who prefers to stay in the closet."

"What?"

"You heard me. I don't plan on coming out. I'm a fighter jock for fuck's sake. This might be the liberal age of the New Millennium, but look around. There are no active duty out gay fighter jocks in the whole United States Air Force. Hell in the whole United States armed services."

"This isn't a joke? You don't have some Go Pro hidden in your hat somewhere?"

“Good God Stretch, didn’t we established that I’m not the Delta Hotel you thought I was. I thought I proved that to you.”

“If it wasn’t for the bet on me being gay with Chester, I might have believed that.”

“I said you got it wrong.”

Casey fell back on the couch and folded his arms. “Go. I’m listening, and hurry up, I get off duty at noon so make it brief.”

“Chester and I made a bet when we were in the academy, a long time ago. We never got to the end of it.”

“Until you found me as an easy target.”

“Yes, I mean no.” Nolan scratched his head and walked the length of the waiting room. “Listen, Chester said anybody who was gay would know I was gay. He said he read in a science journal that all gay guys had a reliable instinct about it. He said the article was about gaydar. I told him he was full of crap, and that any out gay guy wouldn’t know I was gay unless someone told him. And so we made a hundred dollar bet.”

“What about me?”

“I realized when I said you were gay and you admitted it, I could use the conversation to win a hundred bucks. But I didn’t go camping with you to win a bet. I went camping with you because I wanted to go camping with you.”

Casey absorbed the explanation. “So it wasn’t a preplanned scheme to win a bet?”

“Hell no. It was an opportunity I jumped on. It wasn’t a bet about you, it was a bet about me. If any gay guy, you included, would know I was gay or not. And you didn’t. If I was wrong, I’m really sorry. I never meant for you to get wind of this. Or worse, to get your feelings hurt. Come on, can you give me a break here?”

“So you’re really gay?”

“Yes. And another confession while I’m at it. Casey, I like you. I like you a whole lot. Can you give me a chance to prove once and for all I’m no dick head?”

Casey got up from the couch. "Take a seat Captain Kelly."

Nolan plopped down on the couch. "Here we go. The Captain stuff again?"

"I want you to realize something about me. All I've ever done is hurt guy's feelings. I'm a train wreck when it comes to relationships."

"I don't care. I'm tough as nails."

"Do you have any idea how long was the longest relationship I've ever had?"

"I don't need to know."

"Six weeks. Six long weeks."

"That's understandable."

"Understandable? I just gave you the big red flag."

Nolan gave Casey the trademark eye trick.

"What's that supposed to mean?"

Nolan got up. He walked over to Casey and got into his personal space. Standing straight, he whispered to Casey, "You're in big trouble here Stretch."

"What are you talking about?"

"Have you ever had a boyfriend like me?"

"Good God no. You're a one and only."

"So?"

"So what?"

"This."

"This what?"

Nolan used his hands to point inward to his body. "This. You're in big trouble because this is undeniably irresistible." He smiled at Casey with his hands still pointing inwards.

Casey stepped back and put both hands on top of his head.

Nolan also stepped back and sat back down on the couch. "I told you so."

The news flash announced road closings. The road to Nolan's house was closed. "Good thing mom and dad got out yesterday. And Numb Nuts is probably sunning on the beaches of Hawaii. Since I'm your boyfriend, I guess I'm staying at your place tonight."

"Whoa, just a minute here. Who said anything about us being boyfriends?"

"I didn't say you were my boyfriend, I said I was your boyfriend. There's a difference. Don't go and get your panties in a bundle. I'm not going to pressure you into telling me you're my boyfriend until you're good and ready. But I get to speak for myself, and I say I'm your boyfriend."

"This is absurd."

"Relax, you don't need to worry about me, I'm not going to start stalking you or anything like that. My mom and dad raised me right."

"You're on the futon. Period. Got it?"

"Got it."

"God help me."

"You have enough provisions for making a descent dinner tomorrow. After all, it is Christmas."

"Gram. We'll be having dinner with Candy and Gram."

"And Buddy. By the way, did you notice how Buddy liked me right away?"

"Why?"

"Just saying. The dog is smart."

By noon, Nolan finally convinced Casey to leave the Subaru in the hospital parking lot. The Ram truck was ten times better in the deep blowing snow. Casey sat at the fighter squadron until one. At one, Nolan was relieved from duty. All the guys on duty were booked into the Air Force Inn the day before. Nolan was on standby until the day after Christmas. He also had a room at the inn but decided not to tell Casey about it.

They drove the big four wheel drive truck effortlessly past the MP shack at Boniface Gate One. Visibility was very low for the short drive to Casey's place. The wind was up to thirty mile per hour gusts. "This is going to be one of my best Christmases ever, me snowed in with my dude, just the two of us on the futon under a blanket and watching football games on the TV."

Casey slid down in the seat and kept his eyes looking forward. Nolan heard the audible moan leaving his mouth and smacked Casey on his left thigh. Casey jumped.

Nolan parked in the drive. "Do you like to shovel snow?"

"I just love it."

"Good, we can clean some of this snow away later tonight if we can't think of anything else to do." Once again the eye trick. Buddy moved the curtains from the front window and fogged up the glass. His pack was bigger for the Christmas celebration. It was turning out to be the best Christmas for him also.

Casey noticed Candy joined Buddy at the window. She smiled, relieved they made it without slipping off the road.

"Let me get my bag of civvies in the back."

"You have a bag of civvies?"

"Always. One never knows. Right?"

"Right.

They left the truck and pushed their way through the snow in the driveway to get to the back door. Buddy was there waiting for them.

"Hey Buddy, remember this guy? He's gonna shovel the walks for us while we watch." He let Buddy out the door to go pee.

"I don't mind. Just as good as a workout in the gym."

"I was kidding. I'll do it later."

"Do you have two shovels?"

"Yes."

"Then we can knock it out in no time. But I think we better wait until the wind dies down, or else we'll be wasting our time."

"OK."

Gram stuck her head out the door to the stairway. "Well hello Nolan. Will you be staying with us tonight?"

"Yes ma'am. The road is closed to my house."

"How exciting. We're having turkey and venison for dinner tomorrow. Do you like venison?"

"Practically grew up on it. Yes ma'am I sure do."

"Honey, please call me Gram."

"Gram it is."

Casey asked, "Did you say you were making cinnamon apple pie?"

"Candy is. I taught her well."

Candy came into the hallway. "Hi Nolan. I'm glad you guys made it safely. This is one doozy of a storm."

"Hi Candy. Will there be football on TV tomorrow?"

"There will be in this house. Does that mean I finally get someone to watch and drink beer with?"

"If Casey let's me."

"He's all yours. I'd rather learn new tricks in the kitchen from Gram. Well, we better get up. Can you do me a favor and set the temperature at 68 again for Captain Kelly. He's a Southern boy and likes it warm."

"Or not." He threw Casey the one eye up one eye down trick.

Buddy was already waiting at the top of the stairs.

On the way up, Nolan asked about lunch. "Do you want me to make grilled cheese for lunch? We forgot to eat at the base."

"Why not?" They entered the apartment. Buddy did a perimeter check and Casey walked to the living room to drop of his back pack. "You can put your things over here by the window."

"Dude, I thought you were going to get a tree in here."

"I have a tree."

"Where?"

Casey led him to the kitchen window. He pointed to the pine tree with lights. "I decorated that, so it qualifies for my tree."

"I'm hungry. Are you gonna help me?"

"Yes."

"Let me get out of this flight suit. Can I change in your bedroom?"

Casey squinted his eyes. "Alright, but no snooping."

Nolan shook his head repeating the word snooping as he went for the bag on the living room floor. "Don't start without me Stretch."

Casey began pulling out the bread, cheese and the pan.

Nolan returned to the kitchen wearing his baggy jeans and a worn out t shirt with a dirt bike graphic on the front. He hummed the tune to a song Casey didn't recognize.

"I thought you only wore tight fitting jeans?"

"Sometimes I just have to give my boys a break. I call these my commando jeans."

"So glad I asked."

He brushed by Casey the same way he did in the camper even though there was ample room. Casey jumped. Nolan chuckled. "I have a remedy for that."

Casey thought Nolan was putting together the sandwiches like he was in some kind of science lab. He was meticulous in his preparations. "What else do you know how to cook?"

"Lots of things. Scrambled eggs, toast, macaroni and cheese. All cuts of steaks. Pretty much anything."

Casey sat at the table and watched as Nolan moved around the kitchen. Buddy laid on the floor by the entrance wondering if there was a sandwich in the pan for him also.

Nolan placed the finished product on the table and beamed with pride. He sat down. "You first. Tell me what you think."

Casey took a bite. "You're a real chef."

"How long are you gonna to be mad at me for making that bet with my brother?"

Casey finished swallowing. He looked at Nolan. "You're OK. I'm not angry with you. I probably should have said something right away instead of ignoring you all week."

"We're all clear then?"

Casey gave Nolan's arms a glance. "I guess this is as good a time as any to make a small confession."

Nolan moved his eyes.

"That first night at Reilly's, when I met your brother. I might have told a small fib. On purpose, just to tick you off. That was when I believed you were a Delta Hotel."

"And?"

"I said I thought your brother had the bigger biceps, but I think yours were a little bigger."

Nolan smiled. "I know."

"Who won the bet with the weight?"

"Let's not talk about that right now. It's a sore spot."

"Well, it doesn't really matter. The both of you are pretty nice looking. Chester might only have a slight edge on you with the sex appeal."

Nolan stopped chewing. He asked with his mouth full. "What?"

"Forget I said that. I was thinking out loud."

Nolan swallowed. "No way. You can't drop that kind of bomb on me and expect me to let it go. Is it his nose? I knew it, you think my nose is too big."

"No. Your nose is nice. Nice and straight."

"What then. I know. It's his waist. He got my mom's narrow waist, and I got my dad's barrel waist. It's genetics, no mater how many crunches I do, I can't get a small waist like he has."

"No. Not your waist."

Nolan lowered his brows. "What then?"

"Alright, if you make me tell you, but don't go and get mad at me for being honest."

Nolan folded his arms and stared at Casey, waiting for the answer.

"When Chester talks, he sounds a little bit more sexy than when you do. He has that cute Southern drawl. You not so much."

"Are you saying you get turned on when you hear a redneck talk?"

"A little."

Nolan returned to finishing his sandwich. It was obvious to Casey his mind was churning.

"The sandwich is good. Thanks."

Nolan responded with a smile. "I say we go down and tackle some of that snow on the driveway." He flexed his right bicep. "These guns come in handy for a lot of things."

With their Air Force winter parkas on, and their hats and gloves, they grabbed the two snow shovels from the garage and began the chore of removing the snow. Buddy jumped all around thinking they were playing a game. The wind blew snow back on any uncovered pavement they managed to momentarily expose.

Nolan unexpectedly fell back on the fresh snow. Facing up, he called Casey. "Get over here and help me up."

"I can't. I'm busy."

"Come on, I'd help you. Pull me up."

Casey smiled at the guy immobile and on his back. Buddy jumped all around him. He put his shovel aside and extended his hand. Nolan grabbed it with his glove on. Casey pulled, but was unable to pull the 180 pounds of muscle up from the snowbank. Nolan made his move and pulled Casey down on top of him. Right where he wanted him. "And you said you weren't my boyfriend."

"I'm not."

"Then what are we doing here?"

"We both fell."

"Are you sure about that?" Nolan stared into Casey's eyes. He placed both his arms back into the snow, giving Casey the choice to get up.

"I think you might have been right earlier today."

"About what?"

"About being undeniably irresistible."

"Prove it."

Casey allowed his arms to relax and moved down placing his face closer to Nolan's. "If we kiss, will you be able to behave later on?"

"I don't know."

Casey moved his head slightly away.

"I mean, yes. I will behave."

Casey moved back down and reached for Nolan's lips with his own. The cold and snow made the kiss feel all that much warmer. The inside of Nolan's mouth was hot, wet and eager. Nolan used his arms to roll Casey over on his back. It was his turn to be on top and move in for the kiss. But not before exchanging a few words.

He spoke to Casey with a strong Southern accent. "Did I mention I really like you?"

"You did."

"Do you like me?"

"I wish to hell I could say no. If you kiss me, it might help clear my head a little."

Nolan reached down and gave a repeat performance. This time with a free moving tongue. No holding back. "Do you have any hot chocolate upstairs?"

"I do."

Nolan climbed off the tall guy and grabbed one of his hands. He easily pulled Casey up on his feet. "Let's get a path from the front door to the sidewalk and then give it a rest for a while. The wind is still blowing this snow all around."

They took another ten minutes to make a small path from the front porch to the sidewalk. Buddy still thought they were involved with a game of snow jumping, until he saw Casey head for the garage door with the shovels. He rushed to the door to be the first to get in.

Casey led the way up the stairs. Inside the kitchen Nolan couldn't get the smile off his face. "Can I make the hot chocolate?"

"Give me your coat. I'll hang them out by the stairs. They're wet." Casey hung the coats and Nolan dug in to make the hot chocolate, still smiling from ear to ear. Casey looked worried.

As Casey read the latest news on the Kindle. Nolan placed the cup before him, and sat on the other side of the table.

"The first one is the one to remember."

"That's true, but I might want another, is there enough left in the can?"

Nolan moved his eyes into position. Casey didn't look up.

"Really?"

"Really what?"

"The first cup of hot chocolate?"

"It was."

"Captain Link?"

"Yes Captain Kelly?" Casey pushed his Kindle aside. "Fine. You win. So what if I admit I won't ever forget it?"

"We're on the same page right?"

"We're talking about that interlude we had in the snow."

"Interlude?"

"Kiss."

"Now we're getting somewhere. So tell me, did you like it?"

"Damn it anyway. Yes I did. Now go ahead and ask me if it was the nicest kiss I ever had."

"Was it the best kiss you ever had?"

"Yes it was."

"Want some more?"

"Yes. No. Maybe. I need to ask you to do me a huge favor."

"I'm yours."

"Help me not screw this up?"

"Easy."

"Not so much. I need to you to follow my lead."

"Not so easy. I like being in charge."

"I'm sure you do. I want to do this thing different. I'd be lying if I said I didn't want you to take off your clothes and tackle me to the ground. But that would be the norm for me. And I don't want the norm. So can you follow my lead for a while, and allow me to choose the time, place and intensity?"

"Fine. But here's the deal. The moment you tell me you're my boyfriend, all brakes are off. I'm jumping your bones on the spot, so be careful where we are when you decide to let me know."

"Thanks. I think."

"Want another cup?"

Casey slid his empty cup across the table towards Nolan. He got his cup refilled. Nolan got a text message on his phone. "Nice to see someone out there loves me." He gave Casey a look referring to the unanswered messages. "My little brother."

"Is he OK?"

"Things are hot over here and I'm not talking the weather. Merry Christmas big brother." He read off the message and began to make one in return. Casey thought his eyes were getting glassy. "I better send one to Numb Nuts before he sends one to me. He'll never let me hear the end of it." He composed another test message for Chester.

"I hope you plan on calling your mom and dad, instead of sending a message."

"I will. The twins are there and my sister too." He looked up at Casey after pushing the send button on the second message, thinking but not saying.

"I know what you're thinking. I'm working on a plan, but I need someone's help."

"TV?"

"Have you seen the Christmas special for the Midwives?"

"Midwives? A series about having babies?"

"Not good huh. What about Downton Abbey?"

Nolan made an expression that would have Casey believe he was in extreme pain.

"Dr. Who?"

"Phew. Saved by science fiction."

Casey got up to get the futon and TV ready. He put pillows on one corner for Nolan, went to the bedroom to get more for the other end.

"At different ends?"

"Yes. Separate blankets too."

Nolan gave another expression of pain.

"You made a deal."

"I know."

Casey got the two of them situated before firing up the Netflix app on the big screen. He sat with the remote in his hand without pushing any buttons. "We could talk instead. Dr. Who's not going anywhere."

"You first."

"Is it really that important for you to stay in the closet as a fighter pilot?"

"Absolutely."

"Elaborate."

"I don't want to be the one to pave the way."

"Do you feel like you're keeping secrets from your friends?"

"Who doesn't have secrets in their life. It doesn't bother me. My turn."

"Go."

"You're in the medical career field. The first place where guys started coming out of the closet. They even have gay married couples living on base housing. Why not you?"

"I like keeping people at bay. My being gay isn't the only thing I prefer not to share with my peers at work. I do have a good friend though."

"I know. Am I supposed to pretend like I don't know who Ines is?"

"Yes. But let me ask about that one, I'll get back with you."

"Do you watch porn?"

"Really? Isn't that personal?"

"We kissed."

"I can't answer that. But I have seen some."

"I do. But if I had you to take care of me, I don't think I would want to. Would you believe I've already jacked off thinking about you in my bed. You got those long legs. I love long legs."

"Don't you think I'm a little bit on the skinny side?"

"No. You're just right. You're my fantasy guy."

Casey was blushing.

"What about me. Do you think I'm hot?"

"Too hot for comfort."

"Explain."

"Your nose."

"My nose? What about these?" He lifted his arm and flexed his bicep.

"I accidentally saw something when I was drawing your blood."

"Go on."

Casey kept his mouth shut.

"And you liked it?"

"Can't say."

"All the guys on porn have their balls shaved. Does that turn you on?"

"No. I like a guy to look like a guy down there." Casey was getting uncomfortable with the direction of the questions.

"Are you sure? You heard what my brother said."

"What about you? Do you like a guy who shaves?"

"Not really. Unless he's got a lot of pubes growing on the tip of his cock."

"No such thing."

"How often do you jack off?"

Casey turned red in the face. "I think I'm getting embarrassed."

Nolan gave him the eyes. "Almost every day. But that would change if you were my boyfriend."

"I think we better watch TV."

"I wish I had someone to bet with on how long you last."

"You better not."

"Can I make a bet with you?"

"Not about that."

They watched TV well into the night. With two separate blankets.

"I'm going to turn in. Let me take Buddy downstairs and I'll be right back." Before he left, he went to get the sweatpants Nolan used before. "I don't want you to get cold in the middle of the night."

"I remember."

At about 1:00 a.m., Casey heard someone by the door to his bedroom. He glanced over to see two red eyes looking at him. It was time to play dead again. Then he awoke. Looking for the red eyes, it took him a few seconds to realize it was one of those dreams. He laid in bed, not wanting to fall asleep for a few minutes, hoping the night visitor would stay away. Then he remembered. "I wish we were neighbors when we were kids. Because if we were neighbors, I think I could have protected you from the Boogeyman."

Casey pulled the top goose down quilt off the bed and grabbed his pillow. He walked to the futon in the living room. Nolan was sleeping on his side. Casey moved very carefully to get next to Nolan by his back. He threw the quilt over them both. Nolan reached back and took one of Casey's arms to drape it over him. No words were exchanged. They both fell back asleep.

Casey was the first to wake up. He loved the way Nolan smelled. He played with the stubble on the side of his head, the Army buzz cut he wore ever since a young teen. Nolan turned around.

"Did we have great sex or what?"

"No. We had a good night's sleep."

"Damn, I must have been dreaming because what you did to me last night was out of this world." He reached between his legs. "In fact, you still got me harder that a rock."

Casey jumped out of the bed and moved to the kitchen.

"Merry Christmas Stretch."

"Merry Christmas Flexer."

"Can you get back here and give me a Merry Christmas present?"

"No."

"Not even a prelude to what I can expect?"

"No."

"I'm using my down home Southern drawl, in case you haven't noticed."

"I noticed."

Nolan began to hum the same tune he hummed before. He got up to go to the bathroom. Casey heard him brushing his teeth. He returned and crawled back under the quilt.

"What's that song you hum?"

"Just a tune. Do you recognize it?"

"No."

"Have you heard of Zack Zeet?"

"I think so."

"It was one of his number one hits. My dad wrote it for him."

"What's it called?"

"If you get back in here with my coffee, I could sing it for you."

"You will?"

"Yes I will. But don't go and expect me to sound like my dad. I'm not cut out for the music business. I'm more the fighter pilot type."

Casey entered into the living room with two cups of coffee. He sat in the chair opposite the futon. Nolan took a sip. "The name of the song is 'I'm Gonna.' I think my dad wrote this song thinking about you and me."

"Are you saying your dad knows you're gay?"

"Of course he does. I don't keep any secrets from my dad. Or my mom either. Chester, sometimes." Nolan began to sing the song to Casey. The recurring phrase of the song had the words, 'I'm gonna make you want me.'

When he finished, he smiled at Casey. "So?"

"You have a nice voice."

"Thank you, and what did you think about the lyrics?"

"They can't be about us. Your dad wrote that song before we knew each other."

"The world works in mysterious ways." He grabbed his cup for more coffee. The coffee cup went back to the coffee table. He put his hand inside his sweatpants and felt his private parts.

Casey noticed. “Ah, Flexer, you have your hands down your pants.”

“I know. My balls hurt. And I’m not just talking a little, I’m talking a lot.”

“Did you hit your testicles when you fell in the snow?”

“No.” He kept his hands under his sweats. “Damn, my balls are swollen too.”

“Does your penis hurt, or just your balls?”

“My balls, and my stomach too. And I didn’t do any crunches yesterday. I feel like someone blew air up my nuts”.

“Nolan, you said we had great sex last night. Do you remember if you had an erection?”

“Of course I did. Spoiler alert here Stretch. When I think of you, I get hard. Really hard. Then I have to jack off.”

“Did you jack off last night?”

“No.”

“Why not?”

“If I tell you, you’ll get mad. And it’s Christmas, I don’t want to wreck the day.”

“Nolan, I’m a big boy, I don’t care if you or anybody else masterbates. I do it too.”

“Did you last night?” Nolan asked.

“No. But I thought about it.”

“So you promise not to get pissed off at me?”

“I promise.”

“I thought you would crawl in my bed and I’d be fucking you. So I didn’t want to blow it. Then I fell asleep and had this really hot dream. You were amazing. It was one of the best fucks of my life.”

Casey twisted his mouth.

“You promised.”

“I’m not angry. I know more than anyone else we don’t have control over what we dream. So, did you ejaculate in your sleep. A wet dream?”

“No.”

“Are you sure?”

"Dude, I need to give you a heads up here. I'm a really heavy comer. I've logged in over six shots, and I'm talking consistency here. Thick too."

"Did you wake up and masterbate?"

"I tried, but I couldn't come, the thought of you crawling all over me took away the pleasure of my right hand. It didn't work."

"Right hand?"

"Yes, right hand, and for your information, I do sometimes jack off with my left hand too. I told you I'm ambidextrous, regardless what Numb Nuts told you."

"Epididymal hypertension."

"What the hell is that?"

"Flexer, I'm sorry to say, you…" he paused for effect.

"Hello, I'm right here. I would like a clarification any time now."

"Fine, Flexer, you have a bad case of blue balls."

"What? There's no such thing."

"Yes there is. The medical term is epididymal hypertension."

"If that were true, why is this the first time I've ever had it?"

"Understandable. You said you jack off almost everyday."

"So?"

"Do you have an orgasm when you jack off?"

"Ah, hello, what would be the point of jacking off without coming?"

"Well, did you have an orgasm last night?"

"No."

"Then, you have blue balls. Do they feel swollen?"

"Yes." Nolan moved so fast Casey couldn't stop him. He slid down his sweatpants and exposed his genitals to Casey with no inhibitions whatsoever. He moved his dick up and showed Casey his balls. "See, they're swollen."

Casey was taken aback. He tried to put on his professional nursing hat, but the image of what Nolan had between his legs was taking his breath away. True to what Chester said, Nolan had a very thick bush, yet only rising up slightly and stopping abruptly as though there was a line drawn on his lower abdomen. His light brown hair was so dense, the skin on his scrotum was barely visible. His cock was thick with a very pink head.

"Let me guess, too much hair and you can't see my balls?"

"Correct. As much as I would enjoy looking at you with your pants down all morning, you better pull them up now."

"Oh, sorry. So you really say blue balls is a real condition?"

"The arteries that carry blood to your genitals enlarge while the veins that leave the genital area constrict, allowing less blood to escape."

"Let me guess Doc, a boner?"

"Exactly. The uneven flow of blood causes an erection. The testicles can swell also. As much as twenty-five to fifty percent larger. If not emptied, this blood in the area builds up through vasocongestion, thus, you get blue balls."

Nolan slipped down his sweatpants for the second time. He lifted his cock and looked at his ball sack. "They're not blue."

"Like Chester said, you got an Amazon jungle going on down there. But I imagine the blood in the area is without oxygen, and the hue would be somewhat blue."

"Look out the window. Do you think we can make it to the base hospital. I'm telling you, my nuts really hurt. My gut too."

"Amputation."

"You got to be fucking kidding me?"

"Sorry. That was unprofessional of me. There's a simple solution. Go into the bathroom and jack off. When you have an orgasm, the blood in the area will leave, and you'll be as good as new."

"Can't."

"Nolan, I told you I don't think anything bad about masterbation. Go ahead, I'll get breakfast together while you're preoccupied."

"I told you I can't. I tried, but I wanted you too bad, my hand failed me. I can't come."

"Well, you're going to spend the rest of the day in pain."

"Didn't you take the medical oath?"

Casey laughed. "No. That's what the doctor does."

"Captain Link, I'm sorry, but you're going to have to help me out here. You have to jack me off."

Casey looked at his hands. "If I touch you there, I'll lose all my control. I'll lose my plan."

"Sorry, but you're a medical professional. And besides, I'm your boyfriend. You have to jack me off." Nolan felt his groin area. "Damn it, I'm getting hard again."

"Get up."

Nolan got up off the futon and stood with an obvious erection pushing up from under his sweatpants. He took off his shirt.

"What's with losing the shirt?"

"I'm getting hot."

Casey pulled the back of the futon up to make it into the couch. He placed pillows on the corner. "Sit here and put your leg on the sofa."

Nolan stripped off his sweats and was completely naked in front of Casey. Casey loved what he saw and didn't tell the guy to put his shirt back on. By now, Nolan was completely erect. He was the kind of guy who went straight out. Not big, not small, on the thick side and very hard. His penis was uncontrollably bobbing up and down with every beat of his heart.

Nolan sat in the corner of the couch like Casey told him to do with his eyes set on Casey, not knowing what he was about to get. Casey sat at the other end of the couch and looked at Nolan.

"Captain Link, I need a hand here really bad."

"I know." Casey lifted his leg and put his bare foot against Nolan's genitals. Nolan jumped.

"I have a solution for that."

Nolan kept his eyes on Casey's foot. Casey began to rub the cock before him in an up and down motion, similar to what a hand would do in the same situation. Careful to not apply much pressure to his sore testicles, he managed to get the end of Nolan's cock, right before the head between his toes.

Nolan moaned. "God that feels so fucking amazing. Keep it going Stretch. Push a little harder."

"Yes sir." Casey kept with the movement of his long foot up and down the underside of Nolan's cock.

"Oh fuck, you're gonna make me come." He grabbed Casey foot and guided the movement to his cock. Sliding down a little on the couch, he pushed Casey's foot where he wanted it, moaned and let out his first of many squirts. His whole body jerked with every release. Seven in total. Casey marveled at the man's ability to ejaculate. Covering his torso with thick slow running fluid. Nolan kept both his hands on Casey's foot and raised it to the surface of his stomach. Casey let his foot be guided to wherever Nolan wanted it. He felt the bottom of his foot slide all across the front of the guy he was staring at. His foot got a tour of the guy's somewhat hidden six pack under a thick skin. The smell of Nolan's bodily fluid invaded both their nostrils. The smell of Nolan's come was beginning to over excite Casey. He pulled his foot back and tried to make it to the bathroom sink on one dry foot, having to use the heel of the sticky one.

"I told you I was a heavy comer. We might want to have a towel handy for our next adventure." Now that Casey was at the bathroom sink with the door open, Nolan had to raise his voice to be heard. "Thanks Doc, I feel better now. I owe you one. Any time, anywhere, anyway you want. Let me know. And I hope to God it's sooner that later. I don't think I can endure another case of epi hypertension."

Casey walked back into the living room with a dry towel and two dry feet. "Epididymal hypertension. And you're welcome." Casey threw him the towel.

"Damn, that was an extra big load. Did we just have sex?"

"I'm not sure. But I might have to take care of business in the shower this morning, or I might end up like you did."

"I got a better idea."

"By the way, can you do me a favor?"

"I'm all yours."

"Don't shave. You have the sexiest genitals I have ever seen."

"Or touched. And wish granted. Chester wrong again."

"Well, Chester said chicks hate it. Guys on the other hand might be a different story."

"I feel bad."

"I thought you said you felt better."

"No. Bad. This was the first time I had sex without getting kissed. It makes me feel cheap."

"Is this a trap?"

"Of course not. So what do you say? A little after sex kiss?"

Casey slowly approached the futon. He looked at Nolan's bare chest. He was rock hard, with a slight barrel belly like he claimed, and very little chest hair. A small amount at the top between his pecs, and a very small amount surrounding each nipple.

"You promise to behave?"

Nolan was still naked. "I promise."

"Can you put your sweatpants on?"

"Do I have to?"

"Yes."

"What the hell. He grabbed the sweatpants on the floor and slipped them over his very hairy front. "Now?"

Casey walked towards him and straddled his legs on both sides of what was now covered up. He leaned down close to Nolan's lips. "You are the hottest guy I've ever seen Captain Kelly."

"I know." Nolan pulled him in for a kiss. Casey took the opportunity to touch both his biceps. He felt them get hard. Nolan flexed to show off. He took Casey's hips and moved him around on his crotch. "Doc, I'm getting hard again. I don't want another bad case of blue balls. What do you say?"

Casey jumped up and moved to the kitchen. "Get that thing under control. Do you want to shower first?"

"Alright. Don't go and get your undies all in a bundle." He got up to go and shower.

Casey held his cup of coffee and stared out at the snow in the trails across the street. It was still nautical twilight, but there was enough light to marvel at the winter scene left behind by the Christmas Eve storm. His thoughts were interrupted by the sound of Nolan singing the words to the song in the shower with his strong Southern accent, "I'm gonna make you want me."

Nolan shaved, brushed his teeth for the second time and enter the kitchen with his shirt off.

Casey remained by the window marveling at the fresh blanket of snow on the trails. Someone entered with a snow mobile, possibly a Christmas present for some lucky soul. Nolan surprised Casey by giving him a surprise hug from behind. He jumped.

"I told you I can take care of that." He kissed Casey on his neck. Casey took the second opportunity in one morning to feel Nolan's arms as they wrapped around him. He closed his eyes and breathed deeply. Nolan did the same.

"This is a great Christmas day Captain Link."

"Thanks for protecting me last night Captain Kelly?"

"I don't think that guy will be back at Reilly's anymore."

"I hope you're right."

"You need to put your t shirt on. You'll freeze."

"I need you to help me out."

"Again?"

"I haven't said anything yet."

"I'm listening."

"I need you to shave the back of my neck. I don't want to make an uneven line."

"Maybe I can safely do that. Your back is so smooth and you have thick skin over muscle."

"I know it's not easy, but control yourself Captain Link. Come on." He led the way to the bathroom.

Casey got his razor and shaving gel. He worked some onto the neck area. "I like your hair cut this way."

"I know."

"Finished."

"Not yet. One more thing." He turned around to face Casey. Casey pretended not to notice Nolan was semi erect under the sweats. "My nipples. I want you to shave my nipples. I cut them the last time I tried."

"Why?"

"Because when I shave my nipples, they get twice as sensitive."

"You have sensitive nipples?"

"Doesn't everybody?"

"To some degree. Me only a little bit."

"Well, another lesson about Flexer's body. My nipples are hot wired to my dick. I can come just by playing with them. No hands on the rudder if you know what I mean."

"You're making things very difficult on me. Alright." He put some gel on his hand and rubbed it into Nolan's left nipple. Nolan closed his eyes and made a noise coming from deep inside his chest. Casey carefully took the razor and moved it around the small amount of chest hair that followed the dark brown perimeter of his nipple. It jumped out right before his eyes. With two fingers, he gently squeezed the protruding nipple. Nolan leaned back and moaned. The front of his pants reached Casey's front. Casey ignored the poke and worked the other side. Nolan had his eyes closed and continued on enjoying the event.

“Done. Amazing, I think your nipples are more reactive that any women God made.”

Nolan turned round to face the sink so Casey was at his back once again. He slipped down his sweatpants, grabbed Casey’s hand and placed it on his cock. This time he didn’t have to beg. Casey put his nose on the crook of Nolan’s neck and began to move his dick in the manner he would have moved his own. He could feel the hard ass of the guy with a very clean looking crack. As if he shaved there, but Chester said his ass was hairless. The guy’s bush around his hands was exciting him so much that his own sweatpants were fully extended in the front. He used one of his hands to get a good feel of the balls while the other jacked him up and down. His balls were big, but slightly swollen from his blue ball event. The bush under his ball sack went further down, but Casey kept his hands out of that territory. It didn’t take long for Nolan to get his second release, this time aimed conveniently right in the sink.

Nolan turned around and kissed Casey for the third time in the morning. He pushed Casey against the bathroom door, reached low and pulled down Casey’s sweatpants. Before Casey could get out a protest, he had his cock in his mouth. Casey was tall, and was long below the belt. Nolan was undeterred by the challenge. He went the whole way without gagging.

With both Casey’s hands on the side of the guy’s army buzz cut head, he gave a warning. “I’m going to come. I can’t hold it back.”

Nolan never stopped until he had a mouth full. He got up and spit in the sink what was shot in his mouth. He leaned over to get a mouthful of water from the faucet, and spit again.

Leaning on the edge of the sink, he looked at the tall guy with an expression of being hit by a hurricane. “Sorry about that, but I did control myself to some extent.”

“No need to apologize. It’s my fault. I never should have believed things would go my way.”

“Can I shower with you? I have shaving cream on my neck.”

“Can we not have anymore sex?”

“Compromise?”

“How?”

“Just a few hugs, and a few kisses.”

They showered together, with plenty of hugs and kisses. Turning off the water, Nolan sang the tune from the song ‘I’m Gonna’ while he grabbed a towel and dried the both of them off.

“I’m treating you to my special recipe of scrambled eggs this morning to show my immense appreciation for saving my life, or for at least saving my nuts.”

“Do you want me to help?”

“No. Sit at the table and watch. I’m a work of art on the kitchen canvas.” He gave Casey his trademark eye movement and began preparing his special scrambled egg breakfast.

“Nolan, I’m seeing a therapist. That’s why I wrote in the journal.”

Nolan stopped with the fork in the bowl of broken eggs. “That’s a good idea.”

“I was going to stop after the first time.”

“So you’re going back?”

“Yes. I decided yesterday when I knew we were on a crash course to connecting that I need to discuss some things with him. Things about how I deal with guys in my life.”

“Is this you saying you’re my boyfriend?”

“No. This is me telling you not to get offended while I hold you off with any under the sheets events or those against the side of the bathroom wall.”

“Oh no. I’m afraid to ask.”

“I’m going to put on the brakes until I get a good chance to go over issues with this guy. His name is Sawyer. Ian told me about him.”

“In this phase of self discovery, you’re OK if I talk to Numb Nuts about whatever we are?”

“I am.”

“We still go camping?”

Casey didn’t answer.

“What am I supposed to do if I get another case of the blue balls?”

Still no answer. Nolan put the plates of scrambled eggs in front of Casey. “Come on, tell me what you think.”

After breakfast, Nolan recovered a little of his lost confidence.

Casey got a call from Ian in Vancouver. “Merry Christmas Ian. How is your family?”

“Merry Christmas to you too. My family, I don’t think this will go down in history as their best Christmas ever.”

“So you did it?”

“Yes I did.”

“Are you OK?”

“Yes I am. They both hugged me and said they loved me, but I know it blew them away. They said they never had any idea. I hope I did the right thing.”

“I think you did. Ian, you have to be the bravest person I’ve ever met. Whatever you need, I’m here for you.”

“Thanks, I’ll call you when I get back. There’s been a development in my life I can’t wait to tell you about.”

“OK. Merry Christmas. Take care.

“See you soon.” They both hung up. Casey came back into the kitchen to find Nolan.

“Everything alright?”

“Yes. Ian is visiting with his family in Vancouver.”

“We need to clear the driveway and the walks. The street plow shoved a shit load of snow up the backside of my truck.”

“The two of us can knock it out in no time.”

They collected Buddy by the back door on their way out to the garage. He was happy after waiting for what seemed to him a lifetime in the morning. Civil twilight already began and there was no sign of Casey.

“Check it out, I guess a foot and a half?”

Casey added, "About three up against the truck."

They tackled the small mountain made by the snow plow blocking them in first. Buddy was marking all the fresh snow by the windows with his legs tearing up the smooth shiny surface. It looked like there was a heard of deer who spent the night.

They finished clearing the back of the truck, and leaned up against the side to take a rest.

Nolan looked at Casey with a serious expression. "You're not going to forget I really like you, right?"

Casey gave him some of his own medicine. "Of course you do. I mean, look at this." He used both hands to point inward. Nolan gave him the eye trick. They moved to the front of the house to clear the sidewalks.

Nolan took a break and let his body fall backward in the fresh deep snow. He laid there while Casey kept clearing.

"Captain Link. I need a hand getting up."

"Alright I'll be right over." Casey kept shoveling.

After a few seconds, "Captain Link, I'm waiting."

"Right away Captain Kelly."

"Come on. Give me a hand. It's cold down here. And my nuts still ache from what you did to me last night."

Casey approached and offered the handle of his shovel for Nolan to grab and pull himself up.

"Give me your hand."

"Do you think I'm stupid or something?"

"Come on, I'd help you."

Buddy swooped in to lick his face.

"At least Buddy loves me."

"That's because you're undeniably irresistible."

"I'm getting frost bite on my ass."

Casey gave in and offered his hand. "Behave, Gram is watching from the front window."

Nolan let himself get pulled up and ditched his plan to pull Casey down for a hopeful repeat of the day before. Once up, he looked at the front window and there was no sign of Gram or Candy watching. "You tricked me Doc. Now you must pay." He grabbed Casey and flung him in the fresh snow, jumping on top before he had a chance to roll over and get up.

"I believe I said I really like you Captain Link."

"And I believe I said I know." Casey kept his stare void of any expression.

"I'm not letting you up until you confess your true feelings for me Captain Link."

"If I do, you let me get up with no hanky panky involved."

"What the hell is hanky panky?"

"Anything involving skin on skin contact."

He gave Casey the eye treatment. "Deal."

"Alright, I understand you really like me. After all, I've been told a few times in my life I'm really hot."

"Sorry, that won't do." He lowered his face a little closer and stared right into Casey's eyes without blinking. He also managed to get in a little grinding with his hips conveniently located right where he wanted them to be.

"I thought I explained to you this morning the ground rules."

"I'm not asking for a fuck in your front yard Captain Link."

Casey tried to move his arms. Nolan had them locked down to his side in the snow.

"I can stay like this all morning."

"Fine, what is it you want to hear."

"You know what."

"I think I like you Captain Kelly."

"Not quite there yet Captain Link. Why not give it another shot?"

Casey pushed up with his hips. He gave Nolan a jolt between his legs.

"Very nice. Dry humping." Nolan moved around in a way that would excite them both.

"Dry humping is the major cause of epididymal hypertension, Captain Kelly."

This time Candy was watching out the window with intense interest. With a huge smile as well.

"Fine. I like you Captain Kelly."

"How much, a lot or a little."

"Between a little and a lot Captain Kelly."

"That's a good boy. I guess I can let you up now." He crawled off Casey, but not before giving it one last hump motion. He extended his hand to Casey, who took it, and pulled him upright.

Casey moved to the front of Nolan and brushed off the snow. Without warning, he pushed Nolan back over who landed right on his back in the same position that started it all. "You're a dick head Captain Kelly. A real Delta Hotel." Casey ran to the garage to escape any countermeasure the other guy might have. Candy laughed from her warm and dry front row seat.

Buddy was at the door before Nolan could get up. Casey followed the dog up the stairs. He heard Nolan shut the door below. "Hang your coat on the hook outside the door, Captain Kelly. We need to get ready and go downstairs to begin the festivities."

"Don't think you're clear from this Captain Link. I'll strike back when you least expect it."

By noon, the sun was up and reflecting brightly on the fresh fallen snow. Casey knocked on Candy's kitchen door.

"Merry Christmas boys, come on in." She gave both Casey and Nolan a kiss on the cheek with a hug to go with it.

Nolan inhaled through his nostrils. "What smells to good."

"My cinnamon apple pie. It should be out of the oven in a half hour, then my part is complete. Beer and football games on the TV."

Casey frowned at her. "Aren't we supposed to watch the New York Macey's parade?"

Nolan looked at Candy for support. "For real?"

"Yes, for real. It's supposed to be every American family's tradition."

Nolan raised his hands to Candy and shrugged his shoulders.

Gram came into the kitchen wearing a snow woman apron adorned with a mistletoe design at the bottom hem. “Merry Christmas boys. Thanks so much for shoveling the walks. That was some snow fall we had last night. I hope it wasn’t too much trouble for you.”

Candy folder her arms. “Don’t worry about that Gram, I think they were having a good time out there. I was watching them from the window.”

Nolan lost any expression from his face. He kept it as neutral as he could.

Casey added, “I had to take charge a few times to keep Nolan on task. I even knocked him to the ground once.”

“I saw.” She threw them both an accusing glance. “Come on Flexer, let’s grab a beer and hit the games.”

“Don’t worry Gram, not everyone is jumping ship. I’m here to do whatever you want me to do. I’d rather cook than watch a bunch of boys in tights knock into each other.”

“You’re such a dear.”

Buddy kept nudging Casey’s hand. He had a rubber ball the size of a softball with a bell on the inside. Casey walked to the living room where there was a large tree decorated with multi colored lights and a history of glass ornaments Gram collected over the years. “Did Buddy get nice things for Christmas?”

Candy shook her head at him. “He’s a dog.”

“You mean this is it?”

“That’s it.”

Gram hollered from the kitchen, “don’t forget our hugs and kisses.”

Casey sat on the floor by the tree. “Come on Buddy, this is for you.” He gave the ball wrapped in a green paper with Santa Clause faces. Buddy sniffed the object, looked at Casey for permission. “Go ahead, it’s for you.”

Buddy began pulling off the paper and found the rubber ball. He put it in his mouth and ran to the room where he could guard his new possession.

Nolan laughed. "We're not going to take your ball Buddy. You can come back in here." Moments later, Buddy came back to the living room with the ball in his mouth. He approached Nolan and dropped it on his lap. Nolan jumped. The ball began to leak water. "What the? This thing is leaking?"

Casey looked at Candy and laughed. "About that, Buddy likes to wash his toys in the toilet."

Candy took a swig of her beer from the bottle. "So boys, when did you two decide to hook up. You were so cute this morning in the snow."

"I'm Casey's new boyfriend."

"You guys are boyfriends? I thought Casey was pissed off at you."

"He was, but it didn't last too long. He's admitted I'm irresistible."

"Better go ahead and explain to Candy your definition of being boyfriends. Candy, Nolan here has a very unique approach to being a couple."

"I'm listening."

"I said I was Casey's boyfriend. He hasn't admitted to it yet. I can wait."

"Are you out at the fighter squadron?"

"Absolutely not. Can I rely on you not to let this get out?"

"That depends. Can you convince your brother I'm the best shot he has in life for a happily ever after?"

"Sure. He already said he likes you. And this is between us, I don't want any trouble, him spending a few days at our place is difficult enough as it is."

"Thank you Captain Kelly."

"Don't mention it."

They enjoyed a day of turkey, venison, mashed potatoes, apple pie and egg nog with rum.

Nolan was unsuccessful in convincing Casey to spend the night at the cabin. He wanted to get back and clear the driveway before the next storm was to hit. Both guys were on duty for the following day. So a reluctant Nolan drove Casey at the end of the day to get his Subaru. They brought shovels to dig it out.

The next morning, Casey took Buddy for a run on the streets to the main gate and back. By 6:45 a.m., he was sitting in the hospital cafeteria having a coffee and thinking about the past two days. Top on his list for the morning was to call Sawyer and get an appointment.

"Morning Captain, how was your Christmas?"

"Really nice. How was yours?"

"Great. I made a snowman after the storm and my son loved it." Sergeant Tomlin's son was five. "I'll see you in the office." The sergeant left with his coffee. Casey checked his phone for any messages. There were none.

Up in the office, Major Meyers called Casey in. "Did you have a nice Christmas?"

"Yes sir, I did. And how about you?"

"We missed midnight mass due to the storm. That was the first one we ever missed."

"Mother nature."

"Listen, heads up. I got wind of a possible deployment of one of the fighter squadrons. If it happens it will be secret, but I want to make sure the pilot's records are all up to date. Can you start going through them one by one starting today?"

"Yes sir. Did you happen to hear where they'd be going?"

"No, but if you listen to the news, I'm betting on missions over Syria. Remember, this is all classified. We don't want to be responsible for passing rumors."

"I'll start right away. We should be slow until after the first, everyone is on min manning for the week."

"That gives us more time to prepare."

"Will you be going this time?"

"I don't know Casey. Sometimes they take a flight surgeon from another theater. I started packing my bags just in case."

"Did you mention it to your wife?"

"I didn't have to, she saw me getting ready."

"Alright, let me get to the computer and start reviewing records. Do you have a clue what Fighter squadron it might be?"

"No clue."

Casey left the Major's office and went to his own to get on the computer. By lunchtime, he was still immersed on task when he heard a knock at the side of his office door.

"Hello Stretch."

Casey turned around to see Nolan smiling at him with his flight suit on. He had a bag in his hand. "Hi Captain Kelly."

"Captain?"

"Hello Nolan."

"Nice." He handed Casey the bag. "I made you a grilled cheese sandwich for your lunch. My special recipe."

"That was nice of you. Are you guys busy today?"

"No."

"So you're not all getting ready for a big event?"

"I'll be a slug in the ditch. There's no such thing as a secret in this man's Air Force anymore." He spoke in his thick Southern Drawl.

Casey shrugged his shoulders.

"That is all rumor. The same conditions we always live with. When you're an F 22 pilot in a fighter squadron, you have to be ready at a minute's notice. As for now, it's life as usual."

"Maybe for you, but for me, I've had my eyes stuck on this computer screen for five hours now getting records ready."

"Shouldn't they already be ready?"

"Ha, Ha General Kelly."

"I have to get back. I'm not supposed to be out of the squadron, but I couldn't find any delivery service."

"Well, don't go and get in trouble on my account."

"Stretch, I had a great Christmas. It was amazing being with you." He stared at Casey for a few moments. "Well, see you around. Hope you like the sandwich." He left the office.

Casey sat looking at the bag for about ten seconds before he got up and moved through the waiting room and into the hospital hallway. He made it in time to see Nolan's backside walking towards the exit. "Captain Kelly."

Nolan turned around. They had about fifteen feet between them.

Casey noticed they were alone in the hallway. "Me too."

Nolan smiled and threw him a salute, turned around and continued on his way. Casey watched as his rear end moved in the flight suit with no visible lines. The next thing Casey did was to enter his office, pick up the phone and call Sawyer.

"Hello Sawyer, this is Casey Link."

"Hello Casey. I hope you had a nice Christmas."

"I did. And I hope you have an opening this week to discuss it."

"Can we do Wednesday again? Same time, six?"

"That would be perfect. See you Wednesday at six."

"Good. See you later."

"Bye." He hung up the phone and walked in circles. He picked up the bag and smelled. It was the same sandwich as always. He grabbed his cell phone. "Hello Candy."

"Hi Sweetie. I should have stayed home today. Who in the hell gets a hair cut the day after Christmas?"

"Well, don't go home yet. Meet me for lunch in the food court."

"What time?"

"Now?"

"Alright, stop by and get me. I could use the break."

Casey grabbed his uniform winter parka and hat. "Sergeant Tomlin, I'm going over to the food court to have lunch. I got my cell phone on if anybody is looking for me."

"Yes sir. Enjoy your lunch."

Casey walked to his car with the brown paper bag in his hand. The roads were all cleared on base from the snow storm. He parked at the Military Mall and walked over to the barber shop. The place was empty, since so many were on leave or off duty with minimal manning. He found Candy sitting in her chair.

"You'll never guess who just called me?"

"That cute airmen who got the free haircut the other day?"

"No silly. Chester. He's flying in this Thursday and asked me if I wanted to go to dinner with him. Can you believe I have a date for New Year's Eve?"

"Come on, I'm hungry." They walked to the food court. There was only two tables occupied with single guys having lunch. Candy got a plate from Popeye's and Casey got a coffee from Starbucks.

"All you're having is coffee for lunch?"

"No. I have a sandwich."

"Since when did you start bringing sandwiches?"

"I didn't."

"Well then?"

Casey didn't want to answer her but had little choice. "Nolan gave me this."

"Wait a minute. You're saying Nolan made you lunch?"

"Yes."

"I knew it."

"What?"

"This guy is falling hard for you."

"Damn it."

"Damn it? Are you crazy?"

"Maybe, Maybe not. Have I mentioned to you I started going to therapy?"

"No. The journal?"

"Yes. My homework. I have an appointment this week on Wednesday."

"I'm so proud of you."

"I need to work so many things out, and this guy isn't giving me any time. He showed up a month too early."

"Can't control when the right guy shows up."

"I know. Doesn't matter. I'll sabotage the whole thing in a few weeks anyway."

"Not so fast. Have you ever tackled this issue before with professional help?"

"No."

"Then bite your tongue. Give this Sawyer guy a chance, and be honest with him, and with you too."

"I know." Casey felt his phone vibrate with a text message. He assumed work was calling him back.

"Hey Stretch, did you like the sandwich? My brother just called. Said he was coming in this Thursday. New Year's Eve. Let's go out with him and Candy. A double date? Call me."

"Work?"

"No. Nolan."

"And?"

"He wants to go out with you and Chester this Thursday."

"I love it. Say yes."

"I guess I could say yes if we drive separate cars."

"For real?"

"Yes. Until I get some things worked out. He's not the easiest guy to say no to."

"Come on, send him a yes."

Casey took the phone and composed the response. *"OK. But we arrive in separate cars."*

The response was immediate. *"You don't trust me? I'm crushed."* He had Candy read the reply.

"You hurt his feelings. Now what?"

Casey read out loud, the response he was typing. *"It's not your fault. You're undeniably irresistible. It's me I don't trust."*

"Nice, go on, send it."

Casey sent the message. The response came right back.

"Fine, I've got five days to change your mind."

Casey read the reply. *"Thanks for the gourmet sandwich."*

"You're welcome Stretch."

Candy smiled. "Have you heard any more from Ines?"

"Just what I told you. He's on leave for the whole thirty days."

"Doesn't guys like that give you inspiration?"

"Yes he does. I told him he was the bravest person I know."

"I have to get back to the shop."

"See you later Candy"

Casey drove to the hospital to continue with the records check. He zoned out on the computer screen until the phone buzzed with a text message. *"Stretch, I'm off at four. Cook me dinner tonight. I can crash on your couch."*

"You're crazy."

"Let's meet at the IHOP for dinner."

"You're still crazy. Your truck is too big and I don't trust myself."

"Come on!"

"Fine, meet me at the Iditarod Dining Facility at 1610."

"You're so romantic."

"So I've been told."

"Fine. 1610. Over and out!"

Casey put away his phone and cleaned up his office. Double checking all the pilot's medical records took him less time than what he anticipated. The next duty day he'd be free from the computer screen. He had Sunday off.

By 4:00 p.m., the sun was very low on the horizon. Civil twilight was scheduled to begin at 4:52. Casey locked his office and left for his car. It was a short drive to the Air Force dining facility, over to the extreme West side of the base. He drove down Fighter Drive and spotted the big brown Ram truck parked to the side of the lot away from any other vehicles. Nolan told him he'd prefer a bullet to his leg than a dent to his truck. So Casey parked next to the truck, leaving one space in between.

By 4:10, Casey was walking through the door to the Iditarod Dining Facility. Nolan was pacing the floor waiting for him to arrive.

"Hey Stretch."

"Hi. Are you hungry?"

"Yes."

"Me too. Should we hit the main line?"

"After you Doc."

They both chose prime rib from the main dinner line. The Iditarod was a modern looking chow hall designed to look like a nice restaurant, with a wooden ceiling and plenty of high glass windows. It was a far cry from the old style Air Force chow halls. There were several lines to choose for full meals to snacks.

"So what are we doing after dinner Stretch."

"I plan on a quiet night with a book and Buddy to keep me company."

"For real?"

"Have you finished your book yet about that lieutenant in Afghanistan?"

"No."

"Tonight would be a good time to relax with that book. Start a fire in your fireplace and get a cup of hot chocolate."

"I have a much better idea."

"I made an appointment this week with that guy Sawyer I told you about."

"Can I give him a list of issues?"

"No."

"Can I give him one?"

Casey took a bite of his food. "And what would that one be?"

"Trust me. To trust me."

"OK. I'll give it to him for you."

Nolan worked on his plate before adding. "I can wait. You're worth it. I like you. A lot."

"Thank you."

"Thank you and?"

"Thank you and I like you too."

"Much better. So, when are we going to take down the tree?"

"Do what?"

"You know, the deal we made. You help me decorate the tree. That would include taking it down too."

"Nice move Captain Kelly. You have to wait until Three Kings day is over."

"When is that?"

"On the sixth."

"Can't wait that long. You have to make a sooner date."

"I'll get back with you on that."

"Can you go to lunch with me tomorrow?"

"I have tomorrow off. How about Monday?"

"Can't wait that long."

"Call me on my cell. I can meet you for lunch. We could try the Kenai Dining Hall."

"Deal."

They finished their dinner and walked to the parking lot together, but got into different vehicles to go home.

Wednesday finally arrived for Casey to have his appointment with Sawyer. He was exhausted by having to put off the eager Nolan every day. And he felt like he was losing the battle.

Wednesday night, once again sitting on his futon, with a glass of red wine and his journal. He began to do next week's homework assignment.

Dear Diary
December 30

Tomorrow is New Year's Eve. That time when people make the resolutions they never keep or think about a week later. Not me. Never have and never will.

So Sawyer asked me if I like to cook. Did I really pay money to discuss the Food Network? I told him I do. So, he said the way he sees it, I have three choices. The first is to skip plans for creating a great dish and go out to eat. To let someone else do it. The second option was to perfect the recipe before I start and only then put it into action. The third was to have a plate in mind, yet skip the recipe and experiment with the ingredients as I go along.

Alright, so what kind of cook am I? Sawyer didn't care what kind of cook I was. He asked me what kind of cook do I want to become. I like the adventure of adding the ingredients as I go along. What fun is there following the recipe? Oh fuck, now I get it. Seventy-five bucks later.

Casey closed the journal and went to brush his teeth. Looking through the bathroom mirror, he wondered. *Am I as brave as Ian or am I a man hiding behind the definition of my career?* He turned off the light and crawled under his double goose down quilts. Sleep came fast.

Sometime around two in the morning, Casey became aware of the night visitor with the red eyes. As usual, the knife was on the dresser and he couldn't get it and play dead at the same time. So he decided to play dead. The red glowing eyes glowed brighter. They moved slowly towards the bed. Casey's heart beat accelerated. Yet he knew how to play. Then the unexpected happened for the first time in his life. Without moving his head, he saw a large figure standing at the end of his bed. The figure was dressed in a green cape. He was very tall and muscular. He had the same kind of haircut worn by Nolan, but it couldn't be Nolan because he was so tall. And there was another striking feature besides the man's stature. He looked at Casey with incredible icy blue eyes. It was Capan Iceman. His childhood superhero. For the first time, Capan Iceman came to his rescue like he did for so many others throughout the years. This night was Casey's turn.

Capan Iceman lifted his hand and pointed to the image with the red glowing eyes. A battle wasn't necessary like in so many of his past adventures. All he said was, "Go," and the night visitor with the red eyes dissipated into nothing at all.

Capan Iceman didn't smile. He didn't have to. Casey knew smiling wasn't one of his super powers. Capan Iceman nodded his head at Casey and with a green swirl of motion, he was gone. Casey opened his eyes. He looked around the room to gather his wits. To affirm he was out of the world of dreams. This time he didn't have to get up and walk around the apartment. He rolled over and went back to sleep.

The morning of New Year's Eve greeted Casey feeling strong and ready for a new day and a new year. He laid a while in bed thinking about the dream he had during the night. Finally, the night figure could be defeated. Oddly enough, Casey felt like he was beginning a new chapter in his life, one where the night visitor had less power over him. One where fear would play less of a role. One where being brave like his friend Ian was a reality, not just a trait to envy.

Climbing out of bed, he put on his running gear and found his best Buddy waiting by the kitchen door. He could hear the sniffing through the small crack of space separating the door from the hallway floor.

By seven he was at the hospital cafeteria. Sunday was his day off, but he wanted to go to work. So he went in his civvies. Dressed in his jeans and a green sweatshirt, he sat at the table and drank a large coffee. There were a few other people around but not too many. He picked up his phone and composed a message.

"Good morning Nolan. I'm at work. Let me know if you still want to have lunch." He pushed send.

Seconds later the phone vibrated. "I missed breakfast. Where are you?"

"I'm in the hospital cafeteria."

"Give me ten minutes. I'll be right over. I'm hungry."

"I'll be here." Casey bought the New York Times and began to read the international news on his phone.

"Hey Stretch. I thought you had the day off?"

"I do. I wanted to make sure I finished with the records."

"I'm going to get some scrambled eggs and toast. Do you want anything?"

"A donut. You pick."

"Right back." He left his shiny green flight jacket on the chair and walked over to the line to get breakfast. Casey braved watching his backside as he approached the line. Nolan had a unique way of moving his butt as he walked. Like the cross between a cowboy and a rugby player.

Back at the table, Casey kept his eyes on the news. "Does this mean we skip lunch?"

"Not in my world it doesn't. Anything interesting with the news this morning?"

"The New York Times say the Brits started joining us in bombing raids on Isis in Syria."

"God Bless the Queen. Those Brits always cover our asses no matter what."

"So, have you had any interesting briefings yet?"

"Shame on you Captain Link."

"No matter, I get briefed too. You do realize we frequently go with you guys?"

Nolan got an ornery look on his face. "That would be very nice."

Casey ignored him. "What is it about the name of this group? The President calls them Isil, the French call them Daesh. The Prime Minister of the UK uses that world also. Then our press calls them Isis. I hear the

BBC calling them the Islamic State. What the hell, if we can't figure out what to call them, how do we figure out a plan to defeat them?"

"Good point. Do you know what Isil stands for?"

"No."

"Islamic State of Iraq and the Levant."

"Levant?"

"Levant refers to a large geographic area in the Middle East."

"And what does Daesh mean in English?"

"It's not an Arabic word, It's an acronym. But there is an Arabic word that sounds like Daesh that translates to trample or crush down. The Terrorist group doesn't like being called that."

"Where did you hear all this?"

"We recently had a briefing."

"I knew it."

"Don't make me kick your ass Captain Link."

"As if you could. I'm much taller than you are."

"Is that a challenge?"

Casey considered the repercussions of his next set of words. He kept his eyes on the phone reading the news.

Nolan studied him while he worked on his scrambled eggs and toast. "What is it? Something's bothering you. Did I piss you off?"

Casey moved his eyes away from the phone. "No."

"Then?"

"I went to see Sawyer last night."

"And how'd that go?"

"OK."

"That's not the vibe I get."

"I started having weird dreams since I first went to see him. Last night too."

"Nightmares?"

"Not all of them. Last night was a good one."

"About me?"

"I'm not sure."

Nolan lowered his voice. "You've seen my dick, in all its glory. Was the dick the same?"

"Who said anything about a dick in my dream?"

"You and me have very different definitions of what a good dream is." Nolan looked around to make sure their conversation couldn't be overheard. "If you'd let me sleep next to you at night with my arm around you, that Boogeyman wouldn't dare show his face in your dreams."

Casey wanted to change the subject. "I talked to Candy last night. She said it was impossible to get a reservation anyplace for dinner other than at Reilly's. She had to talk to her friend."

"About that. Chester sent me a text message. He wants me to ask you what she plans on wearing tonight."

"A black party dress and matching high heels. Hair up. If you tell her I told, I'll deny it."

"Cool. And what about us?"

"I'm good in jeans."

"Thank God."

"Your commando jeans?"

"No. I have a pair of Cinch jeans I wear on special occasions."

"I think you better advise Chester to wear something nice."

"He's wearing a new pair of jeans and a nice leather blazer. With a button down shirt. And his dress boots."

"That will do. A nicely muscled man in leather and boots."

Nolan gave him the eye trick. "What time do I pick you up?"

Casey gave him the stare down without answering.

"Listen, I have to drop Chester off to pick up Candy so they can go in her car. What would be the point of my leaving with you following behind in your Super Subaru?"

Casey gave in, in more ways than one. "Alright. I'll be ready when you drop Chester off."

"Nice. By the way, you can drink, I'm on standby. Can't drink a drop all night."

By 6:30 p.m., Casey was in Candy's kitchen with Buddy. Gram was in the living room watching the local nightly news.

"Come on. Hair up or down."

"He already saw you in the red dress with your hair up, why not have it down."

"Good plan. Every girl should have a gay guy in her closet."

"Closet?"

"Just a figure of speech. Not that other closet you live in."

"So we have to go to Mad Myrna's after dinner?"

"Yes. Chester likes to dance with me." The door bell rang. "Casey, they're here. Quick. How do I look?"

"God help me. I'll go and let them in."

"Happy New Year Doc?" Chester had a small bouquet of flowers in his hand.

"Happy New Year Stretch."

"Happy New Year to you both. Come on in. Buddy's been waiting."

They followed Casey inside to be greeted first by Buddy, sniffing at their shoes. Chester took one look at Candy and froze in place. He managed to snap out of it. "You are absolutely gorgeous."

Candy was wearing a tight fitting black cocktail dress that slightly flared out at the waist. The neck and half sleeves were of black lace. Her shoes were a simple black leather high heels. She wore her hair down and had only a touch of makeup on. A very light pink lipstick.

"Nolan, pinch me please."

Nolan pinched his nipple.

"Ouch. What the hell was that for?"

"You told me to."

"Shall we go?" Candy grabbed her little black purse.

"Candy, grab your puffy jacket. You can leave it in the car, but it's not safe to be without it."

"Fine."

They moved to the kitchen door. Buddy made it there first. Casey bent down to give him a hug. "Poor guy he wants to come with us. You just wait and I'll take you for a good run in the morning."

Chester grabbed the car keys from Candy. Casey followed Nolan to the big Ram truck. "Nolan, wait."

"What?"

"Turn around."

Nolan smiled, turned half way and stopped. "I get it, you want to see how my ass fits in these jeans."

"I never saw Cinch jeans before. I like them."

Nolan faced him with his ornery smile. "Your turn." He turned Casey around and pushed him up against the door of the truck. He locked him in with his arms and gave him a kiss on the side of his neck. "You look gorgeous too Stretch. You turn me on."

"I think Gram's watching from the window."

"Sorry, I only fall for that once."

He let Casey free, who looked at the window and waved at Gram.

"Ooops."

They made it to Reilly's Pub by seven, and had to park down the street. Chester dropped Candy off by the door first. Walking in heels with snow on the ground wasn't so easy but Alaskan girls were used to it.

Soon, they were standing at the bar waiting for their table. The place was crowded. Chester told them all, "The Kelly boys are dry tonight. You both can drink and don't worry about the drive back."

"I only want a few glasses of red wine. I plan to be well balanced for dancing tonight."

"I'm going to be fine with a glass of wine myself."

The young guy in charge of the dining room seated them on a nice table over by the window. But for Candy's dress, the air was chilly so close to the glass. The temperature was in the low teens outside. Chester got up, took off his dark brown leather blazer and draped it over her shoulders.

"Thank you young man."

Nolan nodded his head. "Our mom and dad raised us right." He was dressed in his new Cinch jeans with a tight fitting v neck gold wool blend sweater. No under shirt, so that the shape of his pectoral muscles were on display.

Casey wore his new pair of jeans and a long sleeve black shirt with a small gold leaf pattern throughout. He had his shirt tucked in and even wore a belt.

There wasn't anything to choose from on the menu. The special of the night was filet mignon, baked potato, Greek salad and cheesecake for desert. The Kelly brothers drank diet colas while Candy and Casey both had a red wine.

"Candy, I want another wine. Are you ready?"

"Yes. Then I'll switch to cola. Our waitress is really busy. Maybe you should tackle the bar?"

"I'm on it. Guys, another cola?"

Chester got up. "I'll help you." He followed Casey to the bar. As Casey found a place to squeeze in, Chester stood right behind him. "Hey Doc, what's your plans with my little brother?"

"Little?"

"I won the bet by two pounds."

"I guessed."

"So?"

"It's complicated."

"It's all complicated. So?"

Casey turned around to face Chester. "He makes me feel safe. Something I'm not accustomed to feeling. I'm a loner and feeling safe has always been something I accomplish by hiding out."

"He told me about the journal."

"He did?"

"Don't let it get to you, twins tell each other everything. Especially us two."

Casey took a deep breath. "I'm going to try and let him in."

"Do me a favor. Don't hurt him. He's a real softy on the inside. I call it the gay gene."

"I think I figured that out already. Rough as hell on the outside and soft as a baby on the inside."

"That's him. Come on, let's get those drinks."

They made it back to the table each with two glasses in hand. The dinner went great. There were stories of Nolan and Chester back on the farm. "Chester, go ahead and tell Candy and Casey how you burned down the shed on New Year's Eve back on the farm."

Candy gasped, "You didn't?"

"I sort of did, but it was Nolan's fault."

"My fault? How so?"

"You're the one who told me to hang it on the rafters."

Casey asked, "Hang what?"

"Chester made a star out of sparklers. He tied about twenty of them on a bundle."

"Don't look so horrified. We were thirteen."

"So what happened?" Candy was the one to ask.

"Nolan told me to tie it in the middle of the shed on the rafter. I guess it was too close to the wood, and the shed burned down."

"But not before we had a beautiful sparkler star. And then we both got into big trouble. And it was Chester who did it."

"That was the Christmas we got the dirt bikes."

"And it was the winter they sat locked in the garage for two months, isn't that right Numb Nuts."

Casey was enjoying the stories. "Did Nolan ever get into big trouble?"

"No."

"No? What about the time you drove dad's pickup right into the river. Or should I say under the river."

"Oh, yeah, I forgot about that. But in my defense, I was only fourteen."

There were stories of Candy growing up in Anchorage and stories of Casey dealing with fighter jocks afraid of needles. He skipped any childhood tales.

Casey felt his phone buzz. A quick message from Ian. *"Happy New Year."* He put his phone back into his pocket. "Ines. From Vancouver."

Nolan was the second guy to read a text message from his phone. Casey watched him as he made a quick reply.

"From your family?"

"No. I got to go. Recall."

Chester knew what the message would have said. "Not exercise I assume."

"No. Not an exercise. I'll leave the keys to the truck under the seat at the squadron."

Chester got up and moved to his brother. He gave him a bear hug. "Go and keep Little Grunt safe Bro."

"You got it. Casey, can you hitch a ride back with them?"

"No. I'm going with you. I don't want to go dancing. My place is on the way."

Casey and Nolan left the pub. Neither spoke on the way out. Casey was the first to speak after they made it a mile down the road. "I know you're going on a mission to bomb Isis in Syria."

"Could be. And then we could be on our way to South Korea in support of some action."

"No. This one is Syria. That means you'll be heading to the air base in Southern Turkey. Incirlik."

Nolan kept his eyes straight ahead and his mouth shut. A mile from Casey's house, he broke the silence. "I wish we had more time together to get this thing on the road before me taking off." He pulled up in the drive wishing Casey had something nice to say. But he wasn't going to force it.

"Wait here, there's something I have in my car I want to give you." Casey got out of the truck, opened the passenger side of the Subaru and grabbed something from out of his glovebox. He came back into the car with his fist closed. Nolan was giving him an intense stare down. "I've been thinking real hard this week. My sessions with Sawyer shed some light on me and my life. Past, present and future. I want to ask a favor of you."

"Sure."

"I want to be your boyfriend. That is if you let me."

"Happy new year Redneck Nolan. I'm happier than a puppy with two peckers."

"Are you sure that would make a puppy happy?"

"I'm sure. Wouldn't it make you happy if I had double of what I got in my shorts? Now give me kiss to seal the deal." Casey leaned over to give Nolan a passionate kiss from the passenger side of the truck.

"There's something else. You said you would protect me from the Boogeyman. But I was wondering who's going to protect you. So I want you to have this. I've had it ever since I was nine years old." He opened his fist and gave Nolan a small superhero figurine of Capan Iceman. It was about four inches high, and despite much of the green paint being rubbed off, the icy blue eyes were still there. And the superhero had the structural integrity to stand on his own two feet without falling over.

"Thank you Stretch. I'll make sure we take care of each other. Do me a favor and don't go and fall for a nice looking guy while I'm gone."

"OK. Will you be able to Skype with me?"

"Count on it. I'll send you an email as soon as I get to where I'm going. Gotta go Stretch. How about one more kiss?"

They had another kiss in the front seat of the truck. Casey got out and watched the guy drive towards Boniface Gate One. He waited until the brown truck was out of view, then he went inside, got on his cold weather gear and took Buddy for a long walk.

"It's going to be you and me bringing in the new year Buddy. Thanks for being here for me." Buddy wagged his tail.

The first of the new year was Friday and the base looked deserted. The 525th Fighter Squadron was vacant except for a few airmen designated to stay back and run errands. Casey sat at the hospital cafeteria having a coffee and reading the New York Times on his phone.

Major Meyers joined him at the table with a cup of coffee. "Good morning Casey. I see you survived last night."

"I did. Got home early after dinner with my friends. How about you?"

"Nothing big. My wife cooked and we watched movies."

"I thought you were on call today?"

"I am. I hope to get out of the office by noon. Project Fighter Pulse."

"That DOD directed study? Are we going to get involved with that?"

Dave Meyers made sure they were able to talk secrets without being overheard. "The 525th Fighter Squadron has been selected. That means I'll probably be sent out any moment now."

"I read the directive. So if you go, you have to monitor and log fighter pilot vitals every morning. And get them into the data base?"

"That's right. It's actually a fantastic project. They finally started researching whether a fighter pilot can become a victim of PTSD during wartime operations. This will give them an excellent data base to work with. Especially monitoring the blood pressure."

"What about blood work?"

"That too, but not daily. Weekly."

"Can't they have medical personnel from the deployment location provide the data?"

"They could, and they might. It depends on their manning. So I might get called out, or might not. My bags are packed just in case. If I'm out, that puts Major Martinez in charge while I'm gone."

"Yes sir. Does he have a heads up on this?"

"Not yet. I'll brief him this morning. I better get to the office."

"I'll follow you up."

Casey sat at his desk looking at the letter he had in a sealed envelope. Having finished the record checks, he had time to read more news on the Syria conflict. By noon, he picked up the letter again to stare at the address of his childhood home.

Sawyer said to move on, I need to forgive. And to forgive doesn't mean I have to have a relationship with them. But I do have the right to ask for an apology. So enough of playing the normal family game. They can agree to my conditions. Acknowledge and apologize, or I can push them aside, release my anger and cut them out of my life entirely. So all I have to do is drop this in the mail slot. Presto, Done.

Casey left the hospital with the letter in his hand, drove over to the South side of the runway on Kuter Avenue where the post office was. It was closed for the first of January. But the slot to drop mail was always open. Casey stood before the slot on the wall and closed his eyes. He opened his eyes, breathed deeply and dropped the letter behind the wall. His phone buzzed with a text message. Wondering if Nolan had already arrived to his final destination, he looked down at the small screen.

It was Major Meyers. *"Report back to duty, ASAP."*

He replied, *"I'm at the post office. Be back in ten."*

Casey thought to himself, *is he going to leave me in charge for a while if Major Martinez is occupied on the other side of the hospital? I hope his wife is prepared for his absence. There's so much for a spouse to take care of by themselves.*

Casey parked the car and walked up to his office. He found Major Meyers at the computer in the waiting room.

"I guess you got notice. Don't worry about the office, I'll make sure everything is OK."

"Not necessary. I'm not going anywhere. You are."

"Incirlik?"

"Affirmative. The flight surgeon has requested support for Operation Fighter Pulse. He said he's got everything else covered. I want you to take the laptop. Sergeant Jenkins over in admin is finishing your travel arrangements and travel orders right now."

"When do I leave?"

"I think they have you on a KC 135 hop to Lewis-McChord this evening. That should give you time to pack. Do you have someone to take care of that dog?"

"Buddy's not my dog. He belongs to the lady I rent from."

"Good. That could get complicated. Run on down and see what your travel arrangements look like."

"Yes sir."

Casey was caught off guard with the TDY. He assumed they would request a flight surgeon, not a medical technician.

"Captain Link, come in, I have your orders ready. I'm just finishing with your travel arrangement. If you have a seat and give me a few minutes, I'll be right with you."

"Alright." Casey sat in the chair and called Candy. "Candy, it's me."

"Hi Sweetie. You had to work on New Year's Day?"

"I'm military. Listen, I'm being sent TDY tonight. I don't know how long I'll be gone, and I'm worried about Buddy."

"You realize Gram does feed him, right?"

"I know, but who's going to take him for exercise?"

"Oh, that. Me I guess."

"You promise?"

"Yes, but I'm not jogging. Walks only. Now enough about that dog. Where are you going?"

"Adana Turkey. And that's all I can say. I will have email, and we can Skype if you want too."

"And you don't know for how long?"

"Not a clue. I'm coming home in about an hour to pack. I'll see you then."

"Alright. I'll be here."

Casey hung up the phone and thought about what he had to do to get ready. He hated leaving Buddy knowing no one would take him for daily runs.

"Captain Link, I have everything ready. You're going to be spending some time in airports for the next two days." He was to take the military KC 135 at midnight to Joint Base Lewis-McChord in Seattle. Then he was to take a taxi from McChord to the Seattle-Tacoma International Airport. A forty minute ride. At the Seattle airport, he was booked on a Delta flight to Paris departing at 12:51 p.m., arriving Paris at 8:15 a.m. From there he was booked on an Air France flight departing at 12:30 p.m., arriving Istanbul at 5:55 p.m. From Istanbul he was booked on Atlas Global Airlines, departing 10:50 p.m., arriving Adana 12:25 a.m. There would be someone from the base motor pool to pick him up and take him to the Incirlik Air Base.

Casey thought about the itinerary, remembering his recent long flight from Australia to Alaska and how his tall body suffered with the cramped seats. "Is it true there's a DOD directive stating that any military member over six feet tall gets the upgraded seats with more room?"

"Sorry Captain, I haven't been made aware of that one yet. Why not do what I do. I pay the extra price to upgrade on the longest leg of the trip. If you need the space, it might be worth it."

"I think I will. Am I authorized travel in civilian clothes for the KC hop tonight?"

"Since you're connecting to a commercial flight, you are. It's on your orders." Sergeant Jenkins gave Casey his papers. "You'll have to pick up your commercial tickets at the airport in Washington." He walked back to collect the office laptop and get final instructions from Major Meyers.

TWO

By 2300 hours, Casey was sitting on a bench awaiting permission to board the flight to McChord in Washington. He was dressed in his favorite jeans, cotton sweater and a light goose down jacket. He wore his Merrell Moab Rovers. The most comfortable pair of shoes he owned. Knowing what the hours ahead would be like, he wanted to be as comfortable as possible.

By 2330, the crew chief found Casey. "If you follow me sir, we're ready to get you on board."

"What time do we get to McChord?"

"In about six hours after take off."

"I thought it was a four hour flight?"

"We have a refueling mission with the 90th Fighter Squadron first. Then we get on our way." Casey followed the crew chief to the runway where the large aircraft was awaiting take off. The door to the side flipped up so cargo and passengers could get in. It was snowing lightly and the temperature was eight degrees. "I hope you're going where it's warm Captain."

"Incirlik."

"Oh. I think things are getting hot there."

"I'm gonna find out."

He led Casey inside. He was the only passenger getting a hop to the lower forty-eight. The crew chief told him he might as well lay down and get a good night's sleep. The aircraft was equipped with side straps that looked like one long bench on both sides of the fuselage. After getting strapped in, the boom operator stopped by on his way to the window at the back of the aircraft. "Captain, if you want, you can sit in the back with me while we refuel the F 22s. Have you ever seen them air refuel before?"

"No. Is there room back there for me?"

"Sure." He sat next to Casey and strapped himself in. "As soon as we get to the air refueling track, we can go back and set up." They both felt the aircraft move towards the main runway. “Where are you off to, leave?”

“No. I’m on my way to Incirlik.”

“Cool. I was there last month. Refueling F 16s. I think we head back real soon. Syria is getting pretty hot.”

“Was it cold?”

“Not like here. Twenties in the night, thirties in the day. A lot of grey skies.”

The aircraft reached its altitude. Sergeant Clarke unbuckled his seat harness. “Come on, follow me.” Casey did the same and followed the boom operator to the very back of the aircraft. There was a small area for the sergeant to sit in a small seat and look out a glass window. He was checking the frequencies and other controls that Casey had no idea what they were.

“Where does the gas come from?”

“When we get into orbit, I’ll release a long hose with two small wings on the end. I can fly this hose in all directions, and if I’m lucky, I get it right into the hole of the aircraft.”

“What about in the dark? Are there lights?”

“Not too many. You’ll see. I expect the first of three fighters to refuel in about fifteen minutes.”

“Have you ever missed the tank?”

“Only during my evaluation. Just my luck.”

Casey could see the lights from a small village down below. Other than that, it was pitch black. “How do the F 22s find us?”

“That’s the ground radar’s responsibility. Or the airborne radar. The AWACS. They’re supposed to get the aircraft about two miles behind us. Then the aircraft’s radar takes over and they come onto our frequency.”

They sat for another ten minutes. “See those lights? That’s the three ship about a mile and a half out.”

Casey heard the radio. “Tanker 35, Stealth 25 has a visual. Under your control.”

“Roger that Stealth 25. Proceed to fuel.”

Casey saw the long hose leaving the back of the aircraft with one wing on each side. The first of the F 22s approached the back of the KC 135 and seemed to park in mid air slightly below. Casey knew even though it looked like a slow motion operation, they were traveling at a speed of three hundred knots.

The F 22 had a bright green light on the tip of its right wing and a bright red light on the left side. There was a small door that opened to both sides well behind the glass canopy of the jet. The little door was well lit with a white light. Sergeant Clarke used a single black stick control to his side to fly the end of the hose and find the opening of the F 22's gas tank. It didn't take long. Casey could make out the dark image of the pilot with a helmet and gas mask looking up at them

"Stealth 25, you're cleared off. Stealth 26, ready for fuel." The flight lead slowly floated back from the KC 135 and then slid over to the larger aircraft's right side. The next F 22 slid into position so that Sergeant Clarke could fly the hose into the second tank. As the fuel was being transferred, the Sergeant told the pilot, "We have Captain Link with us tonight from the flight surgeon's office."

"Ask the Doc if he's going on vacation. Tell him to watch out for those STIs."

"He hears you. He's on his way to Incirlik."

"That lucky SOB. It should have been the 90th Fighter Squadron on that deployment. We're twice as tough."

"Tell him I'll pass that along when I get there."

After the refueling mission, the boom operator pulled in the hose and prepared his work station for the end of the mission. "How did you like it Captain?"

"Amazing. You must be good at video games."

"I am."

"Thanks a lot." Casey got up and went to the place he left his bag. About fifteen minutes later, he saw Sergeant Clarke grab a blanket and make his bed for the rest of the journey to McChord.

The pilot spoke in Turkish as he told the passengers to buckle their seat belts. Casey figured that's what he said. The Airbus 321 was descending to the airport in Adana Turkey. More than half the seats were empty. Giving him a chance to spread out for the hour and a half flight south from Istanbul. He looked out the window and was surprised to see the city completely surrounding the single runway at the airport. He read the runway was a little over 9,000 feet long.

They left the airport with the portable stairs pushed up to the side of the Airbus. It was cold and windy. It felt like twenty degrees. All the passengers walked to the small terminal. There were no customs. That took place back at Istanbul. So Casey walked over to the area where the luggage would be placed on the conveyer belt.

"Are you Captain Link?" The one stripe basic airman was dressed in civvies as a security precaution.

"I am."

"I'm on time right?"

"I guess so. Did you expect to be late?"

"No. But there's this pilot who called me and said if I was late picking you up, he'd personally come over to the motor pool and rub my nose in it."

"Not very nice of him. Was it?"

"Captain, I'm a one striper Airmen. You wouldn't believe the abuse I get. So I'm counting on you to tell that guy I was on time. What the hell is he planning on rubbing my nose in anyway?"

"I'll tell him. What was his name?"

"Captain Flex. Some Southern guy."

"Flexer?"

"Yeah, that."

"Don't worry, he's a pussycat."

"I'm supposed to tell you he's in room 14. He said he was flying a night mission or he would have come along. Lucky me right?"

The conveyer belt began and the luggage started moving around in a circle. Airmen Tim Miner waited until Casey had his luggage.

"Do you want me to grab that?"

"I got it."

"The van is just down the street." Casey followed Tim out the door. No one was checking the luggage. There was an unmarked white van on the side of the street. Casey climbed in the passenger seat as soon as the door was unlocked.

"Is the base very big?"

"Yes sir. They tell me the base has been on full operation since the fifties. I swear, as long as I stay on base, I feel like I'm living in the USA."

"How many personnel?"

"About two thousand. And about eight hundred dependents."

"What about the facilities?"

"First class. Swimming pool, gym, bowling alley, movie theater, big BX, commissary, food court, schools, family housing, I tell you, it's a small American city."

"Are there any Turkish military on base?"

"Yes sir. They have their own commander, and we have NATO personnel too. The Brits have a bunch of pilots deployed now also. I even think I saw some Saudi pilots hanging around."

"How is the food?"

"Great. The Sultan's Inn Dining Facility. Best food I've ever had on any base."

"Do you have WIFI?"

"At the USO center. There's internet at the billeting too. They change the password daily."

"And here I thought I was heading for a hardship post."

"Not at all. Do you like country music?"

"Not sure."

"Well, Tommy Keith is scheduled to do a concert here in two weeks."

"How far to the base?"

"Half hour. The base is right on the East edge of Adana."

"What about security with all the Isis activity so close to the Turkish border?" Adana was only about one hundred miles north of Syria.

"The base offered a voluntary evacuation for the dependents last month but only eighty people took them up on it. The others stayed. The base commander has put all locations off limits to everyone except for the Alley right outside the base." After a ride filled with questions and answers, the van drove down a street filled with small shops. "The Alley starts here. The gate is a mile ahead. This is where everyone buys Turkish carpets, antiques, clothes, Rolex watches for twenty bucks and stuff like that."

Casey kept his eyes out the window. Right before the gate, they passed a restaurant. "That's the Red Onion. Best place to eat."

"Is the food safe there?"

"I haven't heard of anybody getting sick. I eat there all the time." They passed the restaurant and approached the main gate to the base. "There's no U.S. Air Force MPs at the gate. The Turkish don't allow it. You need your ID." They showed the Turkish soldier with a machine gun in his hand their documents. He looked around the van and waved them through. "Check it out Captain, It's like we stepped through a portal and we're in the good ol USA."

"Is the billeting near the Operations buildings?"

"Not far. They have a shuttle bus. You're going to like it. The Hodja Inn is really nice. Each unit has a living room with a TV and Cable. A private bathroom too. Man, it's like a hotel back in the States."

The van pulled up in front of a yellow painted three story hotel looking building with palm trees by the entrance. There was an American and Turkish flag painted on two large boulders out front.

"This is where I let you off. I'll get your bag so you can check in."

Casey told the Airman, "Thank you, don't worry about the pussycat pilot who rattled your nerves. I'll knock him down a notch or two." Inside the inn was staffed by a young Turkish man dressed in a suit and tie. It was 1:30 a.m. There was no one else around. He took Casey's papers and signed him in. Then Casey took the key and walked down the hallway to find room number 22 on the second floor.

A little out of breath from climbing the stairs with a heavy bag, he used the key to get into his room. *Airman Miner was right. This is really nice.* He fell back on the bed to see if the mattress was firm enough for his liking. It was. He left the room to find 14. Back down the stairs, the hall was free from any activity or noise. He found the door to Nolan's room and put his ear up against to see if the TV was on. He tried the handle. It was locked. Not wanting to wake him if he was asleep, he walked back to his room to get a warm shower, shave and get into his comfortable sweats. After his shower, he turned on the TV to find eight channels available. He chose reruns of The Big Bang Theory. The clock by the TV showed 2:15 a.m. Casey was exhausted and his legs felt cramped. But he was too excited to fall asleep.

There was a knock at the door. He got up to answer it.

"Hello Stretch? I guess you couldn't take more than a day away from me."

"The needs of the Air Force."

"More like the needs of Captain Kelly." He pushed his way in and closed the door behind him. "Come here." He pulled Casey in for a kiss.

"Did you just get off duty?"

"An hour ago. I wanted to shower and get into my comfies before I came to find you. Now I smell nice."

"You always do."

Nolan locked the door. "Come on, I need to lay down. I really kicked ass tonight."

They leaned up against the headboard to watch the TV. "Did you fly commercial all the way here?"

"No. I had a hop on the tanker to Seattle. I flew commercial from there."

"How'd that go for you?"

"Not bad at all. There was this cute guy at the ticket counter for Delta. He put me in the seats with more leg room and I didn't even have a chance to ask. All the way to Paris. He thanked me for serving our country."

"The last thing I said to you before I left. Don't go and fall for some cute guy before I get home."

"He was cute."

"Was he as cute as me?"

"Not quite."

"How long are you here for?"

"No clue. What about you guys?"

"Ditto. But I know they will send the guys from the 90th. This is a great opportunity to test out our aircraft in combat. Us too." Nolan slid down and put his head on Casey's lap. "Stretch?"

"What?"

"I'm like that puppy with two peckers now that you're here." He was out like a light in less than a minute. Casey finished watching the Big Bang Theory. He took the remote, turned off the TV, slid down and settled in next to Nolan. With his back covered by the other guy's front. He pulled Nolan's arm over him, knowing the Boogeyman would never show himself while under the umbrella of the tough guy's protection.

The alarm went off at six. Casey tried to break free from Nolan without waking him. But he woke up anyway. "Where you going? You just got here?"

"To work."

"Damn, I wanted to have breakfast with you."

"You didn't get enough sleep. Let me set the alarm, and you can find me for lunch."

"Set the alarm for nine."

"Alright." Casey noticed Nolan had a cell phone, probably from Operations. If they were to call his room there wouldn't be an answer. He brushed his teeth and dressed in his BDUs. With the medical laptop and his equipment in the backpack, he took one last look at Nolan sleeping in his bed who rolled over on his stomach. An image came to his mind of him getting his neck shaved. Casey whispered. "I'm glad I'm here too." He left the room and walked to the front desk.

"Is there a place I can get breakfast around here?"

The Turkish man answered in good English. "You can take the shuttle bus to the Sultan's Inn. It stops out front every ten minutes."

"Thanks." So Casey walked outside the main doors of the inn and only had to wait for about two minutes before the base shuttle drove up. He climbed aboard. "Can you tell me when we get to the Sultan's Inn?"

"Yes sir said the older Turkish man with a thick black mustache. The inn was about two miles down the road. Casey kept his eyes out the window. The Airman was right, the base looked like a small American city.

"Captain. The Sultan." He stopped the bus in front of the dining hall.

"Thank you." Casey walked over to the dining hall. The place was crowded, but getting breakfast was only a matter of passing through one line and paying the fee. He found a table to himself and sat with a large coffee and plate of ham and eggs, toast and a bowl of chopped fruit.

He thought about how Nolan was wiped out the night before. *He won't like this too much, but I need to implement a plan to keep his mind on the mission. I don't wan't him to get distracted and hurt. I think he'll understand. I hope he does.*

After breakfast, Casey stood outside the dining facility and waited for the bus to make its way back. A five minute wait. There was only a slight wind and the temperature was in the high thirties. Like a warm weather get away for him.

Back on the bus, "Can you tell me when we pass operations?"

"You go to the fighter pilots?"

"That's right."

"Sit. I tell you."

The ride took only a few minutes. Casey got off in front of the fighter's squadron. He looked at his watch. It was 7:10. With his backpack and laptop, he walked into the lion's den to begin his work.

"Sergeant, is Major Edwards or Colonel Nelson in yet?"

"Yes sir. Which one do you want?"

"The DO."

Just then the commander of the 525th passed by the front desk. "Captain Link. You made it here in record time. Are you ready to begin your work?"

"Yes sir. Are you familiar with what we're doing?"

"I am. I like the idea. Major Edwards has already briefed all the guys on their responsibility. Let me know if you need any support."

"Thank you sir."

"Sergeant, take the Captain to the briefing room and get him a table over to the side."

"Yes sir. Captain, if you would follow me." The Sergeant led Casey to their briefing room. It wasn't as high tech as the briefing room back at JBER, but it had a large screen and nice chairs.

"Captain, is this table big enough?"

"This is perfect." They both heard the announcement over the loud speaker. "Attention all 525th pilots. Report to the briefing room for your medical checkup. No one will fly a mission today without it."

"Here goes."

The Sergeant laughed. "It ain't easy with these guys. Let me know if you need anything. I'll be at the front desk."

"Thank you."

The pilots began entering the briefing room with their donuts and cups of coffee.

"Doc? What the crap are you doing here?"

"Is this a spot chlamydia check?"

"No. If you guys will have a seat, we can get this over with. I'm going to check your blood pressure, temperature and I have a question for you all to answer."

"Let me guess, does it burn when you pee?" Some of the guys laughed. Some said to knock it off.

The first guy sat in the chair. "Captain Sandler, you'll need to lower your flight suit so I can get your blood pressure."

"What's this all about?"

"The 525th was selected for a DOD study on the effects of combat missions and if they have a relationship to PTSD further on down the road."

Casey took his blood pressure. 110 over 70.

"Will I live?"

"I think so.Those are great numbers. Now I need to take your temperature."

"Are you going to use a rectal thermometer?"

"I can if you want. It's up to you."

"I'll pass this morning, maybe tomorrow."

Casey waved the Exergen Temporal Scanner over his forehead to get a reading in less than a second. "Good."

"Am I done?"

"One more thing. On a scale of one to ten, ten being the highest, how much stress do you feel this morning?"

"For real?"

"For real."

"Who sees this?"

"Medical researchers somewhere back at the Pentagon."

He used his hand to show the number five.

"Thanks. Don't worry, this doesn't get passed around the unit. Have a good mission today Captain."

"Howdy."

"I thought Howy was your name?"

"It is. Howdy's my callsign. It's better than my name around here."

"Howdy it is."

Casey sat for an hour gathering data on the pilots. He made sure they all understood he'd be doing the same thing every morning. And later in the day for those scheduled for night missions.

By the third guy, it was clear to Casey none of the guys wanted to answer the stress question in front of the others. So he wrote the question on a paper and had each one answer the question by writing the number down on a separate paper with no name. Most of the reluctance disappeared. By 0910 he finished with the last guy for the morning. There were six others scheduled to fly night missions. They would report to duty at five.

The break room cleared out as each mission broke up into small groups to brief their day mission. Casey was about to put away his medical equipment when he saw a guy stand by the table, unzip his flight suit and sit in the chair.

"My turn." Casey smiled at Nolan.

"Are you scheduled for a mission today?"

"Not that I know of. But I am on call. Do you have anything in that bag for a bad case of blue balls?"

"Tell me you're joking."

Nolan gave him the eye trick. Casey shook his head back and forth.

"Give me a moment, I'm going to set you up with the flight surgeon to get a prostate milking."

"Whoah, what the hell is that?"

"The doctor will have to insert his finger in your rectum and find your prostate, then manipulate it until you are able to release the backed up fluids."

"You mean until he makes me come?"

"That's right. Some guys even find it to be pleasurable."

"I was just pulling your leg. I don't have blue balls, but I am horney as hell."

"I figured as much. Have you been masterbating?"

"No. Not yet. And now that you're here, no need."

"Do you want me to take your blood pressure?"

"Not today." He stood up and zipped up the front of his flight suit. "You done here?"

"For the morning. I have to get back here at five to check all the guys for tonight's missions."

"Come on, I'm taking you to lunch. Then we're going for a walk down the Alley. I haven't been there yet. The guys say the food is great."

"Are you talking about the Red Onion?"

"You heard of it?"

"Yes. That nice young man who you scared the crap out of told me."

"What?"

"Airman Miner."

"Oh. Him. Was he on time?"

"He was."

"Good. Mission accomplished."

"I need to log into my email before I go. I might be expecting an important email from my parents."

"For real?"

"Maybe. Time will tell. Candy might be trying to get a hold of me if there is anything wrong with Buddy."

"I'm gonna find the DO and let him know I'm off to the front gate to have lunch. You can log in with your email at the front desk. Come on."

Casey found the computer and logged into his email account. There wasn't any emails from anybody, other than from Netflix informing him of a new program.

"You ready Stretch?"

"I'm ready."

One of the other pilots passed them in the hallway. "Hey Flexer, I heard you did a sierra hotel job last night."

"Yes I did Klinger. Now let's see if you can do the same today."

"I'm counting on it. But don't forget, you got em while they were sleeping."

"No excuses dude. See you later."

They bumped their fist together.

"What's with the keys?"

"The DO gave me the keys to the truck."

"You're not going in your flight suit are you?"

"No. We have to change. No one is authorized off base to the Alley in uniform. Come on, I'm starving."

Casey followed Nolan to the old white pickup truck. A truck with no back seat like his huge brown Dodge Ram. "I'm on a mission. I need your help. My mom wants a Turkish rug. I'm not too good at picking nice things out."

"Did she give you a color scheme?"

"Blue."

"Size?"

She wants to hang it on the wall where there is an old wool blanket hanging now. I think about six feet long will do. Not as wide."

"Do you have money?"

"Yes."

"Is there a place I can cash checks?"

"You can cash checks at the billeting office."

Nolan parked the truck by the front of the Hodja Inn. They walked in together. Nolan was full of smiles.

"Go ahead. I'll meet you by the front desk in ten minutes."

"Unacceptable Stretch."

"Fifteen?"

"You can take as long as you want, but I'm coming with you."

"I can see we are going to have a nice little chat at lunch today."

Casey used the key to get inside room 22 on the second floor. Nolan was right behind him. With the door locked, Nolan pushed Casey on the bed and crawled on top. Casey was pinned down.

"How much do you like me Captain Link?"

"This again?"

"Get used to it."

"I like you Captain Kelly."

"That wasn't my question Captain Link."

"Yes it was."

"No it wasn't. You forgot the how much part."

"Oh, that again. Alright. I like you more now than when I first met you."

Nolan moved his eyes in the same manner as always. "Not good enough. On a scale of one to ten, ten being the highest."

"No way."

"Fine. I'll just stay like this and maybe even start dry humping for some relief." He moved around his hips and Casey could feel he was getting hard.

"How about this. I like you because you make me feel safe. And I really like the way you smell."

Nolan reached down and kissed Casey full on the lips. He released the hold he had on his arms. "Good for now."

"Can I get up Captain Kelly?"

"Alright. You earned it." Nolan rolled over to let Casey get off the bed. He laid there and watched as Casey threw on his jeans, sweater and civilian shoes.

"Did I ever tell you those long legs of yours really turn me on?"

"Can't remember." Nolan made a move to get him back down on the bed. "I remember now. Come on, we need to get out of here and buy a rug."

Casey reluctantly followed Nolan to his room on the first floor. They passed a few guys from the previous night's mission.

"Flexer. Doc. Damn, didn't we kick ass last night?"

"We sure as hell did. I hope we're on schedule for a day mission tomorrow. I want to see those bastards run."

"We'll find out at five."

Nolan stopped at his door. Casey followed him in. "No hanky panky Flexer."

"Says who?"

"Me."

"Come on, take off my boots for me." Nolan sat on the sofa in the side living room.

Casey rolled his eyes but did as he was asked. He got off each boot and put his feet to his face. "Your feet smell nice too."

"They do?"

Nolan stood up and zipped down his flight suit. He had a military t shirt underneath, a pair of socks and that was it. Casey sat on the bed and watched. Nolan approached him. He put his hands on his hips and leaned closer to Casey. "This is what you do to me Captain Link."

"Well, in that case, you better wear your undies under your jeans."

Nolan left him alone and put on a pair of jockey shorts. The tight fitting type that went down the leg like boxers. "I might need your help getting my boys in my jeans."

"You're doing just fine by yourself." They finished and left the room with their winter jackets. Casey cashed a check for three hundred dollars. They would buy on the Alley with the American currency.

"Can we eat first?"

"That's fine with me. The nice airman who picked me up said the food was really good at the Red Onion."

"When we're finished, we can get a Rolex for twenty bucks."

"Nolan, for real?"

"Yeah, for real."

"You know they're fakes, right?"

"Who cares? For twenty bucks? I might get one for my brother."

"How nice of you to think of him."

They approached the front gate and drove over to the side where they could park and leave the truck inside the base. It was easier to walk out since the restaurant was only a few yards from the gate.

The Red Onion had seating on the second floor of a worn out looking two story cement building. The building was painted in a mix of colors, everything from the bright pink metal stairs to the blue and gold windows on the first floor. They were seated at a table on the second floor.

"The guys said the lamb and rice dish is really good."

"I think I like the chicken and rice. Are you sure we won't get sick eating here?"

"It should be OK. This is the place everyone comes to and there aren't any war stories about food poisoning."

The waiter took their order and they both ordered a Coke.

"So, Boyfriend. How's it going so far?"

"Good Nolan. Can you tell me anything about the mission last night?"

"It was an eight hour mission."

"Did you refuel in air?"

"Yeah. Over the Med. Those night refueling exercise missions back in AK were worth their weight in gold."

"I got to see one on my way to Seattle. The pilot said he was pissed the 90th wasn't in Turkey instead of you guys. He said they were tougher."

"Who said that?"

Casey laughed. "I didn't get his name. He was wearing a silver helmet and a face mask. Maybe that helps out a bit."

"Tougher my ass."

"Could you see anything last night?"

"Hell yes. With the night vision goggles, I could see ground fire being exchanged."

"Were there any Americans down there?"

"This is secret. But yes, a group of SEALS and Green Berets."

"God. Green Berets. Your little brother."

"I know it. But it's what he wants. Anyway, he's not started training yet. He's in Afghanistan."

"Eight hours. What happens if you need to urinate?"

"Piddle pack."

"What?"

"We have a piddle pack. It's a bag with a gel inside to absorb the liquid. Now you know why the flight suit has a zip up from the bottom."

"Remember what you told me about being one with the aircraft?"

"I do."

"Does it take a lot of concentration to maintain that relationship?"

"Yes."

Casey looked around. They were alone in the restaurant for lunch. He put his hand on top of Nolan's. "Flexer, I don't want to be the reason for you losing focus here. Can we please make a pact to put the physical side of our relationship on ice until we get home?"

"For real?"

"For real."

"Blow jobs?"

"No."

"Hand jobs?"

"Not even."

"This sucks."

"This is for you Captain Kelly."

"Are we going to have repeats of last night?"

"And how do you expect to keep in the closet at the fighter squadron by sleeping in my room at night?"

"We could alternate."

"You won't be able to behave. And if you could, all it would take is for one guy to see one of us leaving the other's room and put two and two together."

"Your food is getting cold."

"How is your lamb?" Nolan ordered the lamb tava, a dish with lamb, rice, tomatoes and spices. Served with a pita bread.

"Good. How about your chicken?"

"Excellent."

They both finished without talking until, "Are you going to be mad at me?"

"No. Fuck it anyway, you're right."

"If you're not flying tonight, why do you have to report at five?"

"I have to brief my mission with the crew going out tonight. Lessons learned."

"As soon as I finish getting their vitals, I'm off until the morning. What about you?"

"I should be out of there by six."

"I think we'll have time after shopping to run to the commissary. We could fill up the room with snacks. Chill out with some TV?"

"Good plan."

They finished dinner and left the restaurant for the shops in the alley. "Nolan, have you ever been to Tijuana?"

"No. Have you?"

"No. But this looks like the pictures I've seen. Did any of the guys tell you the best place to look at carpets?"

"Up there. Nigel's Carpets."

Before they could arrive to the carpet shop, Nolan pulled Casey inside the Rolex watch store. They left with a blue faced Rolex Submariner on Nolan's wrist. "Damn, it's only January and I already got some of next year's Christmas shopping done."

"Let me guess, Chester?"

"You got it."

They passed a man trying to sell them a box of Cuban cigars for twenty bucks. "Sorry dude, we don't smoke."

Two shops away from their destination to buy Turkish carpets, Nolan pulled Casey inside a clothing store. "Check this out. I got to have it." Nolan had in his hand a black t shirt with BLOW ME in white letters written on the front.

"If you buy that, I never will."

"Come on, just for sleeping?"

"Your decision Captain Kelly."

"Alright. Let's go and get a rug." On the way out, Nolan spotted a rug that caught his eye. "Hey, that one has a lot of blue in it."

"Which one are you looking at?"

"That one, right in front of us."

"The one with the unicorn in the middle?"

"Yeah. The blues are perfect for my mom."

"Nolan, that is a polyester rug from China. Are you for real?"

"Well. What the hell? You pick then. I told you I wasn't so good with shopping."

"Come on. You let me do the talking." They walked two more shops down until they reached Nigel's Carpets. They entered and the store keeper got up from his chair watching TV and greeted them in fairly good English.

"You buy nice Turkish carpet today?"

"Maybe. If the price is right. If not. we're just looking then."

"No worry. My prices are the best in Alley. Much better than shop on base."

"We want a carpet about six feet long in blue."

"Blue? I have the right one for you. How about a beautiful Yahyali? Very dark blue. Gold, burgundy and little white. Best wool in Turkish carpet."

"Let's see."

"Please sit here. Would you like some Turkish coffee?"

"That would be nice."

The man called a small boy from the back room. He said something in Turkish and the small boy disappeared out the front door. Then he went to the side and pulled out a rolled carpet and opened it up on the floor. The carpet was mostly dark blue, with traces of yellow ochre, pale raw umber, and a lot of burgundy in the middle. There were white lines outlining the outer design with a hexagon motif.

"I like this. What about you?"

"I liked the unicorn."

“Do you have two that are similar?”

“Yes of course.” He went for another roll. The rug was the same size but had more yellow ocher in the middle. The first one was a village scene around the edges, and the second one was a fruit motif all the way around.

The young boy came back with a tray and three coffees. The tiny cups were filled with a coffee black and thick as mud.

“Stretch, this is going to keep us up all night.”

“Fine with me.” Casey took a sip of the coffee. “If we buy two rugs, do we get a better price?”

“Yes, for you, the best price. You pilots?”

“He is, I’m a nurse.”

“My best price for today is only nine hundred dollars.”

Casey looked at Nolan and spoke slowly so the man could understand. “I think the man at the BX has much cheaper prices.”

“This man has poor quality rugs. Big mistake to buy.”

“They looked nice.”

“Today, I can make special deal. Only seven hundred dollar.”

Both guys finished the coffee. “I can’t tell you what I want to pay. You will get offended.”

“No offended. How much you pay?”

“Are you sure you won’t get angry?”

“Very sure. How much you pay?”

“Five hundred for the two.”

The man got up off his chair and cried out loud. He said something about Allah above.

“I’m sorry. I told you you would get mad.”

“Not mad. But my heart. Not too strong.”

“Listen, we have to get going. The man at the BX will sell for much cheaper, with no heart attack.”

“Come. Please, what is best price you pay me?”

"I'm sorry, I don't want you to have a heart problem. Thank you so much for the coffee. We must be on our way."

"Please."

Casey got up and pulled Nolan with him."

Nolan lowered his eyebrows at Casey. "Stretch, my mom. She's loaded, who cares."

"Come on, trust me." They left the shop with the man almost in tears. They walked down the street. "Fine, then we buy the one with the horse in the middle."

"Hold your horses, I want one of those we saw in that shop. We can take pictures and let your mom pick which one she wants. I'll take the other one."

"Stretch, you fucked up the deal."

"No I didn't. Come on, let's walk to the end and back." They walked down to the end of the block and looked in all the windows. Many children came out to pull them inside, but they refused. On the way back, Casey said, "Watch and learn Flexer."

The man saw them coming down the street and began to cry again. "Come. I give better deal."

"How much for the two?"

"Seven hundred."

"Well, I can pay six hundred. But no more. We have to get back to the base."

"Come inside." They followed the man inside where the little boy was sitting in front of the TV.

"Six fifty?"

"Six hundred. So sorry."

"Very well, I give you both for six hundred. My family eat rice for two weeks with no meat, but I can do."

The man rolled up the rugs and tied them with string. While Casey was giving the guy the money, the little boy tugged at his father's arm. He was desperate about something he saw on the TV.

The man said something again about Allah and watched the screen. Both Casey and Nolan knew the news wasn't good.

"Bomb. Daesh make big bomb at train station in Ankara. Many people go died."

"I'm so sorry." Casey and Nolan left the shop with two eight foot rugs for three hundred dollars apiece. "I bet that attack was the Isis."

"That or the Kurdish. We better get back to base."

"Do we still have time to hit the commissary?"

Nolan looked at his watch. It was only 3:00 p.m. "We do."

By 7:00 p.m., they were both dressed in their sweat pants and t shirts in Casey's room watching TV. "I can't believe you stopped me from buying that t shirt. Blow me. Probably two of my favorite words."

Casey shook his head. "Let's take a picture of both rugs and send them to your mom. Be sure to tell her your good buddy got the best price."

"OK. Roll them out on the floor."

"You realize we bought these rugs in the knick of time. The base commander has put everyplace off base off limits, including the Alley."

"I bet Isis is all over this country. Just waiting to attack."

"I agree. It doesn't look so good for Turkey." They snapped the pictures. "How am I supposed to get Candy and Gram a gift now that we can't get back to the Alley?"

"Don't fret. The shops outside the BX have good stuff. What were you thinking of buying them?"

"A colorful scarf for Gram and a wild shirt for Candy."

"Grab the chips and let's watch TV."

Casey went to the dresser and selected a bag of chips. He opened the little fridge and took out the chip dip. They both sat upright on the bed and looked for something to watch on the TV.

Casey felt the short hair on the side of Nolan's head. "Your brother said you had this grunt haircut ever since you were thirteen. What's up with that?"

"Are you saying you don't like it?"

"No. It suits you well."

"Capan Iceman."

"He does have short hair like that. High and tight."

"He knew I was gay and had a talk with me on the farm. Chester had a big mouth. I was only thirteen, but from that moment on, I wasn't afraid of being different from my brother or all the other boys."

Casey frowned at Nolan and turned off the TV. "I used to have conversations with Capan Iceman, but truthfully, he never talked back."

"Get your laptop."

"My laptop?"

"Yes. Get it and log into the WIFI."

Casey crawled off the bed, grabbed the office laptop and sat back down.

Nolan waited until he was in. "Now google General Wade Bowden."

Casey did a search. Several lines came up. "Take the second one with the images." He did.

"Is that him? Man he's really nice looking. Is he that big?"

"Yes he is."

"This is the General you told me about."

"Yes."

"The one that helped you and Chester get into the Academy?"

"Yes."

"How did your dad meet this guy?"

"Casey, that guy is Capan Iceman."

"I don't understand. Capan Iceman is a comic book hero in graphic novels."

"Yes, and yes. See that guy standing next to the general in this picture?" He pointed to one of the pictures in the second row. "Select that one." Casey had the picture fill the screen. “That’s my dad’s best friend, Sandy Spencer.”

“Sandy Spencer? The author of the Capan Iceman books?”

“Yes. My dad served with that guy in Berlin right before the fall of the Iron Curtain. When the wall came down. My mom was good friends with Sandy. They served two years in the Peace Corps in Samoa before going to Berlin?”

“He was stationed in Samoa?”

“No. He was a teacher, then he got a commission in the Air Force and was sent to Berlin as the head of the AFN Berlin Radio.”

“Your mom was in the Peace Corps?”

“Yeah. Now get this. Those two have been a couple for the past twenty-six years. Sandy got out to be a writer, and Wade stayed in. He made three stars before he retired and took the job with Peg Leg Securities down in Texas.”

“Are you telling me Capan Iceman is gay?”

“Very much so.”

Casey never cried but finding out his superhero was a real man, and a gay one to boot almost made tears run down his cheeks.

“What’s wrong?”

“Nothing. It’s not every day one finds out their special protector is gay. Gay like me.”

“Like me too. It was Wade who talked to me and told me never to be ashamed of who I was. He told me the world wasn’t ready to accept guys like us yet, but that I should march on, like he did. From that day, I was proud to be gay. After that, never a day passed where I felt ashamed of who I am.”

“And he’s been in love with the same guy for all these years?”

“Absolutely. He showed me it can happen. Aside from all the bad press gays get for having multiple partners, it can be done.”

“Thanks.”

"For what?"

"For sharing this with me. It means more to me than you could ever imagine."

Nolan put his arms around Casey. "My pleasure Stretch. I understand. It's always meant a lot to me too."

Casey set the alarm for 4:30 a.m. to have a good run with Nolan and to get him back into his room before the other guys left theirs for the day.

"Who set that thing for four?"

"I did, and it's not four, it's four thirty." Casey got up to go to the bathroom and turned on the light. It flickered on and off.

Nolan's duty cell phone rang. "Yes sir."

"Who was that so early?"

"The DO. He said to meet in the inn's break room in thirty minutes. For all military personnel."

"Do we have time to shower?"

"You go ahead, I'm going to slip back into my room and get ready."

"In uniform?"

"I think civvies are OK. He didn't say."

"Alright."

Nolan opened the door a crack to peek into the hallway. The coast was clear so he slipped out and made way for his room on the first floor.

Casey took a hot shower with the lights flickering on and off, shaved and threw on his jeans. He left for the inn's break room. Nolan was already there in his commando jeans sitting with the other pilots from the squadron.

Casey found a seat by himself and sat waiting for the DO to speak. There was an air of excitement with all the fighter jocks ready to gear up and go.

The commander entered with the DO and all the men stood up to attention. "Take your seats men. We have some exciting news for this morning. The first news of the day is we're all grounded until further notice." There was a murmur of complaints responding to the commander's news. "Let me get right with it and turn the meeting over to our intel officer, Lieutenant Wells. The floor is all yours Becca."

"Thank you sir. Good morning. The classification of this briefing is secret, yet I will be discussing some things I read online this morning. Last night at approximately 10:00 p.m. local time, certain members of the Turkish military and police force made an attempt to overthrow the government. We have reports of several hundred persons being killed and more injured. President Endovan quickly turned to the social media app, FaceTime, and urged the citizens of Turkey to fight back. And as far as we can tell, several thousands did. The coup attempt failed."

The lights were flickering on and off. Becca pointed up to the ceiling. "This is a result of the attempted coup. The Turkish government has cut all power to the base and we're entirely on base generators."

There was another low murmur of complaints from the guys.

"We can't confirm the following news, but we believe the Turkish commander of the base has been arrested this morning by Turkish police loyal to the government. We do know there has been a direct order from the Turkish government for a no fly order in Turkish airspace. Unfortunately this is all the information we have at this time. Colonel."

"Thank you Lieutenant. I want all of you to remain at the inn unless I have directed you to the operations building for support. You will have permission to use the shuttle bus for trips to and from the Sultan's Inn for chow. Other than that, all other locations are off limits until I tell you otherwise. No one will be in military uniform. The base schools are officially closed until further notice. I've been briefed that we all are to keep electric usage to an absolute minimum. No TV other than in the break room. That's it men. Sit tight and wait for further details." The Colonel left the room and everyone stood at attention.

The DO remained. "You all heard what the commander said. You might as well start catching the shuttle bus for chow. I called the motor pool, and they'll be adding a Blue Goose for runs between the Hodja and Sultan's Inn. Keep vigilant. Dismissed."

The guys got up and began discussing the various scenarios. Casey remained seated and listened to the collage of conversations. Nolan was watching him from the other side of the room instead of actively joining in on the conversation in his small group. Casey left for the second floor.

He unlocked the door and decided to check his email. Sitting on the bed, he began to read. There was one from Candy.

"Hello Sweetie. Just to let you know, I'm taking Buddy for walks when I get home and Gram has taken him for a few in the mornings. Miss you."

There was another one from Netflix. Two from Amazon reminding him about the products he looked at two years ago. And the last one to read took his breath away. He read the message and felt as if he was going to cry. There was a knock at the door. He got up to answer it.

"Hey Stretch. The news really sucks doesn't it?"

"Yeah."

"Come on, it's not that bad. It's all part of the big picture. The Turks are turning more and more towards the other radicals in the region. It's to be expected."

"I know. That doesn't bother me."

"What then?"

"I got an email this morning. It upset me. I want you to read it and tell me what you think." He led Nolan to the bed and placed the computer on his lap. Nolan began to read the message out loud.

Dear Casey,

I hope you are well. I have to write you this email so you can know what happened. And I want you to forget about me. Go on with your life. No doubt you will not understand, but all I ask is you follow my wishes and let me be.

I have decided to leave my position in the Air Force, begin a new life. They'll call it AWOL, I call it finding the new me. I've taken only a few of my possessions. Hopefully the world will meet the new me and forget the old one. I wish you the best. Please honor my wishes and don't come looking for me.

Forever,
Love Ines

"Damn. The guy has balls, but to go AWOL? I think that's really stupid of him. Her. Will you do as he requested and leave her alone?"

"I don't know. Right now, I'm too confused to think straight. I can't help but believe if I was home I might have had the chance to talk him out of it. He's not finding freedom, he's finding a jail sentence."

"You hungry?"

"Yeah. Maybe you better go with your buddies?"

"I am going to breakfast with my buddy. Grab your coat Stretch."

Casey grabbed his jacket. Nolan took the opportunity to put his hand on Casey's shoulder for a few brief seconds while the door was being opened. There were about ten other guys waiting for the bus in front of the inn.

Nolan joined the conversation inside the bus, while sitting next to Casey. Casey kept his eyes out the window searching for any signs of Turkish police arresting suspects. There were none. The bus stopped in front of the Sultan's chow hall. A group of British pilots approached them to get more information. There was a lot of excitement surrounding the group. Casey kept quiet. He followed Nolan through the line to get a plate of eggs and bacon. They sat at a table with two other guys, Fatal A and Uckoff. Frank's last name was Zuckoff, so it was inevitable he'd end up with Uckoff at his tactical. The lights were all but a few turned off. The ones left on were flickering. Uckoff told them, "I read online from the German news DW dot com that the President of Turkey is blaming the U.S. for the coup attempt. They said the U.S. was accused of secretly working with that cleric guy hanging out in Pennsylvania, Gulan."

Nolan shook his head. "The next thing we'll know is the Turkish government will be inviting the Russians to use the base for their support of the Syrian regime."

"No doubt," admitted Fatal A.

Casey listened to what they all had to say without joining in on the conversation. He got up to get a fresh cup of coffee and a pastry. While all the military in the room was focused on what the next move would be by the president of Turkey, he was stuck on the email Ian sent him. He decided to forward it to Candy and see if she got one too. After all, she was his life coach.

Nolan made him jump. "I have a solution for that."

"I know."

"Looks like we're going to be stuck in our room for a while. Oh well." Nolan had an ornery smile on his face.

"I can't get my mind off the email I got this morning."

"Let it go. The guy has to make his own decisions in life, whether they're the right ones or not."

They took the bus back to the Hodja Inn to await further instructions from the DO. Some of the guys stayed in the break room to watch the TV, others decided on catching up on some sleep. Casey and Nolan slipped away to the room on the second floor.

"I'm going to send Candy an email about Ian. I wonder if he sent her one too?"

"Don't take too long. We need to figure out what the hell we're gonna do all day."

Casey sat and composed a quick email.

"Hi Candy. If you've heard the news about Turkey, don't worry about me or Nolan. We're safe. I received a communication from Ian that was very disturbing. Did he send you one also? I'm going to forward his last email. Take care, and please give Buddy some exercise."

In five minutes, he got an email response.

"Casey, I'm so worried about you two. I saw the news today. Are you sure you're not in any danger? I can't believe that email from Ian. He better send me one too. After all I'm his coach. What a huge mistake this guy is making. What the hell, does he think it's romantic to live a life on the run or something? I'll let you know if I hear anything from him. You two keep safe. Tell Nolan to email his brother. Better yet, I will. Bye Sweetie."

Casey read the email to Nolan. "I agree with her Stretch. Now what do you suggest we do while under house arrest?"

Casey went to sit on the couch. "If you don't mind, I think I want to be alone."

"I was thinking more on the line of tossing a coin up in the air. If I win, I get to chose anything I want in bed tonight. If you win, you get to chose."

"What about our deal we made to put that stuff on ice?"

"There's no mission. No reason to act like two priests now." Nolan got up to make sure the door was locked. He came back to sit on the couch next to Casey.

"Really Nolan, I want to be alone."

"I thought you were going to tell me about that letter you're expecting from your parents?"

"Later."

Nolan stared at the wall for a few seconds before he got up without saying anything and left the room. Casey never moved.

Five seconds later, the door opened and Nolan walked back over to the couch. "Casey, what are we doing here? None of this makes any sense to me?"

Casey kept his eyes where they were when he came back in.

Nolan walked back and forth twice. “Listen, I know you’ve had rough times in your life. But I can’t be with a guy who won’t let me inside. And I’m not talking dick here. I’m talking this.” He pointed with both hands to his self.

Casey looked at him.

“That’s it? No I want you inside, or I need you, just a look?”

Casey thought to himself, *I told you the longest relationship I had was six weeks. Why all the confusion?*

“Maybe we need to be honest with ourselves here. I’m sorry Casey, but I’m not interested in a one way street.” Nolan left the room, but this time he didn’t come back. He got up off the couch and went for the laptop.

“Dear Ian, I read your email this morning. I’m out of the country on a TDY. As I see it, you’re on leave until the end of the month. Was it the twenty-fourth? So please don’t make any decisions yet. Wait until I get back and we can talk about all the possible alternatives. Candy would love to talk to you too. Remember, she’s your life coach. Please give her a call or an email. Come on, I want to talk this thing through with you before you make any big decision. Let me know. Please. I’m your friend.” He pushed send.

That night, neither Casey went to room 14 nor did Nolan go to room 22. At 0600 the following morning, there was a knock on Casey’s door.

“Captain, there is a briefing with the DO in the break room scheduled for 0630 hours.”

“Thanks. I’ll be there.”

He took a shower, shaved, then stood in front of the mirror naked and stared at himself for several seconds. From there he went to dress in his civvies and join the group in the break room. He found the same place to sit. Careful not to get caught, he looked around to see if Nolan was in the room. He was talking with a group of guys at the far end. He wasn’t looking around like Casey was.

All the guys jumped to attention when the commander, Colonel Nelson, entered the room.

"Take your seats."

They all sat down to hear the latest news.

"I've got good news and I've got bad news. The government is lifting the no fly order to take effect at noon local time."

There was a murmur of approval. The guys were itching to get back on their bombing raids.

"The bad news is all F 22s will be departing the country at that time. Same flight plans, stay over at Ramstein in Germany until the following day."

Now there was a murmur of disapproval. There were a few guys who didn't even get in one run.

"I received a heads up from the Turkish police this morning. They expect a mass demonstration outside the main gate at any time. I want the pilots to pack their bags and get over to operations as soon as this briefing is finished. For the rest of us, we're scheduled to depart on our mission's KC 135 this Sunday morning. The tanker is required for refueling the F 16s until their replacement is on the ground. So admin and maintenance personnel sit tight and check in with Major James for any updates. The base is going to be a busy place starting right now. The Secretary of Defense gave the evacuation order for all DOD dependents to pack their bags and be ready for departure. We expect three 747s from Atlas Air to arrive tomorrow morning along with six C17 Globemasters from the Air Mobile Command. All dependents should be gone in no less than two days." Colonel Nelson gave the floor to the DO, Major James.

"I want all flight leads to start on the flight plans as soon as you get to Ops. Same arrangements as made during our deployment preparations."

There was a hand from Jammer, one of the flight leads. He was given the floor. "Sir, is it alright if I place Rabbit as flight lead. He's ready for his evaluation."

"If you think he's ready, go ahead. Are there any other request for changes to the formations?" There were none. "This briefing is over. Get a move on."

The guys got up and talked in small groups on their way out. The level of disappointment was obvious. Casey caught Nolan talking with the guys in his flight. No doubt they had a lot to do before departure.

Back in his room, Casey paced the floors. Thinking about what Nolan said to him. *He's right. I don't let anybody inside. He made the right decision.*

He grabbed his laptop to check if Ian left a response. The only mail he had was from Candy.

"Hello Sweetie. Guess what I'm doing right now? I'm watching TV where there are hundreds of Turkish people burning the American flag outside the base. The same base where you're at right now! My God. Are you and Nolan going to be safe? I am so worried about you.

Send me an email as soon as you can. I'm frantic.

I went with Gram to the thrift store downtown last night. You'll never guess what I bought. Check out the picture.

Casey, this is, or was Ines' black dress. The one where I had to stitch the strap. What the hell is going on? Be careful and write me as soon as you can."

Casey composed the message.

"Hi Candy, we're OK. I can't give you details yet, but safe. About Nolan, if we were a couple, I think that's over now. I'm not what he's looking for in life. Better he found out now than later.

Are you sure that dress is the same one? That makes no sense at all. It was his favorite dress. Can you drive by his house on the way to or from work and see if his car is parked there. He took it with him and left it at the airport in Anchorage. Got to go, don't worry. Send Chester an email and tell him Nolan is safe. Later. Take Buddy for a run! I miss him so much. And you and Gram too."

He sent a quick email to his boss back at the hospital, telling what he could without sending classified information. He closed the laptop and went to sit on the couch in the small living room. He leaned back and closed his eyes. With his eyes open, all he could see and hear were Nolan's last words right before he left and closed the door for good. He awoke with the rumble of jet noise. The F 22s were taking off in their three ship formations to get back to guarding the skies over Alaska.

There was a knock at the door.

"Captain, the DO wants to see you over in operations. He said to stay in your civvies. I have the truck. You can come with me."

"Let me put on my shoes and grab my coat." Casey followed the sergeant out of the building to the older white chevy truck in the parking lot.

"Has there been any changes with our departure date?"

"Not that I know of."

The sergeant dropped Casey off at the front of fighter Ops and took off to park the truck.

"Major, you wanted to see me?"

"Pull up a chair."

Casey sat in the chair facing the DO's desk.

"I got a call from the vet on base, Major Owen Henty. He asked if I had anybody available to help out with the evacuation. I'm sending all my men and women to help out with the tasking."

"The vet?"

"Are you comfortable with dogs?"

"Yes sir."

"He needs some help. It's not only people who are getting evacuated. There are over seventy dogs that need to get checked out for the flight home. I figured since you're in the medical profession, you might be able to help the guy out."

"I'll do whatever I can sir."

"Good." The Major got a laugh. "I bet it's not what you planned on doing for this deployment."

"No sir, not at all. But if I can have a hand in helping families get their pets out safely with them, then

I would be really happy. I sort of have a dog back at JBER. The thought of having to leave him behind would kill me."

"That dog you run on base with?"

"Yes sir."

"Let me call Sergeant Arnold back in here. He can take you over to the vet's office so you can meet Major Henty. The restrictions have been lifted somewhat. However, stay in civvies and absolutely no off base. In fact, stay clear from the front gate."

"Yes sir."

Sergeant Arnold gave Casey a ride over to where the vet had his office, right next to the hospital. "Captain, do I need to wait for you?"

"No. I'm going to walk over to the BX after this then I'll take the shuttle bus back to the Hodja Inn."

"See you later sir." He took off with the truck.

"Is there a Major Henty around?"

There was a young senior airmen manning the front desk. She was immersed in a pile of documents a foot high. "Can I say who's asking for him?"

"I'm Captain Link. I'm going to be helping out with the evacuation starting tomorrow."

She led him back to the Major's office. "Captain Link. You're on the flight surgeon's staff?"

"Yes sir. I'm a registered nurse. I hope I can be of some help. The DO said you have over seventy dogs to check out before they leave."

"At least. I hope there aren't any I don't know about. I don't want to be the guy to tell the kids they can't take their dog home with them. The ones they adopted while being here and not having me check them out with shots and all."

"Well. Just tell me what you want and I'll do my best to help you."

"Can you be at the flight line tomorrow morning? Say around seven?"

"Yes sir. In civvies?"

"Right. The base commander wants everyone in civvies for a while."

"Seven it is. Nice meeting you." He left the Major to his phone and documents. The walk over to the BX was less than a mile. There were signs of life beginning to show on base. He hoped to find good gifts from Turkey to bring Gram, Candy and Buddy too.

The BX was packed with moms shopping for essentials to get them by on their journey. Things like diapers, activities for the kids for the long flight, snacks, cookies. Everything in each shoppers basket looked like what would be needed for a mass evacuation.

Casey found a vender outside the BX inside the building that sold clothes. he was able to find a colorful scarf like the ones Turkish women wore to cover their hair out of doors. Not all women did. And he found a bracelet with Turkish coins for Candy. The gift for Buddy came from China, but he'd not know the difference. It was a ball with a nylon rope attached to one end for swinging around. He was about to leave but a black t shirt caught his eye. The one that said in large white letters, BLOW ME. He bought it without thinking, placed it well inside the bag to hide the white letters from view. Then he made sure he had enough snacks to keep him happy inside his room. After shopping, he stood by a group of other guys waiting for the shuttle bus.

Back in his room, he opened the laptop and checked his mail. There was a message from Candy.

"Hi Sweetie. I drove by Ian's place before work, and there was no car and no lights on. Do you want me to ask his landlord if he was around? Take care. I mentioned to Chester about you and Nolan. He said Nolan already wrote him. Chester said he was really down."

Casey answered her email.

"Hi Candy. I leave soon. Can't say details. Wait until I get back and we can both go over and ask his landlord if he's been home. Candy, I don't have his

parents email or phone number. They might know what is going on.

I'm helping the vet on base check out over seventy dogs tomorrow so they can evacuate with their families. Can you believe, over seven hundred family members will be off base in a few days. I can't imagine the logistics of this.

"Take care. Talk later."

Although the movement restrictions on base were eased up a little, the base was still without power other than the generators. TV was only allowed in the break room. With nothing much to do but play solitaire, eat snacks, read and sleep, he decided on a hot shower. By late in the evening, finding himself exhausted from nothing to do, he fell into a deep sleep.

Sometime during the night, he was startled by an image standing at the end of his bed. It was the big man with the icy blue eyes. So he immediately searched the room for the other eyes. The red glowing ones. But there were none. Capan Iceman had his hands on his hips, chin tucked in, and shook his head back and forth slowly with the expression of disapproval written on his face. He woke up. Heart beat accelerated, but for a different reason. One that would take time to figure out.

The alarm buzzed at five. He showered again and shaved, dressed in his jeans and grabbed his jacket to catch the shuttle bus for the Sultan's Inn. Breakfast at 0530 was less crowded than at seven. He took his time, read an old copy of the Stars and Stripes newspaper. He checked his watch. Thursday, January seven. The newspaper was only a week old from the first of the New Year. After three cups of coffee, and a good breakfast, he left the building for the shuttle bus to take him to the flight line. He could see the aircraft parked on the side of the runway before he got to his stop. There were two commercial 747s and three Globemasters lined up one behind the other.

Casey jumped off the bus and walked over to the building where the passengers and their pets would meet for boarding. He found Major Henty was having families place their dogs in the crates in a row.

"Major, I'm ready." There were two lines formed.

"Good morning Captain. You take the line to the left and I'll take the line to the right. Get the records from Sergeant Cahn. We need to check their heart rate and temperature. And give a look into the eyes, ears and mouth. If you see anything that looks like they shouldn't be traveling, let me know. If not, sign off their health certificate and get to the next one."

"Yes sir." Casey went to introduce himself to Mark Cahn. He already met the Senior Airman, Denise Clarke the day before in the office. "Are you ready Sergeant?"

"Let's go sir. The first one is a mixed breed, fifteen pounds. You're lucky day, we have the auricular thermometers for use in the ears. Have you used these before?"

"What, no rectal thermometers? Yeah, I've used similar thermometers on our fighter pilots. If I can hold them down, I should have no problems with the dogs."

Casey walked over to the cage and spoke with the owner. A fourteen year old girl. Mary. "Hi Mary. Is your dog stranger friendly?"

"Yes. She won't bite."

"What's her name?"

"Princess."

"Alright, let's get her out and check out her heart rate." The dog was wagging her tail at meeting a new person and let Casey do what he had to do, including putting the thermometer in the ear for a few seconds. She also let him open her mouth for a quick inspection. "You have a very nice healthy dog. I sort of have a dog as friendly as her back home in Alaska."

"Alaska?"

"That's right. Anchorage. Where are you off to?"

"My grandma's house in Wisconsin. My dad has to stay behind."

"Well, I bet Princess will love the snow up there. Most dogs do."

"She does."

Casey signed the health certificate. "Sergeant, this one is a go. Who's next"

Casey worked for three hours without a break until he had to go to the bathroom. He managed to check fourteen dogs. By lunch time, the seemingly endless stream of mothers with their children walked across the runway to climb aboard the first 747. All the dads walked them to the stairs, gave the family members hugs and sent them off to anywhere USA. Some to base housing, many to grandparents houses like Mary, Princess and her mom.

"That's it for today Captain. Can you be back here tomorrow at the same time?"

"I'll be here at seven."

"I think we're going to have a bigger crowd tomorrow. They plan on filling the other two 747s and three globemasters. By the next day, everyone should be gone."

"Do you have a family here?"

"Yes I do. My wife and son leave in tomorrow's group. I can't even be home to help her pack."

Casey noticed his eyes were getting watery. "They must be very proud of you. Where will they go?"

"They catch a commercial flight from the Baltimore-Washington airport for North Dakota to stay with her parents."

"Will they be traveling with a dog?"

"Yes. We have a border collie. He's traveled before. My son is old enough to take charge of the dog. The most difficult thing about all this is I won't know where my next assignment will be for over year from now. So we can't buy a house or relocate my family anywhere. She doesn't want to spend a year at her parents place. We really haven't figured this one out yet."

"Sounds like your family is stuck in the middle."

"We are. And my son is in junior high. This could mean another school change after a year."

"I don't envy you Major. I hope America understands the sacrifices those of you with families make all the time. I wish you the best of luck."

"Thanks."

"So you don't need any more help today?"

"We're done for now. See you tomorrow at seven?"

"Yes sir. "Casey left looking at many sad faces in uniform. From those who put their families on planes or were about to. He took the shuttle bus back to the Sultan's Inn for a late lunch or early dinner. Afterwards, in his room he read his email.

*"Hi Sweetie. I got an email from Chester. He said Nolan was in Mildenhall England for the night. Have you left Turkey yet? Chester said Nolan had, and these are not my words, a bug up his A**. I wonder why? I drove by Ian's place again. No car. Be careful."*

Casey wrote back.

"I'm in Turkey for a few more days. Can't say more. Keep an eye on Ian's place. I have his key at home. When I get back, I'm going over there to snoop around. Tell Gram I miss her baking. Did you notice if I have a letter from New York? Later."

He closed the laptop and decided on a game of solitaire. After losing three out of four games, he threw the covers over him and went to sleep. Sometime during the night, he awoke to find the night visitor with the red glowing eyes staring at him from the bathroom door. He looked over to the end of his bed. There was no sign of the superhero with the icy blue eyes. It was back to playing dead. He woke up with a cold sweat. This night, he had to get out of bed and walk around the room. Not wanting a repeat of the dream he just had. After three rounds, he got back in bed, and did something he'd not done since he could remember. He cried. He never felt lonely after a break up. But this time was different. He wanted to hear a smart ass comment from Nolan. A look with the funny eye trick. To feel his hand on his shoulder. Enough tears were spent to wet his pillow.

Back on the flight line for the last of the three days helping out Major Henty, all that was left on the runway to fill up were three Globemasters. There were only about fifteen dogs to check out. It was the easiest of the three days. Casey had time to lean against the table and watch the last of the families walk to the giant aircraft for a quick stop in Ramstein Air Base Germany, then on to the East Coast. From there, all the families would find commercial flights to wherever the turn of events would lead them. After completing the checks of all the dogs, Casey said goodbye to the Major, Sergeant Cahn and Airman Clarke, and walked over to the fence to sit and watch the aircraft take off. With the wheels of the last one up, he looked around the base and thought about how the place would be changed. No longer a small American city, but a place of only soldiers. A duty assignment. A place where the Turkish merchants would experience for the first time since the 1950's what it would be like without the endless stream of American shoppers with the reliable appetite for Turkish carpets, twenty dollar Rolex watches and t shirts with funny vulgar sayings on the front. Spending the green dollar. He wondered how many of them if any were in the crowd burning the American flag only two days before.

Casey took the shuttle bus to fighter operations to check in with Major James.

"How did the dog duty go Captain?"

"Went fine sir. Are we scheduled for departing tomorrow?"

"I sure hope so. The bus will pick up anyone at the Hodja Inn tomorrow at eight. I'd recommend getting a good breakfast in the morning. It's going to be a long ass haul home."

"In uniform, correct?"

"In uniform. We stop tomorrow for the night at the 100th Air Wing in Mildenhall England. Then it's a marathon run to Fairchild in Washington. The next day we depart for JBER. Only three days strapped on the side seats. I hope you have some kick ass music on your iPod."

"I have my kindle."

"See you in the morning Captain."

Casey left the Ops building for the chow hall. And then for the BX to stock up with three days and nights of snacks. At least he'd be able to stretch his legs out with the side seats, unlike a commercial aircraft. And creative guys always found places on the floor to sleep.

By 0900 the next morning, Casey was strapped in the side seats of the Boeing KC 135 Stratotanker along with the 525th Fighter Squadron maintenance crew, admin support personnel, the commander and the deputy of operations.

The aircraft pulled up hard and left behind the F16 pilots from the 31st Fighter Wing out of Aviano Air base in Italy to continue on with the bombing raids against Isis in Syria. When the tanker reached altitude, Casey took out his iPod and listened to his most recent playlist. By chance, the song 'I'm Gonna' was first on the list. The repeating words I'm gonna make you want me brought the image of Nolan singing the song. In the shower, out of the shower, all the places he sang it came to mind.

The Boeing aircraft had a range of eleven thousand miles. One stop overnight in England, another stop to refuel at Fairchild AFB in Washington State, and a four hour leg back to JBER in Alaska.

Casey grabbed his bag and his rolled carpet and walked to the parking lot to find his car. He worried about the car being buried in the snow, but from a distance, it was obvious someone dug it out. And scraped the windows too. It was after midnight and Casey wanted to get home to his own bed and friends on McPhee Avenue. A ten minute drive now that the car was freed from the elements.

He parked the car and looked at the window. Buddy was pushing aside the curtains and fogging up the glass with his nose. He grabbed his bag, went for the back door and let Buddy out. The dog jumped up to lick his face.

"Did you miss me? I sure missed you. Come on, go make a pee and you can come up and visit with me." Buddy ran out in the snow to mark a bush, ran back in and raced to the top of the stairs. "You still like to be the first one to get in." He opened the door, picked up the mail on the floor and walked into the kitchen. Buddy did a perimeter check of the whole apartment to make sure everything was safe. Casey quickly glanced at the pile of mail. Nothing from New York.

Buddy followed him to the bathroom where he prepared a hot bubble bath. In the kitchen he grabbed a glass of red wine. After two sips, he put the glass in the fridge. Thinking a wine buzz might aid the night visitor. His protector Capan Iceman wasn't happy with him and might not ever come back. Buddy laid on the floor and watched as Casey shampooed his hair and relaxed with the sound of the radio in the background.

When the alarm woke Casey at five, Buddy was sprawled out on the end of the bed. He jerked his head up with the prospect of an early morning run.

"OK. Let me get on my cold running gear and we'll go for a run, we can make it to the front gate and back." Buddy jumped off the bed and twirled in circles. Casey figured it would be his first run since being away. They braved the cold thirteen degrees and left the house for a run down McPhee Avenue towards the main gate. By the time they arrived, they both had frost on their face, Casey on the neck scarf and Buddy on the fur around his mouth.

The MP recognized the two and came out to greet them. "Haven't seen you two around for a while."

"I was deployed with the 90th in Turkey."

"That was a fast one. I saw them arrive a couple of days ago."

"The maintenance crew arrived last night on the KC 135. Late. We're all back now."

The MP went to pet Buddy who was glad to get the attention. "Shake." Buddy did.

"Well, better get back so I won't be late for work."

"See you around Captain."

Casey ran back to the house with half the speed they used to get to the base. They took a five minute detour to stop at the garage apartment where Ian lived. He let Buddy off the leash to sniff around. There were no footprints in the snow, no car and no lights on in the apartment. The place looked as though it was vacant for a while. The walks were shoveled in front of the main house. He stood there looking all around and thinking of what was going on. Something wasn't right but he couldn't put his finger on it.

They ran the five minutes back to their house. Casey pushed the reluctant Buddy through his kitchen door. Up in his own apartment, he took a quick shower, shaved and put on his blues for work.

By 0630 hours he was sitting at his favorite table in the hospital cafeteria drinking a coffee and having breakfast of scrambled eggs and toast.

"That was a fast deployment. How'd it go?"

"Hi Major. I only got one day of work in with the tasking. After that it was almost like being under house arrest."

"I got an email from a Major Henty. He said you were a great help."

"That was nice of him. I tried to help out as much as I could. They had to check over seventy dogs for the evacuation."

"Are the dependents all out?"

"Yes sir. It took about three days. The place is really going to miss the family element."

"Well, I'm glad you made it back. Things have been very slow while you were gone. Maybe some of the guys brought some bugs back with them and business will pick up some."

"They all seemed healthy to me when they left." He thought about the bug Candy told him Nolan had.

"I'm going up, finish your breakfast. See you when you're done."

"Yes sir." Casey finished eating and got another cup of coffee. He picked up his phone and wrote a text message to Candy.

"Can we meet for lunch at noon? I went over to Ian's place this morning, Buddy and I looked around outside. I have a theory to throw at you. Text me."

He finished his coffee and made it into the office five minutes early.

"Welcome back Captain. That was a short visit to halfway around the world."

"Hi Sergeant Tomlin. It was a long trip. Everything cool around here?"

"Slow. Nice and slow."

"If anybody is looking for me, I'll be in my office filling out the travel voucher. It got complicated."

"Roger that."

Casey left for his office to fill out the forms for his travel. Twice he checked his email. Nothing. But there was a text message from Candy.

"So glad you're back and safe. Noon is fine. Can't wait to see you."

By nine, Major Meyers gave Casey a file. "Captain, can you run this over to get the commander's signature on his medical waiver?"

"Colonel Nelson?"

"Right."

"I'll run it over now."

"Thanks. By the way, if you have any personal business to take care of, feel free to take the time. Things are really slow here. Just give Sergeant Tomlin a heads up."

"Thank you sir. I might have to run over to the post office and finance." Casey looked at the folder. He wondered if Nolan was on duty. *Well, I can't hide for the rest of my tour here. I'll have to face it sooner or later.*

He drove over to the 525th Fighter Squadron. Parked the car on one of the few slots with no name painted on the curb. He looked around the lot. The big brown Dodge Ram was parked in its usual place. He took a deep breath, tried his best to compose himself and walked to the entrance of what he thought of as the lion's den.

At the front desk, he asked the airman on duty, "Is the commander in?"

"No sir, not yet. I think he'll be in after lunch. He gave all the maintenance personnel and the admin staff until noon to show up today."

He didn't want to leave it with the Airman due to it being personal medical records. "I'll come back after lunch. Can you tell him I have some records to sign?"

"Yes sir."

"Hey Doc, I heard you had dog shit duty back in Incirlik," Howdy was passing the front desk with Flexer and slapped Casey on the shoulder.

"Hi Howdy, Flexer. Dog duty only, no crap."

"Did you have any of them cough?"

"No coughing Howdy. I told you I don't do that."

Nolan looked at Casey with a blank expression.

Howdy told the Airman, "If anybody is looking for us, we're at the BX on official business."

"Yes sir, enjoy your official shopping trip."

They both left the building.

"I'm going to go. See you after lunch."

"Yes sir."

Casey left for his car. The big brown truck passed him as the driver never gave him a second look.

Casey got into his car and turned on the ignition. *Good. Not so bad as I thought. We just pass each other and work goes on as it always did. No embarrassing scenes or body language to avoid. I can do this. Not so difficult.* Casey wondered if he'd ever see the Nolan eye trick again, or was that only an image of the past. He missed it. But he was well schooled in break up emotions. Life would go on. It always did.

By noon, Casey put the Colonel's envelope on the floor of his car and went to the Military Mall Barber Shop to find Candy.

She jumped out of her chair and ran over to give him a hug. "I was so worried about you."

"Yuk!"

"Oh come on, I know you want to give me a hug."

"Well, maybe a little one."

"Follow me, let's get out of here before I get a customer." They walked over to the food court to find a table.

Casey pulled a small box out from his pocket. "I got you a little something." He passed it over to Candy. She took the box and opened it up.

"It's so pretty. I love it." She shook her wrist to hear the Turkish coins make a metal noise.

"How's Gram?"

"She's home baking a cake just for you. German chocolate."

"I can smell it from here."

"So dare I ask? Have you seen Nolan yet?"

"This morning. We're going to be OK. He walked by and didn't say anything. No big scene."

"And that's your definition of OK?"

"It's better for him."

"And that's why he's been acting like a bear?"

Casey shrugged his shoulders. "Let's get our food." They split up to get lunch and met back at the table.

"So, what did you do?"

"Me?"

"Yes you."

"Nothing."

"Not buying it."

"I said I wanted to be alone."

"Ah yes. You hurt the guy's feelings when he was thinking what you needed at the moment was him."

"How do you know that?"

"Because that's how guys are. You should know, you're one."

"Not convinced."

"What else?"

"He said I acted like I didn't want to let him inside."

"Of course. Back to my original theory. Go on."

"That's it. He said he didn't want a relationship that was a one way street and left. End of story. Our little fairly tale came to the end."

"Shame on you."

"How so?"

"Why did you leave that gorgeous cop?"

"Because it wasn't fair to him. I didn't feel anything."

"And how do you feel now about Nolan?"

Casey took a bite from his sandwich. He didn't answer her.

"Just like I thought. You're going to have to be the big boy here and set this thing right. Doing nothing is plain idiotic. Unless you want to be alone for the rest of your life."

"Maybe I do."

"Maybe you don't but you have a pattern of behavior that keeps you that way. Be honest here, that big smart ass is fun to be around."

"What about his double?"

"I think we're really hitting it off great. I love being around him, and I think he loves being around me. Even though he's gone so much of the time. But hey, it's a whole lot more than what I had before I met him."

They worked at their lunch.

"Candy, what if Ian didn't write that email?"

"What?"

"What if someone else wrote that?"

"How? It was from his account?"

"And if someone had his laptop and email password?"

"Why?"

"There could be a hundred reasons. But I know Ian was excited about the changes taking place in the Air Force. He told me about what the Defense Secretary said in an interview. The guy's planning on allowing transgendered persons to serve in the armed forces. That is supposed to be announced this spring. And he only had a few months to finish his four year commitment. And he loved that black dress. Why in the hell was it in the thrift store?"

"You have a point there."

"And there's something else. He told me over the phone that he was excited about a recent development in his life. He said he'd tell me after he got back from leave."

"He never told you?"

"No. If I only had a way to find his parents."

"What if you worry them to death. Is it such a good idea to drop this bomb on them if they are in the blind?"

"Maybe. I need help here. I have to do it, I'm going to give him a call."

"Who?"

"Kevin. Not only is he a cop, but he works cyber crime. He has all the tools we need right now. Did the guy use his credit cards lately? Did he send that email from his house? When did he fly back to Anchorage? All those questions we won't have answers to without some help."

"Will he talk to you?"

"Yes. He's a decent guy."

"Are you being fair to him? Will he think you want to start something back up? I mean, you haven't said a word to him since you broke it off."

"I know. I'll just have to lay the cards on the table right from the start. Then if he doesn't want to help, it's his decision. I'll understand. I don't plan on leading this guy on."

After lunch Casey returned to his car in the parking lot, grabbed his phone and made the call. "Hello, Kevin? This is Casey."

"I know. Caller ID."

"I hope you had a nice Christmas."

"I did. What about you?"

"I did too. I just got back from Turkey last night."

"Where the military overthrew the government?"

"Yes and no. The coup was unsuccessful. But I ended up coming home because of it."

"I saw that on the news. A big demonstration of Turks burning the American flag by some base near Syria."

"That's where I was. In Adana. Listen, I'm in need of some help. You're the only person I know who can, if you're not to angry at me."

"I'm not angry at you. It hurt, but I was never angry. Has anything changed since then?"

"No. I'm still the same old fool. But I have a friend who is so much more level headed than I am, and he's disappeared?"

"Did you call the police?"

"You."

"Is this an official report"

"Not yet. But I want your advice."

"I can drop by your house after work. Say around five?"

"Do you remember where I live?"

"I see you haven't lost your sense of humor."

"Five would be great. And thanks so much. I really need your advice on this one."

"Five Casey." He hung up. Casey did the same.

He started the car and drove back over to the 90th Fighter Squadron to get the commander's signature. It only took ten minutes, and there was no sign of Nolan or the big brown truck. He felt like a fool but drove around the base looking for the truck, not having the slightest idea of what to do if he found it. Then he returned to his office, spending the rest of the day counting minutes. Hoping Kevin would have the magic wand to solve the whole mystery with his friend.

He made it home at fifteen minutes to five. It was snowing lightly, but enough to shovel, so he grabbed one of the two shovels and began to clear the front walk, and then the driveway. There was enough of a clearing for Kevin to pull his Honda CRV in the space.

Kevin got out of the car and smiled at Casey with the shovel. "The fun of living in Alaska." He walked over to Casey and pulled him in for a friendly hug. "It's nice to see you soldier." As luck would have it, a big brown Dodge Ram truck passed by the house at the exact moment. The big eight cylinder engine roared as it moved on down the street without stopping. Casey was careful not to show his surprise at the unfortunate timing of a friendly hug, from a guy who's help he needed badly.

"Have you eaten yet?"

"No. I thought maybe?"

"Better idea. Come on, I'm cooking and rumor has it Gram baked me a chocolate cake." Casey led Kevin to the familiar apartment with the familiar big dog. Buddy was at the door waiting for him.

"Buddy boy, do you remember me?"

"Sure he does. You're not an easy one to forget."

"So have you?"

"I haven't forgotten, but I have moved on. And you can thank God for that."

They entered into the kitchen. "Let me grab your coat." Casey took the coat and threw it on the Futon. Buddy made himself at home on the floor blocking the way to the rest of the house from the kitchen.

"Want a glass of wine?"

"Sure."

He poured them both a glass of wine. "Is steak and salad alright?"

"Sounds fantastic."

Casey began moving around to get dinner ready. He started to tell the story at the same time. Kevin was an accomplished listener.

"I have this friend who is a lieutenant. He works as chief of admin for several sections of the hospital. His name is Ian. Actually his name is Ian by day and Ines by night."

"Oh. Are we talking a drag queen here?"

"No. He's transgendered. He just came out and plans to leave the Air Force at the end of his four year commitment, coming up in a few months."

"Alright. Did he get into trouble with the law?"

"Wait. I want you to read his last email to me." Casey got the laptop and opened his mail. He handed the computer over to Kevin.

"I see. AWOL? That's going to get him thrown into the brig."

"Kevin, he didn't write that email. Someone else did and I need you to help me figure this thing out."

"How can you be so sure?"

"Because I know him. He was excited about the very real prospect of transgendered people being allowed to serve in the armed forces starting this spring. He loved that black dress."

"What dress?"

"Casey told him all about the dress."

"So you suspect foul play?"

"God. I haven't been able to let myself say that. But yes I do."

Casey sat down and waited for the steaks to finish. Kevin got up. "Let me help you with the salad."

They set the table and sat to eat. Buddy had his very own steak on the floor with his red dish.

"Does that dog always eat steak?"

"It's our little secret. Gram thinks he eats less due to the winter blues."

Kevin laughed. "So what is it you think I can do?"

"Kevin, come on, anything you could do is more than I can. I'm clueless here. I don't even have his parent's phone number or email address."

"I'd have to open an official investigation and follow protocol."

"Not yet."

"What about the base Military Police?"

"He's not missing until the 25th of this month. That's when his leave is over and that's when he'll be logged in as AWOL."

"Casey, I don't know about this. You're asking I do investigative work on the side. I could get into a lot of trouble with this."

"Listen, I have his key. I have permission to enter his place whenever I want. Why can't you be off duty going to a friend's house?"

Kevin worked on his steak.

"I don't want you to get into trouble. And I won't hold it against you if you say no. And more than anything, I don't want you to think I'm putting a move on you. That would be so unfair."

"Send me that email you got from him. When do you want to go to his place?"

"After dinner? He lives five minutes from here."

"Under my conditions."

"I'm listening."

"If I find anything that requires the attention of the law, I make it official at that very moment. I'm talking a formal investigation."

"I understand."

"Where's the cake?"

"We have to go down and get some. She'll have coffee too."

"So how were things in Turkey?"

"Wait, I have something to show you." He got up and Buddy followed. He came back with the rolled carpet. "Look what I got."

"A carpet?"

"Yeah. Let me open it up and show you." He rolled it open in the living room. "Damn, I have no idea where to put this thing."

"I do. In my apartment."

"Ready for some coffee and cake?"

"Let's do it." They walked downstairs. Casey had the scarf he bought Gram wrapped in a white paper, the one the vender used to wrap it up. Casey opened the kitchen door a crack. “Gram, you in there?”

“Come on in Casey. I’ve got something for you.”

Casey led Kevin inside. “I bet I know what it is. Your granddaughter isn’t the best at keeping secrets.”

“I heard that.” Candy came into the kitchen, followed by Gram.

“You’re the policeman friend of Casey. Kevin?”

“Yes ma’am.”

Candy eyed the guy. She always said he was the most handsome man she ever saw. “Nice to see you again Detective.”

“Kevin please.”

“I know, but detective sounds so romantic.”

“Sit down you three and we’ll have some cake and coffee.” They all did.

“Candy, do you want to take a walk with us after cake and coffee?”

“Why?”

Casey threw her the look. “I don’t know, maybe to go over and visit Ian tonight?”

“Oh. Sure, I’d love to. You have the key?”

Gram looked at Candy. “Why do you need a key honey?”

“Just in case he’s not home or something.”

Casey threw her another look.

Gram returned her attention to Casey. “Candy and I were worried to death for you in that place you went. It sounded so dangerous.”

“Not really. But the Defense Secretary did make all civilians and their dogs leave the base for the States.”

“They get to take dogs with them?”

“Yes Gram, dogs are an important part of the military family. I actually had to inspect with the vet over seventy dogs for the evacuation. It took us three days. And then, they were all gone. The base was a different place.”

“Well, I’m glad you’re back. Maybe pick a safer place the next time.”

Casey laughed. “I got you a little something.” He gave her the white wrapped paper.

“You shouldn’t have. Really.”

“Go on, open it up.”

She opened the package to find a colorful scarf with a red rose motif. “It’s lovely. It matches Candy’s arm.”

“I’m going to have to borrow that some time. It’s a perfect match.”

After cake and coffee, the three of them walked down the side of the street to find the garage apartment where Ian lived. Buddy was in the lead on the leash.

“Casey, did you tell Kevin about the black dress?”

“I did.”

“Remember guys, if the landlord or any of the neighbors talks to us, don’t introduce me as a cop. We don’t want that kind of attention at this point.”

They stood on the sidewalk looking at the garage apartment. Casey pointed out, “No footsteps in the snow. No tire tracks in his parking spot.”

“Let’s go up and take a look. Don’t touch anything. Let me do the touching. The last thing we want if there is a problem is to add you guys to the list of suspects with finger prints.”

They climbed the stairs and Casey pulled out the key. “Kevin, what about the dog?”

“Has he been here before?”

“Yes.”

“Then it’s no problem.”

They all entered into the large open space. Inside the kitchen, they stood and looked around. They smelled the air. The kitchen looked normal. A few dishes on the counter. Mail on the table. Kevin wore a glove. He opened the fridge. Nothing out of the ordinary.

Then they all walked to the living room. There were signs of packing a suit case. Like how Casey left his apartment for the trip to Turkey. Kevin noticed. “It looks like he was getting ready for a trip.”

"Well, he had thirty days leave planned. He went to visit his parents in Vancouver. I think this is what I'd expect to see."

"Right."

They followed Kevin around. He went to the bedroom. The bed was unmade and Buddy jumped on the bed to give it a full nose treatment.

"Casey, does he leave women's clothing in the closet in the open?"

"Yes."

"All the women's clothing is gone. No shoes either." Kevin used the hand with the glove to move the clothes on the hangers.

Candy made the comment. "No women's clothes. I think they might be on the racks in the thrift store downtown."

"Does he have a desktop computer?"

"No. Only a Mac Book."

They followed Kevin to the bathroom. He looked in the cabinet and all around. "Guys, what it looks like here is someone went on vacation for a month. I don't see anything that looks suspicious."

Casey stood in the hallway with a view to many of the spaces inside. He looked it all over again. "Alright."

They left the garage and walked back home.

"What kind of car does he drive?"

"The same model and year as my Subaru. We bought them together. But his is white. And I don't know what his license plate number is."

"I can get that easy enough."

Every once and a while someone threw a what if scenario at Kevin. There were no answers.

"That's it boys. I'm going inside."

"Take Buddy with you please."

Candy and Buddy disappeared and left Casey outside standing by Kevin's car. "I really appreciate this Kevin."

"OK. Let me snoop around at work on our computers and see if I can find anything out. I enjoyed seeing you again." He went to hug Casey but Casey stepped back. Giving Kevin the same message he already gave.

Kevin threw him a smile, got into his car and drove off. Casey looked at his watch. It was a few minutes after seven. He grabbed the shovels leaning against the garage and began to clear about an inch of fresh fallen snow. The shovel made him feel lonely. Lonely because it was with the two shovels that Nolan and he enjoyed simple moments in the fresh snow. And he realized he felt something else. He missed Nolan.

Upstairs, he sat at the table and looked at his phone, He grabbed the phone and wrote a message.

"Can I drive over to your place? I want to talk to you."

He waited at the table. There was no reply. He went to shower. Out of the shower, he checked for any messages. There were none. So he picked up the phone and wrote another.

"I'm coming over. See you in thirty."

On the drive over to the cabin, he had butterflies in his stomach. He didn't know what Nolan would think about seeing him with Kevin. But he knew if what Nolan saw was left without an explanation, the image could grow into something unmanageable. After a thirty minute drive, he pulled up to the large window covered cabin and parked his car. He looked around. No sign of the big brown truck. He left the car and walked around the driveway trying to figure out how to say what he wanted to say. To explain how he felt.

After a half hour of walking in circles, he saw the headlights of the truck coming up the lane. He stood by the railing of the steps to the front deck.

Nolan parked the truck, grabbed two paper bags of groceries and walked towards the garage door. It opened and closed after he entered. Casey stayed at the bottom of the steps.

The lights came on in the cabin. Casey walked up the steps to the front glass door. He stood there and knocked. Nolan ignored him. The lights went off and Nolan disappeared to a back room.

Casey turned around and used his back to slide down the glass door. He sat on the deck with his back against the glass. It was in the twenties. He sat there and thought about his life. How his life with great guys always ended. Like how it all ended with Kevin. But with Nolan there was a difference. With Nolan gone, he felt saddened. He missed him. Fifteen minutes passed and Casey had too much to go over in his head to leave.

"Captain Link, you need to go home." Casey heard the words through the glass. The lights were all off in the front of the house.

He didn't bother turning around. He sat there thinking of what to say. All that came out was "OK. I'm going." But he couldn't move. A few minutes passed.

"Casey, go home."

"I can't."

The lights remained off. Another two minutes passed. The garage door opened and Nolan came out wearing his parka. He walked over to the front deck and climbed the stairs. "Why are you here?"

"I need to talk with you."

"So talk."

"I didn't mean to push you away. I didn't know I had you on a one way street."

"Who's the guy?"

"An ex boyfriend."

"So you found comfort only after one day back"

"Did you shovel my car out?"

"Maybe."

"He's a cop. I need his help. He works in the cyber crime division. I need him to find Ian. Someone has him and he needs me to find him."

"Ian?"

"Yeah. He didn't write that email. Someone else did."

"How do you know that?"

"I just know."

"Do you always hug your ex boyfriends?"

"That was my first. I don't feel anything other than respect for the guy. He's really a descent person."

Nolan walked over to the edge of the deck and looked out to the stars over the mountains.

"I know you won't believe me, but you got inside of me. In a big way. I really miss you."

Nolan turned around. "Just what exactly do you miss about me?"

"Promise you won't get mad. Or more mad."

"I'm listening."

"I miss your smart ass remarks."

Nolan broke his expression and a small laugh escaped until he got it back under control. "That is so romantic of you."

"I can do a little better."

"I'm listening."

"You make me feel safe. You're like my real Capan Iceman."

Nolan turned back around and gave the stars another look.

"I'll go now. I couldn't let you build up in your mind what you saw at my house tonight. It was nothing more than a friendly hug between two guys with a past." Casey walked down the steps. Ten feet from his car, he turned around to face Nolan in the dark. "Nolan?"

"What?"

"I really wish we were neighbors when we were little kids." He turned and got into his car. Nolan stayed on the deck and watched him drive away.

As Casey pulled down the lane, he felt more lonely than he ever felt in his life. He turned off the radio. A mile down the road, he had to move the rear view mirror. Someone had on their brights. The lights passed his car and braked for a complete stop.

Nolan got out of the big brown truck and walked over to Casey. "Get out of your car Stretch."

Casey got out. Nolan stood in his personal space. "Are you my boyfriend?"

"I want to be."

"Am I yours?"

"I want you to be."

Nolan pulled Casey in for a clumsy hug with two winter parkas between them. There were no words. A car passed them on the lonely road and beeped their horn at being part of the moment.

Casey pushed Nolan back. "I need your help."

"How?"

"I'm not any good at this. But I want to be."

"As long as you want this, everything will be OK."

"Are you really mad at me?"

"Fuck no. I was hurt and confused. When you told me you wanted me to leave, you crushed me."

"When I said that, I don't know what I wanted, but I didn't really want you to leave."

"I didn't leave you. I only needed to make a point. It's all over now. Are you going to work tomorrow?"

"Yes. Are you?"

"I am. I have a mission at nine. Can you meet me in the hospital cafeteria for breakfast?"

"Six?"

"Six it is. Be careful on the way home."

"See you tomorrow. One last thing?"

"What?"

"Do that eye trick."

"This?"

"Yeah, that. See you tomorrow."

Nolan pulled him in for one last hug which turned into a passionate kiss on their lips. They both got into their cars and drove home in different directions. Casey turned on the music. He was on an emotional high never experienced before. He made a mental note to call Sawyer the next day.

Sometime during the night, he woke up to find Capan Iceman standing at the end of his bed. With the icy blue eyes, he stared at Casey and shook his head up and down to demonstrate his approval. In an instant, his body spun in circles to make a green blur. He was gone.

By 0530 Casey parked his car in his usual place at work. He took a good look around for the big brown truck. Relieved it wasn't there yet, he made his way to the hospital cafeteria. There were few people inside, most sitting and having coffee. Mainly the night shift workers.

He sat at the table and pulled out his phone. He sent Ian a text message.

Ian, don't worry. I'm going to find you. I'm assembling a small army to get this done. I won't stop until you're back. He pushed send. Without seeing, he felt the air in the room change. He looked up to see Captain Kelly in his flight suit and jacket entering the cafeteria with a boyish grin on his face.

"Morning Stretch?"

"Good morning Nolan. Did you get a good night's sleep?"

"No. Too much on my mind. What about you?"

"I did. I had a good dream, and not your kind of good, my kind of good."

"You're gonna have to explain that one to me later. Come on, I'm hungry." They moved to the single line to get breakfast. Nolan took a plate of scrambled eggs and French toast, Casey took the eggs and toasted rye. They both grabbed a coffee.

At the table, Casey felt his phone buzz with a text message. *"I'm in LA. Please stop and move on. I have."* He slid the phone across the table to Nolan.

"So will you leave him alone?"

"Nolan, he didn't write that. And my cop friend can probably prove it didn't come from LA."

"OK." Nolan took a few bites from his French toast. "Stretch, I have to apologize to you."

"You didn't do anything wrong."

"Actually, I think I did. I should have realized back in Turkey how upset you were about getting the email from Ian. I'm sorry about that. I should have picked up on it. Listen, whatever you want to do with this, you can count me in, OK?"

"Alright. But don't go and take all the blame. I know I hurt your feelings."

"It's all water under the bridge. The good part is we're here now. Enjoying each other."

Casey looked around to make sure their conversation was staying private. "I have a favor to ask."

"Anything."

"Can we be together tonight?"

"Fuck yes. Where?"

"Let me make dinner. My place?"

"What time do you get off work?"

"I'm taking off early today. Maybe around two if the office isn't full."

"Text me. We can go to the commissary together and get what we want for dinner."

"Alright."

"Damn, I'm feeling like I got those two peckers back."

Casey smiled at the mental image of two Nolan dicks.

Nolan squeezed his legs together under the table. "I don't know if I can wait."

"Do I need to contact your DO and have you removed from flying status for the day?"

All Nolan could managed was to inhale a large amount of air. He exhaled the air and shook his head no.

Casey bought the New York Times to read. "Check this out, the Turkish government restored power to the Incirlik base yesterday."

"Bunch of losers."

They finished breakfast. Nolan had to leave before seven. He got up from the table. "I'll text you when I get off."

"Alright. See you later Captain Kelly. Don't over exert yourself."

Nolan gave him the eye trick.

Back in the office, Sandy was the first to arrive. By 0650, he had his first patient of the day. The base commander.

"Good morning Colonel Price. Do you need to see the flight surgeon?"

"Is he here?"

"Not yet, but if you want, I can get you started?"

"It can wait. I'll come back. Captain, I thought you were TDY in Turkey?"

"I was. Short TDY sir."

He left the office, passing Sergeant Tomlin on the way out.

"Good morning Captain. What did he want?"

"No clue. Maybe it was too personal to tell me about."

"Who in the hell cuts his hair?"

"Not my friend. How do you like that coconut slick?"

"Good morning men. Anything exciting to start the day with?"

"No sir, only the base commander was here to see you."

"Did he say what he wanted?"

"No sir. But he didn't want to tell me. It must have been sensitive."

"Isn't it all. Well, let's hope for another peaceful day."

Casey took a moment to find his desk. He composed a short email.

"*Hello Kevin. I got this strange email from Ian, or the person claiming to be him. I'm going to forward it to you now. Once again, thanks for helping out.*" He forwarded the email along with his message.

While Casey was attending to the first patient, he stopped for a second with the roaring noise of three F 22s taking off at 9:03 and passing over the hospital. It was difficult trying to imagine the world Nolan moved in. With a break after ten, he went to his phone and called Sawyer.

"Hello Casey, I thought you'd be out of the country."

"I just got back."

"How are you doing?"

"Good. But I'm having very strange dreams. And some other issues as well I should start talking about."

"I'm booked for today, but I have an opening tomorrow at five?"

"That would be perfect. By the way, have you heard from Ian lately?"

"Not since before Christmas. I believe he has thirty days of leave, am I correct?"

"Yes. Alright, see you tomorrow at five."

"Five it is. Goodbye."

By 11:00, there were no patients. Casey sent a text to Candy.

"*Hi Candy. You'd be proud of me. I was the big boy last night. We worked it all out.*" He pushed send. The response was immediate.

"*Hello Sweetie. I'm so relieved. I have this fantasy of us five moving to a big farm down South and living happily ever after with Gram baking us cakes. Meet me for lunch.*"

Casey laughed and replied.

"*You better keep that fantasy to yourself. Those Kelly boys aren't going anywhere soon. Both have their rear ends glued to the cockpit. Is noon good for you?*"

Casey drove over to the Military Mall to find Candy for lunch. She was just finishing cutting a young Air Force guy's hair. Casey saw her slap him on the thigh and tell him to get up. She told him it was her lunch hour. The guy laughed and asked her, "Do you want me to take you to lunch?"

"Sorry Cutie, my boy is here waiting for me."

"My luck. The nice ones are always taken."

"You keep that up and you'll end up with a free haircut young man. Now go and defend democracy or something like that."

He paid her and left. "Enjoy your lunch Captain."

“Don’t give up so easily Airman, I’m not her boyfriend, I’m her boy.”

Candy took Casey by the arm. “Come on. Any news from Ian?”

“You won’t believe it. I got an email telling me he was in LA. I already sent it to Kevin.”

“LA?”

“Candy, it’s not from him!”

“Oh, right.” They found a table.

After getting the same sandwich and cola, they sat down to catch up. “So Sweetie, how’s the Kevin thing going?”

“Would you believe he gave me an innocent hello hug and the big brown Ram truck just happened to pass by at the very moment?”

“How did you get out of that one?”

“I had to drive right over and explain it. Then we had a talk and worked everything out. He’s coming over for dinner.”

“What if Kevin drops by with some info?”

“Should I tell him about Nolan?”

“Yes. But you have to do it in person. And hopefully not while Nolan is there.”

“You really know how to make a nice lunch conversation.”

“Well?”

It was a warm day for Anchorage in January. Twenty-seven degrees and sunny, even though the sun sat low on the horizon. Casey returned to his office.

“Sergeant Tomlin, did the base commander return yet?”

“No sir.”

By 3:00, Casey was ready to leave. Before he could get a text sent to Nolan, he got one instead.

“Stretch, you ready?”

“Meet me at the commissary parking lot. Leaving now.”

The truck pulled up next to the Subaru. Nolan got out and waited for Casey. “What are we cooking tonight?”

“Do you have any preferences?”

“Steak?”

“Alright. I can’t forget, I need some beer and red wine.”

Inside the commissary, Casey brought up the subject of the morning email from Ian. “I sent Kevin that email I received from Ian’s account this morning. I’m feeling anxious about what he’ll find.”

Nolan was busy throwing snack food in the cart. “Could it be real?”

“No. It make no sense.” He grabbed a box of microwave popcorn. Stopping the cart, he checked to see if he was in the clear from anybody within earshot. “Nolan, are you going to be OK with Kevin being involved with all this?”

“The guy who was grinding up against you last night?”

“You’ve already shown me what your definition of grinding is. And what you saw defiantly wasn’t grinding. But yeah, him.”

Nolan flexed his right arm. Does he have anything like this”

“Not even close.”

“Then he’s no competition.”

“If he were to show up, and I introduce you as my someone special, are you going to be polite?”

“I’m always polite.”

Casey raised his eyebrows.

“I am!”

“Alright. They filled the shopping cart and headed for the checkout counter.

“You boys planning on having a party?”

Nolan said yes and Casey said no at the same time. Casey pulled out his wallet at the uncomfortable moment.

Back at the car, they put the bags in Nolan's back seat. "You remember the way?"

"So funny today Captain Link."

Casey took the lead with the truck behind him. They both parked in the drive. Candy would put her car in the garage when she got home. There was room for three vehicles in front of the garage door. Casey plugged his engine block into the electric cable on very cold nights.

Buddy was in the hallway waiting for them. Both guys had their arms full with bags and their back packs. He sniffed Nolan before running to get to the door first.

They dropped the bags on the kitchen table. "I have your sweat pants on the chair by the bed. Why not get out of your flight suit while I start putting this stuff away?"

"Yes sir." Nolan threw him a salute and left the kitchen for the bedroom. Buddy followed. Five minutes later, Casey heard the flush in the bathroom. He realized Nolan was standing in the kitchen doorway, bare feet, tight t shirt, sweatpants and nothing else. There was an obvious reaction happening under the sweats.

"Aren't your feet going to get cold without your socks?"

"I'm way to hot and bothered right now to get cold feet."

Sandy turned his head towards the food left in the bags. Nolan came up from behind and wrapped his arms around him. Casey could feel the guy's excitement on his backside. He shivered and placed his hands on the counter without saying a word.

"I think I better help you out of your uniform."

Casey froze at the counter.

"Is something wrong?"

He managed to turn around so he could face Nolan, both in each other's personal space. "No nothing's wrong. But I'm not used to all this."

"All what?"

Casey put his hands on top of Nolan's head. "This." He moved his hands down to Nolan's prize possessions to get a good feel of both biceps. "And this."

"I understand. It's a lot to take in."

"You make me feel something I've never felt before. And it makes me feel like I'm a kid at the circus, but you also make me feel afraid."

Nolan frowned and pulled back. He feared his passionate hug was turning the guy off.

Casey reached out and grabbed his t shirt right at the spot covering his muscular pecs. He pulled Nolan back in. "You moved back. Did I just push you away?"

The only answer Nolan could provide was with the eye trick.

"Can you put your arms around me please?"

Nolan did.

"I don't want distance. I want to be close to you. Very close. The closer you are the better. You're making me feel things I never felt before. Being afraid, that one I'm accustomed to."

"That's a good thing. But I have to say, I'm a little confused here."

"That makes two of us. I guess what I'm saying is, I'm moving very slow. I can't speed it up. If I do, I might blow it like I always do, but please, don't step back because of it. I really like you. I love it when your close to me. You might be the first person in my life I feel like I actually need."

Nolan pulled him in for a kiss on the lips. He was the one to pull back. "I really need you too Stretch. Don't you worry about me. I'm going to do my best to follow your lead. Only one request?"

"What?"

"Every once in a while, tell me you need me?"

Casey bent down a few inches and placed his head in the crook of Nolan's muscular neck. "I need you Nolan Kelly. I need you more than you could possibly imagine."

They remained like that and breathed on each other until Buddy nudged Nolan on the legs. He knew there was steak in the bags and wanted to be sure they didn't forget him in the moment of strong emotions that were bombarding the kitchen walls.

"Let me cut the salad. Go and get into your comfortable clothes."

Casey moved to the entrance of the kitchen while Nolan began organizing the salad. He slipped back in and put both his hands on the back of Nolan's upper arms, giving him a quick kiss on the neck.

Casey returned to the kitchen with his sweats, t shirt and socks. "Do you know how to cook steaks?"

"Get your frying pan, I'll show you."

"Fry? Is that a Southern thing?"

"Maybe."

"Let's try the broiler. You can cut the veggies for the salad."

Nolan kept bumping into Casey. Then he stopped from behind and put his arms around him. "This reminds me of the camper. You have no idea how much I wanted to do this."

"I remember. You were a big tease."

"So when do we go camping?"

Casey managed to get turned around to face him. Their faces were only inches apart. "Do you have the weekend off?"

"I do."

"Can we go where there's cell phone service?"

"Why?"

"The Ian thing. I feel like I need to be by the phone."

"I can do that."

"OK." He made it back around with Nolan's arms holding on. "Captain, can you set the table?"

Nolan let go. "That's no fun."

"By the way, who helped you take down the tree?"

"I'm still waiting for you to complete the deal."

"You're kidding. The tree is still up?"

“Of course.”

“Please tell me you unplugged the timer?”

“Why?”

“Your poor neighbors.”

“Ah, Stretch, there aren’t any.”

“Well, those poor deer.”

“I have a great idea. You convince Candy to offer to help Chester take it down the next time he’s in.”

“I can do that. But you’ll owe me one.”

“I’ll pay.”

“When is Chester coming back around?”

“This Friday. He already has a date for dinner with Candy.”

Casey grabbed the dog’s red bowl and placed it on the counter. “Almost Buddy.”

They sat and ate with the light from a candle. “Stretch, I can’t see the food. What the hell?”

“Now who’s being so romantic.”

“Whatever.”

Buddy finished way before they did. He laid by the entrance of the door to the living room. The moment was interrupted with the phone vibrating on the counter. Casey got up to answer it.

“Hello Kevin. Did you get the email I forwarded to you?”

“Hi Casey. I did. I found something odd. Do you have time for me to come over tonight?”

Casey looked at Nolan. “Can we make it tomorrow?”

“Dinner?”

“How about skipping dinner, and meeting for drinks at Reilly’s Pub?”

“What time?”

“Seven?”

“I’ll see you at seven.”

“Can you tell me anything over the phone. I’ve been on edge for a while?”

"I have the IP address from both emails. They came from Starbucks downtown. I can fill you in better tomorrow."

"Thanks Kevin, bye."

"Tomorrow Casey." They hung up.

Casey took his glass of wine and leaned against the counter. Nolan was pretending like it was an everyday conversation.

"Nolan, I never had the chance to tell him about us. And us only restarted last night."

"I'm fine."

"I'm not going to the pub without you."

"For real?"

"I'm going to send him an email about us and give him the option to pull out. I was really clear last night when he left to let him know I had no intentions of leading him on. I told him when I got back from leave I didn't have any feelings for him. I was upfront."

"What am I supposed to do?"

"Be polite. That's all. I need for him to understand something very important about us."

"Understand what?"

"To understand that I have feelings for you."

Nolan got up from the table. He approached Casey and pulled him in his arms. "Is this guy hot?"

"Well, he's one of the most handsome men I've ever known. But he lacks something."

"What's that?"

"He can't do funny things with his eyes."

Nolan lifted his arm. "What about these?" He moved his one eye up.

"He lacks those too." Casey used one hand to feel the hard bicep. "You on the other hand are the sexiest man I've ever seen, aside from Chester that is."

"What the?"

"I'm kidding. I'm kidding."

"If I'm coming with you tomorrow, we need to arrive in the same truck."

"OK. I can be the designated driver."

"We're talking about a big truck, Stretch."

"We need to take Buddy for a walk."

"A run or a walk?"

"A walk tonight, a run in the morning, at 0430 hours. Can you make it?"

"That depends on how much sleep I get tonight."

"Buddy, do you want to go for a walk?"

Buddy twirled three times in a circle before running to the door. Casey laughed. "You have to wait until Mister Sexy get his jeans on."

"Come on Stretch. We both change at the same time."

"Are you going to behave?"

The eye trick again.

In the bedroom, Nolan slipped off his sweatpants, leaving himself naked from the waste down. He stood there giving Casey a look while he got his sweats off. Casey wore his Jockey shorts. He tried not to look at Nolan, but Nolan made it difficult. He stayed in the same position.

"Oh no. The dog has to go out for a walk. And judging by what's going on over there, you need something else."

Nolan gave in and grabbed his commando jeans. They were safely covered, put on their shoes and winter gear. Finally they made it out the door to go for the walk. Casey stuck his head in Gram's door. "Gram, I'm taking Buddy for a walk."

"How long will you be gone?"

"Less than an hour."

"I'll have coffee and cookies when you get back. The kind of cookies you and Nolan like."

"We'll be ready."

They left the house with Buddy in the lead. "We can walk to the base gate and back. If we walk, that's about an hour."

Nolan kept looking at Casey with a smile. No words, just a smile.

"Alright, what?"

“What?”

“The way you’re looking at me.”

“Can’t I look at you?”

“You got something up your sleeve.”

“I always got something up my sleeve when I think of you.”

“Keven said those two emails, including the one today came from the Starbucks downtown.”

“So Ian never left Anchorage.”

“Nolan.”

“What? Oh, sorry. So the guy who took Ian never left Anchorage.”

“Now you’re making fun of me.”

Nolan stopped them from walking. “I’ll never do that. At least not for real. I’m trying to be with you on this Ian theory. But even if I don’t get there soon, I promise I’ll do whatever you want me to do to help. OK?”

“I appreciate that.”

“Are you going to tell that Sawyer guy about your theory?”

“I can’t right yet.”

“Why not?”

“Because what if it’s him that took Ian?”

Casey could hear Nolan take a deep breath. They continued on much to Buddy’s delight.

“I sent my parents a letter.”

“So what did you say?”

“I told them they had to apologize and acknowledge or I never wanted anything to do with them from that point on.”

“Have they written back?”

“No.”

“So you wait?”

“I honestly believe I’ll never hear from them. And it doesn’t bother me. Truth is, I felt a lot of freedom the moment I dropped that letter in the box. No more pretending at family gatherings. No more feeling like I have to throw up ever time he enters the room.”

“What about your sister?”

“I think she will act the same way. She wants the myth of the happy family. Hell, she lived it. If she doesn’t contact me, then the same goes for her. In the strangest way, she had a role in all of it. I know she’s a victim, but she fits so well into the puzzle.”

Nolan put his one arm around Casey as they kept walking. “You stick with me Stretch and I’ll share my family with you.”

For the second time in his adult life, Casey cried. Not the kind of cry one could hear, but the kind of cry that produced tears running down both cheeks. So much so that he had to use his gloved hand to wipe them away.

Nolan noticed. “You gonna be alright?”

“Better than alright. I just hope I don’t go and blow this like I almost did in Turkey.”

“Come on, let’s change the subject.”

“Tell me about your little brother in Afghanistan. Is he like you and Chester?”

“Not at all. He’s quiet, very sensitive, smart as hell, and more patriotic than Chester and me put together.”

“If he’s sensitive, can he fight?”

“Fuck yes. Chester and I made sure of that.”

“Good God, did you hurt him?”

“Only a little bit. We made him tough.”

“Is he gay?”

“No. When you’re gay, you never jack off with girly magazines.”

“How do you know that?”

“I told you, we all had to share the same bedroom. There’s nothing private in that world.”

“Funny. My whole world was, or I should say is private.”

“Not anymore it isn’t. You’re here right now telling me things very private about your life.”

“That’s right. I am.”

“You tell me anything you want Stretch.”

They approached the front gate. Buddy pulled to see if his MP friend was on duty. He had several of them.

The MP came out in the cold. The temperature now dropped to seventeen degrees. “Hi Captain. Buddy Boy, come here and shake hands with me.” Buddy pulled up to the MP and did as he was told. “Not running tonight?”

“Tomorrow before work.”

The MP stooped down to pet Buddy. “I think we need a police dog while on duty. Why don’t you leave him with us sometimes?”

“I can’t. He belongs to the lady who lives on the first floor of my house.”

“He’d be real good at it.”

“He’d love it too. Well, we better start back.”

They turned around and walked in the other direction to get Gram’s coffee and cookies.

They were quiet for a while. Nolan kept bumping the side of Casey and giving him the smiles.

“Remember what you read that day in my journal?”

“I remember. I’ll never forget it.”

“I have dreams.”

“What kind of dreams?”

“Dreams like what you read in the journal.”

“Was what you wrote in the journal a dream?”

“No. I wish it was. But when I grew up and the abuse stopped…”

“It stopped? Why?”

“Why? I can only guess, but I started growing tall and I think he was a coward. I would never have had the courage to fight back, but he might have thought I would, so it stopped when I was about fourteen. I also think since I was on the feminine side, that it turned him off. He liked macho little boys. And macho men too. He had a lot of guy flings on the side. Married guys who kept it from their wives and fooled around. Especially hunting buddies. The guy really loved to kill animals. ”

“How did you know this?”

“It gets sicker. Are you sure you want to hear this stuff?”

“If you can talk about it, go on.”

"Well, one weird thing about me as a child was adults, especially the normal ones. They liked me. And he knew it. So he always made me come with him on his man outings and I entertained the women while he'd go off in some other place in the house and do his thing. All those women fit into the same profile. Blind as hell to the reality around them. As if they didn't want to know their husbands were off having gay sex. We would just engage in conversations about interesting things. Mostly I would listen to their stories. Like no one else would."

"God Casey, there are monsters in this world."

"Yes there are. And my dad wasn't the only one. I remember one of the places I would have to wife sit while he was off having gay sex. It was the principal of his school. His wife would sit and sew while telling me all about her wonderful sons in college. I heard my dad talking to my mom a few years later how one of the sons moved to India to join a cult and the other one killed himself. I knew why as the two talked like it was such a tragic mystery.

"That's sick."

"I know. What's sicker is the macho guy students that came around from his sports teams. I could tell they were obsessed with him, but I never knew to what extent the obsession went. I didn't want to know."

"How did you ever have a normal conversation with your dad?"

"That's an easy one. We never had a single conversation in my whole time living in that house. Never a one, other than direct orders to do something like clean the garage or be his gofer for tools or something."

"What about your mom? Did you have conversations with her?"

"She had conversations with my sister, but never for me. I think she hated me for the physical attention I got from her husband. That would explain why she loved to see me get beat. She'd always wait until the very end, then she'd act all responsible and try to stop him, but never until the beating was over. Most of the physical beatings were at her request anyway. I think she would rather see me get beat than receive her sick interpretation of love."

"What do you mean at her request?"

"You know, if I did something wrong while he was at work that pissed her off, she'd delight in the words, 'Just wait until your father gets home.' Then when he did get home from work, I'd get bounced off the walls and the ceiling. I got the mock choking all the time too."

"What's a mock choking?"

"That's when he would sit on me and put his hands around my neck to choke me, but not until I passed out. I never passed out with those."

"What's going on with your dreams?"

"Well, I've had these dreams for years. Sawyer said they were a product of PTSD."

"PTSD?"

"I know. I had the same reaction. I thought PTSD was with soldiers only. He told me there is more PTSD in our world among rape victims than there are from military experiences. I'm not so convinced what I dream about is a part of PTSD, but it doesn't matter to me what it's called anyway."

"So go on, the dreams?"

"Right. Well, I've had these dreams where I wake at night and see an image like the devil with glowing red eyes. I have to play dead or he gets me. And the part I hate is I always have the knife on the dresser top, but I can't get to it, so I have to fake dead. Then I wake up in a cold sweat. I have to walk around the house for a while before going back to sleep or I have a repeat dream."

"And you said you have good dreams too?"

"Since I met you and fell for you…"

"When did that happen?"

"At the SDI briefing I had to give at the fighter squadron. When you were smiling at me from the front row. You had me then."

"Sweet. Sorry, go on about the dreams."

"Well, since I met you, there has been a different element to my dreams. You're going to think I'm crazy."

"No way. They're dreams. All dreams are crazy. Go on."

"I started seeing Capan Iceman standing at the end of my bed. He pointed at the red eyed monster, and the monster disappeared into thin air. He's been in my dreams a couple of times now. Stupid isn't it?"

"Fuck no. I get it." He stopped them from walking.

"Get what?"

"Capan Iceman. That's me in your dreams."

Casey took a deep breath. "Well, you have the same haircut."

"Your night time worries are all over now dude."

"Maybe."

"God Casey, like I said, if we were neighbors when we were small, I think Chester and I could have done something."

"I bet you could have. It's why I feel safe with you."

"You do?"

"Yes I do."

Nolan put his arm back around Casey as they slowly walked home. He chuckled. "Yes sir, I'm your very own superhero. I love it."

They walked on for a while in silence. "Nolan, remember when you said you thought we were going to fuck, so you didn't want to jack off?"

"I remember. That was a great Christmas for me."

"I wanted to say something about that."

"Go on."

"About anal intercourse. Would you mind if we not do that? At least not until I feel ready? And if I'm being honest here, I might not ever be ready."

"Stretch, I have to ask, have you ever been fucked in the ass?"

"Yes and no."

"Listen, you tell me if and when. It doesn't mean everything to me, even though I do like fucking a guy in the ass. I even enjoy a poke every once in awhile. But here's the thing. If I get to be naked next to you and feel you want me, physically and emotionally, that's all I need. We'll figure out how to pleasure ourselves as we go along."

"Thanks Nolan. You're my," he paused, "You're the greatest."

Nolan smiled at Casey.

"Nolan, I forgot to tell you about tomorrow night. I have an appointment with Sawyer downtown at five. Should we drive separate cars to the pub?"

"No. Let me come with you. I can wait in the truck."

"Are you sure?"

"I'm more than sure."

"You mind waiting in the waiting room?"

"I can read my book while I wait."

"OK. Can I introduce you to Sawyer as my boyfriend?"

"You better or there'll be hell to pay."

"Cool."

They arrived to the house an hour after they left.

They took off their winter parkas and threw them on the steps. Casey opened Gram's door a crack. "You ready for us yet?"

Gram opened the door. "Come on in boys, Candy and I were just talking about you two."

"Was Candy spilling secrets again?"

"I heard that Casey Link." She entered into the kitchen. "So we're having cookies and coffee?"

"Yes we are. Come on boys, sit down."

They sat at the table. Casey was opposite Nolan. Candy was between them.

"So boys, you're coming with Chester and me this Friday, right?"

"We are?"

"Yes, you are."

Casey looked at Nolan. "Are we?"

"She's the boss."

He looked back at Candy. "Let me guess, Reilly's?"

"Yes."

"Don't you think Chester is getting bored with that place?"

"No. I think he wants to show me off to the other fly boys."

Nolan laughed. "I think she might be right about that."

"Fine. Reilly's it is."

Casey tried not to pay attention to the secret looks Nolan was giving him from across the table.

"These cookies are great Gram."

"Why thank you Nolan. I made a plate for you to take upstairs for later."

Buddy was begging at Casey's side, but Casey pretended like he didn't give Buddy people food in the presence of Gram.

"I don't know what's got into that dog. Such poor manners begging at the table like that. You go lay down Buddy." Buddy put his tail between his legs and laid on the floor at Casey's feet.

"Well, I'm going to leave you young folks to the table. Candy, if you need me, I'll be in my room watching TV. By the way, I have a little surprise for you all tomorrow night."

"Good night Gram," she told her.

Both Nolan and Casey also told her good night.

When Gram was away from the kitchen, Casey told Candy, "We're meeting Kevin tomorrow night at the pub to discuss Ian."

"We?"

Nolan smirked. "Yip, we. Should be a barrel of monkeys."

"And Nolan has promised to be polite."

"My mom and dad raised me right."

"Well, thanks for the cookies. We have an early start tomorrow. A 4:30 run, isn't that right Captain Kelly?"

"You say when."

They got up from the table to leave. "You stay here Buddy. I'll come and get you for our morning run."

"Guys, don't forget Gram's plate. I don't want all these cookies around here. I can't believe I'm not fat yet."

Nolan grabbed the plate. They left for the upstairs.

"Stretch, look at all these cookies she gave us."

"Take some with you to work tomorrow."

"I will."

At the top of the stairs, Nolan followed Casey inside. "Now can we get our sweats back on?"

"Yes. And we can watch some TV?"

"Who picks?"

"We toss a coin, but no sports channels."

"We toss a coin and no PBS."

"What if it's a PBS program on Netflix?"

"What if it's a sports program on Netflix?"

"Do you like to listen to music?"

"Do you have any Led Zeppelin?"

"Led Who?"

"You're pulling my leg."

When they made it to the futon, Nolan grabbed the remote and began looking for a program suitable to them both. After a few minutes, they settled on a program analyzing ISIS. Each guy occupied the far end of the couch. Casey watched Nolan from the corner of his vision. After a few minutes, he stared directly at him.

Nolan noticed. "What?"

"Something is odd here."

"What?"

"I don't know, you're not being you."

He made the eye trick. "You think?"

Casey laughed. "I know what's wrong. Come here." He made room for Casey to lay against him in the corner if the futon. Casey got both his arms around Nolan and settled them right below his rib cage.

"What's wrong?"

"What I said in the kitchen tonight, I want to make an amendment."

"I'm listening."

"You be you. And don't get hurt if I have to stop you or slow you down because you're going too fast for me. But I need Nolan to be Nolan. The one and only."

"Are you sure?"

Casey leaned over to kiss him in the neck. "We can try it, OK?"

"I like it."

They watched the TV for about a minute before Nolan became Nolan.

"So you're sure you want me to be me?"

"I'm sure."

He took Casey's hand and began to slowly move it down. Waiting for a reprisal or some semblance of resistance. Getting none, he continued until the tips of Casey's fingers were below the waistband of his sweats and at the beginning of what Casey came to refer to as the Amazon jungle.

Casey took over. He moved his hand down further until he had the half excited cock in his hand. He massaged it until it was like a rock. "Does your dick always get this hard?"

"It's like iron, isn't it? I can hang a damp towel on it."

"You tried that for real?"

"Come on, what guy hasn't?"

"Me?"

"Oh boy, I can see you're going to need my training skills."

"I can't wait. Towel hanging class 101."

"Can we go to your bed?"

"I'm ready." Casey let Nolan get off the couch with his sweats down to his knees. He kicked them off and left them on the floor. By the time he reached the hallway entrance, he was completely naked. Casey had yet to remove anything. Nolan grabbed him and turned him around. "I need you Stretch." He kissed Casey full on the lips. Casey pulled off his t shirt, sweats and socks. Nolan took a detour to the bathroom to grab a towel.

When the towel was sticky and laying on the floor by the side of the bed, Nolan asked Casey, "It's early, what do we do now?"

"Know what I really want?"

"A repeat?"

"To get warm under the covers and have you tell me stories when you were little on the farm. I love your stories." They arranged themselves under the double goose down quilts, ready for a hot night under the covers with the cold night air all around them.

"Stretch?"

"What?" Nolan was on his back with Casey's head resting on his chest.

"Don't worry about that Boogeyman coming around tonight. He'll know better."

"I believe it."

"So what do you want to know?"

"Tell me about your mom."

"First of all, she's really pretty. She loves the simple things in life. When we…"

Nolan told and Casey listened. The night passed this way while two men began a bond that neither would fully grasp at the moment just how strong it would become.

The Alarm buzzed at 4:00 a.m. "What the fuck is that?"

"Good morning Nolan."

Nolan lifted his head to glance at the red glowing numbers of the digital alarm clock. "You said 4:30."

"That's when we leave the back door. I need a coffee first."

"Did you have pleasant dreams?"

"Probably. I didn't wake up feeling like this for having a bad one. How did you sleep?"

"Like a baby."

Nolan reached in front of Casey and felt between his legs. "Should I solve this problem?"

"I have to go to the bathroom. It's a normal reaction to a full bladder."

"If you say so." He pushed his erection against Casey's rear end. "But this is due to another situation." Before Casey could get up, Nolan slipped his cock between his thighs and began to move. He could have had some relief if Casey hadn't jumped out of the bed into the cold air of the bedroom. "Damn. That was downright cruel."

"Come on. I'll get the coffee on."

"Jeeze, I was just trying to be me."

Casey went to the bathroom to rid himself of what Nolan wanted. On the way out, he threw on his sweats and sweatshirt. He grabbed another sweatshirt and threw it at Nolan.

In the kitchen, he checked his messages. Nothing other than ads. A message from USAA and an email from Amazon. Nolan found his cup.

"Are we going to eat at the chow hall?"

"You know the command hates it when you refer to the Iditarod Inn as a chow hall."

"Whatever. The guys at the squadron call it the Choke and Puke. What do you call it?"

"The dining facility."

"So then, can we go to the Dining Facility for breakfast today?"

"Alright."

They waited for the coffee to finish. The coffee was ready. Nolan got a email on his phone. Casey poured the coffee and Nolan read.

"Love letter?"

"Yes. From my mom. She's worried about Sandy."

"No wonder. I don't even know the guy and I am too."

Nolan sent his mom a text and said the words out loud as he typed. *"D o n't w o r r y mom, S a n d y is a big boy n o w."* He pushed send. By the time he got milk in his coffee, the reply came back. "Good God." He typed the reply and did the same with the words being repeated out loud. *"B e c a u s e you a l r e a d y know I love you. Got a big mission. Write later.”* He pushed send.

Casey stared at Nolan a little too long, half smiling.

“What?”

“Nothing. I’m a little intrigued, that’s all.”

They dressed for a run and left the second floor to find Buddy. He was already on the other side of the door sniffing at the bottom.

“Come on Buddy. I told you we would go for a run.” He spun around both guy’s legs.

They left the house. “Damn, it’s cold enough out here to freeze the balls off a pool table.”

Casey laughed. “It is isn’t it?”

They took off towards the main gait, but at the corner of Pine Street and Mountain View Drive, he took a right turn instead of a left.

“Stretch, do you need a navigator?”

“No. Change of plans, follow me.”

Casey led them in the direction of Ian’s garage apartment at the far Western section of his small neighborhood.

“I should have guessed. Now what?”

“I’m going in to get his mail. There has to be a clue in there somewhere.”

“Is that legal?”

“Of course it is. Friends always pick up the mail for friends when they’re away on vacation. Same thing here.” He pulled out his key. They headed for the steps and Buddy was first to make it to the door. Inside, Casey looked all around without moving. Buddy made his rounds. “Nothing has changed. I didn’t think it would.” He walked to the bathroom with Nolan behind him. “Nothing here. Come on.”

There were about ten envelopes on the table. He took them all and led the others out the door. He locked it, and they took off down the stairs. Right then, a young man left the house to find his car. He stopped and stared at them.

“Hi. I’m Ian’s friend. Getting his mail for him.”

"Right. I've seen you around here. Is he planning on returning soon?"

"End of the month."

"Wait, I'll go in and get the rest of the mail." He returned into the house.

"Stretch, why don't we ask him if Ian's been around?"

"How do I explain getting his mail if I tell him I don't know where he is? He supposedly asked me to get the mail."

The guy left the house with a brown shopping sack. "Here's all we have since yesterday. Got to get to work."

"Thanks." Casey took the bag. The guy got into his car and started it up. He sat there waiting for the motor to warm.

"Come on, we run back, it's too cold to walk." Buddy seemed to complain about the short run. "We'll do a better one later." Casey pushed him through the kitchen door to his house before they climbed the stairs.

"I need to shower and shave before getting to work."

Casey was immersed in reading the return addresses on each envelope.

Nolan leaned against the wall by the entrance to the living room. "I guess I'll go now and get my shower?"

Casey placed every envelope in a pile.

"I'm going now."

"Enjoy your shower Captain Kelly."

Nolan left for the bathroom, mumbling as he moved, "Thank you Captain Link. How nice of you Captain Link."

They drove both vehicles to the base and parked at the Iditarod for breakfast, arriving minutes before six. It was cold and dark out, with few cars in the lot. Half the tables were empty. They both selected a plate of scrambled eggs and a bowl of chopped fruit. Each had toast and coffee.

"I think this is the nicest dining hall in the Air Force."

Nolan raised his eyebrows.

"Well, you've been to a lot more bases than I have."

Nolan looked around. "You make me happy Stretch."

Casey smiled with a mouthful of eggs.

"Want to make me more happy?"

He swallowed. "How?"

"Spend a week with me at the cabin."

"What about Buddy?"

"Bring him along."

"Can't. Gram needs him too. No one would take him for a run."

"We can figure that one out."

"What about this Ian thing?"

"I do live in Anchorage you know."

"True."

"Come on. My DO told me I have to take leave or I'm gonna loose it. I planned on losing it until I realized we could have a good week at the cabin together."

"You have banked sixty days of leave? Don't you ever take a break?"

"No. Never wanted to, until now that is."

"Nolan, I just got back from leave. There's no way the Major would approve more days right now."

"Well, go to work, and come to the cabin afterwards. I'll be home making cheese sandwiches to be ready as you walk through the door. Starting tonight. We can get in some great skiing on the trails around the cabin."

"Tonight?"

"I promise to behave."

"Remember, you're supposed to be you. Behaving and being Nolan isn't very synonymous."

"This is me being Nolan. What do you say?"

"Let me think about it."

They finished their breakfast and drove to separate parts of the base. Casey East to the hospital and Nolan West across the flight line to Fighter Ops.

A quick detour for a coffee in the hospital cafeteria. He stopped to greet Major Meyers having a coffee at a table. “Good morning Major. Anything big planned for the day?”

“Hi Casey. Nothing as of yet. Any big plans for this weekend?”

“Cross country skiing north of town. What about you?”

“Shopping with the wife. A couple Blu Rays. Clean the car. We married men have such exciting lives. Do I ever remember the good old days.”

“I can imagine. Laundry done, dinner cooked, house cleaned, someone to talk to. What a challenge.”

The Major laughed. “I suppose you’ll find out some day. Are you dating anyone?”

“No.”

“What about that red head over at the Mall?”

“She’s dating a friend of mine. I rent the upstairs at her Gram’s house. She lives with her.”

“She’s a nice looking girl.”

“A real good friend too. Did the base commander ever get back with you?”

The Major took a sip of his coffee, the way Casey knew meant to think before giving the answer. The answer was short and to the point. “Yes.”

“Well, I’ll catch you in the office.” Casey left for his desk to check his emails. “Good morning Sergeant Tomlin.”

“Good morning Captain Link. Did you see the Major yet?”

“He’s finishing a coffee and remembering the good old days in the cafeteria.”

“Good old days?”

“Do you ever miss being single?”

“Hell no. Life is much easier when you have help. And having kids can’t be beat.”

“Nice. If you’re looking for me, I’m at my desk.”

“Yes sir.”

Casey went to check his email. There was one from Candy.

"Hi Sweetie. What happened to all the hot water this morning? You know you could conserve hot water if you took one together. Just saying. Gram wants me to remind you and Nolan she has a surprise for all of us after work. Text me."

Casey laughed at the lack of privacy living above Candy.

"Good morning Gladys Kravitz. I have Sawyer at five and Kevin at seven. Any ideas?" He pushed send. Then he sat with his brown bag of envelopes addressed to lan.

First he separated the bills. Disappointed there were no letters from his mom or dad. *Who sends letters nowadays anyway? What was I hoping for?* He took two envelopes from the USAA bank and opened them both. They were bank statements. There was a balance of over four thousand dollars in his checking account. *Alright, who starts a new life and leaves money in the bank? Kevin needs to see this.* There were items ordered from Amazon that were obviously for women. He also had the credit card statement with USAA's American Express card. There was a balance of seven hundred dollars. Unfortunately, the statements were for the time prior to Christmas, so it really couldn't tell him anything he needed to know. *Maybe Kevin can track his card for purchases. They do that in the movies all the time.*

His concentration was broken by a text message from Candy. *"I see an opening between six and seven in your schedule. Text me."*

Before he could, there was a vibration sent from Nolan. *"SO? I'm on desk duty today. We'll have a blast on the trails! Warming up by the fireplace with a hot chocolate afterwards. Please."*

Casey wrote back. "*OK. But you have to help me out. We have to run back from Sawyer's to see what Gram wants to show us, then on to Reilly's at seven to meet with Kevin where you're going to be the politest fighter pilot in the U.S. of A. It's going to be a busy after work schedule. You in?"* He pushed send.

The answer came fast. *"I told you, I'm always polite. I'm in."*

Casey made one more response. *"You're the greatest. Candy complained today about the hot water being gone. I think the next time you stay over we better take a shower together. Lunch with Candy at the Mall at noon?"*

The response came. *"I love her. I'll try."*

Sandy spent the morning with two Army pilots and a pilot from the 90th. During his break, he sat at the computer and wrote Kevin an email.

"Good morning Kevin. I hope you're well. I haven't had much time since I've been back to have a talk with you. I met a guy I think I can connect with. He's a pilot on base. I'm seeing a good therapist to discuss my issues. This guy is helping me out with finding Ian. I want to bring him along to the pub tonight. I'll understand if you don't want to come. I know I haven't been your lucky charm. I never wanted to hurt you and I especially don't want to rub salt in a wound. Text me if you plan on meeting with us at seven.

Thanks"

After he pushed send, he went to the computer to check on some record updates. He sat there and decided to update the base commander's records. He saw what he shouldn't have seen. The base commander was HIV positive. He closed the records and sat back in his chair. Now he had a secret that he'd have to keep from the world. Unless there would be some kind of official statement. But one thing for sure, he'd be gone, at least at first on medical leave within the week. Only he, the Major and the lab technicians would know why.

It was the first day since November the temperature reached above freezing. His car thermometer showed thirty-three degrees. Downright balmy for Anchorage in January. The big brown truck was in the lot. He walked to the food court with no sign of Nolan. So he entered into the BX to see if he could find him.

He was easy to spot. In the home goods department with a couple of towels in his hand. “Hello Captain Kelly. Running short on towels?”

“Hello Captain Link. I might need extra this week. I have a special guest coming over, and I plan on making a lot of spills to clean up after.”

“Why don’t you wash the ones you have?”

“Too much bother.”

“You do have a washer and dryer in that place. I saw them.” Then the light went on in his head. “Oh my God.”

“What?”

Casey made sure no one was near enough to hear the conversation. “I just realized I have a boyfriend with fringe benefits.”

“I already knew that.”

“I’m talking about that huge front loading washer and dryer you have at the cabin. Why didn’t I see this before?”

“Fine with me. Maybe you can give me a hand and help me catch up a little with mine too.”

“Of course. I’m off at three. What time do you get out of here today?”

“I can get out at three.”

“Then we run to my place, strip the bed, all the towels. Oh, and that towel on the floor too. And all my dirty clothes. All the extra blankets too. This is fantastic. Where have you been all my life?”

“Come on, I need to pay for these, you said something about lunch at noon?”

“After you.” He followed Nolan to the cash register to pay for the towels. They found Candy sending messages at one of the food court tables.

“Hi Candy.”

“Hello boys. I just got a message from Chester. He wants to take me skiing around the cabin this weekend.”

Casey looked at Nolan.

“So what? The more the merrier.”

"Good point Captain Nolan. We might as well get used to it, right?"

"Trust me, we've shared space before."

They went for lunch.

"Candy, are you going to tell Gram where you're going this weekend?"

"Yes, to a weekend ski party at a cabin with Casey and Nolan."

"Very convenient, having gay friends, isn't it?"

"You better believe it. Besides, I plan on having Chester over real soon for dinner to let her know about us. I think it's time."

"Good plan."

"Now, if I could only figure out what's she's got planned for after work. She wouldn't give me any hints. I hope she hasn't found a long lost grandchild somewhere, there's no room in that place for more and I don't plan on sharing my bedroom with anyone."

Casey raised his eyes at her. "Guys, I found Ian's bank statements in his mail this morning. His USAA checking account and his USAA American Express account."

"Did you open that mail?"

"Nolan, how else am I supposed to find clues?"

"I just asked."

"I'm giving the bank statements to Kevin tonight. I know he can do a check and see what the activity has been on his debit and credit card."

Candy wiped her face and braved a sensitive question. "Have you prepared yourself for the possibility of what he wrote you as being true?"

"Candy, who starts a new life and leaves the cash behind?"

Nolan suggested, "Maybe the mail you have is because he can't give a forwarding address? Maybe he cleaned out the account after those statements were sent."

"And what about the emails being sent from Starbucks downtown instead of LA?"

Both shrugged their shoulders.

"I guess I'm alone in this quest."

Nolan leaned forward. "I told you I'm in, whether I have doubts or not. One hundred percent. Alright?"

"Me too. You can count on me to do whatever we need to do to find the answers about this."

"Thanks. Thanks to you both."

Nolan got up. "I have to get back. We leave at three?"

"Yes. I'll text you if something comes up and I can't get away."

"Later Candy."

"By Nolan. See you after six."

At 3:00 p.m., Casey was happy to get the message from Kevin. He planned on being at the pub by seven. He sent a text to Nolan who told him he was already in the parking lot waiting.

Casey left the hospital and found the truck next to his Subaru. He threw Casey a salute and followed him off the base to his house. They parked and went for the back door. Nolan grabbed his bag of civvies to change. Casey stuck his head inside the first floor. Buddy jumped out, ready for a run. "Gram, you in there?" She was out. "Come on Nolan, we can make a quick lunch so I can be ready for my appointment at five?"

"Would you rather stop for fast food?"

"We probably should have made a quick stop at the Choke and Puke. Alright, let me grab the laundry." He took out several large garbage bags and began to fill them up with everything from blankets to sheets, towels and clothes. By the time he finished, he had three bags full to the top and Nolan was dressed in his jeans. "Did you send the rug home yet?"

"Yes."

"Did your mom receive it?"

"I don't think so."

Casey bent down and gave Buddy a hug. "I'll be back in a few hours to see you. You be a good boy."

Casey left his uniform ready for the next day arranged on a hanger. He could change after their morning run with Buddy on the way to work. "Come on, I don't want to be late." They dragged the bags to the truck and took off for some fast food.

Nolan had an idea of where to eat. "Micky Dees?"

"Really?"

"What?"

"Let's try the Turkish Delight. Bring back old memories."

"Where in the hell is that?"

"Just south of Merill Field Airport, north of the university."

"Lead the way."

They made it to the restaurant on Lake Otic Parkway. "I heard the food here is really good."

"Better than a Big Mac?"

"We're going to find out."

Inside, Casey led Nolan to a table. The sign said to seat yourself. "Check it out, ambient lighting." The room was lit with purple and red lighting on the side of the wall.

"Better than candle light. My food might look purple, but at least I'll be able to see it."

They studied the menu. Both guys ordered cappadocia chicken kebab with white rice and a salad. Casey ordered a carrot yogurt dish with hummus for an appetizer.

"Nolan, I left the skis at my apartment."

"Well, we have to go back after your visit with the shrink."

"I hate that word."

"Sorry."

"That's alright. Call him Sawyer."

They ate their dinner with little conversation. Casey was nervous about being late. "Was it so bad?"

"No. Now ask me if it was better than a Big Mac."

"Alright, we go there the next time. I thought since Turkey was where you got inside of me, that this would be romantic."

Nolan used his foot to get Casey under the table. "Stretch, I'll go wherever you want to go. No complaints."

"Let me pay for this. I'm going to get some baklava to go for later."

"Baka va what?"

Casey laughed.

In the truck on the way back to Casey's apartment, after his visit with Sawyer, Nolan picked up on him being extra quiet. "He seems like a nice guy."

"He is. He's good at making me admit things I don't want to. Oh well. I guess that's what it's all about."

Nolan put his hand on Casey's thigh. They made it to the driveway by 6:15. "Come on, let's see what Gram wanted to show us." Casey opened the back door. "You go on in, I'm going to run up and get my skis."

Casey leaned the skis up against the back door and entered into Gram's kitchen. He was immediately bombarded with a swirl of brown and white on the kitchen floor. The white part was a one year old female poodle mix chasing Buddy's tail.

"What is this?"

"This is my surprise. I got her from the shelter today."

Candy stood at the entrance of the door with her arms folded. "Nice, huh?"

"Well, you don't have to share a bedroom with her."

Nolan was sitting at the table with a plate of cherry pie. "The more the merrier. This pie is great."

Gram bent down to pick the puppy up in her arms. "Isn't she cute?"

Casey sat at the table, and Candy put a plate of pie in front of him. "Eat."

"Thanks Candy. So what's her name?"

"I don't know yet."

Nolan lifted his fork in the air and said, "Cherry Pie."

"Why Nolan, I like that. What do you think Candy?"

"Sure. Why not."

"It's settled then, Cherry Pie it is."

"Nolan's right, this pie is to die for."

"Thank you Casey. I was wondering. Could you do me a favor?"

"Of course."

"Could you take Buddy for a while? I can't train Cherry Pie while she's too preoccupied with chasing his tail all over the house."

"Gram, what will he do when Casey is at work?"

"Oh. I guess I didn't think of that."

Casey liked the idea. "I have a plan. Nolan has the week off and I'm staying at the cabin after work. Let Buddy come along with us for the week so you can get the opportunity to train Cherry Pie without him being a distraction."

"Oh, what a great idea. Are you sure you don't mind?"

"Of course not. Do you mind Nolan?"

"I could use the company."

"Perfect. When can you start?"

"Tonight?"

"It's settled then. Buddy's going on vacation with the boys." Buddy lifted his ears to try and figure out what just transpired. He liked the sound of it.

"Let me get his bag of food and his Christmas toy."

They thanked Gram for the coffee and pie. With Buddy's food, toy and leash in hand, they left the kitchen door for the stairway. Casey opened the back door. "Buddy, you go pee." Buddy ran to his favorite bush in the backyard. While they waited, Casey wondered about the logistics for the week. "Now that we don't have to stop by and get Buddy for exercise, shouldn't I bring my car so you don't have to give me a ride to the base?"

"We need to arrive in one truck tonight. We can start that tomorrow. I'll come with you and we can have breakfast at your favorite dining facility."

"You mean the Choke and Puke?"

Nolan laughed as Buddy ran back inside. "Will he behave in the truck while we meet with Kevin?"

"Of course he will. Are you going to leave the engine running so he won't get cold?"

"Stretch, he has a winter fur coat."

"Are you sure?"

"I'm sure. Come on, you don't want to be late." They took off in the truck down the street. Buddy was sitting on the bench seat in the back with all his attention focused out the passenger side window.

"What if someone steals my skis out of the bed of your truck?"

"Bring them in."

Casey slid down in the seat. He was overly quiet.

"You OK?"

"I'm OK."

"No you're not."

"Just a little overwhelmed with what I said to Sawyer tonight. I think I should have said less."

"Then you'd be wasting your money. What would be the point of that?"

"Well, if I would have kept my mouth shut, I wouldn't feel so dirty right now."

Nolan took his right hand off the steering wheel and held it out. Casey ignored it.

"I'm not moving my hand until you grab it Stretch."

Casey took his left hand and put it in Nolan's. Nolan lowered their hands to rest on the bench seat. "You're a lot of things Stretch, but dirty isn't one of them."

They parked the truck in the lot where there were few cars, dinner time was over and it was a work night for many Anchorage men and women. "Buddy, you be a good boy and we'll be right back." Buddy didn't look worried, he liked keeping watch over the truck, after all it belonged to his pack. Casey grabbed the skis and looked around for Kevin's car.

"What does he drive?"

"A newer Honda CRV. Dark grey."

The CRV wasn't in the lot, they were fifteen minutes early. They were met by the manager of the club. "Evening guys. Do you want me to put your skis in the back office?"

"Thanks." Casey handed over the long skis to the young man. Nolan took off to get a secluded table where they could talk in private.

"So, Ironman, what do you and Buddy plan on doing while I'm at work all week?"

"Ironman? I like it. Is that because…?"

Casey answered with a shrug of his shoulders and two raised eyebrows.

"I plan on giving Frosty a good workout."

"Frosty? That's a strange name for your penis."

"My boyfriend is so so hilarious. Frosty's what I call the snow blower. I'm a little behind."

"Sorry Flexer, but your behind is anything but little."

"First my nose, now my ass?"

"If you remember, I told you I like your nose."

"And?"

"I like your behind even more."

Nolan's expression changed with Casey's confession.

"I meant to ask you about snow removal. How in the hell do you find the time to clear the driveway to the main road?"

"Oh, that. My dad. He contracted for a snow removal service. They always show up after a snowfall and clear the lane. All I have to do is the driveway and whatever areas I want clear around the house."

"That was very generous of him. I bet he's so proud of his sons in the service."

"He is. Mom too."

"What else do you have planned?"

"To have dinner ready for you when you arrive. To have your comfies laid out. To have your cup of hot chocolate all ready for you." He leaned close to Casey. "I plan on being your very own personal butler. To take care of every one of your needs all week."

"There they go again."

"What?"

"The chills. They just ran up my back."

"Anything you want to tell me about concerning your visit with Sawyer tonight?"

"Maybe later. But I did tell him about Ian after all."

"I thought you were going to keep that from him?"

"I was. Then at the last minute, I decided to talk about it."

"What did he say?"

"I don't think he believed my theory."

"How so?"

"He asked me to tell him what the important people in my life felt about it. Then he asked me if I took into consideration their points of view."

"Did you say yes?"

"I didn't say. He made it his point to let me know that when people come out of the closet to themselves, they frequently act with an overload of emotions. He said those emotions can take over their rational behavior for a while."

"I agree."

"I like it when you do that."

"I can agree with you sometimes."

"No. Not that. It's more fun when you don't agree with me. I like it when you talk like Chester. It makes me feel like you're comfortable around me. And for some crazy reason, that twang makes me feel safe."

"Good evening Casey." Kevin surprised them both as he approached the sensitive conversation.

"Kevin. Thank you for coming. This is my boyfriend Nolan Kelly. I've told him all about you."

Nolan stood up to shake his hand. "Nice to meet you Detective."

"Please call me Kevin." After they shook hands, they all sat down to begin the meeting.

"Can I get you a drink?"

"Thank you Nolan. A beer would be nice."

"I'll be right back."

"He seems to be a nice guy."

"He is."

"What's his specialty? It has to be something to capture Captain Link."

Casey touched his chest. "Here. Don't ask me why, but he made it inside of here."

"Ah yes. The place I couldn't find."

Casey reached over to touch his arm. "Don't go and blame yourself. You're a great guy Kevin. The only mistake you made was to get hooked by a really screwed up one."

Nolan came back with Kevin's beer.

"Thanks Nolan. So Casey tells me you're a pilot?"

"That's right, I fly the F 22 Raptor."

"A man who moves faster than the speed of sound."

"Well, not always, the sonic boom can get us into a shit load of trouble."

"You have a very strong Southern accent. Can I ask where you're from?"

"Georgia. I'm a country boy from the start."

"Well, not the very beginning, he was born in Berlin during the Cold War."

"Are you German?"

"No. My dad was stationed in the Army. He worked at the AFN Berlin Radio station. So I was born on an Army base."

"Very interesting, do you speak German?"

"Only the bad words. I left Berlin before I turned one year old."

Kevin returned his attention to Casey. "I found something out this morning."

"Go on please."

"I have an acquaintance at Starbucks downtown. He works the early morning shift."

Casey leaned forward on the table. “The place the two emails came from? The IP address, right?”

“Yes. My friend told me there was a group of trans people who came into the coffee bar on New Year’s day. He said there was a guy, or gal with Ian’s complexion, height and weight. But he didn’t get any names.”

“How many of them?”

“Three.”

“How accurate would his memory be on customers from the first?”

“I asked him about that. He said he shamefully stared at them the whole time. He said he was fascinated by the trans community.”

“Has he seen the group in the bar after that?”

“No.”

“Did they pay with a credit card?”

“No. Cash.”

Casey took the two bank statements out of his pocket. “Can you check on the debit card and credit card transactions since I received the first email?”

“I can. But only if I open an investigation.”

“Then do it. Can you contact the parents?”

“I will if this becomes official.”

Nolan entered into the conversation. “Don’t you risk freaking out his parents if what lan is doing is by his own will?”

“We do,” answered Kevin.

“If I were a parent, I’d want to be notified. Even if it would cause me great worry.”

“I’m going to talk with the landlord tomorrow. After I turn the case in to my boss.”

“Nolan and I spoke with a young guy in the house. We didn’t ask about lan. He gave me his mail.”

“I’ll need all that mail. Do you have it with you?”

“No. Only these two. You can keep those. I have the rest in a bag at my apartment.”

“Casey, it’s possible my boss won’t agree to an investigation and I can’t do it without his authorization. You have to be prepared for that. We deal with missing persons all the time. And I don't want to upset you, but this is looking like a guy who decided to cut all ties with his old life and begin a new one. Even if it is on the extreme."

"I understand."

"Something else. If I open an investigation, I have to talk with base personnel about this guy's life style. I'll have to expose his transgendered side."

"I know. I thought about that. If he's on the run, it won't matter, and if he's a victim of foul play, then we can't hold anything back that might help him. So do what you have to."

"I thought you would say that."

"What about his car? Isn't it strange you haven't been able to track it down?"

"Maybe."

They discussed options for about an hour. It was obvious Kevin wasn't leaning towards the foul play theory. "Well, I better get on my way. Casey, I'll call you tomorrow and let you know what my boss says. Nolan, it was nice to meet you. You're a lucky guy."

"Nice to meet you too. And I know it."

Kevin stood up and left the table after giving Casey a reassuring pat on the shoulder. He held no hard feelings towards him for being honest.

Casey locked his eyes on the far corner of the bar. Nolan sat saying nothing.

"Thanks."

"For what?"

"For being polite. For coming with me. Maybe this was difficult for you."

"I told you, aah, forget it. Should we get back and start a fire?"

"You have any hot chocolate?"

"You know I do." They left the bar to find Buddy sitting on the back bench of the truck with his eyes glued to the entrance of the bar. The one where his pack disappeared into an hour before.

Casey tapped on the window. “Hi Buddy. Just wait until you see where we’re going tonight. You’re going to love it.”

The drive north took a half an hour. Casey slid down in the seat and said nothing the whole way home. Until they pulled into the freshly plowed private lane. The first thing he saw of the house was the lit up Christmas tree in the front of the glass covered cabin. “Oh my God. We have to do something about that tonight.”

“Tonight?”

“Well. At least pull the plug.”

“Whew. I wasn’t planning on doing any work tonight.”

There were two bags of groceries in the bed of the truck. Mostly snacks. Casey let Buddy out who immediately proceeded to investigate the cabin grounds.

“He’s really going to love it here.”

“So are you.”

They walked up the front steps and opened the glass door. Buddy had to inspect the whole house like a soldier on a top level mission.

“I need to get my laundry out of the truck.”

“Let me pull the truck in the garage for the night. We can get everything after that. I’m expecting a call from Chester. If the phone rings, answer it for me.”

“You have a land line?”

“There, on the wall by the fridge.”

“OK. I’ll start putting the groceries away.”

Nolan left for the garage from the inside and Buddy took off after him. The garage was another new zone.

Casey laughed to himself. *All snack food. We’re going to need a shopping list if we plan to eat good food this week.* His thoughts were interrupted with the ring of the phone on the wall with the cordless receiver. He grabbed the phone and answered it.

“Hello”

“Hello. Am I talken with Casey?”

“I’m Casey. Nolan is parking the truck.”

“I’m his dad. Should I call back?”

"No sir. I hear him coming now."

"Been doin any fishin up there?"

"No sir. Truth is, I don't know how."

"That settles it, I'm coming up there and we gonna cut a hole in the ice. What do you say?"

"I could give it a try. Oh, here's Nolan. Nice to talk with you."

"Same here. Don't go and forget about that ice fishin. We'll make Noley cut the ice. Those muscles have to be good for something."

"Alright." He passed the phone to Nolan.

"Chester?"

"No, it's your dad."

Nolan grabbed the phone and began walking in circles around Casey who leaned up against the counter in awe of who he just spoke to. He'd never even seen a celebrity in his life up close. And here he was talking on the phone to one of the biggest music stars in the world, Bobby Kelly, like family.

"Hi dad. Everything OK?"

"Chester said you sold our dirt bikes."

"Yeah, he's a BSer. I got a plan for that one."

"We're going out with his girlfriend tomorrow night."

"She's a nice girl. You and mom would like her."

"I think so."

"Ice fishing? Dad, we don't get much time off. Maybe on the weekends though. Can't you bring a buddy?"

"He might want to. I'll ask him."

Casey cut in. "Ask him if your mom received the rug yet."

"Dad, did the rug show up yet?" He shook his head yes to Casey.

"Casey picked it out. You know me when it comes to pretty things. I had my eye on a blue unicorn. But Casey put his foot down."

"OK Dad. I love you too. Talk later." He walked the phone back to the wall rack.

"You really love your dad, don't you?"

"I sure do. How are you with ice fishing?"

"Ignorant as hell."

"No matter. Do you want some hot chocolate?"

"I'll make it, if you start a fire."

"Deal." Buddy followed Nolan to the garage to get some dry wood.

Casey found a pan to heat the milk. Nolan worked on the fire. "Hey Ironman, when did you house clean? I was expecting the same condition I found before your parents came for Christmas."

"Oh, about that." Nolan was able to talk across the open room. "Mom wasn't too happy with Chester and my housekeeping skills. She contracted a cleaning service to come once a week, every Thursday. They do everything except the laundry. And trust me when I tell you, they were here this morning."

"You lucky devil."

He stood up and gave Casey the eye trick from across the room where Casey was watching him. "Yes I am." Buddy was completely intrigued by the task of moving wood around inside the house.

"Your dad knew my name."

"I told you, I tell my dad everything, or almost everything."

"Does your mom know about me too?"

"Of course."

"The hot chocolate is ready. Can we push the couch in front of the fire?"

"Done." Nolan moved the couch so it was facing the fire about seven feet away.

"Let me feed Buddy and I'll be right over." He took Buddy's bowl and put two cups of food inside. Buddy heard the bag crinkle and ran to the open kitchen. "Don't worry, starting tomorrow, it's people food. You're on vacation." Buddy had his head above the bowl and probably didn't get the message.

"Come on Stretch, we need to have our comfies on for this. Follow me."

"I haven't seen your bedroom yet. I'm curious." He grabbed his bag and followed Nolan up the stairs. Nolan's bedroom was over to the left side of the house.

"Come on in, this is it."

Casey entered into a large room with a queen sized bed made from an iron frame with copper bars for the headboard. There was a sixty inch TV mounted on the wall facing the bed. The large window faced the forest to the side of the house. The carpeting was dark brown. The walk in closet was as large as Casey's complete bedroom. "You have a bathroom in your bedroom?"

"All the bedrooms have a bathroom."

Casey walked inside the large room. There was an oval whirlpool style tub and a glass enclosed shower to the back. A double sink on the marble counter. The floor was covered with a dark earth toned tile. The walls were a combination of plaster and green tiles. "Is that a bathtub or a swimming pool?"

"I never use it. I like the shower."

"So I guess bubble baths are out of the question."

"Not with you around they're not. Can you imagine what we could do in there?"

"I already imagined it."

Nolan came from behind and began taking off Casey's clothes. Casey moved away to get his sweats out of the bag. "Let's hurry up and change, the hot chocolate is going to get cold."

"OK Stretch. You're in charge this week." They threw on their sweats and left the bedroom to find the fire and their cups of hot chocolate. Buddy was busy giving the whole upstairs his inspection. He followed the guys down the open stairs with a view out the glass front to the mountains. Or the nighttime view of the stars and on good nights, the northern lights.

Nolan picked up on Casey's somber mood in the truck. So he controlled his urge to get naked and grab the tall guy in his arms.

Back by the fire, Nolan turned off the lights and they both sat on the leather couch. In the middle and side by side.

"The hot chocolate is good Captain Link."

"It hits the spot doesn't it?"

There was a huge leather footstool in front of the couch. Nolan placed one of his legs over on top of Casey's. He stared into the flames of the fire.

"Your dad called you Noley."

"He does that. Ever since I was a baby."

"To him you still are his baby. Can you imagine what it would be like to love your children and have to face the fact that they grew up? His three baby sons are grown military men. Risking their lives for their country. And all the time he can see the image of you boys taking your first steps. Or teenagers burning down the garage. I bet being a parent can be the biggest joy in the world."

Nolan put his arm around Casey's shoulder. He kept quiet.

"Can I call you Noley sometimes?"

"As long as it doesn't take the place of Ironman. And you can't do it around others. Especially Chester. With his big mouth, he'll blab that all over the place."

A few minutes passed with no words. Buddy laid in front of the fire and liked the warmth it gave. He kept one eye open on his two pack members close by.

"Today has been a rough day for me. I feel emotionally exhausted."

"I can tell. Does it help having me around?"

Casey slid over to rest his body on the side of Nolan's. "It does."

"I'm your superhero Stretch. Don't forget it."

"I won't."

Nolan slid down a bit to get more comfortable.

"What happens if I run into Ines someday, all dressed up and looking pretty? Maybe in the grocery store, or at Mad Myrna's? Do we pretend like we don't know each other? Do we go for a hug and say how nice it is to see each other?"

Nolan kept quiet and rubbed his shoulder.

"If I skip the run tomorrow, will you make sure Buddy gets some exercise around the house?"

"Sure. Maybe I'll take him for a ski outing on the trails around the cabin."

"That would be nice."

Casey closed his eyes and let the sound of the crackling wood in the fire soothe his mind. He fell asleep nestled up to Nolan's side.

Nolan let him sleep for a few minutes. Until he moved his arm and woke him up. "Come on Stretch, let's hit the sack."

"Did I fall asleep?"

"You did."

"We need to let Buddy out for a pee before we go upstairs."

"I'll go." He led Buddy to the front door and let him out. Buddy ran down to the closest tree and lifted his leg. He ran back upstairs not wanting to get left outside in the unfamiliar place. Nolan let him in, and pulled Casey off the couch. They turned off all the lights and climbed the stairs to Nolan's room.

"Do you have an alarm?"

"What time do you want to get up?"

"Five? If we plan to eat at the Puke and Choke, we need to get there by six."

"It's the other way around, the Choke and Puke. I'll set it for 4:30 so we can have a nice cup of coffee before we leave."

"You're the greatest Noley." He rolled over and let Nolan drape an arm over his side. "The greatest." Casey fell asleep in less than ten minutes. Nolan on the other hand laid awake in bed. Happier than he ever felt in his entire life, as the words "the greatest" echoed over and over again in his head.

Early morning arrived and Nolan didn't need the alarm clock to wake him. He laid in bed for a half an hour staring at the stars out the bedroom window until the buzz caused Casey to roll over.

"Morning Noley."

"Morning Stretch."

"Is it really 4:30 already? I wish I could stay in this bed all day."

"Call in sick."

"Now who's so so silly. You know there's no such thing as calling in sick with the military, and I don't feel like going to the hospital to get put on bed rest."

"Did you get a good night's sleep?"

"I must have. I feel so much better than last night."

"You were really upset. So no bad dreams, right?"

"I did have a dream, but it wasn't a bad one."

"Tell me about it. Was I naked?"

Casey laughed. "You were dressed. That was the normal part of the dream. Damn, now that I'm awake, I see how weird this one was."

"But not bad?"

"No. You got out of the bed, not naked, and went to the dresser. The dresser in my apartment. You took a knife. I got out of bed and waited for you. You brought me the knife and I took it. You smiled at me."

"That was it? You better pay more attention before you fall asleep. I was naked in the bed all night. I should have been naked your dream too. So no sex?"

"No sex. But there was something else. Then I believe I woke up?"

"And?"

"I dropped the knife. It went straight down for my bare foot, but I woke up before it landed."

"Damn. I was hoping I got a nice blow job. Maybe later. Come on, get up, take a shower and I'll go down and make the coffee."

"Thanks Ironman. Let Buddy out first, OK?"

"Yes sir." Nolan crawled naked out of the bed.

"My God you have a beautiful ass."

Nolan turned around to stare at him with his standard eye trick. "Yeah?"

"Buddy needs to go out. He can't wait."

He mumbled something under his breath, slipped on his sweats and took Buddy downstairs.

Casey was surprised Nolan didn't put the move on him as was his usual self. But he didn't complain. His emotions were in a turmoil, and he wasn't even sure what or who was the culprit.

The smell of the coffee greeted Casey as he came down the stairs. "You should have warned me that your shower has six different locations where the water comes out."

"Did you like it?"

"Yes."

"Buddy did his thing."

"Both things?"

"Yes."

"We on for the date with Candy and Chester tonight?"

"If you want."

"I do." Casey sat at the breakfast bar between the kitchen open space and the living room. "The coffee smells great. Is there hazelnut in there?"

"Yes."

"Do you have a pen and paper handy?"

"Why?"

"I think we should brainstorm and make a shopping list. If I'm going to be here all week, we'll need a food plan. Healthy food. And steak for Buddy, it's his vacation."

"Are you coming shopping with me?"

"I can if you want, but you have to go to the base with me, why not do the shopping while you're there?"

"I can."

They both added items to the list while each having two cups of coffee.

"Should Buddy come along with us to the base?"

"If you don't mind him shedding so much in your truck. He'd like it."

"No problem,"

"I'll vacuum and clean the inside of your truck before the week's out. I owe you one."

"For what?"

Casey took a swig from his coffee cup. "For being you."

Nolan threw him the eye movement.

"In fact, you being you has me feeling like someone other than me. I have a plan for you when I get home tonight."

"A surprise?"

"Yes. A surprise, Nolan style."

"Oh damn, this has to be good."

Casey raised his eyebrows without making a smile. "Maybe. Maybe not."

Nolan grabbed his cock through his sweatpants.

Casey got up to go and dress in his blues. "Better keep your hands off that thing while I'm at work."

"Yes sir."

"Do pushups instead."

"Yes sir."

Nolan drove Casey to his apartment to get the Subaru, then they both drove to the Iditarod for breakfast. By 6:50 a.m., Casey was in line at the hospital cafeteria getting his cup of coffee. He glanced over to the corner of the seating area to find the base commander in his civvies, having a cup of coffee and staring at him. He paid for the coffee and left for his office. He decided he would tell the Major of his discovery concerning the commander.

"Good morning Sergeant Tomlin. Is the Major in yet?"

"Good morning Captain. He's in his office."

"Thanks." Casey first went to his own office to drop off his backpack. Checked his email. Then walked across the hall to the Major's office.

"Good morning Major."

"Good morning Casey. TGIF, right?"

"You can say that again."

"Skiing on for this weekend?"

"Yes sir. Do you mind if I ask you a question?"

"Go ahead."

"Do you remember when we had that Staff Sergeant in the summer who came up HIV positive?"

"Yes."

"He was denied his petition to stay on at JBER because it was considered an overseas assignment."

"This is true. They wouldn't bend. Casey, you saw it didn't you?"

"Yes sir. That's what I wanted to tell you. I was reviewing records and I saw it. I didn't want to keep it from you."

"OK. Now one more person knows, but it won't go any farther, will it?"

"Correct. What are his chances of staying on as the base commander?"

"Nil to none. He's got in twenty years, and he purchased a home north of town. I didn't ask but I think he'll retire and stick around here for a while."

"I feel sorry for the guy. Not the way he would have imagined ending his career."

"So true. What concerned me the most is he reacted like it was a death sentence. Like we were living the eighties. I had to explain to him how medication can allow him to live a good life. But I don't think he believed me."

"How long do you think he'll be in his position?"

"I give it less than a week. His results were in right after Christmas. His records have already been sent to HQ ALCOM."

Casey understood any military person acquiring the HIV virus while on active duty was allowed to stay. However there would be no deployments and no overseas assignments. JBER was considered to be an overseas assignment and the DOD was steadfast on sticking with the rule.

"Any idea of who would be his replacement?"

"No clue."

"Well, I better check for patients. I just wanted you to know I saw it."

"Good move. Anybody else on staff know about this?"

"No sir."

"Keep it that way. Now let's hope for a smooth day."

By 8:00, Casey got a call on his cell phone from Kevin while he was in his office.

"Hi Kevin. Any good news?"

"Yes and no. It was nice seeing you last night."

"Is that the good news or the bad news?"

Kevin laughed. "I have permission from my boss to open an investigation."

"Now that's good news."

"I'm on my way over to the base this morning to talk to the commander of the Office of Special Investigations, (OSI). I plan on making a stop at his place on the way to get some information from the landlord. What do you say we meet for lunch?"

"That would be fantastic. Give me a text when you're ready and I can meet you at the Military Mall Food Court."

"Roger that Captain."

"Did you hear that in the movies?"

"Yes. See you at lunch."

"Looking forward to it Detective. We can discuss the Vic over a coffee."

By ten, Casey checked for any messages after attending to a sergeant from the Air National Guard who was a boom operator on the tanker. He had a serious throat infection. There was a text from Nolan.

"Shopping complete. My hands are itching for some action."

He wrote the reply. *"Keep your hands off that thing. Do chin ups instead."*

The reply was swift. *"Fine. But I'm going to need some serious medical attention when you get here."*

Casey laughed. *"Be careful what you wish for, Captain Kelly!"*

After working on a few records for the Army helicopter pilots, Casey received a text from Kevin.

"Mission complete. Lunch?"

He sent the reply, *"I'm ready, on my way to the Mall Food Court now."* He grabbed the paper bag with Ian's mail.

"Sergeant Tomlin, I'm off for my lunch hour. I've got my cell phone if you need me."

"Yes sir."

In minutes Casey was parked at the mall. He forgot to call Candy about the meeting. So he stopped in at the barber shop first.

"Hi Candy. Will you be free anytime soon for lunch?"

"Hi Sweetie. I can take off as soon as I finish up this nice looking Guard guy. Why are the Guard guys so much better looking than the active duty ones?"

The guard guy smiled and Casey rolled his eyes. "I'll be at a table. Kevin is joining us for lunch with some info we need."

"Give me five."

Casey left to find Kevin. "Hello Detective Lippman. Thanks for coming."

"You're welcome Captain Link."

"Any trouble getting on base?"

"No. The shiny badge."

"Right. I brought the bag with Ian's mail for you to take. Should we get lunch before we exchange notes?"

"Good plan."

Both guys decided on a sandwich from Charley's Grilled Subs. They returned to the table to find Candy with a slice of pizza.

"Hi Kevin. Nice to see you again."

"Hi Candy. Likewise."

They talked about the weather for a while as they ate. It was Kevin who began the discussion on Ian. "I talked to the landlord at Ian's place before getting here. He said he spoke with Ian on New Year's Eve morning."

"That would be before I left for Turkey. Before he sent me the email."

"He didn't mention anything odd about Ian, so I asked what he was wearing. He was dressed in men's clothing."

"Is it important we find out if the landlord has ever seen him dressed like a woman?"

"Yes, but not right yet. I'm sure I'll be back talking to them later on."

"Anything else?"

"Yes Casey. He told him he'd be gone for a while and paid the man two months rent in advance."

"Two months in advance?"

Candy was quiet as she listened to every word of the two way conversation.

"That's right."

"So he planned on returning?"

"Maybe. Maybe not."

"More so maybe."

"I talked with the head of the base OSI. He filled out a report. I gave them both your names as points of contact."

"Oh my God, did you give them Nolan's name?"

"I should have, but I didn't. Casey, is Nolan out at the fighter squadron?"

"No. Not at all."

"Alright. We'll leave him out of it. What about you?"

"I'm not out, but it doesn't matter. If I have to out myself to help find Ian, I'm OK with it."

"Alright. Keep in mind, you don't have to out yourself by admitting you have a friend who is transgendered. I don't know the legal UCMJ rules, but I do know it's permissible to be gay and serve your country."

"Yes and no. I think the other pilots would eat Nolan for lunch if they knew."

Candy spoke up. “They’d try, but he’d eat them first. And Chester would grab a fork and help out.”

“Well, let’s hope we can safely keep him out of this. Worse case scenario is he’s a friend of a friend who knows lan.”

“Casey one other thing. OSI will be contacting his parents. They have access to his home records.”

“Alright. Do you think they would pass to them my contact information?”

“They might. Can’t hurt to ask.”

“Could you get it from them?”

“I think I could.”

“I’ll wait. If you get the contact info, you can pass my number to them.” Casey took a deep breath. “This is good. We sure as hell haven’t gotten anywhere up to this point. Thanks so much Kevin.”

“Guys, we’re going to solve the case. We might not like what we find, but at least everyone can move on in the end.”

“I agree Detective. I mean Kevin.” Candy liked calling him Detective.

“Well, I better get back to my office.”

“Kevin, what about the bank statements?”

“I’ll call you later today or tomorrow with that.” He got up from the table.

“Like I said. You’re a great guy Kevin.”

Kevin threw him a mock military salute and left the food court for his car.

“Well, Sweetie, that was interesting. Do you still believe Ian isn’t acting of his own free will?”

“I’m trying to keep an open mind. In the end it doesn’t matter what any of us think as long as we keep objective and take it step by step. Kevin will solve this thing. I’m sure of it.”

“Good attitude Sweetie. How’s Buddy liking the forest retreat?”

“He loves it. How’s Cherry Pie?”

“She peed in my room this morning. Just lovely.”

"Give her a chance. God only knows what those dogs had to endure before the shelter."

"I know. I do like her."

"Gram has a big heart. It shows with her love for dogs."

"And for us too. I better get back to the boys. This world wouldn't be a safe place if the soldiers didn't all have a fresh haircut."

"See you tonight. What time does the Kelly boy arrive?"

"Should be around four."

"You picking him up?"

"I hope to."

"Hey, if he comes in late and doesn't have time to run to the cabin before the pub, take him to our place and have him shower and change in my apartment."

"Nice plan. I'll ask him. Could save some time."

"You packed for the weekend?"

"Been ready for two days now."

"We're going to have a good time. See you at Reilly's."

"Later Sweetie." She left the table and returned to the barber shop. Casey sat by himself at the table and tried to absorb the lunch meeting. He was happy with the progress. But he was a little stressed out too. It was looking more and more like Ian wished him to stay away.

By 2:30 p.m., Casey sent Nolan a text. *"Slow day. Zoomies are healthy this week. Leaving the office at 3:00. Candy and I had a good visit with Detective Lippman. See you soon Noley.*

The reply was immediate. *"Can hardly wait. Been one hell of a long day."*

Casey smiled at the message from the guy he previously knew as Delta Hotel. Now better known as the loving son of a descent, well adjusted family. Noley.

Casey pulled up the freshly plowed lane to the cabin. Nolan was over to the side pulling the snow blower into the garage. Buddy was running in circles looking for rabbits.

"Hey Buddy!"

He came running up to greet Casey. "Did you take good care of our boy while I was gone?" Buddy wiggled his whole body to give the answer.

"Come on Stretch, I have your dinner all ready."

"You do?"

"I told you. Part of my plan for the week."

They both entered into the cabin via the garage door. Nolan grabbed Casey and gave him a hug. "Can you feel that?"

"I'm afraid to ask." Nolan was wearing his commando jeans.

"Very funny. I'm talking about my arms. I busted my ass on my arms this morning. They feel tight as hell."

"You're going to have to get that parka off before I give you a rating." They left the garage and entered into the warm house.

"Run upstairs and get your comfies on. I'll get the soup ready."

Casey raised his eyebrows and did as he was told. Minutes later he entered the kitchen with his sweats on.

"Sit right down Stretch. Almost ready." He stirred the pan. Casey could see the two empty cans of Campbell's Tomato soup. Nolan poured the soup in two bowls and set them on the table. He then grabbed a plate from out of the oven. Four grilled cheese sandwiches.

"This is a first for me."

"No it's not. I've made these for you before. Don't tell me you already forgot?"

"No. I wouldn't forget. I was referring to coming home from work and having dinner prepared and set on the table for me. You're amazing."

"Thank you. Eat up, don't let the soup get cold."

"Did you have time to feed Buddy?"

"Yes I did. He had steak."

"Please tell me you didn't fry it."

"No. I cut it up in small pieces and put it into his bowl."

"Raw?"

"Yeah. He loved it."

"Did you mix it with anything?"

"Like what?"

"I read online we need to mix his food with fruit and vegetables. So that only seventy-five percent is protein."

"We can do that. Oh, fuck, the veggies." Nolan got up to get the pan of corn out of the oven. He put an ample amount into each dish and set them on the table.

"This is great. Did you plan for desert?"

"Of course I did. It's a surprise."

"The sandwich is superb."

"Thank you."

"Candy and I met with Kevin for lunch today at the food court."

"I know, you told me."

"His boss approved to open an investigation."

Nolan shook his head up and down with his mouth full.

"He talked with the landlord this morning. The landlord said Ian spoke with him on the thirty-first. He told him he was going to be away for a while, and he paid the guy two months rent in advance."

Nolan stopped chewing and stared at Casey. He didn't say what he was thinking.

"Kevin also spoke with the OSI on base. He gave them mine and Candy's name as a point of contact."

Nolan stopped chewing again and stared at Casey.

"He didn't give them your name. He said he'd keep you out of this."

Nolan shook his head up and down.

"I might have to out myself during the investigation. Will you be able to hang around with me if I do?"

Nolan swallowed. "Fuck yes. Let anyone try and stop me. Dude, my definition of being in the closet is me not saying I'm gay. Period. I don't care if someone sees me blowing you in the truck. As far as I'm concerned, if I don't say I'm gay, I'm in the closet."

"Alright. But just to be safe, let's be careful with that truck scene."

They finished the main course. Nolan smiled and went to the cabinet. He got out a package of Oreos. "My favorite cookie. Aside from Gram's that is. Do you want coffee or milk to go with them?"

"Coffee. And thank you. I love those too."

"Don't mention it Stretch."

Casey noticed Nolan was walking funny. "Did you hurt yourself today?"

"No. Why?"

"You're walking like you fell down or something."

"No. It's my balls. They're a little sore."

"And why?"

"It's nothing. I think I have a mild case of epy hyper balls. Go ahead and enjoy your cookies and coffee."

Casey rolled his eyes and jumped off the bar stool. He walked up to Nolan who was busy getting the coffee ready. "Hold still." Casey put his arms around Nolan and reached over to his front. He slipped both hands under his baggy jeans and down to the place where the Amazon Jungle began. Nolan froze in place, with his breathing greatly accelerated. Casey went farther down, past his cock and to his furry balls. He began to feel both testicles. To make the evaluation easier, he slipped the hands back up and undid the snap and zipper of the commando jeans. The jeans hit the floor and Nolan was now naked from his waist to his ankles.

Casey reached below his balls and pushed with his fingers in the space between the ball sack and what Nolan referred to as the sweet spot. "Turn your head and cough."

"For real?"

"Turn your head and cough Captain Kelly."

He did as he was told. "I thought you said you don't do this."

"Only with special patients. Now cough once more."

Nolan coughed.

Casey stood up. “Pull your pants up Captain Nolan and finish your dinner. There is nothing wrong with you or your testicles.”

“Ah, Doc, I don’t want to complain about the service, but you didn’t have your hand on my balls when you told me to cough.”

“The cough has nothing to do with your balls. Your balls feel hard as rock. There isn’t any fluid backed up in those to cause you any pain. Remember, I know what your balls feel like when they’re engorged. Your balls are fine. I think your discomfort is all in your head.”

“Suit yourself, but I say my balls need a release. And why did you tell me to turn and cough if you thought there wasn’t a problem?”

The coffee was ready and they both sat for desert. “Do you know why the doctor has you turn your head and cough?”

“Yes. So you don’t cough in his face.”

“That’s part of it. He’s not checking anything about your testicles. He’s checking for a inguinal hernia.”

“And here I thought he was trying to cop a freebie. I mean, straight or gay, who wouldn’t want to get their hands on my boys.”

“He’s not trying to get a freebie. He’s trying to feel your inguinal ring.”

“You’re speaking Chinese Stretch.”

We have a place on both sides of our lower abdomen. The inguinal canal, right above the testicles, where the torso meets the leg. It’s the same canal where the spermatic cord passes through, attached to the testicles, where there’s an opening. If there is a tear in the wall, soft tissue, particularly the lower intestines can come through. Thus, a hernia. It’s very common among men. Seventy to eighty percent of all hernia cases fall into this category. But don’t worry, your inguinal ring is in top shape. Same as your balls.

“Well thank you for the evaluation Doc, but I still say I have a problem with backed up fluids in by balls.”

There was a text message from Candy. *"Hi Sweetie. Chester is an hour late. I'll take him to your apartment, scrub him up, change his clothes and we'll drive over to Reilly's from my place. See you soon."*

"Candy. Chester was an hour late. She's going to scrub him up at my place and they'll meet us at Reilly's."

"Scrub him up?" Nolan lifted his one eye.

"Change his clothes too."

"Maybe you better send her a message telling them to go ahead and order without us. We can meet them for drinks."

"OK." Casey sent the reply.

Nolan got up to massage Casey's neck. "Did you like the dinner?"

"One of the best I ever had. Actually it was the best."

"Cool."

"Oh. Where did you learn to do that?"

Nolan ignored the question and leaned down to get in a good hug and a kiss on the neck.

"I have that surprise I told you about in my bag upstairs."

"The surprise is in a bag?"

Casey smiled. "Yes. Want to follow me up and get it?"

"I'm right behind you." Casey heard him mumble the words, "In a bag?"

"Did you say anything?"

"No sir. So let me guess what's in the bag. Rubbers?"

"No."

"Lube?"

"No."

They entered into Nolan's bedroom and Casey went to his bag. He pulled out a small package wrapped in white paper. "I hope you like it." Casey went to the door and told Buddy, "Go and find your toy." Buddy took off down the stairs and Casey shut the door behind him.

Nolan opened the package to find the black t shirt with the white letters BLOW ME on the front.

"No way. I love it."

"Put it on."

He took off his t shirt and replaced it with the new one.

Casey shook his head.

"Well?"

"I think it's crude to give a guy oral sex without getting kissed first."

Nolan grabbed him. They pulled in tight with their arms to kiss. It was Casey who pushed back. He used both his hands to slip down Nolan's commando jeans. He was already hard. Casey took his time with getting the hard cock in his hands and feeling his balls. He played with the guy's dense bush, making sure any loose hairs were knocked to the ground. One of the disadvantages of oral sex with a hairy guy before taking a shower.

Nolan was breathing hard. His tight belly was moving in and out. Casey slid down and placed his nose deep in his bush and inhaled. Nolan pulled off his present and threw it on the floor. Now all that was left were the two white socks.

Casey placed both his hands on the guy's hard smooth ass cheeks. He put the head of Nolan's cock in his mouth and swirled his tongue in a circular motion.

Nolan moaned with his hands on top of his head. "Damn it Stretch if you don't have me hornier than a two peckered billy goat."

Casey went further. He made it the whole way. Standing up, he pushed the guy back. "Get on the bed Nolan Kelly."

"Yes sir Captain Bossy."

Casey took off the guy's socks, then took off his own. After getting completely naked, he crawled on top of Nolan, putting both hands on the muscular chest. "You have beautiful muscles Nolan Kelly." He bent down to lightly tease a nipple with his tongue.

Nolan grabbed him and rolled him over. He straddled Casey with his hips. He flexed both his biceps. “Are you saying my body turns you on?”

“Completely. Now scoot your butt up here and get your cock into my mouth.”

“Yes sir.” Nolan scooted his ass up to Casey’s chest. He stopped at the right place for Casey to do what he wanted to do. Nolan looked around for the towel. He forgot it. But Casey’s t shirt was on the bed. He grabbed it and put it by his side. It didn’t take long for Casey to get the first taste of salty fluid in his mouth. It was Nolan’s decision to pull back. He moaned and began shooting squirts aimed at Casey’s neck. Several thick shots of hot come hit his body. Nolan grabbed the t shirt and cleaned part of it away, but not until some dripped down and reached the blanket on the bed. He finished. He sat back on his ass so Casey could feel the hottest part of his rear end pressed tightly against his chest. Nolan moved his ass cheeks in a way to make that happen.

He reached over and kissed Casey full on the lips. Then he reached back and grabbed the guy’s long slender cock. “My turn.”

Nolan crawled back as he stuck his thumb in his mouth to lube it with spit. He found Casey’s sweet spot with the soaked thumb and gently pushed. Casey reached down and pulled his hand away. So Nolan move on with getting a cock in his mouth. Casey lifted his legs on both sides of Nolan’s face. The stubble added to the excitement, the combination of his soft lips with his rough face made things go faster. He gave Nolan the warning, but Nolan kept at it, not letting go. Casey came in his mouth. Nolan used his hand to finish the task while spitting in the already soaked t shirt. Throwing the t shirt on the floor, he scooted up and covered Casey’s body with his own. His muscles were heavy.

“Would it be a risk of over inflating your ego if I told you you’re the sexiest fighter pilot in the squadron?”

"No. Because I already know it." Nolan was giving his version of grinding his private parts against Casey's.

Casey had his hands on Nolan's ass. "Are you sure you don't shave your butt?"

"I'm sure. But when you get a closer look, you'll find what I got up front does reach my sweet spot."

"I already noticed." Casey moved his hands up to the top of Nolan's back. Then to his biceps. "I'm worried about something."

"What are you worried about Stretch?"

"Us."

Nolan lifted his head up to get a good look into Casey's eyes? "What the hell for?"

"I'm worried I won't be able to give you what you need."

"Are we talking about sex?"

"Yes."

"Damn it anyway. Didn't I already tell you all I need is to be next to you naked, and to know you want me?"

"You did. But sometimes you say things to be nice."

"What I said, I meant. What the hell do you think I was doing before I met you?"

"Not sure."

"Well, I'll tell you. I was jacking off to porn. Every night. Do you really think that compares to what you just did for me?"

"But you said you liked fucking guys in the ass."

"I do. But I also love getting a blow job from my boyfriend. Casey, please don't get me started worrying about you worrying about me."

"OK."

"Good. That's settled then."

"I really need you Noley. I don't ever want to feel like I felt when I heard your jet take off from Turkey. When we didn't say goodbye. It hurt. I never felt like that before."

"We need each other Stretch. Life sucks without that special someone. It really sucks."

"You said you were going to take care of all my needs this week."

"And I meant it."

"Then shampoo my hair."

Nolan grabbed the dish soap and put some in the palm of his hand. He told Casey to close his eyes and began to do what Casey asked of him. When he finished Casey took the bottle and did the same for him. Before long, they were both squeaky clean from the Irish Spring and the blue bottle of Dawn.

"I think we better finish and get dressed for tonight."

"Come on, I want to try out the towels I bought." He passed through the glass door of the shower first and grabbed a towel folded on the table to the side. "Come here Stretch." He dried Casey's body from top to bottom, taking extra care to dry everyplace between his legs.

Nolan handed Casey the towel. "I think you better make sure my ass crack is dry." He turned around and leaned on the sink. "It won't bite Captain Link."

Casey laughed. But he liked the idea of getting a good look at the most perfect ass he ever saw. In and out of the flight suit.

He dried off both butt cheeks, especially the top part of the crack.

"I think you missed a part Captain Link."

Casey used the towel to dry the full length of his ass crack, getting a good look as he did. He already knew the crack was as smooth as a baby's ass until he reached what Nolan referred to as the sweet spot. Then the Amazon jungle took hold. "Done."

Nolan turned around. "Do you still like my crack?"

Casey raised his eyes and shook his head yes. "What are you going to wear tonight?"

"I thought my special Cinch jeans."

"Those really compliment your rear end. Almost as much as your flight suit when you go commando."

"It's settled then. Cinch jeans it is. Do you want me to go commando?"

"Not in close fitting jeans. But a tight t shirt would go nicely with them?"

"I'm here to please you Captain Link."

"I'm finding that out."

"Chester sent me a text to ask if we were going with them after dinner to Mad Myrna's?"

"Yuk. I don't like that place. Too crowded."

"We don't have to."

"Do you want to?"

"It might be fun with Chester and Candy."

"OK. We go. But I hate dancing."

"I don't care. We can sit and watch. I'm not as big on dancing like my brother is. He must have got the dancing gene while I got the double dare me gene."

They both got dressed and left the upstairs, much to Buddy's delight. He didn't understand being kept out of a room.

"Do you think we have enough food for the weekend?"

"If we don't, I can send my brother out on a shopping spree."

"Can we make a stop at the drugstore on the way to the pub?"

"Why?"

"Because I want some candles. And some shampoo. And some bubble bath too."

"What's wrong with my shampoo?"

"Nolan, that's dish soap. It's going to dry out your scalp. Besides, I want something that makes your scalp smell like fresh fruit."

"You want me to smell like a fruit?"

"Would you prefer flowers?"

"Fruity will do just fine. Jeez. I guess we're going to start eating in the dark."

"I was thinking of the swimming pool in your bathroom. Surrounded by bubbles and the light of candles. So romantic, right?"

He gave Casey the eye trick.

"Nolan, I don't mean to snoop, but is Chester's room in order?"

"The cleaning service goes in there. It should be."

"What about clean bedding? You said they don't do laundry."

"I don't know."

"Alright, go in there, strip the bed and get the sheets in the wash. Come on, I'll get the washer ready."

"He never did any of this for me."

"Make him buy you drinks tonight."

"I will." Nolan went upstairs mumbling all the way.

Casey took Buddy out for some exercise. He threw the ball in the snow. After five minutes he came back in and found Nolan waiting in the laundry room.

"I thought you said you were going to get the washer ready?"

"I did. Come on, the soaps in. All we have to do is touch go."

After a quick stop at Walgreens, they parked the truck on the street outside Reilly's pub. Nolan didn't like the idea of some drunk dinging his truck door getting into theirs.

"I'm leaving my coat inside."

Casey was wearing a sweater. "Might as well."

They entered the pub around 8:00 p.m. Candy and Chester were on their desert. Casey and Nolan joined them at the table.

"Hey Bro. How long are you in town for?" They did a fist bump.

"Until Sunday morning."

"Dad called last night."

"What he have to say?"

"Not much. He wants to come up and do some ice fishing. Casey answered the phone and made the mistake of telling him he didn't know how to fish. Oh, and he said the dirt bikes were well protected under the tarp in the barn."

"Damn. I thought he told me he sold those. He must be getting forgetful."

"Sure he is."

"Sandy leaves this week. His deployment is up."

Casey jumped in on the brother's conversation. "How long was he there?"

"Eight months."

Candy asked, "Does he have a girlfriend or boyfriend back home?"

Chester answered. "He's as straight as an arrow."

"Poor guy," mumbled Nolan.

"And if he does, he hasn't told us about her."

Nolan continued, "He starts training for Army Special Forces as soon as he gets back. The fucking Green Berets."

Chester shook his head. "Damn it anyway if he didn't go and do what he said he'd do. Be just like Uncle Wade."

Nolan took a fork and ate some of Chester's pie when he wasn't looking.

"What the fuck? Didn't Mom teach you better manners?"

"Relax. You owe me."

"How so?"

"Because I laundered the sheets on your bed. So drinks are on you tonight."

"Well, they'll be finished in the washer when we get back. We can have a nice glass of wine while they're in the dryer," Casey explained.

Candy was a little embarrassed. "I'm going to the ladies room. I'll be right back. Don't start a fight without me." She smiled and moved in her special way. Chester watched.

"Damn, that girl is scorching hot."

Nolan looked down at Chester's jeans. "Dude, stand up."

"Why?"

"I want to see those jeans."

Chester stood up.

"Damn Bro, those jeans are so tight, if you fart, you'll blow your boots off."

Chester sat down. "It's the style. Not like those baggy jeans you still wear."

"I'm wearing Cinch. They're aren't baggy."

Casey decided to come to Chester's defense. "Nolan, if I have to admit, he looks pretty damn good in those jeans. He's got that narrow waist. Those jeans do him justice."

"Thank you Casey. Maybe you can go along with my brother and help him shop for clothes. He's a little behind."

"Well, he picked out the Cinch jeans by himself, and they also do him justice."

Candy returned to the table. "Come on, what were you three discussing in the absence of a girl?"

Casey answered. "Tight jeans."

Candy threw in her two bits. "Not every guy can pull it off. But this guy?" She slapped Chester on the thigh. "Shit hot dude."

Nolan took a sip from his beer in the bottle. "I'll be a son of a bitch." He had his eyes at the other end of the bar. "Chester, do you see who I see?"

Chester looked over. "Fucking hell. Do we go over there and throw the pencil dick out?"

Casey looked. "Oh, guys. Pretend like you don't see him. Please?"

Nolan looked at Casey and twisted his mouth.

Candy said, "No bother boys, he saw me and took off. He must know I have an appointment to kick him in the nuts."

"Smart move."

"I agree." Chester threw his brother a high five.

"I appreciate you two saving our butts that night, but maybe a little restraint if we don't perceive a threat? I'm the one who called you guys. Anything wrong, and it's my fault."

"Relax Stretch. Guys like that are used to getting the shit beat out of them."

Chester shook his head in agreement. "They expect it."

Candy folded her arms. "Are these guys hot? Or what?"

Casey exhaled. His phone rang. "Sorry guys, I wouldn't normally do this, but I'm waiting for a call from Kevin."

"Hi Kevin."

"Hello Casey. Can you talk? Sounds like you're at a party."

"I can talk. I'm at Reilly's with Candy, Nolan and his brother."

The other three listened in on the conversation. Their table was far enough away for Casey to put Kevin on the speaker phone.

"You're on the speaker phone."

"I found some information with Ian's bank statements."

"I knew you could. Anything interesting?"

"Not really. At least nothing out of the ordinary from my point of view."

"Go on."

"With the American Express card, there was no activity since the twenty-seventh of December. On the debit card, there was a withdrawal of three thousand dollars on December thirty-first. The day he paid two months rent in advance."

"That's it?"

"That's it Casey. Nothing to lead me to think anything suspicious was going on with his accounts."

"Alright. Thanks Kevin. I really appreciate it."

"Good night Casey. Enjoy the evening with your friends."

"Bye." He put the phone down to discover the three at the table were all giving him the same look. He twisted his mouth, grabbed his beer and took a drink.

Candy changed the subject. "What time are we going skiing tomorrow?"

Chester answered. "I thought after breakfast. Nolan, you did fill the fridge with breakfast food, right?"

"Yes I did."

Casey added, "We have beer, wine and lots of fun food. Snacks. And hot chocolate too."

"Wait until you see what's in the car. I'll give you a hint. Gram."

Nolan answered first. "Chocolate chip cookies?"

"Yes. And one apple pie, one chocolate cake and two loaves of multi grain bread."

Casey licked his lips. "That does it, we have to take her out to dinner the next time Chester gets in town."

Candy put her hand on Chester's arm. "What do you say, Flyboy?"

"I'm in. I'll email you as soon as I get the schedule."

Casey asked, "Does she have a favorite…"

"Hello young men, young lady. Do you mind if I join you?"

They looked up to see Colonel Price, the commander of the 673rd Air Base Wing. The base commander.

Nolan jumped up, Chester didn't know who he was and Casey decided protocol didn't require it. "Please do sir." Nolan pulled up a chair from an empty table.

"Thank you Captain Kelly. Let's see, I know Captain Link, Nolan, and the pretty young lady who keeps our men looking sharp. Candy, right?"

"Yes sir. I've cut your hair a few times."

"Yes you have. You're a talented young lady. And I'm sorry but this guy I don't recognize."

Nolan answered. "Chester, this is Colonel Price. He's the base commander. Colonel, this is my brother, Captain Chester Kelly."

The Colonel extended his hand. "I haven't seen you on base. What's your unit?"

"I'm a pilot with the 22nd Airlift Squadron out of Travis."

"The C 5 Galaxy. One hell of an impressive aircraft."

"Yes sir, it is."

"Are you on leave?"

"No sir, I fly the run from JBER to Hawaii, and sometimes to Australia. I lay over while on crew rest."

"I see. And the young lady?"

Chester answered first. "She's my girlfriend."

"Lucky man." The Colonel looked at Nolan and Casey. "And where does that leave you two?"

Casey got to the answer before Nolan. "We're all friends here. I mean the four of us."

"Friends are what makes the world go round. Look at this place. A civilian Irish pub. The only place we can go and let off steam. You boys are too young to have experienced the joy of the officers clubs. They were an institution. The wives had their officers wives clubs meeting there. The officers had their raw egg eating contest. It was a place where we could let loose after a stressful time on the job with no prying eyes. We acted like fools and our subordinates never saw us. Now this is all we get."

The four at the table listened to him recall the good ol days.

"Well, I better get the hell out of here. I hope you all enjoy your evening." He got up, Nolan and Chester stood up to show their respect. Casey kept in his seat. He didn't like the way he questioned Nolan and himself. Neither did Nolan, but he tried to hide it.

Candy waited until the Colonel was out of sight, then she lifted one leg up for the guys to see. "Look, I have my dancing shoes on. Are we ready to cut a rug?"

Chester answered, "I'm ready for anything you want."

Nolan rolled his eyes.

Casey moved back his chair. "Might as well get this part over with. Mad Myrna's, here we come."

They paid the bill and drove the ten minutes it took to arrive at Mad Myrna's. The crossdresser, gay, trans, bi, straight, anything goes bar in town. The best place for dancing if one didn't mind bumping into someone different from one's self.

They were early enough to get a table. Casey made the announcement. "I volunteer to be one of the two designated drivers. Who's going to be the other one?"

"I don't mind, as long as Chester stays balanced enough to twirl me around the floor."

With the two designated drivers appointed, Chester and Nolan ordered a beer. Candy and Casey ordered a cola.

They weren't seated for five minutes when Candy pulled the smiling Chester off his chair and dragged him to the dance floor.

"I think your brother is really happy."

Nolan reached for Casey's knee under the table. "So is his brother."

"Stay here a moment will you? Watch the drinks."

Nolan gave Casey the eye.

Casey walked over to the bar and approached one of the crossdresser entertainers talking with another. "Hi. Can I have a word with the two of you?"

"What do you say Rosie, six two, six three?"

"Six two. One eighty-five?"

"Give or take a few."

"My name is Casey. I have a friend who recently came out as transgendered and he's, I mean she's been missing since the first of the month. I wonder if you've seen anybody fitting her description in here lately?"

"Honey, look around you. You're in a drag bar."

"Well, my friend would stick out because she's not very good at it yet. She's not in drag, she's in the first stages of transition."

Rosie extended her hand. "My name is Rosie."

Her friend did the same. "I'm Carla. What does your friend look like?"

"Not tall, dark eyebrows, but light skin. On the thin side. Probably wearing purple lipstick."

Rosie looked at Carla. "No."

Carla shook her head. “Honey, I’m afraid you’re looking for a dark hair in a blond bush. But we’ll both keep our eyes open if you want to check in from time to time. Is that your date sitting over there all by himself?”

Casey looked over to the table to find Nolan watching him with his arms folded. “Yeah, he’s all mine.”

“Well, I suggest you get back over there. Not smart leaving a hunk of muscle all alone in a place like this.”

“Thanks Rosie. Carla. Her name is Ines. And she has a slight Canadian accent.”

“Now there is some info we can use. Good luck honey.”

“Can I leave you my cell phone number?”

“My lucky night. I haven’t got a number in almost a month now.”

Casey asked the bartender for a paper and pen. He wrote his name and number twice for each of the drag queens to take with them. Then he returned to a brooding Nolan at the table.

“Do you want me to get you another beer?”

“No. I’ve had enough. I want to drive home and you probably won’t let me if I have another.”

“Can I get you a cola?”

“Alright. Better yet, let me go. Those two pretty ladies have their eyes on you.”

“No they don’t. They have their eyes on you. They warned me to get back to the guy with the muscles at the table.”

“They did?” Nolan had a big smile on his face.

“They’re not the only ones. You can’t expect to be the sexiest guy in a gay bar and not get hit on all night.”

“So does that mean you’re going to protect me?”

“They can look all they want, but if they start touching you I will.”

Nolan got up to get two colas. Rosie and Carla couldn’t take their eyes off of him. Casey smiled and threw them a thumbs up sign.

Candy and Chester returned to the table. "We need a break. I think Chester has been practicing."

Chester smiled. He sat and pulled Candy on his lap.

By 11:00 p.m., Candy was ready to go. She wanted to relax by the fireplace and hear Kelly brother stories. Chester stopped after two beers so he drove. They left Mad Myrna's at the same time. The truck took the lead north to the cabin.

"Stretch, what did the commander mean by his comment, the two of us?"

Casey was slouched down in the passenger seat. Nolan's question brought him back to the moment. He was stuck thinking about Ian's banking activity. "I'm not sure, but it appeared to me he was questioning our relationship. As if he knew about us."

"Fuck. How could he?"

"Because I think he's gay. And you know, we gays have a sense about these things?"

"How did you come up with that?"

"Nolan, don't worry about him. He's out of the picture?"

"What does that mean?"

"Oh crap. I said too much."

"Not enough. Come on, let it all out."

"Alright, if you have a deployment to a secret location, are you going to tell me where you're going?"

"You know I can't. It's the nature of the job. And I know you understand that."

"I do. There will be times I find out things about military members that I can't tell either. This is one of those times. And I should never have said as much as I did. So keep it between us, OK?"

"OK. I get it. But, you think whatever he thinks about us, we don't have to worry?"

"That is what I think."

"Did you have fun tonight?"

"I did."

Nolan turned off the radio and began to sing the song, "I'm Gonna."

Casey cut him off. "You don't have to sing that anymore."

"Why?"

"Because I already want you?"

"Alright. I'll sing another one. Any request?"

"Sing me one of your father's favorites."

"OK. His biggest hit, 'Wild Rose on the Fence Line.'" Nolan began to sing the song. He didn't have a voice that would get him on the radio, but he sang with conviction and joy. His singing voice was lower than his speaking one. Casey closed his eyes.

"So?"

"I think you're a really good singer. I loved that."

"Do you know what the wild rose is in the song?"

"No."

"It's my mom. When my dad fell in love with her, he wrote the song. She was the wild rose in his life."

"Your mom and dad told you how they fell in love?"

"Of course they did. My dad was head over heels for her first. It took my mom a while. I think the song did it."

"I bet they're wonderful people."

"They are."

"Do you know how to play the guitar?"

"Yes I do. Now you. You sing me one."

"No way Ironman. I do not have a singing voice."

"It's not about the voice. It's about how you feel when you sing the song. And how you make someone else feel. Come on, give it a try."

"My singing voice is so bad, when I was little and we went to church, I only moved my lips to the words so no one would hear me."

"Sad. I'm gonna work on that. So you went to church?"

"Ironic isn't it? We went every Sunday as the respectable family. Never missed."

Nolan answered the call from Chester on his truck infotainment system. "Go head Numb Nuts."

"Flexer, I think we've been followed ever since we left Myrna's."

"Who do you think it is?"

"Some kind of SUV. Can't get a good look though. He's staying too far back. Are you thinking the same thing I'm thinking?"

"Pencildick?"

"Exactly."

"Sandwich?" suggested Chester.

"Let's do it. Leave this line open. I'm pulling off in a quarter mile on the left."

"Copy."

"Sandwich? What the hell is a sandwich?"

"Just like it sounds. We get this guy locked in a sandwich, then we convince him never to follow us again?"

"Oh my God. What if he has a gun?"

"Grab my handgun from the glovebox."

"You have a gun in your glovebox?"

Nolan turned off the lights in the truck and took a left turn down a snow covered street. He drove a few yards until they passed a curve in the road, then stopped.

"You just passed us Bro. I'll tell you when Pencildick goes by."

"Copy. He should be the first set of lights behind me."

"Roger that. Heads up, I'm packing."

"Copy."

The next set of lights passed. "Pencildick passed by. I'm heading for the main road."

"Copy."

Nolan left the lights off the truck and pulled around to get back on the main road. He took off towards the SUV, with the lights off.

"Nolan, can you see where you're going?"

"Relax. I can see just fine. Start decreasing your speed Bro, I'm in position."

"Speed set. I think he slowed down."

"Wait until I get into position. I think he's tagged me. Alright, put her in reverse." Nolan pulled up behind the older model SUV and turned on his high beams. The SUV stopped. Casey could see Candy's car driving in reverse with the backup lights on. Before the driver of the SUV could turn his vehicle around, Nolan had the bumper of his truck pushed up to the back of the SUV, and Chester had his back bumper touching the front.

Nolan grabbed his handgun. "You coming?" Casey got out of the car. Not to be the observer, but to stop Nolan from doing anything more reckless than what he was already doing.

Chester approached the car, watching the driver's every move. It was the guy they saw in the pub earlier. The same guy whose nose Nolan broke back in December. "Get out of the car Pencildick."

The guy left his window rolled up and didn't say anything.

Nolan took the gun from under his belt. "Should I start shooting out his tires?"

"Let's give him one more minute to get out of the car. Then go for the rear left tire."

Nolan aimed his gun at the tire.

Casey spoke. "Roll down your window a bit, and I'll convince them to let you go. But I want to know why you're following us first."

The guy rolled his window down about five inches.

"So let's hear it?" Casey asked.

"I'm not following you. I'm going to a friend's house."

Nolan waved his gun at the tire. "Not good enough!"

"Because you broke my fucking nose you Army grunt."

"Bro. Would you say his manners haven't improved since the last time we met?"

"I fully agree. Bad case of poor manners."

Casey cut in. "You can't be this stupid. Do you really think you can take these two maniacs on?"

He didn't say anything.

"I'm going to cut you a deal. You interested?"

"What?"

"You promise to stop this right now. Leave all of us alone, and I'll make sure these guys do the same. It all ends right here."

"OK."

"But one condition. You give me your driver's license."

"No fucking way."

"Well, I tried. I guess this is going to get very ugly. Worse than the last time you acted so stupid."

Casey saw the guy reach for his wallet. He took out the drivers license and held it in his hand, inside the car. "What the fuck do you plan on doing with this?"

"Your address. If you continue to harass us, then the deal is off. My boys will know where to find you."

"Fine." He gave Casey the driver's license and put both hands on the steering wheel.

"Good move," he read the name off the license, "Mark Kendall. I really hope this stops here, for your sake. And I think it would be a good idea if you stay away from Reilly's." Casey grabbed his cell phone and took a close up picture. He handed the license back through the window. "Guys, let him pull out and turn around. He's going that way." Casey pointed back down the road in the direction he came from. Nolan stayed in his spot, Chester moved Candy's car up enough to allow the guy to make a U turn.

Nolan and Casey watched as the guy disappeared down the road into the darkness of the Alaskan night.

Casey was fuming mad. He got into the truck without speaking to Nolan.

Nolan spoke to his brother over the speaker phone. "You take the lead, we'll keep our eyes out the back for any further conflict."

"Copy. I'm hanging up."

"Here, put this back in the glovebox."

"I'm not touching that thing."

Nolan reached over and placed the handgun where it was before. He kept his eyes on the road, with the headlights on, glancing over at Casey every few seconds. "Want me to sing you a song?"

"Oh, I don't know. Can you sing me a funeral march? As long as we're in the mood for dying."

"Ah, come on Stretch, we're having a great night. Don't go and piss on it by getting all upset over some Pencildick following us home."

Casey gave Nolan a dirty look. He kept quiet the rest of the ten minutes it took to get to the cabin. Nolan hummed the tune to the song 'I'm Gonna' while focusing his eyes on the headlights of Candy's car down the road.

It was a warm Anchorage night for January. Twenty-four degrees. The stars were out and there was a hint of the northern lights swirling green to the north. Nolan parked the truck outside and Chester put Candy's car in the semi heated garage. Casey left the truck and walked up the front steps to the main entrance of the cabin. Nolan waited until the garage door shut, took one last look down the lane for anyone stupid enough to follow them, then followed Casey up the stairs who was leaning against the railing watching Buddy watching him through the glass door.

Nolan tried his best to be cheery. "There's our big Buddy." He used the key to let him out. "You go on in, I'll wait for the dog."

Chester turned on the lights. Candy made herself at home leaning up against the kitchen bar top. Nolan shut the door and Buddy ran around to make sure he properly greeted everyone in the cabin.

Candy noticed the tidiness of the place. "I think you boys have improved on your housekeeping skills since I was last here."

Chester folded his arms. "Nice, huh?"

Casey rolled his eyes.

"Boys, what's with the Christmas decorations?"

No one answered.

"Well, I was responsible for putting it up. I guess I can take it down."

Casey glanced over at Nolan. "I bet if you asked Chester, he'd be glad to help you. After all he's ready for anything you want?"

"That's OK, I can do it by myself."

"No you won't. You might fall off the ladder. I'll take down the ornaments, you can but them in the storage box."

"Alright, maybe we can get it done tomorrow after breakfast and before we go skiing."

Casey smiled at Chester. "That guy is pretty damn handy if you ask me. He put it up, now he's taking it down. I bet his mom would really be proud of him."

Chester threw him a dirty look. Nolan gave Casey a thumbs up sign. Casey left for the laundry room to put the sheets in the dryer.

"Candy, grab your bag, I'll show you where you can get into some comfortable clothes."

They walked up the stairs with Buddy taking the lead.

Casey grabbed a pan to get the hot chocolate ready. Nolan came up and put his arms around him. "So, is this our first fight?"

"We're not fighting. Besides, I think Turkey would qualify for our first fight."

"Oh, right. So you're OK with me?"

Casey managed to turn around to face Nolan with his arms remaining in place. "You and your brother were reckless tonight. You put Candy's safety in jeopardy. All of our safety. Am I suppose to just blow that off?"

Nolan dropped his arms. "I'll go get some wood and start a fire."

Casey turned back around. Candy walked down the stairs with Chester. "You making hot chocolate?"

"I am. I can't wait to try those cookies." The baked goods Gram made were displayed on the counter top.

"Where's Nolan?"

"He better be making my bed. I bought the drinks."

"I don't think that's going to happen. You might want to do it yourself. Grab your cups, the hot chocolate is ready."

Nolan was almost ready with the fire. The sound of the kindle wood crackling helped set the mood for ending a hectic day.

Casey put a plate of chocolate chip cookies on the foot stool. Candy and Chester were comfortably arranged on the end of the couch. Nolan was on the large easy chair, and Casey sat on the floor. He stared into the flames while Nolan stared at him, worried if he'd done any irreparable damage to their relationship.

Candy had the boys telling farm stories. Casey stared at his phone. "Mark Kendall."

Chester repeated, "Mark Kendall. We should have beat the crap out of that guy."

Casey kept his focus on the flames of the fire. Nolan threw his brother a head shake sign to keep his mouth shut.

"I think you boys might have scared him enough to stop his nonsense. Saves me from having to kick the guy in the nuts."

"What if he's the one responsible for Ian's disappearance?" The other three all exchanged the same expression of doubt. Casey picked up on it right away. "You guys enjoy the fire. I've had a big day. See you all in the morning." He stood up and walked towards the stairs. "Nolan, please let Buddy out one more time before you turn in. And get your handgun out of the truck. It won't do anybody any good in there all night." Buddy watched Casey climb the stairs but decided after careful deliberation to remain with the group.

Casey put on his large t shirt for sleeping and remained in his tight fitting boxers. After brushing his teeth, he crawled into bed. Ten minutes later, he heard the door open and close. Faking sleep he listened as Nolan entered the bathroom, flushed the toilet, brushed his teeth and turned off the light. He could hear the sound of a man throwing his clothes on the floor. There was the sound of hard metal being placed on the wooden nightstand. Buddy made his noise getting comfortable on the carpeting. Nolan crawled into the bed and laid on his back.

"You awake?"

Casey kept quiet.

"I'm sorry. I had such a great day with you, it's too bad to have it end this way."

Casey rolled over and put his head on Nolan's bare chest. He usually slept in the nude. "I'll get over it. It was still a great day for me too."

Nolan put his arms around Casey and gently squeezed. "So we're alright then?"

"We're alright. I only hope you include me in on the plans the next time you decide to teach someone a lesson. With a gun in your hand."

"Yes sir." Casey fell asleep with the sound of air being taken in and out of Nolan's lungs, through the muscle and bones of his chest.

Casey woke up without the assistance of the alarm clock. He cautiously slipped out of bed, went to relive himself, threw on his sweatpants and led Buddy downstairs to have his morning pee.

The wall clock showed 5:11 a.m. He made the coffee, took one of Gram's cookies, and opened his laptop to write Kevin an early morning email.

"Good morning Kevin,

I found a possible lead to our case last night. His name is Mark Kendall. He's a violent guy who has a history with myself, Ian, and my other friends. It all started one night when we took Ian out for the first time dressed as a woman to a place other than Mad Myrna's."

Casey told the whole story, right up to the point of Nolan breaking his nose on the surface of the bar to an applauding crowd of patrons.

"I'm sending you an image of his drivers license. Let me know if you think I'm pushing the limits with this new angle. I should be around my phone until at least

nine this morning. I'm not sure what kind of cell phone service there is on the trails around here. Once again, thanks for all your help."

Casey sat at the counter separating the kitchen from the living room remembering how hate filled the guy was at the pub with his friends that first night. To him, his new angle made perfect sense. The early morning in the cabin was quiet. He looked over at the fireplace and decided to start a fire.

With his chore complete, the silence of the cabin replaced with the crackling sound of burning dry wood, and his cup of coffee, Casey sat on the floor with Buddy curled up between his legs. He didn't notice Nolan leaving the stairs for his morning cup of coffee.

"Good morning Stretch."

"Good morning Noley. Did you get a good night's sleep?"

"I did. What about you?"

"I did."

Nolan joined Casey sitting on the floor with his cup of coffee and two chocolate chip cookies. He passed one over to Casey. "So we're good for sure?"

"We're good. I wrote Kevin an email this morning."

"About what?"

"I told him all about that violent homophobe."

"All?"

"Yes. I send him a picture of the guy's license too."

"Won't I get into trouble with a cop when he finds out I broke a guy's nose?"

"Not with Kevin you won't. He won't give a gay basher any support."

"What are we doing for breakfast this morning?"

"I thought steak and eggs?"

"Isn't that Buddy's steak?"

"It is. We need to buy chicken for his food. He needs to have some variety, fish too. He can have some steak and eggs also."

"Who's going to be the cook?"

"I have a feeling it's going to be you and me. Chester might be busy taking down the Christmas tree."

"Damn, if you aren't a genius. You got him to put it up and take it down. I fucking love it."

Chester came down for his cup of coffee. He was all smiles.

Nolan noticed. "We're going to have to keep Candy around. He usually wakes up in the morning acting like a grizzly bear."

"It is a wonderful morning in Alaska. Beats the sunny beaches of Hawaii any day of the week." He grabbed a cup for his coffee.

Casey stood by the front window. "I see there is a fresh coat of snow on the ground. Should be great for skiing."

"Since Chester weighs the most, he can cut the trail."

"No problem. Just leave it to the man of the house."

Candy came down the stairs in her pink sweat suit. "Good morning boys. Please tell me the coffee is ready?"

Chester had her cup filled. "Just the way you like it."

"Thank you Dolly."

Nolan laughed. "Dolly, I like the sound of that. Dolly. So cute."

Candy had her coffee by the fire. "Who's making breakfast?"

"We are. Nolan and I thought you and Chester could take down the tree while we make the breakfast."

"Good idea boys."

Nolan went to the garage to get the box for the decorations. He came back and placed the box by the tree. "Here's the box Dolly. I'd give you a hand, but I think this is the perfect task for two love birds.

Chester smiled at Nolan. "Thank you Bro. I will enjoy myself." He smiled at Candy. "Anything I can do with my girl is a joy."

By now all four were sitting by the fireplace with a cup of coffee. Casey's phone rang. He jumped up. "That might be Kevin." He grabbed his phone and answered.

"Hi Kevin. I guess you got my email this morning?"

"I did. And I have some information for you also."

"Great. I have you on the speaker phone. What did you find?"

"I was able to contact Ian's parents this morning."

"Go on."

"They received an email from Ian telling them he planned to disappear for a few weeks. He told them not to worry and everything was under control. He said it was all a part of his transition."

"When?"

"On the second of January."

"Are you able to get the message and check the IP address?"

"No. They said they deleted the message."

"So the same guy who sent me the email could have also sent them one too?"

"That's one scenario."

"Do you plan on checking out that guy I sent you this morning?"

"I'll do my best."

"Thanks Kevin,"

"Talk to you later."

"Bye."

No one said anything to Casey. He was the one to speak first. "None of this makes any sense to me. He specifically told me over the phone on Christmas day he couldn't wait to tell me about a recent development in his life. He was excited to tell me. He would have told me."

Candy tried to give her support. "Sweetie, whatever the situation is, I think we've been moving forward. Every day we get some new information. I believe Kevin when he said we'd get to the end of all this."

"Perhaps. Nolan, you ready to get the steak and eggs cooked?"

"You're the boss. This might be over my head."

Casey moved to the kitchen to begin making a good breakfast. He hollered over to Chester and Candy, "Take your time. We can't go skiing until civil twilight starts at nine."

Chester found the ladder in the garage and began making preparations to get the Christmas tree down, but not before playing the newest music from his favorite group Brothers Born.

Casey pulled out the pans. "Can you break a dozen eggs in this bowl? I'll get the steak ready."

"Yes sir."

Buddy was glued to Nolan's bare feet.

Candy noticed. "Don't worry boys, I won't tell Gram you're the reason for his lost appetite this winter."

Casey raised his eyes at Nolan. "Busted!"

Nolan kept glancing over at his brother and Candy working like a team by the tree. He nudged Casey and pointed at the two with his chin. Casey stopped and shook his head up and down with a smile.

The cabin soon filled with the smell of breakfast, especially with the first set of toast Nolan burned in the toaster. He cut more slices from the home made bread and finally managed to get it on a plate.

"You two can take a break over there. Breakfast is ready."

Buddy was busy with his bowl of eggs, steak, bits of homemade bread and an added dose of chopped broccoli.

The four sat at the kitchen bar and enjoyed a good morning meal. Chester eyed the baked goods Gram sent along. "I plan of having some of that cake for desert."

Casey raised his spoon in the air. "Me, I'm going for the apple pie." He was interrupted with the ring of his phone. "Guys, I have to get this. It's Ian's parents." He grabbed the phone and answered. The conversation at the table came to a halt.

"Hello." Casey put the call on the speaker phone without telling the caller.

"Good morning, may I speak with Casey Link please?"

"I'm Casey. Are you Ian's dad?"

"Yes I am. I was given your number this morning by a detective from Anchorage. Detective Lippman."

"Yes. Detective Lippman is a friend of mine."

"He told me you filed a missing person's report on lan."

"I did. Ian is my good friend. We work together at the base hospital."

"He told me about you. You're the only friend in the military who shares his secret."

"Yes sir."

"You must imagine his news to us this Christmas was a real shock for my wife and me."

"Yes sir. It was one for me also. But I was happy for him to start the process. So he could feel like a complete person."

"Are you saying he wasn't happy?"

"Yes. From what I've learned about transgendered people, they're miserable when they don't take the steps to change their lives and gender. I think he was very unhappy until he made the decision."

"He told us he would be safe. Did he tell you the same thing?"

"Maybe. I can't be sure though. He was excited to tell me about a development in his life, and he hasn't. That bothers me. I wanted to be sure so I called the dectective."

"His mother believes everything is alright. I'm not so convinced. Will you keep me informed of whatever you find?"

"Of course I will. Do you have my email address?" Casey passed the address over the line and got his in return.

"Thank you Casey. Keep in touch."

"I will. Goodbye." He hung up and placed the phone on the counter top. "So his dad has his doubts."

None of the other three made a comment.

Nolan poured the coffee for everyone to go along with their desert. "So Bro, since we cooked the breakfast, you gonna do the dishes?"

"Wrong. We do the tree, you do the breakfast. All of it."

Casey laughed. "We got it."

Candy looked over to the side. "That's a dishwasher, right?"

"I don't think my brother has learned how to use it. He has difficulty with technology."

"Right, like the F 22 Raptor."

By 9:15 am., there was enough light in the sky from civil twilight. The sun would pass the horizon at around 10:00. They were all dressed with cross country skis attached and poles in hand. Buddy was ready to take the lead.

Chester took the path he knew well leading by a stream heading south from the cabin. The snow was packed enough to allow Buddy to run up front, only sinking down occasionally on the soft spots.

Candy was second in line behind Chester, followed by Casey with Nolan acting as the rear guard.

After a mile, they stopped for a break. There was a large house over by a lane off the main road to the city. Nolan pointed. "That house over there belongs to Colonel Price. I was invited to a party there last year. He had both fighter squadrons over for pizza and drinks."

Casey looked at the odd roof on the house. It was a blue shingled roof with a huge patch of red shingles in the middle towards the back. "What's with the roof?"

"The guy thinks he's a Jack of all trades. He patched the roof with the wrong color shingles, the same on the front of the house too. He tried to install a wood floor by himself and made one hell of a mess with it."

"Is he married" Casey knew the answer.

"No. He's a real party boy. Drinks a lot too."

Casey was the only one who knew the guy's tragic secret. And that he'd no longer be the base commander in a few days.

They skied for two hours, no one complained about wanting to stop, but it was cold and feet were beginning to feel the effects. Back at the cabin, Nolan volunteered to get the fire going.

Casey swept the needles off the wood floor from the dried out Christmas tree. Candy took charge of the hot chocolate, and Chester selected the music.

Nolan announced his plan for dinner. "Lunch is up to whatever you can find in the fridge. I'm in charge of dinner tonight. I promised Casey to make dinner for the whole week."

"Can I help?" Casey worried his plan would include grilled cheese for the main course.

"You can help, but I'm in charge."

Candy asked, "What's the menu?"

"Chili."

Chester moaned. "And delivered pizza."

"Hey, it's gonna be good."

Casey smiled. "And don't forget, I get to help."

Chester and Candy grabbed a blanket and sat by the fire.

Casey announced. "I'm going to follow Buddy's lead and take a nap." He raised his eyebrows at Nolan and took off for the upstairs.

"I could use one myself." Nolan followed right behind him.

Casey jumped on the bed and Nolan did the same after shutting the bedroom door. He maneuvered his body on top of the taller guy. "Do you believe me when I tell you you make me hornier than a peach orchard boar?"

"I do, even though you tend to exaggerate sometimes. A peach orchard boar?"

Nolan lifted his head up from the small of Casey's neck. "I never do. I have never fed you a line of BS ever since I first met you."

"Never?"

"Never."

“Do you want to try the bubble bath with me before we start our nap?”

“Yes. Thank you God.” Nolan jumped out of the bed, pulled off his shirt, and threw it on the floor. He took off his socks. He unbuckled his pants and stopped. “Stretch? Are you planning on taking a hot bath with your clothes on?”

Casey laughed. He climbed off the bed and began removing his clothes. Nolan was totally naked with his clothing scattered all around the floor. He stood at the doorway of the bathroom waiting impatiently for Casey to get ready. “You do realize I fly an aircraft faster than the speed of sound, don’t you Stretch?”

Casey kept his comment to himself. Finally with his clothes off and put in place, he went to the bathroom and prepared the bath with bubbles. “Oh no, the candles are in the kitchen.”

“Stretch, I don’t know if you’ve noticed, but I’m harder than a rock. There’s no way I’m running down stairs with this boner between my legs.”

“Alright, we can turn off the lights and use the light from the outdoors to help set the mood.”

“I’m always in the mood.”

Casey prepared the water with the bubbles and got into the water first. “Come on Mister Sexy, right here.”

Nolan slid into the tub and arranged himself to fit with his back against Casey’s front. “My first bubble bath since I was five years old.”

“I don’t think you did when you were five years old what we’re about to do.” Nolan slid down and let his body relax in the near darkness, nestled up against Casey’s front. He inhaled deeply through his nose. “What’s that smell?”

“It’s the smell of the ocean. That’s why it’s called Algemarin Foam Bath. And the bottle is blue.”

Casey took the bottle of shampoo and put a small amount on Nolan’s head. “I bet this grunt haircut saves you a ton of money on hair care products.”

"What hair care products? I prefer Dawn from the kitchen. The one they use on the little duckies."

Casey lathered up his scalp. "Close your eyes so I don't get any soap in them."

"I want to see."

"Close them please."

Nolan quit complaining and closed his eyes.

Casey used the hand held attachment to rinse the shampoo from Nolan's head.

"It smells like girlie perfume."

"It's supposed to smell like fruit."

"It doesn't."

Casey shampooed his hair as well.

Nolan played with Casey's legs. "Did I ever tell you I think your long legs are really hot?"

"I think you did. Did I ever tell you you have really great ears?"

"No. You said you liked my nose. All the damn work I do on my muscles, and the guy I fall for likes my nose."

Casey laughed. "I told you about the other parts I like."

"Tell me again. So I don't forget."

"Remember when I had to take your blood pressure when you came in to finish your flight physical?"

"Of course I do."

"I saw something so beautiful and hard."

"My biceps."

"No. Your butt crack. You really have a hard muscular butt, and a perfect crack."

"All those damn squats I do paid off. Now we're talking. What else?"

"Your five o'clock shadow."

"Do you like it when I don't shave?"

"Yes." Casey moved his hands to feel his hard chest. He let his fingers excite both nipples. The nipples that always jumped to attention with the slightest touch. "And these."

"Careful there Stretch. I told you about those."

"I know. But if I have to be honest, I didn't believe you."

"I told you I don't BS."

"I never heard of that in a guy before."

"So, you never had a guy like me before, did you?"

"No. Never."

"I'm pure Georgia horney. All the time. So what's the wager Stretch?"

"A wager?"

"Yeah. Come on. You play with my nipples, I shoot my load right into the air without touching my dick. If I make it, what do I win?"

"If you don't, what do I win?"

"Ask away."

"Let me think. If you can't do what you say you can do, I win…" he thought about it. Looking in front of him, he saw Nolan was as hard as a rock, sticking out of the bubbles. "I win lunch in the parking lot with your camper."

"Fine. If I win, you go camping with me next weekend."

"Only if we get to eat with candle light."

"Oh crap. Not that. What the hell, OK."

Casey kept moving his fingers over Nolan's tight chest. He did his best to massage the guy's nipples. He gave them a pinch.

"Don't do that, just keep with the same motion. God, you got me so bothered. You drive me fucking crazy, even if I do only have one pecker."

Casey watched as Nolan used his stomach muscles to move his erection back and forth. He noticed after a few minutes that Nolan got a tighter grip on his long thighs.

"Keep your eyes open Stretch, you're about to lose a bet."

Casey felt his muscular body tense up, and as he let out a moan, the first shot of come took to the air. Followed by two more. The rest took its time dripping down his shaft.

"Can I touch my dick now? I don't want to get stuck with blue balls with any juice left inside."

"You won, fair and square. If I didn't see it with my own eyes, I wouldn't have believed it."

"It's what you get with a Georgia country boy. Damn, that felt so frigging good. Now what about you?"

"In the bed?"

"You're boss all week."

They soaped up. Nolan gave Casey some assurance with his experience level. "Don't worry about the come, mine always stays on the bottom. It won't float."

They left the tub and dried off. Nolan handed Casey the towel.

Candy waved goodbye to Casey and Nolan watching from the window Sunday morning. She had a container of chili for Gram. Chester had to confess it was the best he ever had. They watched as Chester drove her car down the lane on their drive back to the base. He had to report by noon for his flight to Australia.

"I'm really happy for your brother. They make a perfect couple. Candy never complained before she met him about being lonely, but I know she was. Everybody needs somebody in their life, isn't that right Noley?"

Nolan put his arm around Casey. They watched the snow fall gently to the ground before moving to the fireplace.

Monday morning, 6:30 a.m., Casey laid on Ian's bed in his garage apartment. Looking up at the ceiling. *Ian, where in the hell are you? I won't stop until I know for sure. I just want you to be safe and happy.* He got off the unmade bed and stood in the dark bedroom trying to put the few pieces of the puzzle together. He smelled something he couldn't put his finger on. Finally leaving the apartment, careful to not cause suspicion with the lights on, he left for his car to make it in time to work.

By 6:45 a.m., he stood in line for a coffee at the hospital cafeteria. Finding a secluded table to sit, enjoy the coffee and to reflect on his personal life, he decided to make the attempt not to think of Ian any more for the rest of day. He needed the time to go over the events with Nolan and what they meant. His near obsession with Ian was getting in the way of moving forward with the new development in his personal life. He left the cafeteria on the hour and walked to his department. On the way he passed Ian's office, stopped, stared at the shut door, shook his head and continued moving. His thoughts were interrupted with a strange smell in the hallway. A smell he thought he knew, but definitely not one of the regular hospital smells.

"Good morning Sergeant Tomlin. Did you have a nice weekend?"

"Yes sir. We went to the Anchorage Museum yesterday. Have you been there?"

"I have, I enjoyed it."

"What about you? Do anything exciting?"

"Hit the trails with my friends skiing. The snow was perfect. Is the Major in yet?"

"No sir."

"I'm in my office if you need me." He left to check his email. Afterwards he dowloaded the song 'Wild Rose on the Fence Line' from iTunes. He had his first patient from the 90th Fighter Squadron at eight.

"Lieutenant Kling, how can we help you today?"

"My foot. I think I might have broken something. It's swollen and blue."

"Come on in, we'll have a look."

Jack Kling, better knows as Jack Shot, limped into the examination room.

"Can you climb up here? I'll get your boot off." Casey carefully took off the guy's left boot as he winced a little. "How did you do this? Skiing?"

"No. I fell off the balcony at my apartment."

"Please tell me you live on the second floor?"

"Third. But there was a lot of deep snow below. And I won a hundred dollars."

"Fell or jumped?"

"I have to stick with fell, or I'll get may ass burned royally."

Casey pulled off his white sock.

"I wasn't completely stupid. I checked the snow pile that morning. It was soft all the way down. No ice or anything like that."

"You're a genius."

"Come on Doc, haven't you ever wanted to jump into a big pile of snow?"

"All the time. Alright, let me finish getting your records prepared and the Major will be with you right away."

By ten, Jack Shot hobbled out of the hospital with a cast on his foot and two crutches. He was removed from flying status until further notice.

With no patients waiting, he stared out the window of his office. The snow stopped. There was an additional two inches of white powder on the ground. Anchorage always looked so clean in the winter. No matter how hard he tried, he thought of Ian. He came up with the idea of sending a bait message. If someone had his personal accounts, then they were reading all his messages. He began to compose the draft.

"Dear Ian. Hold tight. Nolan and I have put together all the facts and I believe we know who is responsible for your disappearance. All we need to do is get our mission ready. We're coming to get you. Hold on, it won't be long now. We won't give up until we have you back and safe."

He sat staring at the message. Not pushing send. Then he began another message.

"Good morning Kevin. I am sending you this draft I want to send to Ian's phone as a text message. I believe it might pull the person or persons responsible for Ian's disappearance out of the shadows. Let me know what you think.

Thanks so much."

He attached the draft and sent the message to Kevin via email. He glanced at his calendar. January 18. Ian had two more weeks of projected leave. No one would really get serious about his disappearance until that date passed. He jumped with the vibration of his phone.

"Good morning Stretch. Just wanted to say I had a great weekend with you. I'm taking Buddy with me to the Red Apple Market. I have a killer plan for dinner tonight. Text me if you want anything. That includes me."

Casey smiled. He returned the text. *"I had a great time with you also. You know I do."* He pushed send.

Not one minute passed before getting a reply text from Kevin. *"Absolutely not. That is too reckless. No need to add more victims to the case. Text me and tell me you won't send that message."*

Casey looked for the words to send. *"Thanks for your advice. I appreciate your expertise."*

A few minutes before eleven, Casey was still bothered by the smell that was following him all day. He picked up his jacket and smelled. Nothing. He picked up his backpack. Nothing. He picked up his blue silver braided flight cap. The smell was on the inside. He stared at the cap for several seconds before dropping it on his desk. *Son of a bitch. Coconut oil.* He reached up and rubbed the short hair on the back of his head. *The pillow. Ian's bed. Coconut oil. Colonel Price.* Casey sat down and took in a deep volume of air. *That's what he wanted to tell me on Christmas day. The new development in his life. He was seeing someone. Not just any someone, but the base commander.* Sitting at his desk, he wondered who he should tell first. *If something bad happened to Ian, the commander would have valuable information we don't have. Kevin. He should know about this immediately.*

Kevin answered the phone on the second ring. "Casey, if you want to debate your crazy bait message, the answer is still hell no."

"Hi Kevin. You won't believe what I just figured out. The biggest clue to Ian's disappearance yet."

"Go on."

Casey lowered his voice to a near whisper. “Ian was having a physical relationship with the base commander, Colonel Ed Price.”

“Who told you that?”

“No one. I figured it out on my own.”

“Casey.”

“I was in Ian’s apartment this morning. I laid on his bed for a few minutes looking for clues, and I got coconut oil on the back of my head.”

“Casey?”

“Listen, the base commander is the only guy I know who slicks his short hair back with coconut oil. I also know other things about the commander that fall right in line with my theory. No, it’s not a theory, it’s fact.”

“Let’s say it’s true. You do realize people get together every now and then. Socially and physically, right?”

“Come on, are you saying we should ignore this lead?”

“No. I’m not, but I have better leads as of an hour ago. Leads we might want to put our energies into first.”

“What.”

“The guy you tangled with. Mark Kendall. He has a prior record. Actually two of them. He was sentenced to a year in jail in Washington State for gay bashing at a gay bar in Seattle. He got out of jail only six months ago.”

“Oh my God. I knew it. What now?”

“Wait, there’s more. Three years ago he was arrested in a murder case in upstate New York. There was a transgendered person who went missing. He was the last to be seen with her in a bar. But they couldn’t get any evidence on the case, so they had to let him go. They never found the body.”

“Never?”

“That’s right.”

“So what if he’s an expert at hiding bodies. My God, I’ll never find Ian.”

“Don’t get ahead of yourself.”

"Are you going to arrest this guy? Get a search warrant and look inside his house? Inside his car, and his friends houses too?"

"I can't. Not until I have evidence he might be involved. I'm bringing him in for questioning as we speak. If we get anything, then I have to get a warrant approved by a judge. This could all take some time."

"Kevin, we might not have any time."

"This is how the system moves. I'll call you with any info I get."

"Alright Kevin. I know you're the only hope I have here. Thank you."

"Sit tight. Got to run." He hung up. Casey walked in circles around his office. He sent Candy a text. *"Lunch at noon?"* Then he thought about the bait message. With the draft prepared, he hit the send button. The message was sent to Ian's phone. Not wanting to be dishonest with Kevin, he sent him a text confessing what he did.

By 11:45, he was in his car and driving over to the Military Mall Food Court to have lunch with Candy. He had a call on the way over. It was Kevin. He answered through his Subaru audio system. "Hi Kevin."

"Casey. I thought you understood me when I said not to send that message."

"Don't be angry. Nothing will come of it anyway. I'm on my way to have lunch with Candy."

"Keep me informed." He hung up. Angry at Casey for being what he said was reckless.

After parking his car, he went to find Candy. She was already at a table texting Chester. "Hi Candy. Having a busy day?"

"Hi Sweetie. No. Really slow. These Air Force boys have started to copy the grunts on base and are cutting their own hair. I can tell the business is slowing down some."

Casey put his military hat over to the side. "Have you ever been haunted by a smell?"

"Haunted?"

"Yeah, I've had this smell following me all day and I couldn't put my finger on it. Until I did."

"And?"

"Are you ready for this?"

"And?"

"Candy, remember Ian wanted to tell me about a new development in his life?"

"Yes. Probably a new color wig."

"Wrong. He was having a physical relationship with the base commander, Colonel Price."

"No fucking way! How do you know this?"

"That smell. Coconut oil." He told Candy everything about the period from laying in Ian's unmade bed to connecting the dots in his office.

"So you're telling me the Colonel is our prime suspect?"

"No. I called Kevin and he told me what he found out on our homophobe Mark." After he told Candy what Kevin said over the phone, he added, "Maybe I should have let Nolan shoot the prick."

"So what now?"

He didn't tell Candy about his latest bait text. "We wait until Kevin gives me a call. He sent an officer over to get the guy and have him questioned. If they find any evidence, they go to the judge for a search warrant."

"Do you think…?"

"I can't think that way. I have to keep hope alive. You too."

"The power of positive thinking. Make sure you call me with any new leads. Promise?"

"I promise." Casey found the need to change the topic. "Did you enjoy your weekend?"

"Did I ever. Casey, I think Chester and I are getting serious about our relationship. Am I making a mistake?"

"Good God no. Chester is a great guy. A great guy with a great family. You know what that means?"

"What?"

"I think it means he'd make a great dad, just like what he grew up with?"

"I guess it takes a great parent to be one."

"Candy, I didn't mean it like that. I know you'd be a great mom. And besides, who wouldn't want a role model like Gram in their life?"

"I'd like to be like Gram with my children."

"I have to ask, if this thing went further, what would you do about Gram? I mean if you had to relocate. Chester can get assigned all over the world."

Candy got teary eyed. "I won't leave Gram behind. Somehow I have to convince her she has to come with me. Do you think Chester would mind?"

"Not at all. He grew up with an extended family. And if you had kids, can you imagine how much help she'd be? But you have to have the conversation with both him and her if things start moving in that direction."

"What about you?"

"What?"

"Come on. I'm talking about you and Nolan. What if you get different assignments?"

"I can take care of that. My nursing degree makes me employable almost anywhere in the world. But it's too early to think about those things now."

"I disagree. Time flies when you're having fun."

By three in the afternoon, the sun was low in the sky. It was to set by six. Casey sat in his car with the temperature reading twenty-five. He let the engine warm a little before taking off. While putting the car in gear, he found the song 'I'm Gonna' on his iPod and turned up the volume. Past the gate, he turned down the volume and tried to sing along with the words. Deciding no one would ever know, he turned the volume so low it was barely audible. Then he began to sing the song out loud, with his windows fully rolled up. It was the first time in his memory of ever hearing his singing voice. He decided it was between horrible and not too bad. Remembering what Nolan told him, "It's not what your voice sounds like, it's how you make someone feel."

Not far from the cabin he received a text from Nolan. Breaking with his usual protocol, he read the text while driving. There was no one on the snow covered road besides himself.

"Casey, hurry up and get home. I'm hungry. Can't wait until you get dinner on the table. Let me know your ETA."

Casey put the phone down and felt completely confused. He pulled into the lane of a nice house off the road and stared at the text. *He was excited about making me dinner tonight with a surprise. This makes no sense. Whatsoever."*

He sat in the drive wondering why the strange message. Then he thought of the bait message. He composed a reply.

"Nolan, are you sure you want me to cook tonight, especially after the disaster I had with dinner last night?" He sat with the engine running, turned the car around and faced the entrance to the road. The reply was quick.

"I'm sure. So what's your ETA?"

It was 3:15 p.m. He made the reply. *"Got a little hung up at work. I'll be at the cabin by four-thirty."* He pushed send and then called Kevin. His heart was racing so fast he could hardly talk.

"Kevin, I'm so glad you answered. That bait message. They have Nolan. I think Mark Kendall and his gang has him somewhere. They might be at the cabin now. They want to know when I plan to get there."

"Casey, calm down. Take a few breaths. Tell me what's going on."

"I got a text from Nolan. He wanted me to get to the cabin and start dinner."

"Casey. Where are you right now?"

"I'm about five miles south of the cabin."

"Are you parked?"

"Yes."

"Listen, what is so suspicious about cooking Nolan dinner?"

"You don't understand. He was making dinner today. All week."

"Maybe he decided to have you do it instead."

"Kevin, please, something is wrong. Let me guess, when you sent the officers out to get Mark, he wasn't in, am I right?"

"That doesn't mean they've kidnapped someone. Casey. I think you're letting this get out of hand…"

"You don't believe me. No one believes me. I'm in this all alone."

"Alone? No frigging way Captain Link. I've been in this with you the whole way. What do you plan on doing now?"

"I'm getting help. I know a guy nearby who can help me. I'm sure he has a few guns in the house. That homophobe Mark and his friends are out for some serious revenge."

"Who is going to help you with guns?"

"Colonel Price. He lives one mile south of the cabin. He'll help me. I know he will. This guy is reckless and reckless guys make great warriors. I need a warrior right now. I have to go." Casey hung up with Kevin and took off again in the direction of the cabin, but with the intention to find the house with the red roof patch in the middle, situated down a lane on the left side of the road.

The glare from the low sitting sun interfered with finding the lane to the commander's house. The sun would disappear at 4:30 p.m., but there would be ample light until the end of civil twilight at 5:25.

With the turnoff visible, his phone rang. It was Kevin. The call went unanswered. The lane was plowed, probably the same snow removal service Nolan had at the cabin.

Casey parked his car by the front entrance. The house was an older looking farmhouse, with several wooden sheds off to the side. The attached garage was big enough to accommodate three vehicles. The wooden doors were old and probably cumbersome to open. The porch was small, with an overhang to help keep the snow from banking up against the front door.

Casey climbed the stairs and rang the doorbell. He noticed a small electronic box. One of those front door caller IDs. A newer model of the Ring. *Come on Colonel, please be home. I need your help.*

His attention was shifted to the front of the garage. The small wooden door was moved outward about five inches, just enough for the movement to get noticed with peripheral vision. Next he saw something else. About two inches of a dog's muzzle stuck out, trying to push the door open more. Casey stared at the dog's muzzle. He walked down the stairs to get closer. The dog whined. A familiar noise. The whine came from Buddy trying to get out.

"Buddy? What are you doing in there?"

Buddy barked. Not his happy bark, but a nervous anxious bark.

Casey opened the door and Buddy jumped out. He circled Casey, then ran back inside the now opened garage door. Casey followed. Buddy ran to the large white box by the side of the wall. He put his paws on top of the white box. Casey walked over to the freezer. "What's the matter? Alright, get down." Casey opened the large freezer. He stared at the meat inside. "Oh dear God." He froze in place, much like the body that was frozen inside, naked and curled up in the fetal position. Ian's face looked waxy white. Minus any recognizable expression. Casey slammed shut the lid. He leaned against the side of the freezer and tried hard to gather his wits.

"Kevin. I have to call Kevin." Before he could get his phone out of his pocket, Buddy ran to the door leading to the inside of the house. Casey followed. Buddy was sniffing the floor and whining. The old farm styled kitchen had another door leading to the basement. Buddy scratched at the door.

"Buddy, is Nolan in the house. Where's Nolan?" Buddy scratched at the basement door. Casey opened the door. The basement was dark, with some light coming through small windows. He hollered down. “Nolan, are you down there?”

Buddy ran down. Casey quickly followed. At the bottom of the stairs he saw what he feared most. “Nolan, God please no. Please no.” He bent down to touch the body laying still on the basement floor. There was a pulse. He lifted an eyelid. The pupil showed some kind of a reaction to being drugged. Nolan was alive, but heavily sedated. “Don’t worry Noley, I got this. You’re going to be OK.”

Casey grabbed his phone. He called Kevin.

Kevin answered on the first ring. “Casey, damn it, you answer that phone when I call.”

“Kevin. It’s not the Mark guy. I found Ian. It’s the commander.”

“Is he alright?”

“No. He’s naked and frozen in the freezer. In the garage.”

“Where are you?”

“I’m at the commander’s house. Nolan is in the basement. He’s been drugged. I need cops and an ambulance, really fast.”

“Where is the commander?”

“He’s at Nolan’s cabin, but I saw he has one of those Ring doorbells. I’m sure he’s on his way over here right now. Probably about a minute or two away.”

“Casey, you have to get out of there.”

“I can’t. Nolan is in the basement, I can’t lift him. I can’t get out of here.”

“Can you secure the door so he can’t get in?”

“Maybe.”

“Look for anything. Boards, anything. I’m leaving you on the speaker phone while I get squad cars dispatched. Go. Secure the door.”

Casey left the phone on the cement floor and ran to the work bench to look for anything to keep the commander from getting down the stairs. He found a long segment of old cotton rope. Racing against time, he climbed the stairs and looked for a way to tie the door shut. He wrapped the rope securely around the round door knob, and then used the post on the railing to tie the other end. He tried the door. The rope only allowed the door to open about an inch. Not enough to get a knife through. He ran back down to look for a board. To try and make a wedge.

Kevin was on the speaker phone. Casey heard the sound of Nolan's truck pull up in front of the house and stop. "Kevin, he's here. He drove Nolan's truck."

"Did you get the door secured?"

"Maybe. I'm looking for a board. I already tied a thick rope to the door handle."

"I have help on the way. It should take about fifteen minutes. I'm on my way in the car. Sit tight. Whatever you do. Don't let him talk you into opening the door."

"OK. Please hurry. And send for an ambulance too."

"It's on the way."

Casey found a two by four board and looked for a way to jam it into the step to keep the door from opening if the rope was to fail. He managed to get it sideways between the railing and the wall, giving him about six inches of extra protection if the rope gave away.

He heard footsteps in the kitchen as the wood flooring creaked while the commander approached the basement door. Casey moved to the bottom of the stairs. He found an old knife on the work bench, about seven inches long. He held it firmly in his hand, ready to use it in hand to hand combat if he had to. Hoping the guy didn't have a gun.

"Open the door Captain Link. I know you're down there."

"Why? So you can shove us in the freezer in your garage?"

Kevin was listening in on the speaker phone.

"I said to open the door Captain. That is a direct order."

"Why did you do it? Ian was a good guy. He didn't deserve to die." Casey heard him try to open the door. He pushed hard, but the rope held.

"It was an accident. I didn't want to kill her. I loved her."

"A freezer burial isn't the best way to show your love Colonel. I'm not buying it."

"Captain, you have to believe me. Open the door and I'll tell you what happened."

"You can tell me from where you are."

"She wouldn't let me have her the way I wanted. I got tired of the games. So after a fun night at the drag queen bar, I slipped a little something in her drink before we turned off the lights. My plan worked, but in the morning, she was stiff. Must have had a bad heart."

"Or maybe you killed her with the drugs. Colonel, I need to know, what was in the drug? Did you give Nolan the same thing?"

"He's sleeping. Don't worry about him."

"What did you give him?"

"My special cocktail. Propofol, fentanyl and a little midazolam."

"My God, were you planning on sedating a grizzly bear?"

"He's strong, he'll be alright. Unlike poor Ines."

"Why don't you get in your car and drive off? You have about fifteen minutes before the police get here."

"I have a better idea. You probably know about my medical condition."

"What condition?"

"I have AIDS. I'm going to die soon."

"You don't have AIDS. You're HIV positive. There's a huge difference."

"So you say."

"Why did you get Nolan today? He has nothing to do with this?"

"I could have dug a hole this spring, and no one would have even know about this little accident. But you had to persist. You sent the text saying you and Nolan knew who did it. I had to find out what Nolan knew. So I invited him over for lunch. He was an easy target."

"So you planned to kill Nolan too?"

"No. The truth is, I don't know what I planned to do, but it's all perfectly clear now. I know exactly what I need to do."

"Colonel, get in your car and take off while you still can."

Casey heard the sirens and saw the red, white and blue lights flashing through the small basements window. It made an eerie light show in the dark basement.

"Well, you're other friends are here. Looks like it's show time. Tell your boyfriend the keys to his truck are on the passenger side floor "

"Kevin, are you still there?"

"I'm out front Casey. You did good. Stay put."

"Did you get the names of the drugs he gave Nolan?"

"I passed that on to the ambulance. They're about a mile behind us."

"Kevin, I don't know if the Colonel has a gun or not. He didn't say. But I think he's planning something stupid to end it all."

"I got it. Stay put."

Casey heard the loud speaker coming from the front of the house.

"Colonel Price. We have the house surrounded. Come out slowly with your hands on top of your head."

Casey heard the wooden floor creak in the living room as the Colonel walked towards the front door. The front door opened, and the next thing he heard was a volley of gunshots. It all lasted for about ten seconds. Then there was silence. Until Kevin's voice came over the speaker phone next to Casey.

"It's all over Casey. You can open the door now."

"He's dead isn't he."

"Yes, he took the suicide by cop route out of his problem."

Casey realized he had the knife in his hand the whole time. His knuckles were between red and blue. He stood up and dropped the knife on the floor, barely missing his foot.

"Hold on Noley, it won't be long now." He walked up the stairs, so weak his legs could barely get him to the top. He managed to get the board and the rope off the door handle. The EMTs were in the kitchen with a stretcher waiting for him to get the door open. Buddy never left Nolan's side until Casey called him away. He gave the two EMT men a slight scare with his teeth showing.

They rolled Nolan onto the stretcher and struggled to get him up the stairs and out of the house.

Kevin and Casey stood at the bottom of the stairs for a moment. Casey gave Kevin a huge hug. "You did it Detective. You saved our asses. I only wish I could have done the same for Ian. He was so happy to start his new life and never got the chance."

"I'm sorry Casey. I'm really sorry. I never met the guy, but I really grew to like him."

"Can you have one of your guys drive my car to the hospital?"

"Sure."

"I'm taking the truck with Buddy. If anything happens to the truck, Nolan would probably have a cardiac arrest."

They walked up the stairs with Buddy taking the lead. Casey notice there were more cars arriving to process the crime scene. One of the shed doors was open and he could see the white Subaru parked inside. The sounds of the ambulance disappeared into the distance with Nolan on the way to the civilian hospital. Casey stood and watched as it faded into the darkening sky of nautical twilight.

"Come on hero. We have to get to the hospital." Buddy listened to his new nickname with both ears cocked. They drove off towards the city.

Casey called Candy and told her as much as he could while driving. "Can you drive to the hospital and get Buddy out of the truck?"

"I'm leaving now."

"One other thing, don't text Chester. I'll write a complete email for Chester and he can forward it to his parents. I don't want to panic them with not enough information."

"Alright. Sweetie. See you in a few minutes."

THREE

Buddy was on his leash confused to where he was. He's smelled Casey's suitcase on other occasions, but he never followed one to a place completely new to him.

"Noley, are you sure these little jets are safe?"

"Little? This baby seats fifteen people, and it's just you, me and Buddy. Relax. This is the only way to travel. By the way, when do we schedule my next milking relief?"

"Nolan! Quiet. What if someone hears that?"

"Oh crap, it's a medical procedure. Don't get so jumpy Doc."

The nicely dressed man in a black jump suit addressed Casey and Nolan. "We're ready to board sir, if you will follow me?"

Another man took their bags. Buddy stuck to Casey's side as they walked across the runway to the sleek private jet, not sure if he liked the idea of air travel.

They all followed the man in the jump suit up the steps to the jet. Buddy let Casey take the lead. "Noley, what if he has to pee?"

"Then he pees. Who cares? Besides, we refuel in Idaho. We can let him out to pee on the tires. He'll like it."

Casey looked around inside the cabin of the private jet. "I've seen this in the movies but never so close. This is amazing."

Buddy laid on the floor between Casey's feet with his ball on a rope secured in his mouth.

Casey and Nolan strapped themselves in.

The man in the jump suit asked them, "Can I get you anything to drink?"

"I'll have a beer."

Casey said, "Same here please."

When the man went to get their drinks, the pilot came out of the cockpit to greet them. "It's a pleasure to have you aboard. I've never ferried two Air Force captains before. It's an honor. I hope you relax and enjoy the flight. We take off in about five minutes."

"Thank you." They both said at the same time.

"Is it true you fly the F 22?"

"Yes sir, I do."

"Impressive. Well, let me know if you need anything." He left for the controls.

Nolan slapped Casey hard on his thigh. "One weeks leave in the beautiful state of Georgia. This is going to be great."

"I hope your family likes me."

"They're going to love you. Stop sweating about it. I can't wait to get you on the dirt bikes. I'll take Chester's and you can take mine. In case you bend metal."

"I can hardly wait."

The jet rolled to the assigned runway. Within minutes, the jet took off and headed south. Buddy looked nervous until Casey put his hand on his head. That did the trick. He trusted the members of his pack.

"Thanks again for coming with me to talk with Sawyer last week. It meant a lot to me."

Nolan gave Casey a loving smile. He picked up his bottle of beer to clank bottles. "To our future Stretch."

"To us."

THE END

Other books by Jon Swank

BERLIN Book 1: Hot and Cold
BERLIN Book 2: In and Out
BERLIN Book 3: Langsam und Schnell
BERLIN Book 4: Light and Dark
BERLIN Book 5: Loud and Clear
BERLIN Book 6: Over and Out
NEVADA CAIN RANCH
DELTA HOTEL

ABOUT THE AUTHOR

Jon Swank is a thirteen year veteran of the United States Air Force where he served as an officer in radar operations. Jon now lives in Northern Nevada spending his time writing and hiking in the mountains.

Feel free to contact the author with any comments at:

Jon@SwankNovels.com

Made in the USA
Middletown, DE
07 March 2017